- THE LANDSKAPË SAGA -
BELL ELEVEN

Nina J. Lux

To those who have always insisted,
"Yes, you can."

PROLOGUE

No QUEEN LIVED on the splendid Queen's Parade, despite its deceptive name, but that was only the second thing that struck the man. Once the light rain of pixels that had bitten his surroundings into tiny colourful squares had fallen to the ground, the sucking *click-click-click* as they pieced the image of the new world back together had ebbed out and the drizzle dispersed, he found himself in urban scenery with tall square buildings, wide concrete roads and elevated sidewalks. It was the monochrome twin of the place from whence he had just come.

The first thing he noticed was the sharp odour. He could smell vast amounts of energy in the air, but of two kinds. There was the organic and green power that he knew well from his own realm, the one he had left to step through to this place; it was cool and fresh against his nostrils.

Then there was another kind, a grey and dusty sort of energy, like burnt-out coal. Drawing in its intoxicating scent, he had to check himself not to become too affected. For many years he had been told of the corruptive influence of this darker source of power. Dead coal and fire instead of what was still living—

humans would never cease to disappoint him.

He pulled up his scarf to cover his mouth and nose, leaving his forehead and slanted almond-shaped eyes clear. He couldn't risk anything. Not tonight. The people sleeping around him within their protective walls had no idea what was about to begin outside on their own streets, and perhaps for the best. If nothing unexpected happened, they would never know.

The alley in which he had landed was dark and grimy, and he crept out with caution, even if there was little risk of meeting someone at this time at night. Still, before leaving his hiding-place, he looked several times up and down the street. A dusty sign sat on a corner of a lower brick building, more ancient than its neighbours, and the man peered up to read it. Queen's Parade—just where he wanted to be. Under the shadow of skyscrapers and through the old industrial landscape in the centre of the capital, his steps echoed precariously in the silent night as he trudged the streets. He navigated via the moon, round and full in the sky. Having expected it to be smaller, of lesser importance, it was with disappointment that he had to admit it looked just the same as his own, not privy to any partial judgement.

The man was dressed according to custom in this new place: stiff bulgy trousers in a washed-off blue hue, white short-sleeved t-shirt, and a dark leather jacket topped with a third layer—the scarf—to keep the early spring cold out. He had asked to wear another colour, any colour, rather than blue for the trousers, but his superiors had insisted that it was abso-lutely necessary. He couldn't shake the feeling that he was being mocked. It disgusted him, all of it: the sticky feeling of ridicule and these clothes and the itchy facial hair stuck onto his face in the current fashion of this godforsaken land.

More, he thought as he peered around another corner and turned into an alley-way trailing the street of his destination.

More. Humans disgusted him. That disdainful race without a shred of conscience. Thirsty for power, greedy and cruel, these people knew nothing of balance and harmony. It was up to him and his kind to punish them for their mistakes, though he was merely a corner stone in the larger picture.

Stealing away along the walls, past shop windows and front doors, slick and soft like a slithering snake, the man soon found numbers on the doors—79, 81 … He went further along. The cobble stone made his steps uneven and he almost twisted his ankle once on the strange surface, but he kept his narrow eyes on the numbers on the doors.

83 … 85 …

There it was. A green wooden door, just like he had been told, with the number 87 carved in golden letters and a large brass knocker in the shape of a lion, the capital's protective symbol. There was not so much as a guard to protect the inhabitants and at first he thought there had been a mistake, but the gilded plate on the right side of the door told him he had found the right place. It seemed to glow in the dark, its glimmering details shining as though they wanted him to find it.

The absent monarch was the second thing that the man noted about the new world that night: the Queen's Parade had no Queen at all, but a President, whose name he now read in curly letters on the plate outside her house.

Eileen Colerush, President of Vildaell.

The man felt the handle. Locked. Again, as he had been told. From an inner pocket of his jacket he extracted one of the three precious willow leaves that the Lord had provided him with before leaving. His fingers were gentle as they pinched a corner of the elongated leaf, careful not to make the slightest dent in its surface.

"Only three," the Lord had said in a grave voice, his eyes lunging deep into the young man like only a Lord's eyes could.

"Use them with caution and care."

Instructions concluded, the Lord had placed the three leaves in the young man's hand. They had been light and soft to the touch and had felt like an invaluable treasure to carry. This strange power over him did not diminish even when one of them now rested in his open palm, ready to come to his aid. The moonlight gave it a matte silver hue, though he knew it was green as well in its ambiguous nature.

Of power and destruction; of power and creation. So the Lords said.

Gathering his focus and mind power to the task in hand, the young man placed the leaf in his palm, securing it with the thumb, and reached out for the door handle. In his mind he concentrated on the energy inside the leaf, felt its organic power pour through its delicate veins like low-key thunder. A pounding signalled the waves of power venturing from the leaf into his veins, blending with the blood and inherent force within, resulting in low crackling and small sparks of light as it happened. It spread through his body and gathered somewhere deep in his core where it whirled with a dull sound. Though not a novice (they had practised it many times), the sensation still presented him with some peculiar discomfort which, at the same time, was almost pleasurable. Each surge swept in him like a drum beat in his lower abdomen. It was almost complete: the contained energy from the leaf had been transferred straight into his bloodstream.

Soon the thudding subsided and the next stage began: he left this trance-like state and focused all the collected energy, now mature and controlled, into his hand. He reached out and touched the lock on the door. It clicked open as the mechanism malfunctioned.

It was an ancient method of his kind, those of the Essence, and a more experienced Master could perform it all in one breath. This man was yet too young to hope for such skill.

In his hand, the leaf had cracked into a small heap of dry brown ashes. He let the residues fall to the ground, stepped over them, and went in over the threshold.

Inside, he met an unprepossessing interior. A simple rag rug in the hallway welcomed the visitor into a small area with a cloak hanger and an oak bureau upon which a row of photographs stood in perfect alignment, set right by a careful hand. At closer inspection, the man recognised the President's family. One of them depicted a smiling woman with dark hair and a nose like those horrid beaks of crows—Eileen—together with another, slightly older, woman, presumably her partner who also held some position in the government. Between the two stood a young girl, their daughter Sofia. It was an old photograph; Sofia was in her twenties now. The man stared at the youngest of the family. A sole child, he knew she must be spoilt rotten. Such were the customs of humans. But there was some spark, an icy glimmer, in her pale eyes, such a contrast to her dark brown curls that framed her oval face, which struck a chord within him. They were like shimmering pieces of silver, in the most captivating nuance he had seen. His own eyes, dark as the night, were absorbed in the light grey and lingered there, hooked beyond the flat surface of the photo image.

A crow cawing outside returned him to the present and he tore his gaze away from the photo of the girl.

Ignoring the photographs lining the wall in an ascending formation, he sidled up the stairs with his hand on the smooth mahogany railing, careful not to make the steps creak. The carpet dulled his steps and he soon found himself at the top, facing four closed doors lined against a rounded space. Four doors, four possibilities—and only one chance of getting it right.

At first he cursed the Lords for sending him out into such

uncertainty, but then he felt a swelling pride at their trust. They trusted him to use his instincts; to use his Essence.

He put an ear to the first door on the left. No sound. When he pushed it open he saw that it was, as expected, the storage room. A faint creak in the old hinges on the way back caused him to freeze and listen for restless sounds in the unnerving silence, but nothing else broke the sombre sleepiness of the house. Content, he closed the door and stepped back.

The second door was a carved wooden port with gilded handles and lock, and its surface was more meticulously ornamented than any of the others. Before pressing the handle, he leaned against the door and listened. A slow steady breathing could be distinguished from within. It came from more than one person, but no more than two. This must be it, he thought—the President's suite.

From an inner pocket he plucked one of the remaining silver-shaded leaves and enclosed it in his fist. Just as he felt the power once more drain the leaf and enter his blood, a creak from his right made him cast his eyes open and swing around, pausing the photosynthetic process. The fourth door had opened and on the threshold stood a young woman in only her night gown, a loose-fitted pale blue dress in shiny material. Her hair was long and curly and dark, almost black, and her fierce grey eyes glared at him with mixed surprise and suspicion.

They truly were silver, the young man thought.

The girl, a woman now, knew how to ride a horse and had seen the world, but she did not yet know who the man was, or exactly how much he knew about her.

Rubbing sleep from her eyes, she eyed him from top to toe. "Who the devil are you?"

From the room next to him the young man could hear bodies shuffling on crisp sheets. Something wild and untamed flew into his mind, clouding it with bad premonitions. He had to subdue it, crush it. Kill it.

"Tell me who you are or I will scream," she said. "You're not the first stranger to enter this house unauthorised. One word is all it takes." She scanned his outfit and frowned. "You aren't from here, are you?"

"I am a messenger from Jahran," he lied, lowering his voice almost to a whisper, hoping she would follow his lead. "There has been a coup d'état and the Prime Minister is in trouble. I was sent here to ask for our neighbour's good graces, to ask of Eileen, President Colerush I mean, for help."

Sofia seemed to weigh her options. When she did reply, the concern in her voice was braided with residual suspicion, but the young man could tell that she would swallow his bait. He merely had to reel her in. The simplicity of humans was astonishing. "Nothing happened to Mr Erdavan, I hope?"

"Oh, Miss Colerush, I am afraid I have bad news …," he began. Words were held in little regard where he came from, but he had learnt that humans valued them highly. He ought to keep it simple but the story came alive as he spoke, widened and deepened, gained more dimensions and more colour. The lie became larger and more complex with his every word. Next he knew, he became the messenger and described how Prime Minister Erdavan had been overthrown by the opposition. There had been an uprising against the poor conditions, a mob, a strong mob attacking the leaders (he almost said 'Lords'), forcing them out on the streets to be assaulted by the people. There was blood! Gore! Screaming! The young man's heart was beating with the development of the story.

"That is truly terrible," said Sofia, and the man shook his head as if it was terrible, indeed. "And all this took place by the river bank, at the main square?"

The young man nodded. He suppressed a self-satisfied smile and focused on staying in character. In his hand he searched again for the energy in the leaf. When he met the dove's eyes of Sofia, they were once more locking, nay clawing, into his. Just like the photograph had done downstairs. The sparkling ice was cracked by natural clefts in her irises, witnessing the deep abyss in which one could get lost if not careful. A lesser man might, one of weaker earth.

"And what if I say the stench of your lies alone is enough to wake up both my mothers?"

A heavy lump congealed in the man's throat and made it hard to breathe. He forced himself to remain calm. "What do you …?"

"The only river in Jahran runs along the border of Vildaell, which is why the poor people are starving," she said. "Furthermore, the Prime Minister—my godfather—is, as he told me in a wired message this afternoon, on official business in Buria. Hence, your story reeks of rubbish though I'll give you points for creativity."

In her smirk all Sofia's beauty transformed into slyness that he'd failed to recognise before. Humans were unpredictable creatures. The man swallowed the initial shock of astonishment, and became himself. "If I were you, I would not underestimate the extent of my creativity."

To his bewilderment, she laughed. It was a ringing and a delightful laugh. Not sarcastic or menacing, though he saw now she was equally capable of such ugliness. He gritted his teeth, moving his hand slowly towards his belt where a dagger sat waiting. If he could help it, he would rather not use the despicable weapon welded from the filthy energy that tainted this air. He'd rather not, but when in the human world, do as humans do …

In the other hand he held on to the leaf. Considering the turn of events, he would have to try the feat he'd attempted for many moons without success. Only the most accomplished of his kin could master it. Without breaking eye contact with Sofia, he transported himself into the tiny veins of green and silver, into the cells of the leaf, and accessed the flow of energy; with heat from his hand the photosynthesis moved through layers of skin, peeled them away; left the pores in the smooth surface; and immersed itself in his blood. He would know in a moment if it had worked.

As the last rings of Sofia's laughter left her lips, he felt the green power synthesise within. Seconds remained.

"One last chance, boy," Sofia said, the glistening eyes luminous with unyielding calm. "You cannot be much older than I am. What is your name? What is your business here?"

The circle was complete. A dull throbbing resided in his abdomen and now spread to every limb. It was infinitely faster than he had ever done it before, though not perfect. Before long he held the power to destroy and to heal in the palm of his hand.

He shrugged his shoulders, made as if to sigh, and stretched out his hand towards the girl. "My name is not important," he said with a smile. "But I will tell you my reason for being here. There is no reason to be alarmed. Please do take my hand. We can become friends, you and I, if you let us. If only you will give me your hand. Greet me!"

His smile widened as she approached the hand with caution. When he at last answered her question, it was already too late. Sofia's delicate fingers had touched his and although there was no flash of light, no thunder, no crackle, not an inkling of a sound, the energy from the leaf leapt into her with a quick surge and she collapsed into his arms. He held her slender body and felt its weight tugging him down. Careful not to hurt her, he peeled one of her eyes open and admired the shimmering grey irises, now vacant and blank, but as radiant and captivating as if they were still seeing. He leaned into her hair and drew in her intoxicating human scent, whispering,

"My dear Sofia—I am here to change your world."

With his face still buried in Sofia's hair, the young man felt the disruption in the energy field before the impact.

But he had no time to react.

The walls detonated in an ear-deafening implosion, and he tumbled to the ground, Sofia still in his arms. The heat wave hit at the same time as the ceiling collapsed, and debris and smoke and all sorts of sizzling, crunching, acid mist surrounded the open sky and the city below. Dust and dirty smoke seized everything in its path and when it was all over, a ghost-like stillness overlaid a capital void of life.

PART I
CURFEW

NOTICE

§34.2:1. May 4, —th year of the Lion. The Republic of Vildaell hereby includes the *Curfew Restriction Legislation,* (from here on referred to as the *Curfew Law*), §34.2:1, as part of its constitution. The Curfew Law demands a twelve-hour curfew between 6:00PM and 6:00AM (from here on referred to as *Curfew hours*) every day without exception. During Curfew hours, all citizens and non-citizens present within the borders of the Republic of Vildaell must remain inside. Doors must be locked according to §34.2:2 (see below) and each house must from May 4 —th year of the Lion, be equipped with a Signaller (§34.2:3). Curfew hours will be signified by a total of ten bells in a sequence starting at 5:00PM concluding at 5:45PM, and end at 6:00AM with bell eleven.

Anyone found outside premises during Curfew hours will be removed.

CHAPTER 1

5:10PM

THE CITY OF Amérle was still alive. A faceless driver concealed under a dark helmet thundered over the aqueduct, over the frothing river, and into the central parts of the capital. The motorcycle slalomed between honking cars and clumsy trucks that were all in a hurry, all racing against the setting sun, now a rich orb cast in silks of gold and red in between the tall city buildings. Every citizen here had one destination and one destination only at this time and would—as they must—arrive there before their Signallers blinked red at six o'clock and Curfew began: behind a locked door.

Zooming past the Great Square, through the underpass, the motorcycle soon escaped the highways. Instead of slowing down, the driver pushed the speedometer up to its limit, only releasing it back towards lower figures when entering a quiet residential area on the northern outskirts of the city. It was a neighbourhood with rows and rows of identical houses, distinguishable only by colour and the number on the mailbox, long since emptied for the day.

An elderly man, Mr Nagel by name, lingered on the street

corner with a watering can in his hand, and glared at the approaching vehicle. When the driver lifted a hand in greeting, the stooping man did not wave back, but only growled to himself, shook his head, and continued to shuffle back to his own house.

With graceful skill, the motorcyclist shot left past Mr Nagel and entered through a gate into the parking space in front of the red house at Mauve Road number 15. The mullioned windows were still open and let the fresh summer evening air into the house before close-up, the curtains fluttered in the June breeze, like napkins waved in welcome of the long-lost soldier. The fiery glow of the sun bathed the house in its honey-coloured light, like a halo over its rooftop sinking into shades of honey-suckle flowers in full bloom. From the street one might think the house quite wholesome, but close up the flailing paint became obvious, revealing a darker hue underneath and telling of a long winter gone past. It was a dwelling for the humble, but as homely as houses got.

The rumble of the engine and the crushing gravel under the weight of the motorcycle reached all the way into the two-storey villa, and a moment later a handsome man in his forties appeared on the doorstep. Otto Evenson was tall and poised—and he smiled at what he saw.

"You drove carefully, I hope?" he said with unveiled concern as the noisy engine came to a full stop.

"Always do, Dad," the driver replied and pushed up the tinted visor to reveal a pair of blue eyes just like the ones belonging to the man on the threshold. Now Otto recognised his daughter.

When she pulled off the dark helmet, her blonde mane flowed out and settled around her shoulders, its edges resting on the collar of her leather jacket. Freja Evenson ran a hand through her hair, feeling the moist sweat that followed the skin at her hairline.

"Good, because you might want to have a look inside," Otto said, a teasing grin showing off attractive creases around his mouth. "That's all I'll say. No, you can't make me say another word. See for yourself … Fitzie."

In Freja's stomach gentle butterflies came alive and started flapping their wings like maniacs. It couldn't be … Could it? The summer holiday had just begun and only school kids were off—working people would still be toiling away for another few weeks before taking leave, at least in Amérle. The idea seemed too good to be true, but her father knew better than to joke about such a thing, surely? He was a joker, certainly, but he wasn't cruel.

She jumped off and pushed the motorcycle, a Thunderball X770 of last year's model, to the side of the garage into its usual space and swept the plastic cover over it before hurrying after her father into the house.

As it turned out, neither the butterflies nor her father had misled her.

"Peekaboo, Fitzie! Missed me?" Robin smiled and wrapped his arms around her in a long hug.

"I haven't missed being called Fitzie, that's for sure." She laughed and broke free from him. "Why didn't you tell me you were coming?"

"And miss the look on your face right now? Not a chance."

He was tall and gorgeous by anyone's standards, with jet black hair, rich dark brown eyes and an irresistible smile. Still, he had the air of somebody who wasn't aware of how attractive he was, and who wouldn't have made a big deal out of it even if he had known. Other boys in school would saunter up to girls, hand in their hair as if they were the answer to all life's questions. It was the last thing Robin would do. His fingers ran through the waves of his hair to adjust, not to show off. His humble nature was one of the reasons Freja had been less than enthusiastic about his move to Fink, a city miles from Amérle down the south-east coast of Vildaell. That was ten months ago. In between his work, Freja's final year in school, and the constraint of Curfew, time had swept past both of them like a missed train. He already looked different. Older. Rebellious stubble lined his chin in a casual kind of way. It was likely Robin hadn't even noticed it himself: he wasn't the mirror type of guy.

"I bet Nagel will be happy to see you," said Freja and Robin threw his head back in a laugh. "He was glaring at me just now as I pulled up. Don't think the Thunderball helped either."

"We might, just might, have to pay him a visit," said Robin in a conspiring voice.

"You remember that time with …"

"… the pink daisies," Robin filled in. "Boy, was he mad. 'Young rascals, crooks, and thieves!'" Mr Nagel's accent was spot-on. They continued to make various imitations of poor Mr Nagel, one crueller than the other. His precious roses and daisies had barely had time to bloom before Freja and Robin, as children, would roam his garden, steal his flowers and then offer them to unsuspecting neighbours at a bargain price. Only on warm summer days could he relax, as they would rather play hide-and-seek among the streets of the neighbourhood, or on school days when Freja would wait for Robin to finish and they'd race each other home, pretending to be sprinting against Curfew even if it was just two o'clock.

As he went on to tell her about his work as a sales representative, Robin's eyes lit up just like they had done then for each rose stem they ripped off, for every dishonest silver crown in their pockets and for each time he had found her hiding place and uttered an elated 'peekaboo!' before running off to hide himself. When he spoke he laughed, so that two dimples, one in each cheek, appeared and Freja grinned back at him. "It sounds great, Robin—and so does Fink. Maybe I should go there when

I graduate," she said, musing. "Are there any good roads?"

"Final year now, huh?"

"Eight months and I'm out of here."

"You wouldn't leave Amérle."

She didn't object, because he was right: she wouldn't leave her father alone, not yet anyway. It was still too soon. Over two years gone by since her mother was removed, and still Freja fretted that her father would crash and burn without her. Behind his smile she sometimes spotted the grief, lurking and burning underneath the happy surface. If she left … She shrugged off the thought.

The ensuing silence, as natural as conversation, was cut short when the door to the kitchen swung open and a rich scent of sugar and buttered oat entered the living room. When Otto came in holding a steaming tray of newly baked biscuits, oat with white glaze, Freja and Robin exchanged amused looks. Neither was surprised: because whoever said never to bring your work into your home had clearly never met chef Evenson. Crammed between his elbow and chest was a hot bag full of biscuits. His hands were occupied by a large plastic bucket from which steam was rising in swirling formations, spreading the warm familiar scent that always seemed to linger inside the house.

"Did you just make these, Mr Evenson?" said Robin and stood up to relieve him of the burden. "That's some sort of record, surely."

"Oh, it is nothing," said Otto in his formal way of speaking, waving off the compliment, extending yet another bag of delicate oat crumble. "You better take them home though—we do not want you out too close to Curfew. You are here for a few days, correct? —So you can speak more another day." Without waiting for a reply he ushered a reluctant Robin out into the hallway, with Freja stalking behind. While Robin put his loafers on, Otto read some figures off the Signaller box on the wall. "Seventeen minutes, forty-three seconds. Are you sure that will be enough, Robin?"

"You're welcome to stay here otherwise," Freja offered. "Right, Dad?"

"Yes, yes of course you are," Otto said and put a hand around Freja's shoulder. "But your parents and your sister might want to see you too, when you've been away for so long."

"How is Cecelya?" Freja asked. "I haven't seen her in ages. Doesn't she miss me?"

Robin cleared his throat. "Well, you know what my sister's like, always up to something weird. Last time we spoke she was on her way to Jahran—I know, right?—with some boy she met in art class." Robin laughed and shrugged. "She just packed her stuff and left a note on the kitchen table saying that she'd hitchhike there. Mum's furious, obviously. I wouldn't want to trade places with Ceci when she gets back."

"But you have heard from her," said Otto, his voice divulging the same apprehension that Freja felt. "Since then?"

"Trust me," said Robin with a smile, though Freja could tell he was worried too. "We've been through this at home. She called from a payphone in Rim, that's just on the border to Jahran, so she should be across it now."

Freja dared not look at her father, knowing that they were thinking the same thing. She hated that gut feeling she had sometimes—it was like a sixth sense.

"When was that?" She meant to pose the question innocently, as though it was coming from nothing but pure interest, but could tell she failed.

"Two-three days ago?" said Robin. "Really, don't worry. I wouldn't expect her to get in touch now. Can't imagine Jahran has many payphones, right? She's probably having the time of her life with that boy, Kale-something. You know him, Freja?"

"Kale Kolbjorn? He's from a wealthy family, that's all I know."

"Excellent. Any trouble, he can buy them out," Robin said with a laugh. "That'll come in handy in Jahran, it's that kind of place, right? Look, I understand why you'd be ... worried about it." He spoke with caution, but not in fear. "Mum's the same after my uncle ... you know. But I think that after all our stories, Ceci'll be too traumatised to risk Curfew, don't you think? I know I'd be."

Freja smiled at the memory. Another one of their pranks. When Robin and Freja came in with their daily earnings from Nagel's flowers, Cecelya would tip-toe up to them, gracefully like a two-legged cat, and ask what they had been up to, desperate to be part of her older brother's life. Wide-eyed, the then four-year-old Cecelya would wrap her arms around her little knees and gape at them as they told one story after another about space monkeys who climbed up through the ground during Curfew hours to spy on humans.

"I'm sure it'll be fine," Freja said without quite meeting Robin's eye. Even so, she knew he could see right through her pretended faith; he knew her too well.

"Fifteen minutes," said Otto. "Better get going. Give my love to your folks, will you? And let us know if you ... if you hear anything."

Robin promised he would and shook Otto's hand before heading out through the door. As he reached the gate, Robin waved back at the house before turning onto the street and disappearing behind the hedge. His house was on an adjacent street to theirs, under a minute's walk away. In the distance the last bells rang out over the city, a hollow symphony accompanying the concert of colour in the sky. Otto closed the door.

He continued to lock it three times: once at the top, once in the middle at the main keyhole, and then finally at the bottom where he slid a heavy metal lever to block the door from the inside. With quick fingers he then entered a four-digit code on the Signaller, and a yellow light started blinking. After a few seconds, the blinking stopped, and even though he knew this meant that the procedure was complete, Otto tugged at the door which didn't budge. He turned to Freja.

"Can you get the windows upstairs?"

While her father went into the living room, Freja ascended the stairs to the second floor to close and secure the windows in their two bedrooms and the bathroom. Every window required the same procedure: after first pulling a knob and making sure that the lever was in place, she tugged a tough white string at the side so that the double blinds fell and blocked out a last glimpse of the garden outside. Her hands moved with ease and with habit, and within a few minutes all the windows on the upper floor were shut, locked, and blinded. Downstairs, she found her father securing the last window in the kitchen, which was still oozing with hot steam from his baking. She drew in the scent as the last blind fell down between the glass panes with a rushing sound, and felt the familiar cosiness at once enclose their inner world.

"You ready for a round of Rhyffle, old man?" Freja nodded towards the half-finished board game by the dark window. They had played it in the family for as long as she could remember. A board battle between red and blue pawns across a colourful playing field. "But no 'skipping' this time—I keep telling you, it's not allowed."

"More and more like your mother every day," her father sighed with a smile. He grew serious. "What if Cecelya …"

"No," said Freja. "Don't."

"I can tell that you are thinking the same."

"Of course I am, Dad, but I can't be thinking it. Mum … I just can't be thinking it. Can't we just play?"

"Just promise me you won't go hitchhiking to Jahran."

She promised. "Can we play now? Please? I'm sort of winning."

"You are not," her father said and turned to the board where the pawns from last night's round were waiting patiently. "Are you?"

As they sat down by the game under the warm light from the table lamp, the hands of the grandfather clock in the corner showed six o'clock and the yellow light on the Signaller in the hallway switched to red.

It was now past Curfew.

CHAPTER 2

A WEEK LATER, Robin was still in town. He had taken time off work, he said, to visit his family, even though public summer holidays were less than a month away. His return to Amérle was peculiar, and perhaps it was wondering what he really was doing back that had set Freja's sleep on edge. Every morning, she woke up with a jerk after yet another nightmare in which Robin went out to meet someone—and never came back. Sometimes his sister was with him, sometimes his brother, and sometimes all three Aitken siblings, but the dreams all ended the same way: a blinding light like headlights from a truck, a groan as if the whole world was in pain, and a falling sensation.

On yet another morning, the cold sweat was sticky on her skin and she woke up with her body tangled amongst the sheets, needing a few minutes to fight off the white prison. She threw a glance at the digital clock on her nightstand, its red stripes glaring in the dark. 05:55AM. Five minutes before Curfew was lifted and the eleventh bell would ring out over the city from the TV tower at Linden square.

Ten bells, divided into each quarter of the last hour before Curfew, anticipated the city lock-down. The bells rang once at five o'clock, twice at quarter past, three bells at half past, and finally the quartet of bellows at fifteen minutes to six. There was no ring once Curfew had set in. A deep quiet lowered itself over the still lands until morning, when the eleventh bell rang and signified the new day.

In her nightmares, bell eleven never rang.

She stared into the ceiling, trying not to count the seconds. *One, two …*

Amérle was far from a big city, despite its capital status, and more or less every soul here had felt the cold touch of Curfew in one way or the other. For Freja, the connection was close: 25 months and 16 days ago, her mother, Marja, left the house with their dog Mops and never came back. Over two years had passed, but her father would still hover on the doorstep each day before she came home, staring out into the street as though in fear that Freja would follow in her mother's lost footsteps. Robin was right—there was no way she could leave Amérle. Not yet.

05:59. She had been staring at the clock, feeling each second pass like the precarious edge of a blade. In that last minute, Freja was clutched by the usual cruel and suffocating fear that the final bell wouldn't ring, that her nightmares would come true, and Curfew would be eternal.

Only when the angry red figures on the clock switched to 6:00AM and the distant bell, one almighty toll, sounded outside the walls did the stifling feeling lift, even if it took her several minutes to shake it off completely. While shrugging on a sweatshirt over her pyjamas she heard her father open the windows in his room next door. Winter or summer, rainy or sunny, he opened the windows first thing in the morning. For the past two years, she had done the same.

Breakfast was on the table when she got downstairs. A warm scent of toasted bread and sweet jam swirled from the kitchen and met Freja as she descended the stairs.

"Morning, sweetheart," her father said when she entered the kitchen. "What are you doing up? Already bounced back from the humiliating defeat?" He popped a piece of bread in his mouth. "Toast?" he asked in an innocent voice. She made a face and slumped into a chair by the table, snatching a piece of bread from the basket. The sore loss from last night's Rhyffle game still stung, but she refused to let him know that.

"I'm seeing Robin later," she said with a yawn. "Is there marmalade or jam?"

"There's plum and fig. Might be a jar of apricot left as well in the fridge." He pushed the last piece of his bread into his mouth and scrambled to the fridge, where he poked around for a minute or two before fishing out a glass container with shiny orange content. "Can I tempt you?"

She took the jar and spread a thick layer on top of the bronze slice of toast, almost relishing the heat burning her fingers, and watched it melt into the bread. At the opposite end of the table, her father was watching her like he always did, especially in the mornings. With love and a bottomless bone-shaking fear that it was the last time he saw her. Though it sounded sinister, you just never knew in Vildaell.

With her mouth full she asked, "Wn eulivn?" and her father's patent daughter-face broke into a smile, but he said nothing, leaving Freja chewing in the silence, chewing until her jaws hurt and she finally could gulp down the processed mix of bread and jam. "When are you leaving?" she said again, this time articulating carefully.

"Seven," Otto replied and checked his wrist watch, a lavish accessory with precise accuracy. "I will be back in the afternoon."

"I'm seeing Robin, like I said, so I might be out," she said, hoping that he would not rush home to find an empty house and be worried for her. In the tiny frown between his eyebrows, she saw that he would anyway.

"Call me if you need anything," he said and turned back to his coffee and newspaper. The frown remained.

*

They met in town and wandered around the old part, where many surviving buildings had been spared in the rebuilding of the city and now acted as historical landmarks of Vildaell's past. Nostalgia and sentimentality put aside, they were incredibly ugly. Often square constructions with three or four storeys, the brick boxes were punctured along the side with even squarer windows and square balconies where hardly one person would fit. But it was still a popular area, a token of what had been. They had coffee in a dingy little place just south of the old main square, and bought lunch from a soup stall close to Freja's college, where Robin also had been a student until last year.

It was late when they strolled back into the Great Square on one of the bridges, each holding a paper cup of the second coffee of the day. The Great Square was the main square in Amérle and a memorial site for the nuclear accident. It stood as a hollow in the city plain, like an inverted building digging a hole into the ground, and was surrounded by a grid of bridges and suspension pedestrian paths above. Around it were the main shopping streets, business quarters, and connections to the highway. It linked the south and north parts of the city by the long Queen's Parade, a street name Freja never had understood, considering Vildaell had not had a queen, or king for that matter, in over two hundred years.

A loud signal from the top of the TV tower, piercing the sky from a few minutes' walk away, rang out three times to note the thirty-minute window left to return home.

"Half past," Freja said with a light sigh. "Dad'll be climbing the walls by now."

"Better get going then," Robin replied in between the final gulps of his coffee. "You can hardly blame him for worrying."

"I guess … just imagine though, if we *could* stay out. Until … whenever."

Even Robin, usually the realist between the two, seemed struck by this dazzling prospect for a second, and then gave her a more characteristic sobering look. Freja too struggled to envision it. To stay out until the sun rose again … It was an idea almost too inconceivable to reflect on at all.

"Curfew …," she said, gazing absently out over the square where the daily routine of Vildaell played out: like puppets steered by the same strings people twisted their arms to inspect the time on their wrist watches, and most of them sped up at the sound of the bells. "I wonder what would happen if everyone just decided one day not to go home, if everyone stayed out."

"That's crazy, Fitzie."

"Sure—but what would happen?"

"You know what would happen—same as with everybody who's done it before. They'd be removed."

She could tell that he regretted his words, the way he bit his lip, as though chewing down an apology he knew wouldn't help anyway. He said nothing else, and neither did she. It wasn't his fault, she knew that, but it was always going to be easier for him. He didn't have to deal with the aftermath of a family member being removed: the mandatory paperwork and the reproving looks from neighbours and friends, knowing that they secretly considered your family irresponsible in the midst of all their sympathy. She bet he didn't know anyone who missed Curfew in Fink.

They walked in silence to the parking space at the end of the bridge, where she had left her motorcycle.

"You know, it's ridiculous," she continued while unlocking

the Thunderball, opening the compartment under the saddle and taking out two helmets, offering one to Robin. "Eleven bells, day after day, after day …"

He declined. "Enton has a case he wants to show me so I'll stay there tonight," he said and she replaced the helmet, closed the compartment. "Yes, I've told Mum and he's only about two minutes' walk from here."

Plenty of time, Freja silently noted, for Robin to get to his brother before the full hour. Of course her father's fears were justified—she only had to think about her dream, about waiting in vain for him or Robin, watching the Signaller light turn red, and she wanted to grab Robin's arm and walk him to Enton herself, just to make sure.

Helmet secured and her backpack fastened, Freja mounted the motorcycle, careful not to scratch the sides. She adjusted the rear-view mirrors and got ready to leave, when Robin placed a hand on her arm, sending electric sparks through her nerves. He flicked open the visor to reveal her eyes again. Something was worrying him.

"Fitzie—even if it's ridiculous, and it is, it's still a law. You can't break it." He was staring into her eyes as if searching for some sign of defiance.

"I think I know that." She winked. "Robin Aitken, you sound like one of those Curfew enthusiasts." He acknowledged neither the accusation nor the joke.

"Then you promise not to do anything stupid?"

"Like what?

"Like … I don't know."

Like go look for her. The words didn't come out of his mouth, but they might as well have. Well, she thought, he wouldn't have to worry. You only miss Curfew once—those were the rules. Besides, if Freja needed discouragement, she didn't have to look far. Her father had told her about their neighbour Mr

Nagel, how he had never been able to come to terms with the loss of his family to the Curfew Law. When his wife missed the hour and was removed, their son Jaspir, a hefty boy with famous red hair and beard, who was Freja's age at the time, went to try and find her. A few days later, Jaspir missed his first dinner too.

"Promise," she said curtly. She pushed the visor down once more and the world became slightly darker. Robin nodded and backed away as she kicked the stand, opened the fuel supply, and ignited the power with a roar. She felt the purring vibrations of the engine as she bent over the metal body. With a quick gesture she ushered the motorcycle forward. As it took her away, she felt a stab of bad conscience. Lying to Robin was not admirable, but she wanted to keep the door open and it would only hurt him to know that she did so. If she one day found a trace, a real trace and a real possibility of finding her mother, she wouldn't let a one-word promise stand in her way, that's for sure. Perhaps Robin also knew this, but decided in his naïve vanity to believe her? That was his problem, not hers. She couldn't help but to feel irritation sizzle along with the engine's grumble.

'Promise me you won't do anything stupid', he had said. What did he know?

The sun set quickly now and traffic was getting lighter as Curfew sped closer by the second. Not until forced by a red light did Freja slow down and zig-zag between the few queuing cars to the front of the line. From living all of her life under the Curfew Law, she had developed a sort of internal clock, and it told her that she had twenty minutes left. It should be enough, she quickly calculated, but there was no time to delay. She sped up at the green light.

She turned into Mauve Road at the sound of four bells, and a movement on the kerb caught her attention. At first she thought it might be Nagel again, but he was even worse than her father when it came to Curfew: except on Thursdays when he watered his roses in the evening, he was usually inside an hour in advance, locked and ready.

But it wasn't Nagel. Though it was no more than a shadow in the corner of her eye as she rolled past, it was enough for her to force the Thunderball to a screeching stop and swing it around full circle. Only, now the woman was nowhere to be seen.

Her head was pounding, throbbing, refusing to grasp what her eyes had just perceived. It had been too quick to be sure, and every one of her senses went to war over exactly what—or who—had been on the kerb. Her heart joined in the battle, beating so loudly it resonated through her every bone. She decided that it must have been an illusion, fashioned in her mind by her conversation with Robin.

His comment struck at her again, fiercer this time, and with more acidity than she remembered it.

Promise me you won't do anything stupid.

Except what she had put in her letters to him, he didn't know, couldn't understand. Other than an uncle he had barely known, his family was safe and unharmed in Amérle. She was being unfair, of course, but she couldn't stop the wrenching sensation of resentment from spreading like toxic waste inside. It was a barrier between them and she hated how it kept them infinitely, inexorably apart. But what could she do? It was built by matter strong as platinum, and nothing could ever break it down.

She swung into the driveway at number 15 with ten minutes to spare.

*

The next morning Freja woke up in a cold sweat after yet another nightmare. This time, she had found herself inside the TV tower for some unknown reason and, again, the final bell never came. Instead, the city remained dead and she stayed trapped inside the tower, forever enslaved by the absent bell.

She sat up in bed, chilled traces of the dream prickling her forehead. The clock showed 07:13. She had forgotten to set the alarm, which meant she had not witnessed the bell herself. A cold fear running through her body, she scrambled out of bed and bolted downstairs, calling her father's name. Nothing.

A note on the kitchen table said he had left for work already. The windows were slightly open both there and in the living room, she saw from the open door. She took a deep breath and trembling put the note down, plunging into a chair. The night-mares remained nightmares.

Out in the hallway, the doorbell rang once, twice. Three times. Urgent presses on the button. She frowned, wondering who would come at this time.

When she opened the door, Robin pushed past her without greeting, hastened into the living room and threw himself into one of the armchairs.

"Good morning to you too," Freja said and closed the door.

In the living room Robin kept silent for a long time, resting his elbows on his knees and his face buried in his palms while Freja watched him with growing unease. He did look different, but it wasn't just that he'd aged. He looked wearier. Tired. Only now did she realise that the stubble he'd had on the first day was now thick and almost qualified as a proper beard. Casual had gone careless. Robin who always said beards were for guys like Jaspir Nagel. And the dark circles under his eyes were merciless.

"Hey champ," she coaxed, nudging his shoulder as she sat down on the sofa next to his armchair. "What's wrong? Did someone die?"

He cleared his throat and scratched the stubble-beard.

Wetted his lips. Swallowed again. The words didn't come easily, at first. They never did; they hadn't done two years ago either.

"No, nobody … erm …"

When Robin finally shifted so that she could see his face clearly, he didn't have to say anything. She recognised that look and maybe she had seen it the second he walked into the room, but without taking notice. It wasn't a look you expected or wanted to see. It told of the unthinkable; that which only happened to 'other people'. A chill ran down her back.

"No …," she whispered and felt her eyes glaze over with tears, blurring Robin's face. "Who?"

She hardly dared to ask the question. Robin licked his lips again and inhaled, as though trying to push down the truth, force it back into the depths of blissful oblivion. At last he surrendered and clasped a hand over his mouth, leaving just enough space to blurt out in a half sob, half gasp, the name Freja subconsciously expected.

"We hadn't heard from her so …" His voice broke. "The Jahranian border control … she never crossed, she never … We don't know where …"

Tearless eyes met hers. The barrier between her and Robin had crumbled, and although she had wished over and over that it wouldn't exist, it broke her heart to watch it fall.

There was no bravado or mischief left in his dark irises; the rose-stealing boy was gone. Left was only his broken ghost-like twin. "Freja, Ceci's gone!"

CHAPTER 3

Robin's seat was now empty. He hadn't said much, and neither had Freja, so at last the hollowness between them had become too unbearable. Mumbling something about his brother, Robin had at last stood up and left the house without as much as a goodbye, leaving Freja on the sofa, paralysed by what she had just been told.

It all started almost thirty years ago, at the beginning of May of what was commonly known now as the Year of the Lion, before Freja was born. One of the older nuclear plants in Vildaell, placed in the south of its capital, exploded without any forewarning. President Colerush had long been pushing an agenda to dismantle the power plants and later that week, the leaders of the free countries were supposed to come together in Buria, the infamously rich nation and headquarters for world politics, and discuss the issue. But then the explosion happened and Colerush never made it there. The waste from the plant rendered much of the land in Vildaell, or Amérle at least, uninhabitable for a time and left the immediate area around the plant levelled to the ground. The city was evacuated. Since then, Amérle had been built up in stages by enthusiastic volunteers and it now at least bore the resemblance of a place without fatal levels of radiation in the air, so high that it could kill or cause diseases after prolonged exposure, though that was the true nature of the city. As an additional consequence of contamination, energy supplies ran low for a long time and the smoke lay thick over Vildaell for years as coal, oil and gas became the main sources of energy. Advocates of more sustainable sources had had little success and, instead, notices to reduce driving, electricity use and wasting water still came weekly through the letter boxes of Amérle, thirty years on.

To solve the imminent energy crisis, and as a 'safety measure' against exposure to the radioactive traces still poisoning the air, the next government with President Fiende, a sturdy man with a furry moustache and a terrific beard, recommended a twelve-hour Curfew taking place during the hours with the highest radiation. Less energy used and less exposure to radiation, "For the sake of the people." Abandoning Amérle, or the country, was not an option, he had explained in a famous live broadcast speech with his fist punching the air and the beard bouncing up and down with every lively gesture—"because this is our land." The crowd had cheered. Freja's father had switched off the TV. Curfew was implemented as soon as the protestations from the Queen and people of Buria had been subdued and the demonstrating population of Vildaell had gone home, their placards with raging messages written upon them discarded in piles soon to be washed away by the toxic rain.

After its implementation, few of the initial supporters cheered.

The punishment for transgressing the twelve-hour house arrest was severe. Nobody would be able to tell first-hand what happened if you broke the law, because nobody who did was ever seen again. 'Removed' was the word used in the legislation. These days, the past penalties, effective education in schools and rather gory road signs depicting faces torn apart by radiation or grieving families who'd had a member removed had encouraged the citizens to obey. The occasional demonstration still happened, but active anti-Curfew activity was considered alternative; just like its opposite, the Curfew Supporters, or 'Cursers' for short. Though they were rare and rather disproved of, the Cursers saw no wrong in the legislation, and even endorsed it. They were notorious for plump defence arguments, which they gladly shared, expressing sentiments that Curfew victims deserved punishment for breaking such a vital law that ensured our continued survival. Needless to say, it made them extremely unpopular.

Thankfully it was quite rare that people were removed these days, but many sleepless nights had been passed and countless longing looks had crossed the thresholds since the law had been put into practice.

Freja gazed towards the front door and the threshold where the memories of her mother lingered like indelible ink, and thought that now Robin's house had that ink too. If Curfew had taken Cecelya that mark would never go away from their threshold either.

A dangerously pretty girl of fifteen, Robin's sister Cecelya was a character of her own measure. She had dimples like Robin and doe-like eyes dominated by dark blue, but with tints of brown in them as well. She also had the sharpest mind of the family and carried herself like royalty, on spindly skinny legs, not yet fully grown, always stroking a black stray hair out of her face with delicate fingers. Her impulsive nature, infamous among her circle of friends, was cause for much worry for her parents and her two brothers.

The last time Freja had seen Cecelya was the day before Robin's departure to Fink, almost a year ago. It was a vivid memory. It had been a few hours before Curfew and Freja had stopped by the moss green villa to say goodbye. Cecelya had been dashing, as always, and in one of her most graceful moods. She opened the door before Freja could reach the knocker.

"FREJA!" Her cry rung through the house; all the way from the entrance, up the stairs, and to the bedroom from whence Mrs Aitken came scuttling at the sound.

"Your most dedicated fan, I believe," she cooed coming down the stairs, and laughed so that the family heirloom appeared in her cheeks. "Tell her off if she's too much, dear."

"Don't worry, Mrs Aitken," said Freja and gave Cecelya a hug. "She's like my baby sister."

"I am *not* a baby, darling," said Cecelya, grabbed Freja's shoulders and pecked her three times on the cheeks while Mrs Aitken went into the kitchen. "Freja, how a-a-are you doing? You look positively *glowing*."

There was not a word Cecelya Aitken couldn't place emphasis on, should she feel like it.

Freja replied she was well, and thought that, to most people, Cecelya must come across as haughty and snobbish; the way she elongated vowels and sang them melodiously in tune with exaggerated hand gestures. Her royal manners would surely sting in many eyes, but Freja had always thought she was endearing.

"Is school over for you kids yet?"

"Oh, yes," Cecelya replied with the regal air and fingertip scorn only a fifteen-year-old could achieve and believe in. "Easy as anything, really. 'Tis middle school, not true academics."

"Ceci, don't be a brag," said her mother from the kitchen, the reproach finding its way through to the hallway. Cecelya rolled her eyes with pursed lips and steered Freja to the little living room.

"You are here to see Robin, I suppose?" Freja said she was, but that it was always a *delight* to see Cecelya as well. "Oh, but of course. My brother, dear brother, isn't in—or, he is, rather he isn't up yet, the lazy bastard."

"Language, Ceci," came from the adjacent kitchen.

"Sorry, mother," Cecelya called and suppressed a smile to Freja. "I'll let him know you're here."

Cecelya sauntered off, leaving Freja at the window in the living room, where she admired the blooming fruit trees in the garden. How many apples and pears had she eaten from those trees? A lifetime's worth, surely.

"I've told her to come straight home from school." Mrs Aitken's sudden whisper made Freja jump. "I'm sorry, dear; I didn't mean to startle you." She fiddled with a kitchen towel. "I've told her, she must come home right away, especially now … especially since …"

Mathes Aitken, Robin and Cecelya's uncle, had left a young son and two sisters—one of them standing right in front of Freja—behind. Freja said it was sensible. "But she won't listen," added Mrs Aitken and twiddled the towel. "Maybe you could …?"

"Oh, he is impossible," came Cecelya's ringing voice as she ambled into the room, a delicate hand, its back arched, resting on her chest. Mrs Aitken returned to the dishes with her creased tea towel. "He's up, sort of," Cecelya said with a pondering face, "but let me play you my latest piece while you wait. I made it yesterday and mother said it was pretty—didn't you, mother?"

"Yes, it is a pretty one, dear."

A creative prodigy of sorts, Cecelya played the violin better than most professionals and certainly she was more skilled than people her own age. To her, however, it was merely a 'cultivated afternoon pleasure', as she might put it. Time and time again she was told by instructors that she was the new generation of concert violinists. Cecelya wouldn't listen. In an orchestra, she used to say, she wouldn't be allowed to play her own sheets— only those of antique gentlemen. And she had no interest in antique gentlemen. The best part about it all was that Cecelya was by no means conceited.

She played beautifully for Freja for almost half an hour before Robin came thundering down the stairs and stopped halfway, his head peering through the steps.

"I thought I heard the noise from hell," he said with a grin. Cecelya grimaced towards him and played a final series of notes to finish the piece. "Very nice, Ceci." She bowed with a whirling hand gesture and went to put the violin away in the walk-in closet next door. "Sorry you had to sit through that," Robin said and yawned. He descended and slouched down next to Freja in the sofa, yawning again, and rested his head on her shoulder. "Let me sleep. Please? These trainee exams are killing me."

"She's very talented," said Freja. "I quite enjoyed it."

"Don't let her hear you say that, or she'll be *absolutely gaze-boe'd* over the top of her head—it's her new expression of the week," he added at Freja's amused look. His impression of his sister was so lifelike that Freja had to cover her mouth not to laugh. Cecelya came back into the room wearing a suspicious countenance.

"Is he mocking me again? I swear, Robin, I will …"

"Relax, sis—I was imitating the Queen of Buria."

Cecelya had grunted, unconvinced, but had let it slide.

And now, less than a year later, the unofficial Queen of Vildaell might be gone.

Though, as she had told Robin once the initial shock and the black spots had ceased dancing in front of her eyes, there was no way of knowing for sure. Not yet, anyway. Even if she hadn't crossed the border and even if they hadn't heard word from either her or Kale, they wouldn't know if she'd been removed until the List came out.

The List, the weekly list of names of people who would

never be seen again. Of those who had missed Curfew. The next one was three days away, on Thursday.

But Robin had shaken his head. "She's a tool … but since uncle Mathes   The waiting, the List, the wondering … She saw Mum, she knows. She wouldn't let us wonder." He'd frowned and his nostrils had flared momentarily. "I never understood …," he had started but then trailed off. Then he had raised his head. Freja wished he hadn't, because in it she had seen the pain and the anguish taking over.

The empty seat still wore the imprint of his presence in its indented surface. Only the silence spoke of his absence. It was a silence patented to Curfew; nothing else could muster up the same sense of void.

*

Hours later, half one to be precise, she stood in front of the mirror, trying to decide what to wear. She was going to Robin.

"Just doing my duty as a friend," she told herself as she shrugged on the tenth alternative for top—a light fabric t-shirt—in the past five minutes. Her father was still at work and the house had never seemed emptier. Well, maybe once.

She thought about what she would say to Mrs Aitken, whom she'd inevitably bump in to. That it was going to be all right? That Cecelya would come back? The words were simple enough to form, but it didn't make them any less false. Despite everything, Freja wasn't a cynic. Cecelya could, in theory, turn up at any moment. There were dozens of possible explanations. Sometimes her mind even wandered to theory and her mother could, *in theory*, show up one day with a perfectly good and logical explanation for her absence. The problem was that when you had encountered Curfew on a personal level, you recognised its presence everywhere. No matter how much Mrs Aitken wanted to hope, she would know in her heart what had happened to Cecelya.

Freja's mirror image stared from behind the glass, asking questions Freja would rather have left alone. Did she know in her heart? She thought back to yesterday and the thing on the kerb. Shaking her head, she dispelled the thought and forced her brain to focus on the present. Clothes.

She considered leaving a note for her father, but decided against it. This wasn't the kind of news you gave over the phone or on a post-it. Besides, they didn't know yet. Not until the List. For a brief moment she felt grateful that her own disaster had struck quickly. At least they hadn't been forced to endure the wait—her mother had appeared in the List the next day. Marja Evenson, 41 y.o. Silver linings, she thought to herself as she decided on a striped t-shirt and jeans and headed out.

Within seconds of Freja ringing the bell, Mrs Aitken opened the door. "Oh, Freja," she said and embraced her. "It's so kind of you to come. Come in. We're all here."

Freja was led into the kitchen where Robin's father and his brother Enton sat in front of half-empty coffee cups, an untouched sponge cake—and last week's List on the table. It had been longer than usual—six names lost for good. Freja knew that they imagined how their daughter's, sister's, name would look on there.

Robin was not with them, and a low murmur of heavy-base music from the ceiling told Freja he was upstairs in his room. The two men acknowledged Freja with tired eyes.

"Good to see you, Freja," said Robin's father.

"You too, Mr Aitken. I'm …" She paused, not a clue of what she would say.

"Thank you," said Mr Aitken and lifted his cup as if to take a sip, then changed his mind and set it back down on the table when Enton snapped,

"It's not …! Not yet." He pushed out his chair with a sudden screech as the wood scratched against the tiles, and veered towards the window. "Stop acting like it is."

"Enton, sweetie … it's —," tried Mrs Aitken.

"It's not over," said Enton without turning. That was all. Nothing else was said and a dense silence lowered itself over the room. Outside, the sun was shining, thoughtless and indifferent to what was going on inside the house. Birds flittered and chirped as though it was a day as any other, which of course it was to most.

"Is Robin upstairs?" Freja said in a low voice, hoping it wasn't rude to ask. She felt like an intruder in this private moment and wanted, if possible, to flee the scene. Mrs Aitken said he was in his room and offered to go fetch him. "No," said Freja, a bit too eagerly. "I'll go—you stay here."

With that she dashed upstairs, away from the kitchen, glad to get out, pushing away the guilt pounding at her temples for leaving them so abruptly. But how could she comfort them when there was no comfort to give?

Music was streaming from behind Robin's door and she had to knock several times before she heard the desk chair being pushed back, the gentle spur of the springs and the approaching footsteps. When he opened the door, it was by a narrow crack. "Oh, it's you." Leaving the crack open for Freja to enter, he turned back to the room and threw himself back in the chair by the desk, which moaned under the sudden weight. The music was loud. It was a song from the top-lists, a squalling rock tune by a Jahranian band.

Freja closed the door behind her. She stayed by the entrance, feeling some chilly distance between them which stopped her from acting like usual, where she might lunge down on the bed and comment on the corny music posters on his wall. He liked old music and wasn't ashamed of his large collection from bands to which not even his parents listened. In the corner, by the bed, stood an old guitar, even though he didn't play himself.

It was signed by Rupert Giles, the famous guitar player, and that thing was Robin's most precious possession. On another day Freja might pretend to touch it and send him into a fit and make him wrestle her to the ground and pin her there until she vowed not to lay a finger on it.

On another day she might have done so.

"What are you doing?" she asked. He was on some strange website, Curfew-related, but she couldn't read the exact words off the screen.

"Nothing." He slammed the laptop shut and spun on the chair, leaning back into it. His hands were passive in his lap and he didn't quite look at her.

She cleared her throat. "I'm not sure I helped downstairs."

"You did what you could. Not much to say, is there?"

"How are you? I know it's a stupid, stupid question …"

"Oh, you know that, do you?"

"Yes, I do." Robin mumbled a sorry. "But I'm asking it anyway. You're up here shut in your room while your family is downstairs. You need to be with them."

"I can't. They're just arguing."

"They're arguing because they're upset."

"Well, I'm upset too, but at least I have the decency of being upset up here on my own."

He turned back to the screen and remained distant and reticent for half an hour or so, until Freja had had enough and got up to leave. All the words she had heard herself two years ago, those that she had stuffed away in a remote part of her mind, refused to come out to Robin, though she urged them to. Because she knew they didn't matter. There was nothing she could say to offer respite to him or his family.

When she finally left the Aitkens in peace and reached the end of their property, she allowed herself a long-contained sigh of relief, and dug her hands into her pockets to keep them from the cold air. Clouds had taken over in the sky and were holding the sun hostage. The early summer wind was not unfriendly but mild. She hoped that Robin at least had appreciated her coming.

The square shape of her phone met her fingers and she fished it up by instinct to check the time, see if her father would be back yet. There was a new text—from Robin.

Meet me at the Look-Out on Thursday, noon. R.

She turned back to the house and thought she saw the curtains on the upper floor tremble. It might just have been the breeze pushing through the gap of the open window. Freja turned the corner of the hedge and hurried away.

CHAPTER 4

THE LOOK-OUT—your view of everything.

That's what the sign said. It was a hill in the east part of Amérle from whose top you had a panoramic overview of the otherwise flat city. Skyscrapers and parks all became small islands in their own right in the sea of swarming pedestrians, cars, and bikes rushing here and there in the landscape. Benches dotted the grassy hill, there was a communal yellow phone box covered in splashes of colourful graffiti, and a small kiosk— mostly unmanned—to provide hot drinks and chocolates. It was a love bird hot spot, most of all, and a place for the other leaders to be photographed when they came to hold council with President Fiende.

And of course, all the green areas visible from up there, as well as the one comprising the Look-Out itself, were artificial; since the nuclear disaster, nothing green grew on its own accord in Vildaell.

Freja arrived at the Look-Out twenty minutes to twelve.

The three days since she last saw Robin had been an infinite drag but she had resisted the temptation to call him. As well as the temptation in that morning's newspaper. It sat deep in her pocket now, the List, and that's where it would stay until Robin arrived. It didn't feel right that she should look without him. It was in a sense more personal than a diary.

At home, the walls had felt invasive and the List had been glaring at her from within the morning paper, as though it would burn its way through. She wanted to look, so desperately, thinking over and over that it was possible, that her name might not be on there. But instead she had grabbed her backpack and stuffed the paper inside it along with some of her school books, even though there was no class that day because of the June Solstice. Instinct, perhaps, or a subconscious need for this Thursday to be like any other Thursday, and not one with more darkness than necessary made her push down biology and chemistry books, pens, and folders on top of the List.

She had sped up towards the Look-Out well ahead of time.

Up here the air didn't seem so bad and she could watch her city bustle with life as its people went to work, went to lunch, and went home. In the middle of the web of streets and buildings stood the TV tower which in itself was harmless, but was the source of the bells, and so hateful to her. The bells were minions of Curfew—and the tower kept them. The sun was at its highest point, yet Freja hugged her arms, shivering in the chilly wind. Even for Amérle it was cold, considering it was late June. It was as if the sun was as despondent as the people were and that from now on, after the solstice, it would have less work to do in the sky when night took over more and more every day.

It was just after twelve when he came. Robin's breathing was heavy as though he'd run up the steep hill. The buses went all the way to the top, but perhaps he had felt the idea of closed walls too confining as well.

"I haven't looked," he said when he reached her close to the end of the hillside, a folded newspaper cramped up between white fingers. "They were just staring at it, wouldn't open it. So I left ... Bought this one on the way. I should probably call when ... if ... There's a pay phone here, right?" Freja nodded, feeling the weight of her own copy of the List like a lump of lead. "You didn't look either?"

"We'll open it together," she said and Robin's face sunk into some kind of desolation, as if he'd wanted her to have looked for Cecelya's name and tell him it would be all right. She said nothing, as chances were high it wouldn't be 'all right' anytime soon. They both knew that if Cecelya had been removed, her name would be on that List. It was one of its less despicable features—since the Curfew Law's implementation, Freja hadn't heard of a single mistake. People who were listed were gone.

Robin brought out the newspaper and flicked through one page at a time, like a TV show host looking to draw out as much anticipation as possible from his audience. The News, the Sports and the Finance sections glided by as he approached the TV guide, behind which the List would be placed. An article covering the high and increasing crime rates in Jahran rolled past, the ever-increasing wealth of Buria as a nation bearing the headline *Of Queens' Gardens: Planned Surge for Buria Green Index* which had a large photo of the Queen, waving with a smile, covered half the page. The TV guide; through the thin paper of the Sunday viewings, Freja could see the outline of the List and shadows of its ethereal letters.

Two rows. Two names only.

She stopped Robin's hand when he had two fingers pinching the corner of the last page. She stopped him because, like Mrs Aitken, who had also felt Curfew before, Freja sensed in her heart what would appear in that List, and she would do anything for Robin not to see it. For one single moment more she wanted him to feel the spark of hope, real hope, and let him hold on to that hope for just one more shred of his life. In his raised eyebrow she recognised that naïve wish—conviction, even—that it would be all right. With her premonitions she felt like an accomplice in telling a child Father Christmas didn't exist, only this truth was miles worse, and infinitely more painful. She wanted to scream at him. Nothing would be all right again, ever. But she didn't. When she couldn't hold off any longer without good reason, she let him turn the page. A dry crumbling sound followed as the paper bent and curled at the will of his fingers; or was it the world falling apart?

"One at a time, okay?" she said and quickly covered the two names, then slid her hand to reveal the first one:

Benna Hjalmar, 82 y.o.

Freja knew her. She was a brutish old lady who ran a local charity shop and whose favourite distraction was chasing children and the occasional beggar from her street. Not much to grieve for, Freja thought, but instantly felt bad for thinking it. Maybe there was someone who would miss Ms. Hjalmar.

She glanced at Robin and let her hand glide down to disclose the second name. He didn't utter as much as a whisper as they read it and Freja dared not look at him, in fear of what she'd see. She held her breath. The curved letters glared from the dirty white page, unforgivable.

Cecelya Aitken, 16 y.o.

"She's not sixteen," said Robin, staring at the inky letters, somewhat smudged from his hand where he stroked them. "She's sixteen next month, July 21, not now. She's fifteen. She's *fifteen,* Freja!"

"Robin, I'm …" Her voice faltered. With one hand inside the bag, she found her wallet and retrieved a small golden coin which she held out to him. "Whether they've seen it or not—" Her eyes were still set on the name— "Call them. Here's ten—that'll give you fifteen minutes."

"Is that enough?" he asked. "Is fifteen minutes long enough?

Fifteen *years* was clearly enough for her to live—not sixteen, Freja, fifteen, they got it wrong. I guess fifteen *minutes* should be just right for me to tell my mother that ... that—" He crouched down and slammed his fists against his head, as if dispelling the many thoughts that were gathering like ominous clouds in there. Freja stood over him watching, blinking away tears in her eyes. She had no right to cry—it wasn't her sister—and she had to be strong for Robin, like he had been for her when Curfew touched her house.

"Ten," she said again. He glared at her but snatched the money from her hand and stalked off to the pay phone which was close by. While he was on the phone, Freja closed her eyes and let the wind surge through her, let it wipe away the waste and the toxic residues with its own poison. Far on her left, southwards, was the old nuclear power plant, the source of all this evil. She did not dignify it with her attention, chose not to see that, or the tower. For a brief moment, neither existed, and the world was good.

"Well, that's that," said Robin with a sigh when he came back and Freja's blissful spell was broken.

"What did they say? Had they seen it?"

"The neighbours were already there, with food and other useless stuff," Robin replied and sauntered right past her, surpassing the yellow sign reading DANGER! STEEP BLUFF! without as much as a glance at it. With confident strides he went down to the thin railing that formed the only barrier between safety and a hundred metre drop, and leaned against it as though daring it to break and let him fall.

"Careful there," Freja said, her voice reproachful but weak. Speed was nothing to her, but heights? They were like the antidotes of comfort. She blamed Robin for it—he always pushed her too high on the swings and she had fallen once and broken her wrist. "Your family needs you now, now more than ever, and you'll do no good as a wet splat in the middle of the road."

Robin turned around and his eyes wandered to Freja's chest. It took her a self-conscious second to realise what he was looking at. Her necklace. A drop shaped charm she always wore, day and night, all year round. It was a gift from her mother, who had told her it was a lucky drop of water. Personally, Freja thought it looked more like a tooth, or a leaf, but despite the poor crafting it was her most precious piece, even more so now.

"You know, I never understood the outrage," Robin said to her surprise, still leaning on that godforsaken railing. "It was just a law to me. A law like any other—you break it, well, you face the consequences. Simple. When Mathes disappeared I blamed him for putting Mum and aunt Pristina and my cousin through it. It was his fault for missing Curfew after all. I never said that to Mum, obviously." He shrugged as if his reflection was the most reasonable in the world, and squinted with a frown like he always did when contemplating something in detail. It made sense that Robin wouldn't let these opinions out in the open, given that few stamps were worse than that of Curfew endorser, but Freja felt cheated. Suddenly she wished that the railing wouldn't be so stable.

Her best friend, a Curser?

"Now I'm not so sure," Robin continued, but Freja couldn't help the new light this revelation had shed on him. "Ceci doesn't deserve this. She didn't do anything wrong."

"But your uncle did?"

My mother did? she added to herself. It came out more as a spit than actual words, but Freja didn't care. His words were so deeply insulting and careless and even though his sister had just been removed, she felt every inch of her skin crawl with what he had just said.

"That's not what I said —"

"Except it's exactly what you said, or implied, or whatever."

"Fitzie …"

There was a symphony of ringing in her ears, and his previous words echoed over and over. She said, "I never took you for a Curser, but I guess I was wrong." He opened his mouth, perhaps said something, but his words were lost in the swell inside her head. "Honestly, I can't believe it. I can't believe you!"

Robin watched her with calm eyes. He didn't even try to defend himself. She had a good mind to push him down that bluff herself, to punch him right in his Curser-loving face. Then he spoke again. His voice nigh on drowned in the roar of her pounding heart but she strained to listen. She had to listen, because part of her still knew that this was Robin, her Robin with lustrous brown eyes and black hair who couldn't possibly be one of *those people*.

"Curfew isn't fair," he said, "but what if they're right? What if it's true that the radiation levels are so high between six and six that you will die if you're outside?"

"Well, that's what they're saying," Freja snapped. "And in that case, they could at least return the bodies for a proper burial."

"What if the bodies are so damaged by nuclear waste that … that nobody should see them? What then?"

"Then they could tell us that. There'd be no need for all the secrecy."

Robin rubbed his chin where the beard had grown yet another layer. "True. So why don't they?"

She met his eye with a frown, now without malice. "Because it's not true."

Robin nodded. "But people go missing, they're *removed* to somewhere."

"That makes no sense. You must be right; the damage is too horrible and they hide away the victims."

"In that case, like you said: why cover it up? Does that make more sense to you? It doesn't to me."

She sighed. "Look, we'll never know," she said. "I know it hurts, Robin, trust me, I do, but we'll just—never—know."

A slight beat before Robin replied, "Unless we go find out." At this, Freja inquired as to what in the devil's name he was talking about. "Late last night when neither of us could sleep Enton and I got talking and we decided that if Ceci's name was on the List, we'd go find her."

Freja's mouth fell open. "What?"

"He's onto something, Freja. It's kind of, well, not illegal but not quite legal either, dubious. Lately he's been doing research around Curfew—history, legislation, that kind of stuff. That's what I went to look at that day, what he wanted to show me. He's found information that could lead to more information. I didn't quite understand it but it's a start." He took a step forward, eyes glowing. "Fitzie, it suggests they might still be alive!"

For a second time that morning, Freja could not quite grasp the words thrown her way. A few days ago this same boy had been lecturing her on the irreversible consequences of Curfew, and now he was planning to do the most risky, most stupid thing a Vildaell citizen could do?

"You're unbelievable," she said and Robin's smile froze. "What happened to 'don't do anything stupid' and 'it's a law, you can't break it'? I've wanted to look into my mother's removal for the past two years and you've always, without fail, been there to stop me. What's changed?"

"I told you—I know now, I understand. Nagel's son didn't go about it right, that's why he disappeared too. I shouldn't tell you, but Enton and I have a plan, or the outline of one anyway."

"Care to share? We're in the same horrible boat after all." He hesitated. In that hesitation his betrayal was naked and bared.

Her heart sank and whatever he said next she didn't hear. She scoffed. "Are you actually serious? You cannot possibly kid yourself that I'm not coming with you?"

"It's not that simple."

"Enlighten me, Robin. It seems pretty simple to me."

"Your father," he said and Freja let out a laugh, a loud artificial laugh whose black mocking couldn't evade Robin. He was watching her with infuriating calm and the desire to push him off the hill returned, stronger than before. Instead she turned on her heel and, wind rushing in her hair, reached halfway to the parking lot before she swung around. Robin was still at the railing, not so much as reaching out to stop her from leaving.

"I'm sorry about Cecelya," she yelled over the whining wind. "I really truly am, but if you go without me I will never forgive you. Ever. Even when you're removed because this plan of yours fails, I will not forgive you. Here's a tip, champ—*don't do anything stupid.*"

With those words she sprinted up with her heart in her throat and, after brushing strands of hair from her face, pushed on the helmet, visor down, and raised the engine of the Thunderball to a roaring start. She needed to get out of his sight so that Robin didn't see the tears now flowing without constraint down her cheeks. He would not know he made her cry. Wheels screeching on the tarmac, she left the Look-Out.

When she veered into the empty streets of her neighbourhood, a dark figure on the kerb once more demanded her attention and she slowed down. It was the same one as before, of that she was certain. Though Curfew was still hours away, Freja's brain beseeched her to turn left, to go home, to see if her father was back yet. Curiosity was not a deadly sin in Vildaell, but not far from it.

But then she caught a closer look at the woman, as she passed right by her side, and Freja's heart made a triple beat.

It couldn't be.

The woman moved swiftly, so gracefully it appeared she was gliding across the pavement ghost-like and ethereal, past Freja and to the end of the street behind her, around the corner and out of sight. Freja swung the motorcycle around and rushed after her, careening around the same corner, out of the neighbourhood, and tailed the woman onto a narrow gravel path wedged between her street and another residential area. Strangely, every time she fixed her gaze on the woman, she seemed to appear further away again. Robin's—her own—words echoed in her head, drowning out her adrenaline-nourished heart: don't do anything stupid. This might qualify as stupid, she thought as she took another corner on spitting gravel. Despite her head's insistent imploring to turn back, she couldn't convince her heart to leave no matter how hard she tried. It was holding the reins now, and it said: move forward.

Because now Freja was sure. The flowing auburn hair, the slender silhouette, the tubby pug on the leash … It was her—it was her mother.

All kinds of explanations bounced and leapt like flipper balls in her brain as she slipped across the gravel around another corner, deeper into the wooden area. Given how little they knew about Curfew, wasn't it at least possible? Hadn't Robin said there were peculiar circumstances, evidence that the victims were still, against all odds and information, alive?

The woman appeared again on the path ahead, and twisted her body so that Freja met at last the kind eyes, set in the face that she had painfully longed for ever since it left her sight. In a fluid moment her mother bent down and picked up little chubby Mops, whose cocked ears wiggled in recognition of his favourite Evenson. They disappeared behind another bend and Freja sped up, skating on the tiny stones underneath.

Too late did she realise where the path had taken her: the

Gravel Dump—a bowl-shaped site where residents disposed of their garden waste. Her speed was too high around the last corner, sharp like a pin, and she lost control over the motorcycle for no longer than a few seconds. It was more than enough. It lurched right, then left, slipping and sliding on the growling gravel, forcing her to hold on so tight to the handles that her knuckles stood out like white dots. The motorcycle jerked and turned; she begged the tyre in vain to sway back straight; a branch smacked her helmet and got stuck on the visor, blocking her field of vision. In the scrubby shrubbery in front of her eyes, she felt herself plummet towards the pit, the falling taking a firm grasp in her stomach and wrenching it good as sharp thorns shredded her shirt and tore into her skin as she tumbled through the large piles of rubbish.

A hard spot. Jerks. More jerks. Cast off. Falling.

Gravity clawing; calculating her body mass and multiplying it with the constant vector to determine how fast she should be falling. The closer to the ground, the quicker the object falls. Gravitation laws were absolute.

A blinding silver shade of light appeared before her eyes and she pressed them shut. She had read enough magazines and novels to know what it meant. It was that light at the end of the tunnel.

One thought alone possessed her mind: she was going to die.

And then there was a clicking sound and she fell through.

CHAPTER 5

IF THIS WAS death, she thought, it was a lot less impressive than she had imagined. She rolled over to her back, breathing heavily; rolled to her stomach again and pushed through the pain to a seated position, leaning against a large block of stone, the base of the mountain behind. A groan escaped her when the movement sent a stab through her side; she had landed on hard ground and her left side had taken the hit, especially her hip. Also, she was a mess: her hands were grimy, her t-shirt was dusty and dirty and enamelled by grey and black, her jeans were torn at the side. Though her head felt fine, her helmet was gone. The backpack, however, was by her side.

She remembered having been flung off the Thunderball ... But there was another fact that was even more remarkable. Gone were the Gravel Dump and Amérle, as was her motorcycle.

The space in which she had landed was no wider than one of the winding alleys in the Old Town of Amérle. It would fit three men abreast at most and created a narrow corridor between the massive chain of snow-peaked mountains behind and a tall brick wall of a dirty yellow colour, like tarnished gold.

The wall stretched far in each direction and curved before reaching its end, leaving it infinite, eternal, and detaining whatever was on the inside.

The way into which, by some splendid stroke of luck, stood before her very eyes: an enormous dark wooden doorway with black metal bars in a rigid grid over its surface.

With nerve-wrenching effort, she managed to get to her feet. Her hip protested, though not too insistently. Even as little an action as slinging the backpack on was full of effort, but she did it anyway—she had to find out what in the world had happened. With resolved steps she stumbled up to the door and yanked the handle. The cold metal sent bolts of shivering through her nerves. It refused to budge. She used her right shoulder to heave the massive wood, thrusting so hard she imagined bruises forming with every hit, and her hip screamed for her to stop. She did stop, but only when the rusty hinges had loosened with a reluctant screech, and the door swung open to reveal an expanse of sunlit ground.

The valley into which she stepped was so entirely different from Amérle—or any other city she had been to before—that she inferred, impossible as it sounded, that it must be another country altogether. Every bit of land available to the naked eye was covered in green and flowers and natural splendour. Grazing animals strolled without constraint across the green fields and into the forests, and through the skies soared birds of all kinds and colours. Eagles, sparrow-hawks, seagulls, and martins, all zig-zagging around each other, plunging down towards the ground only to turn at the last moment and shoot up into the sky again. A giant tree stretched high in the far distance, higher than the mountains, up towards the blue sky and the sun itself, and lingering on the north-west horizon, just visible, was the blueness of the ocean. There were no tall buildings and not a sign of concrete anywhere; the air was fresher; the sun brighter;

and she had never seen mountains like those she saw surrounding the outer part of the brick wall. How she'd gone from fatally crashing into the sharp debris of the Gravel Dump to landing in this place, she dared not guess, but here she was. Her father had oftentimes told her that there was no pain in death, that it was calm and peaceful and pain-free, so she closed her eyes and pinched her arm, hard. The sting made her wince. Alive. That was a good start.

This discovery confused her even further and pretty as the valley was, it was a strange place so she turned to find her way back. Only, the gate had closed of its own accord. No matter how hard she pressed down the metal handle, heaved, pushed, or jerked, the gate refused to open. There was no other portal in sight in either direction, only the forest to her left and right, the tree far beyond the wooden area, and the ocean ahead. Climbing was not an option either, given the sharp arrows that lined the metal frame.

"Now what?" she said out loud to herself, feeling rather silly.

Her mobile phone. Of course! She plunged into her backpack, groped around until she found it. But it was dead.

"Great," she muttered and threw it back and stood up in face of the landscape. There was one path leading forward and, with no other options to choose from, she ventured upon it. After a while she realised the most curious thing of all: there were no people to be seen anywhere. Green, green, green, the impossibly enormous tree, and lots of animal inhabitants—but not a human in sight.

A whirring sound, like a hum, filled the air and for a second Freja's mind leapt to an incredible yet enchanting thought—the landscape was singing. The next moment she was almost run over by the source of the sound, and just about managed to avoid the approaching vehicle. Flinging herself out of the way, her hip took yet another impact from the trunk of a rowan tree by the side of the path, distracting her so that she merely got a glimpse of the near hit-and-run. Stood on top of a strange kick-bike, with the two wheels turned sideways, the person—whether woman or man, Freja could not see—sped past without apology, so fast that the two-wheeler seemed to hover above ground, sending the gravel into small whirlwinds underneath. The whirring, she realised, came from its engine.

"Wait," she shouted and pushed herself away from the tree, rushing after the two-wheeler. "Wait!" Even though the vehicle did not stop and though it was moving at too high a speed for Freja to catch up on foot, she picked up her pace and hurried after it. At the very least, she thought, maybe the person could tell her where she was—and how to find another gate. Besides, where there was one person, there was bound to be more.

Just as she worried that she had got lost—if it's possible to lose your way when you never knew it in the first place—Freja began to discern a collection of small houses. The little village was situated in front on the edge of the ocean, in a curved bay. Out on an island, seemingly without any connection to the mainland, stood a larger building, separate in both appearance and structure from those in the village. It was square and alone, as though the very island was built for its convenience.

Eager to see the village closer, Freja broke into a run, ignoring her painful hip, though soon she had to stop and rest, out of breath in the searing heat. Panting, she wiped her forehead, she was really sweating. The sun was rarely this strong back home and she almost felt dizzy. She needed water.

The two-wheeler was long gone and it took Freja another hour to reach the village which rested lazily and peaceful in an arched bay over-looking the still water surface. She entered through a delicate archway and came into the square. The smaller houses in the village were simple wooden cabin-like constructions and appeared to be shops of some kind with large windows showing an array of items on display. There were a few people moving around, all dressed in colourful overalls and all minding their own business, not noticing Freja or even seeming to notice one another.

Before she could decide who to ask, or look closer at the shop windows, a firm hand grabbed her from behind and nails pierced her skin as she was jerked to the side.

"Come with me," a low female voice hissed in her ear as the hand dragged Freja into a dark and cold alley squeezed between two houses. "Or they will discover you."

Freja squirmed to get out from under the woman's hold, and managed with a final pull. She sprinted towards the square again, towards the light. A pounding inside reminded her that she was still alive and had a life to lose—so the pain in her side would have to wait. When the hand seized her again she was so close to the light that she could feel the heat of the sun on her face. The woman snatched Freja back and pain shot through her shoulder. For a moment the socket threatened to unhinge, but it stayed in place and Freja once more felt a hot body behind her. The woman's grip was even firmer now and she found it hard to breathe at all with the woman's other hand covering her mouth. When she finally remembered that she had a nose, breathing got easier, but the panic did not subside. She squirmed, kicked, and swore in muffled words, but the voice murmured for her to stay still. She felt hot breath stewing on her neck as the woman pulled her close, further into the alley, pressing them both against the wall. Cold sweat trickled in large drops down Freja's forehead and added a salty taste in her mouth.

"Calm down. You're lucky you met me first," the voice hissed as Freja made yet another attempt to break free. "Do you have any idea what they would do to someone like you? Quiet!"

Outside on the street, Freja saw how three people—two women and one man—dressed from top to toe in white tightly fitted boiler suits came into view and convened mere metres away from where she was standing. Freja saw her chance and gathered strength to cry out for help. But something stopped her. An icy chill poured over Freja's insides as the three people in white spoke in deep-toned whispers. The three shadows blocked out the sunshine and behind her, the woman's heartbeat pounded into her back, accelerating with every beat. If they had turned their heads and glanced into the alley for even a second, they would discover more than just the darkness in which the two females were engulfed. Though not sure why, Freja's racing heart was thankful they didn't.

Once the three people in white were out of sight again and the sunlight spilled over the ground, the woman waited a few minutes before releasing her grip, and gestured for Freja to remain quiet. Freja, in turn, now felt she had no reason not to oblige.

"You shouldn't have come to the village," the woman, who Freja now saw was probably in her late twenties and quite beautiful with burgundy hair, olive skin, and three gem stones at her temple in the same deep red colour as the jumpsuit she was wearing, whispered, "—too many Masters around."

Before Freja could ask what Masters were, or what the danger with them was—or even *where* she was—the woman pushed her out in the open street. There were more people now, as if the village had awakened, and they were all wearing the same garment, only in different colours. Freja felt profoundly out of place in her torn jeans and filthy t-shirt. A few of the villagers eyed Freja hurriedly from top to toe, but nobody's glance lingered for long. The woman held her close. "Be quiet and stay with me," she murmured and pushed her forward. "I'll take you to Topster. I'm Éloyse, by the way."

"Freja."

"I know."

Freja followed the woman, the thought of the white-clad people still haunting her mind. Within seconds Éloyse had guided her onto a two-wheeler like the one Freja had seen almost too close up before, and concealed her under a cape made from light fabric which Éloyse then attached to her own collar. A humming escaped the vehicle as the engine came alive.

"Letting Topster use you to do his dirty work again, I see," said a man's voice, which must have surprised the both of them because Freja felt Éloyse's muscles stiffen. "Why, I cannot fathom."

All Freja could see from under the cape were the man's light grey legs (she assumed it was part of a boiler suit) and black boots. With her slight frame, Freja must have been well concealed, for the man did not acknowledge her presence at all.

"I thought you were still in the Queen's court?" Éloyse shot back with some subtle acidity. "How is the old lady?"

The man laughed, but his voice was void of any humour. "The Lords have asked me to kindly remind you of your position," he said. "A position you have, according to the Lords, been neglecting as of late."

"The Lords say so?"

"They do." He spoke in a deep and pleasant voice. "They wish to see results, and soon. Lord Eden is concerned …" He paused, the rest of the sentence hanging like spider web in the air.

"Yes? What is Lord Eden concerned about?"

The man cleared his throat. "Not only Eden, but all three Lords as well as other parties of the Élan, worry that there is bias to be concerned about."

"*Bias?*" Éloyse killed the hum of the engine in an instant. "How dare you even—?

"—but I said there was no reason to be alarmed. Is there?"

"This is not a good time, Elflock."

"It seldom is with you, Éloyse. —Master." With the last word the man walked away from Freja's sight. Éloyse said nothing more, only re-ignited the two-wheeler and the whirring again growled from its interior as they rolled off. She wondered what it had all been about, but dared not ask. Soon they were moving so fast Freja's mind was occupied with holding on to Éloyse's waist so as not to fall off.

Once the giddiness had subsided and she had found a comfortable position, Freja could feel the rush of the speed inhabit every cell of her body. It was like nothing she had ever experienced on her Thunderball. The cape covering her flapped in the wind and revealed the scenery. A little blurred, she could at least make out that they had left the village behind and were now flying through the open landscape. In the distance, to the right, she could still see the ocean leading into a seemingly endless horizon. She craned her neck and saw that they were rolling towards the giant tree, now towering before them not very far away.

The landscape soon turned flatter and wider; the road itself became narrower and wilder, with growth roaming the sides untrimmed and uncontained; every now and then marvellous deer skipped alongside them until the speed became too great even for their strong limbs. Forests rose to the right, where the ocean curved off into a peninsula, and the mountains came closer.

At last the road came to a stop and a house appeared before them, as though it was its only destination, and the two-wheeler slowed down until it came to a full stop. Freja felt the jelly in her legs as she stumbled off.

"We have arrived," said Éloyse. "Come."

CHAPTER 6

INDEED, THE COTTAGE stood at the end of the valley, with the tree and brick wall within walking distance and the mountain range just beyond. In the garden patch in front of the house danced a small flower bed moving in the breeze, its neat array of ordered delicate roses, foxgloves and clematis, swaying solemnly, still mere buds waiting to bloom. The yellow buds reminded Freja of her illicit business with Mr Nagel. It was a sore reminder. She had to find out what on earth was going on.

Ahead, Éloyse climbed the steps up to a creaking porch and knocked three times on the door, paused, then knocked once more. Despite the sheer curtains, preventing her from seeing any details of the interior through the round windows, Freja could detect movement behind the glass. When the door swung open she leaned to the side, curious to see the man called Topster.

Whatever she'd had in mind, however, it wasn't what appeared in the doorway. It was indeed a man, if he could be called such a generic term. The height of a child, his face and skin were the only signs that he was older than that, with their wrinkled and crinkled texture. From top to toe he was an image of the best-before-date gone by: a few lonely strands of light hair remained on his otherwise bald skull; his half-open mouth revealed a gaping black hole where all his teeth would have been; his clothes were whole but worn, and ill-fitting as though he had lost a lot of weight in a short period of time; and his slightly hunched back gave him a sinister appearance altogether. He was leaning on his right leg a bit more than his left, and held a tight grip around the latter, as though it caused him pain or needed the extra support. Freja had never seen a stranger man in her life, and he reminded her more of some mythical creature than a human being.

"Master Éloyse," the man growled and lightly touched his chest with his right hand, like some kind of greeting which the woman did not replicate.

"Tell Master Topster I am here to see him," said Éloyse and crossed her arms.

Unsure what to do, Freja remained anonymous behind her. Not that she would rather have shook the man's hand, mind. She was content with hovering in the background.

The man, who clearly hadn't noticed Freja yet, glared at Éloyse with an ugly grin, revealing his mouth did indeed contain a marginalised set of teeth, all as subject to decay as the rest of his body. "The Master en't in," he said and looked around as if he expected Topster to pop out of thin air. "Can I 'elp ya?"

Éloyse took a step to the side and revealed Freja. The man glowered and inspected the girl through narrowed eyes. Her heart must have been beating a thousand beats per minute, but Freja compelled herself to remain calm and confident, and not appear lost or helpless at all. Whether she succeeded or not, she didn't know, but the man broke out in a foul grin.

"What's this, Master? *Hooman,* is it? The *hooman* business, eh?"

"Even if it is, that is hardly *your* business, is it Klobb? Stop your twaddle and tell Master Topster I need to speak with him right away."

"I told ye, he en't in. Go see for yourself if you want." He offered the door.

"That will not be necessary. You will let him know I was here."

Klobb pursed his lips hard, grunting that he would pass on the message, yes indeed he would. Apparently content with his word, Éloyse turned to Freja and released her stern expression into a kind smile. "I must see to something, so for the time being you can stay here. It's safer than the village."

"You're leaving?" Freja blurted out before she could stop herself.

"Klobb will take good care of you until Topster comes back —won't you, Klobb?" He might have agreed, or not, it was hard to tell when all he did was grumble and shuffle back into the shadows within the cottage. "Be nice," Éloyse warned him and pushed Freja up to the porch. "Tell Topster I will come back tomorrow."

"Wait—what do I do with it 'til then?" Klobb yelled from the inside and came out limping, his left leg dragging behind. It was too late. Éloyse was already on the two-wheeler, roll-ing down the road in an invisible cloud of whirring. Whether Klobb or Freja was the more unhappy to see her leave, Freja didn't know.

"'It'?" she said, arms across her chest, trying to hide the cold fear swirling around her veins, making her skin shiver. "I usually go by Freja."

Without replying Klobb turned back inside, gesturing for her to follow.

From where Freja was standing it looked like the entrance to some dark haunted house with the monster not hiding under the bed or in a closet, but inviting you in himself. Klobb must have sensed her fear, like an animal could smell out its prey. He stuck out his head from the murky interior and showed off his brown-stained teeth in a laugh. "Come in, come in," said the beast with glee and summoned her with gnarled hands.

The house was humble in all its sparse decoration, but cosy. The bedroom to which Freja was directed had nothing but a bed, a full-length mirror, and a night table with two drawers, nothing more. No books, no paintings, no ornaments at all. Not even a lamp. Having disposed of her backpack on the bed, Klobb yelled at her to come out the back, and she wasted no time in following his raspy voice. His growling led her through a narrow corridor to the back of the house and into a little garden. This, as opposed to the interior of the house, was overflowing with life and colours: flower beds on both sides with buds of all the rainbow waiting to bloom; a stream with clear water trickling down natural steps of rounded stones; fruit trees dotted at the end of the lawn; and grass soft to the touch stretching across the space.

"If yer staying you better make yerself useful. The Master en't coming back 'til later," said Klobb and shuffled across the grass to the washing line which was tied between two trees, hanging from the lowest branches so that the poor man could reach up even if he had to stand on his tip-toes like some ghastly ballerina from the underworld to do so. For Freja, the line hovered at eye-level. Klobb pointed to a basket of wet clothes standing underneath the line. "There, get to it. But I'm warning ye – no talking."

He fished up a towel from the basket and clipped it onto the washing line as demonstration. Though he was small, he was forceful, so Freja gave him a hollow smile and dove down to the basket. It couldn't hurt to humour him, and besides, she thought, she wasn't sure whether he was human or a human-shaped bomb about to go off. So she 'got to it'. The first garment she pulled up was one of the blue jumpsuits that filled the basket. Holding it up, she estimated that it would have fitted two of Klobb in height and barely half in width. Its blue shade blended in with the sky above, where not a cloud disturbed the peaceful canvas of heavenly paint, until the two colours were indistinguishable. For a bird, it was the outfit of invisibility. The illusion was quite hypnotising.

"Whose—" she began but was immediately smacked by a crooked finger pressing against her mouth. A dry *tsch* sound from Klobb's throat accompanied the coarse touch, whose imprint she would feel long afterwards.

"No talking, lass, I mean it! First thing ye need to learn here—those who speak more than they have to, are liars."

Stumped by his physical reprimand, Freja swallowed about a dozen counterarguments and bent down to the basket and continued in silence.

Because the line hung so low, some of the items reached down to the grass and the hems got smudged. Klobb only glared at these and muttered to himself, but did nothing about it. Whenever she could, therefore, Freja folded the hems of the jumpsuits before handing them to him. She must have done something right because if he noticed, at least he didn't object.

Afterwards they sat at the low table in the kitchen, where a simple fireplace was the only place for cooking and a kettle with water from the stream outside hovered over the crackling flames. There was a glass cabinet along the wall on one side and baskets full of vegetables on the other. No fridge, no freezer, no oven—in fact, no electrical appliances at all.

Before long, Klobb slammed a steaming mug in front of Freja. The mug had a single green leaf drenched in the water.

"Drink," he said.

"Thank you," Freja whispered in one word as he sat down opposite her with his own mug. She wasn't sure whether she was allowed to speak now or not, and deemed it safest not to. If possible, she would rather not give him reason to silence her again: the taste of his shrivelled skin still lingered on her mouth.

All the exhaustion and confusion that had bottled up since the accident came over her at once like wild lava. The woman on the kerb, this strange place, Masters, Éloyse, Klobb, and the mysterious Topster—it was all too much for one person to contain. She glared at Klobb. It wasn't his fault, surely, but he wasn't helping with his twisted idea of hospitality. He glared back, drinking his tea in loud smacking gulps.

The memory of the day her mother was removed flashed in her mind: her father leaning against the closed door, the Signaller's light glaring red. The then fifteen-almost-sixteen-year-old Freja had been perching at the top of the stairs two years ago, waiting to say hello to her mother like they always did when she stepped over the threshold after an afternoon walk with Mops, a few minutes after five o'clock. That time it had been a few minutes to six instead and Freja was waiting for her to come through the door, in denial of the black weight sinking like an iron block into the depths of her stomach as the Signaller beeped and turned yellow. The tenth bell had been long gone and they had had to close the door, or the house would have entered the Zone—that's what they called houses that failed to lock up. A security mechanism in their door ensured it was locked before Zone happened, and Otto had been fighting it, knuckles white from the effort. He lost. The Signaller's beep loud, almost unbearable, and the door slammed shut and her father collapsed on the floor, helpless.

An ice cold metallic chill had filled Freja then at the top of the stairs and it returned now as a reminder of what her father would be sitting through right this very moment. It bruised her heart to think that he would have to go through it all again—

this time alone, without anyone to pat him on the back or hug him and say it would be all right, even though it was a lie. Then there was Robin, who would think she had defied Curfew at last, spurred on by their argument, despite her promise not to. She remembered the uneasy terms they separated on, and understood, because she knew him well enough, that he would blame himself for her disappearance, and felt the steam of the tea go to her eyes. And finally the woman—the shadow of her mother who had led her to the Gravel Dump and to this world.

However much she tried to connect the pieces, they drifted apart again and again.

Staring into her mug, lost in her flurrying thoughts, Freja didn't notice the knock on the window. Only when Klobb returned to the kitchen carrying a heavy basket of apples and, if possible, a more sourly expression on his face than before, did she snap back the present. The horrible unfamiliar present.

"Master Topster sends a message," he said and heaved the basket onto the table with a bang. In his hand was a furry little creature, black like soot, about the size of a skinny rabbit, but uglier and with sharp teeth hanging out like on a vampire through its thin mouth. It had ears and bulging eyes like a bat. A batsër, Klobb explained like it was the most natural thing in the world. "This one's Pollux, though we en't supposed to give 'em names. Pollux is me special one, aren't ya? Trust 'im to deliver a message, 'cause he does what ye tell 'im. Oi! Be careful. 'E dun like to snuggle all that much."

Freja had reached out a hand to let the creature smell it as you would with any pet, but flinched and retracted it at Klobb's warning. The batsër nicked an apple and leapt onto the table and down to the floor, scuttling like a spider through the kitchen door. "Pollux," cried Klobb, but too late. The creature was already out of sight. Klobb sighed and pushed the basket of apples towards her.

"Master says he en't coming back tonight either. And that I ought'a feed you summat." He grabbed one of the apples. "The Master knows I en't of much use in a kitchin'—so he sends apples for ye to eat. 'Ere, take one."

Freja smiled and took one of the fruits and watched with disgusted fascination as Klobb gobbled down the whole thing in a smacking fashion, core and all, as though he hadn't tasted food in a long time. The fruit devoured, he noticed his guest merely nibbling at her green orb, and huffed. "Like a bleedin' Master ... Break's over, lass." He hobbled out again and returned with a bucket of water which he slammed in front of Freja along with a brush. "Back t'work. Do the front porch while I see to th' garden. There, off y' go."

She felt her patience melt away like butter in the sun. Next she knew, it was gone. Enough was enough; she had to go home. She bit off a large chunk of the apple, chewing loudly while speaking. "I'm not your cleaner, Klobb. And I'm not touching that until you start telling me what I want to know."

Klobb seemed equally unenthusiastic by her revolt. He snatched the apple from her hand and smashed it on the table with a loud *CRUNCH!* It caved in like an aluminium soda can, breaking into wet pieces which skated across the table surface. "Y'are what I say y'are until the Master comes back. And if ye don't do what I tell ye I'll toss ye out on yer *hooman* behind to find yer own way back!"

"Great idea," said Freja and stood up. "I think I'll leave." It worked better than she had anticipated. Before she had time to put her threat in motion, Klobb flung up his arms and let out a wet gurgling sound, like a sneeze from the throat. His arms then sunk down and he allowed for a heavy sigh. "Now," Freja continued without hiding her smugness over calling his bluff. "How about we start easy? Where am I?"

"Lass, y'heard the Master—it en't my business. Master

Topster …"

"That's next—who's Topster? Why am I waiting for him?"

"Cannae tell ye."

"How did I get here?"

"Nah-ah." He shifted his weight, leaning on his right leg instead and pounded his left thigh with a closed fist.

"Then how about what happened to your leg? Surely that's your business."

"That's none of *yer* business," he snapped. "Listen—just get t'work and I'll ask the Master, Master Éloyse that is, to tell ye whatever ye want afterwards."

"You promise?" He pushed the bucket towards her. As she felt it was as close to a promise as she could hope for, Freja snatched it from his hands. She would make sure Klobb kept his word.

Later, all chores concluded, Freja asked if she could take a walk. With suspicious enquiry as to the reason, he sullenly consented when she threatened to run away again.

"But dun' go into the forest," Klobb barked. "The fenrirs will eat ye alive if ye so much as close yer eyes for a blink, ye know. And watch out for the deerdjur. An't as friendly as they seem."

"Fenrirs? Deerdjur?"

"Ye know a fenrir when ye see one. And deerdjur are them big fellas, with horns in their heads."

Deer sounded all but dangerous, but she cast away the doubt, deciding that Klobb had no reason to lie. If anything, he'd probably prefer if the deerdjur got rid of her for him. "And dun' even think about running away," he added, a dark look in his eyes. "Ye can run from me, but dun' think there's anywhere t'hide from them."

"Them? Masters?"

"Dun' wanna get on the wrong foot with them, that's all I'm

sayin'. My company will seem like the bleedin' Queen of Buria compared to 'em if ye do something stupid."

Freja gasped. "Is this Buria?" Klobb snorted and laughed for a long while after that. So it wasn't Buria. That was one place ruled out.

After promising not to do anything stupid (with a twinge of guilt she remembered having made a similar promise to Robin), Freja went out.

The sun had begun to set a while ago and although there was no clock in the house, nor would Klobb give any indication of the time, her inner clock, though feeling somewhat thrown off balance, told her that it must be at least six in the evening. That usual restlessness brought on by Curfew had instilled itself in her bones, a subtle ache penetrating to the marrow. The mere act of turning the door knob sent her insides twirling again and her heart beat as if she was committing a crime, even though she had Klobb's permission. In this world, there was no Curfew Law.

The outside landscape was dressed in sombre twilight and glowing insects were singing in every bush around. She didn't go a great distance from the house, keeping her word to Klobb, but enough to inform her of her surroundings. The journey with Éloyse had taken them far in a short period of time, unsurprisingly considering the speed of those two-wheelers. What had Klobb called them? Transporters, she thought and snapped her fingers. That's it. In the distance she could still discern the peninsula and the great sea and if she peered carefully she could just about make out the contours of the peculiar island with the lonesome building. It was so quiet that the insects' melody seemed to be the only sound in the entire world.

She sat down and considered her situation. If she tried to escape into this vast landscape, she realised she wouldn't get far.

Klobb's comment about supposedly wild and lethal animals had stuck with her. She didn't know this world. Say he was telling her the truth for once? For all she knew, the insects now singing so beautifully could be fatally poisonous. Not to mention Masters. Éloyse had been all right, but what about those three Masters in white in the village? Had she been sitting there at all watching what she realised was her first full sunset if she had bumped into them instead of her? She shuddered at the thought and forced it out of her mind. No, she would have to stay put until she could figure out a thing or two. Until Topster came back, perhaps, and explained everything. Or maybe she could coax Éloyse into talking. Until either of those occurred, she decided that the cottage was the safest place to be.

Squinting, she saw the blue ocean and wondered what was on the other side; where was this place in the world? There was a sea separating the mainland of Vildaell, Jahran, and Buria from Muspeldal, the second, distant, continent. She wasn't in Vildaell, nor Buria, and she had a hard time imagining a place like this in Jahran, a country worn down and torn down by poverty, where beggars and criminals lived in anarchy under a powerless state. From TV images she knew it was urban and ugly, nothing like this. So that left Muspeldal, with countries she knew nothing about. But how in the world had she gone from the Gravel Dump across the sea to Muspeldal? It hurt her head just to think about it, and she decided not to, at least for the moment.

Once the sun had disappeared over the horizon, she went back inside. Already on the threshold she heard voices from the garden, and she tip-toed through the corridor, as quietly as the floor allowed, prowling closer to the back, thinking it might Topster who had returned after all. At the back door she discovered that there was one sole voice—Klobb's own.

"I en't letting those horrible deerdjur spoil you, m'dear Sora, don't you worry about it one inch."

He was crouching in the dim moonlight in front of a particularly blossoming bush with small dainty flowers of every colour of the rainbow, the trumpet-shaped flowers opening up to his face like a good friend. In his hand was a clipping tool, and he was grooming the plant with gentle movements. Smiling to herself, Freja left him in peace and retired to the plain bedroom.

Unable to sleep, she dug in her pockets and found the List, crumpled and smudged. In the flickering candle light she read the names. Benna Hjalmar and Cecelya Aitken. Two more names to the long list of missing people. In some central register they would be added somewhere beneath Mathes Aitken and Marja Evenson. Robin's theories were outrageous, but his brother had found something. She just hoped they didn't go off on a blind treasure hunt before she could get back and tell them her theories. She replaced the List and blew out the candle, lay down and stared into the dark ceiling. The seed of a thought had formed in her mind earlier, a thought that had seemed impossible until a few moments ago. But she needed more information to be convinced. When Topster came back, she thought, as sleep wrapped itself around her.

Finally she fell into a dreamless sleep, giving her last waking thought to her father.

*

Rain was hammering down on the roof tiles of the cottage when she woke up the next morning, and she found Klobb standing on a low stool, peering through the round windows out front. Guessing from the bucket beside him, he had been cleaning the windows again. As usual he was mumbling to himself and she could only catch parts of what he was saying.

"Will Topster come today, you think?" she asked.

It would be no exaggeration to say that Klobb nearly fell off his stool in surprise. He jumped, stumbled, and grabbed hold of the curtains to steady himself, an expression of relief spreading across his face when he temporarily prevented the fall and thought he was safe. The next second the fabric tore from its holdings and he fell, landing with a splash in the bucket of water which tipped over, splattering water all over the floor. He spat and swore and threw the window cloth in the puddle. Freja suppressed a bubbling laugh.

"Dun just stand there! Clean this mess up, will ya," he yelled and shuffled to his feet, indignant, all the while muttering curses under his breath and his face contorted in a foul grimace. While he hobbled into the kitchen to dry himself, Freja picked up the abandoned cloth and started drying the floor, laughing to herself.

There was a knock on the door—three times, then once more—and Klobb yelled at her from within to see who it was. Freja stepped over a wet pool and peered through the round glass.

It was the Master again.

CHAPTER 7

FREJA WAS SNARLED at to stay in the hallway while Éloyse and Klobb went into the kitchen. Luckily, she had no difficulties hearing their conversation through the open door while she pretended to wipe the floor. First, Klobb told Éloyse of the message from Topster, saying that he would most likely not return today either, what with the weather and all. A moment of silence followed before Éloyse ordered Klobb to close the door and he did, glaring at Freja who pretended to be busy at work. As soon as the door slammed shut, she dropped the cloth and crouched by the wall to listen.

"You were to keep her out of sight," she heard Éloyse say and Klobb began to protest. "No, be quiet. What if it had been one of the Élan?"

"Meh," grunted Klobb. "The Élan hasn't bothered with this region since pre-wall times."

"Still, we have got to be cautious. I've got bad news." Éloyse paused. "It's like I thought ... I went out there and there is no doubt about it—the latch is closed. I knew this would happen—in fact, I told Topster it would."

"Big whuff," said Klobb, unconcerned. "There are other ones."

"The Élan will not grant me one, not again." Éloyse let out a frustrated sigh. "They are getting suspicious—I have no business there. Also, if they continue to pull strings for me Master Ravn will grumble and trust me, that's the last thing we need right now."

"Infinite?" Klobb said.

"Don't be silly," replied Éloyse. "We might as well speak of fairies."

"If you say so, Master." The sentiment behind his words was hard to determine; it was smug and inferior at the same time. "You know best."

The kitchen fell silent.

"Klobb, where is Topster?" Éloyse asked the question with urgency and scrapes from the floor sounded as she stood up. "He assured me he would be back by now."

"The message, Master …"

"… says he is gone, but gives no indication of where or when he shall return."

"Do you really wish to know, Master?" A tense pause. "Really?"

"As if you would tell me," Éloyse said, not entirely without bite. "Klobb, they sent Elflock to talk to me."

"Elflock? Hum … Tall, square, dynamite teeth? Yes, I know 'im. Bit of a tool, that one. What did he have t'say then?"

"Does it matter? The Lords are clearly not pleased."

While she had no idea what a latch was or why it was important that it stayed open, Freja realised that something had gone wrong since her coming here. Then Klobb said something that really caught her attention.

"Tell me, how did the *hooman* get through? Correct me if I'm wrong 'ere, Master, but Master Topster told me no one but Masters can use it alone."

"According to basic latch physics, that is true."

"Then how—"

"Unless you want to share the details of this master plan of Topster's that I'm risking everything for," Éloyse snapped, "I can't help you." Klobb did not want to share evidently, for he kept quiet. "Didn't think so. Can you get her in here?"

It was a good thing Freja heard this exchange, because she had just enough time to react and hurl herself down on the floor again before Klobb's ugly snout appeared in the doorway. Something sharp, like a splinter, pricked her right knee, but she did her best to conceal the wincing behind strands of hair hanging down in front of her face. When she looked up as the hinges squeaked, Klobb was eyeing her with suspicion. "Drop that and c'mon in," he barked.

Once he had turned on his heel, when she pushed herself up, Freja saw what had caused the pain: the charm from her necklace had fallen off its chain and had torn yet another hole in her jeans. A brief memory of Robin staring at her chest touched her mind and sent a wave of flushed heat through her cheeks. She picked up the charm and put it in her pocket for safety, thinking that she would put it back on its chain later.

In the kitchen Klobb had pulled out a chair for her at the short end of the table, in front of a steaming mug of leaf tea, and wordlessly pointed to it. Éloyse and himself were seated opposite each other on the long sides.

Éloyse was smiling now and spoke to Freja in a soft voice. "Do you know what a Master is, Freja?"

"No," Freja said, glaring at Klobb. "Klobb said he'd tell me stuff if I helped him out around the house, but as it turns out he's not a great promise-keeper." Neither was she, but that was beside the point.

"I didn', Master," cried Klobb.

"I am a Master," said Éloyse, cutting Klobb's tantrum short. "And Topster is a Master. In fact, you are in a world of Masters, in Ma'zekaï—we are all Masters here. Well, most of us." She glanced at Klobb, who scowled in return. "Topster will tell you more when he comes back, but this valley right here is Valley of Wood, one of four valleys in Ma'zekaï which, in turn, is one of the three *landskapës* in what we call the Trinity."

"Landscapes?" Freja attempted, but it didn't quite sound the same as when Éloyse said it. The Master repeated the word—*landskapës*—and Freja tried again, pronouncing it more correctly this time.

"They are," said Éloyse, "let's say, countries within the Universe. We are all of the Master race here, as you are all human in your world, and every *landskapë* is unique. Nature is our element across the valleys of Wood, of Wild, of Water, and of Wind—all of Ma'zekaï. You are from Vildaell, is that right?" Freja nodded. "Well, Vildaell is part of the Heim *landskapë*, as we call it, and a world of coal and steel. Of impure energy, some would say."

"Heim?" said Freja, frowning. "How did I even get here in the first place? There was an accident …"

"The worlds are connected," Éloyse broke in carefully, choosing her words with evident care. "It is a complex link, far too much so to go into details, but the three *landskapës* in the Trinity are all part of the natural force as branches of the Energy Harmonisation Network, or Network for short."

"The Energy– what …?"

"Energy Network," sighed Klobb and rolled his eyes as if it was the most obvious thing in the world.

"I see …," said Freja, clearly not seeing at all. "But the other countries in the world—in my world—are they *landskapës* too?"

"They are all part of Heim," replied Éloyse.

Freja rubbed her temples, trying to massage away the throbbing confusion. This wasn't a different continent—it was another world! Or a *landskapë*, whatever the difference was.

"Dun tell 'er, Master," suggested Klobb, poking Éloyse across the table. "Take 'er to the Willow—the tree will show 'er."

Éloyse didn't seem too pleased with neither his poking nor his suggestion, but she must have seen no other way, because she reluctantly agreed.

*

The Willow, the giant tree she had seen before, rose upon a little elevation at the outskirts of the valley, close to the wall itself and not far from the cottage. It didn't take long to reach on foot, but almost as soon as she came into the fresh air, Freja felt tiredness creep up on her again like some woolly blanket, pricking and suffocating. She said nothing of it, however, for the Master had pulled on such a stern expression and Freja had to admit that she was somewhat afraid of making her cross. There was something ferocious about the way she held herself—straight as a nail and gracefully elegant at the same time with her shoulder length burgundy hair tied up in a short pony tail for the journey, and deep dark brown eyes. So Freja struggled on and as soon as they reached the tree, her fatigue vanished in an instant.

It was an impressive sight. From below it looked as though the drooping tree tops reached all the way up to the few white cotton-like clouds in the sky, and the trunk was as wide as ten regular willows in one. Already metres away from it, Freja had to check her steps so that she didn't trip over one of the thick roots sticking up, concealed here and there by moss and grass. The immediate surroundings, stretching all over the elevation, were greener and more radiant than any other part of the valley Freja had seen so far; it was illuminated with some strange witch-light—as if it was glowing in broad daylight. Éloyse explained the radiance wasn't a trick of the eye, and that its reason lay in the thick and regular flow of energy within the trunk and the leaves. "The leaves fall one day and grow back the next," she said and then crouched and pointed to a little brook flowing from within the hill. "See that? The water is so clear, it is white."

A wind blew past and from above came a rustle as the leaves danced in the breeze, twirling in the light from the sun. It was a beautiful day. A sound like a familiar song emanated from the tree crown, and Freja closed her eyes and let her ears absorb the melody. Soothing tunes entered her mind and gently stroke her consciousness, whispering about comfort and safety, about belonging.

"Hold a moment," said Éloyse, her gaze wandering up towards the tree crown.

The breeze passed and everything seemed still in the world. Then Freja spotted it: a tiny motion above. It was coming nearer by the second. Something was falling from the sky—Freja crossed her fingers it wasn't a dead bird. But as it came closer, and closer, she realised it was no bird—it was a leaf. It must have come loose in the wind and it now descended effortlessly in the most unconcerned manner through the skies towards the ground. Freja stretched out her hands and let the leaf come to a gentle rest in her open palms. It was strangely warm, as though the sun had given it a temperature of its own, and it reposed in the concave of her hands in complete comfort. From a distance it had appeared deep green but up close the real nuances came out bright and clear: silvery emerald, with a whole spectrum of shades shifting as you observed it from different angles. It was the same kind of leaf from which Klobb had made their tea.

"It's beautiful," Freja said and looked up at Éloyse. "This whole place is."

"It used to be," said Éloyse and caught the next falling leaf, observing it closely in her palm. "This valley is the last one in Ma'zekaï. All these mountains used to be covered with forests reaching all the way to the top where the white peak touched the skies. You see them now—barren, deserted, dusty, and grey. Such is the case with Wild, Wind, and Water. Those valleys are not for Masters any longer and when that day comes to this valley too ... Our world is dying before our very eyes." Her candour was unanticipated and Freja wondered what had made the other valleys fall, where they were located, and what had happened to the people there, but Éloyse continued before she could decide which question to ask first. She pointed to the roots, which Freja now saw were pulsating in a regular rhythm. "What you see is the heartbeat of the Universe. Flows of energy leap through these roots, every second of every day and they go to your world, the Red World, and to ours—to all the *landskapës*."

The heartbeat of the Universe. Freja watched the pounding roots and imagined them like pipes through which energy surged like electric waves. It struck her that if those roots could reach to Vildaell, then there was a way back. She resolved to find it, no matter what.

"What happened?" Freja asked. "To the valleys? Isn't there anything you can do?"

"The Network balance is disturbed and has been for a long time," Éloyse said, crouched, and lay a hand on a large root, feeling its pulse. "The valleys ran out of energy when other places demanded more and more. Our valley is alive because of the Willow." She stood up and placed that same hand on Freja's shoulder. It was warm. "But yes, Freja, we do have one chance left—one single opportunity to change the future. Topster will tell you about it when he returns."

Obviously Éloyse had information. If Freja could only make her talk ... It was her sole hope for the moment and perhaps that was why her pulse accelerated to a sprint when Éloyse turned around, apparently content with what she had divulged so far. "Please," Freja spluttered, causing Éloyse to stop mid-step. "Only Masters can go between the *landskapës* alone—you said as much yourself. So tell me—please—how did I come here?"

"You were eavesdropping," Éloyse said without turning around, as if not speaking to Freja at all. Freja's first instinct urged her to deny it, but Éloyse's voice wasn't reproachful. If anything, the Master sounded amazed as though the realisation amused her.

"Please," Freja repeated, pleading now, because she had to know. The idea that had been growing in her mind had now extended to a full theory and she was desperate to find a method of trying it out. "Is this where they all disappear to? Is this Curfew?"

Did her mother lead her here?

"It is not my place to tell you," Éloyse replied in an echo of Klobb's words earlier. "Topster is your authority, he must answer any questions. As he will, that much I can promise you. But we must go back now or Klobb will think we are lost."

Freja snorted at the idea of Klobb worrying, but Éloyse looked like she honestly meant it so she cut it short. "He's more likely think I ran away."

"That would be exceptionally foolish." Five small words but Freja felt the weight of their truth, believing every single one of them. She nodded, sensing that subtle ferocity in Éloyse simmer close to the surface. The cold change in the air lasted for only a few moments, until Éloyse spoke again. "Keep the leaf—it is full of energy, and that is always useful to have at hand here."

Disappointed at the lack of answers, but glad to keep the leaf, Freja put it in her pocket and silently followed the Master back to the cottage. Éloyse left soon after, promising to return once Topster was back. As Freja was resigned to the fact that

Klobb would tell her nothing that wasn't "his business," they spent the rest of the day in mutual silence.

That evening Freja cooked while Klobb kept peering in, tempted by the succulent scent of fresh herbs and boiled vegetables cook up on the fire.

They had had an argument over whether it was right or wrong to eat animals—Klobb for, Freja against—but the discussion had come to nothing since both of them refused to concede. It all ended in Klobb storming out when Freja wouldn't listen to his all-too-colourful narration about bloody steaks and he was now tip-toeing (as much as a man like him could tip-toe) outside the kitchen door, not speaking, but shuffling back and forth with his great nose sniffing like a hungry dog. Every now and then he would utter peevish growls as well. Freja paid no attention, thinking that if Topster shared Klobb's self-proclaimed incompetence in cooking, perhaps good food was a rarity in the cottage. Judging from the past few days, she'd say it was.

The heat from the fire wrapped itself around her mind and she drifted off to memories, happy ones, of home. Playing Rhyffle with her father after Curfew, racing through the city on the Thunderball, strolling around the Great Square with Robin … Even Nagel's face would have been a welcome familiarity at that point. Her mother's spirit hovered somewhere in there as well, separate and distant from other memories, and no matter how she tried to bend her mind, Marja Evenson remained elusive.

The sound of a slamming door brought her back to the present, all her memories turning to ash in the licking flames of the fireplace. Klobb must have gone out, she thought, too impatient for his dinner. Seeing that the potatoes were finally ready, she dried her hands on a towel and turned to call him in, and almost dropped the towel at what met her eye.

Without any introduction, she knew that the man in the doorway wearing a heavenly blue fitted boiler suit was none other than Master Topster.

CHAPTER 8

H E WAS TALL, at least two heads higher than Freja and certainly a few above Klobb's ugly snout, though that was nowhere to be seen at the moment. The soft blue suit created a stark contrast to his sharp features: deep brown eyes that were almost black, high cheekbones stretching under his slanted eyes, separated by a straight nose. His peroxide blonde hair, close to white, tied back in a bun, made the contrasts even stronger. In a way he reminded Freja of the Willow tree. There was the same essence—grand and impressive, yet slender and sly at the same time. In his eyes there was a warm fire burning like cinder, alive and with residual heat to spare. It glowed and observed Freja from top to toe with interest.

She decided to be firm, to demand answers straight away, but the words would not come out. "I'm Freja," she said instead and cursed herself for sounding like a five-year-old.

"Of course you are. Your fire has gone out."

"My fire ...?" She scrambled around metaphors but then his eyes wandered to a spot behind her—the fire place—where the crackling flames had died out, leaving the pot steaming rather than boiling. Fumbling, Freja looked around for lighting material. Klobb had lit it for her earlier, but she couldn't find any matches, lighter or anything else to reignite the flames.

"Here," offered Topster and was suddenly right behind her, so close their bodies almost touched. He reached a hand over her shoulder and into the fire. A moment passed and the ashes came to life once more. Freja stared at the now crackling flames in disbelief.

"How—? Is that magic?" she blurted out. Topster let out a small laugh, almost inaudible, and she felt stupid. He was smiling, but only just.

"It is not magic, Miss Freja," he said and opened his closed fist. In it lay the remnants of a dead leaf, brown and dry, cracked into uncountable pieces as though it had itself been burnt by the fire it ignited. "Merely the power of Nature." Freja gaped, at a loss for words, until Topster discarded the leaf in the fire. "I assume Klobb would have used his own methods."

"So," she said and cleared her throat. "Where is he, where's Klobb?"

"Klobb has gone out on an errand," Topster replied in a calm voice as he sat down by the table. He leaned back in the chair. "Would you prefer if he was here, Miss Freja?"

She shook her head, ignoring the voice inside her whispering the opposite, while at the same time feeling some thrill at being alone with Topster—the man she had merely heard spoken of until now. The man Éloyse was doing "dirty work" for, according to the man in grey from the village. She watched him as he watched her. Like with Éloyse, she sensed some underlying power, hibernating under a wall she was unable to break through or even touch. Even as he sat opposite her with one foot on top of the other knee, with the friendliest appearance imaginable, she felt this force, at rest for the moment but always ready to strike.

When he seemed content that she was quite comfortable

with the arrangement he stood up and took a splash of water from the container, pouring it into a mug in which he then placed another small leaf. "Klobb says you enjoy tea, Miss Freja," he said and placed the mug on the table. "Have you tried it cold?"

"You can just call me Freja," she said and accepted the tea. "No need for 'Miss' or anything." She clutched the mug with both hands and felt the chill spread through her body. It was cold as ice. Topster returned to his silent state of observation. The silence was broken by Klobb who came rushing into the kitchen, his face patched by soil and dirt.

"Master," he said, panting. "I thought I heard yer voice in here." His hand moved to his chest, like it had done with Éloyse. "Ah, mm, *hooman* food," he said, turning his nose to the fire where the stew was back to boiling.

"Can I offer you some?" Freja was happy to turn away from Topster and his searching gaze. Soon Klobb was gobbling away with tell-tale smacks and slurps like a dog while Topster satisfied himself with tea. Freja, on the other hand, ate the concoction with one self-conscious spoonful after the other, cherishing the warmth of cooked food.

"You must have many questions," said Topster. "I am sorry I have not been here to answer them until now."

"Klobb hasn't been very helpful," said Freja and shot a glance at Klobb who bared the inside of his mouth at her, showing off a semi-chewed mass of hot vegetables. She scowled at him.

"Our dear Klobb understands plants better than humans," Topster said calmly with a small twirl of his hand in the air, and Klobb returned to his food. "Ask him to hum a tree to sleep and he has sung it into a deep slumber within the blink of an eye, but I am afraid he has lost touch with his own kind."

So the creature was human after all, Freja thought as she watched Klobb's mouth move up and down and sideways as he worked the few good teeth he had left. It was disgusting, even more so now that she knew he was just like her. She forced herself to look away.

"So." Topster opened his palms upwards towards her in a gesture as though he was handing her something. "I will give you three questions for now. Then I will ask you a favour."

Freja considered this proposition. Despite the fact that she still felt marginally kidnapped, it was more generous an offer than she had been given so far. However, she must choose her questions with care. The first one that came to mind was regarding location, but Éloyse had told her that already. Though now Freja could not for the life of her remember the name. Msomething. The name evaded her. She wanted more than yes or no.

"Do you have your first question ready?"

"Yes." She paused and considered the wording one more time. "What is this place?"

Topster smiled. To Freja he looked content, proud even. His eyes hooked into hers when he replied in a soft voice, like a murmur that she had to lean forward to hear. There was no hurry, no ill-considered words, just the even flow of syllables rolling off his tongue like water in a stream. It was as if everything he did, he did moderately and modestly. "We call it Ma'zekaï and it is a land of Masters. Our race is divided in four groups—the Élan, the Trew, the Flÿght, and the Lords. Together we form one Master race and this, Ma'zekaï, is our homeland."

Careful not to blurt out another question without careful consideration, Freja nodded in acknowledgement. She had heard the word 'Élan' before, though she didn't know from where or what it meant. As to the three other groups, she had no idea but the details were of lesser importance. "How did I come here?"

"Through an energy latch, portals between the *landskapës*,"

Topster replied, once again, without hesitation and then fell silent, apparently content with the answer. Another question tickled on Freja's tongue and she couldn't stop it from jumping out.

"How does that work? Like, where's Vildaell from here?" She clasped both her hands over her mouth, but it was too late. Her final question was supposed to be regarding Curfew and she already regretted spoiling her last chance at information, at least for now.

"Those are two questions, so I will only answer your first one," said Topster. "Latches transfer energy, and use internal power to create links across the Network." He repeated what Éloyse had told her before: latches connected the three *landskapës* and worked through the transfer of energy from one place to the other. When a latch came in use, protons, fields of energy, 'latched' (hence the name) on to the connecting worlds, then shifted the flow in the direction of the transportation, leaving a tiny gap in the Network in the source of origin and moving it across to its new position. "Did you see a light, a silver light, when you came through?" Freja nodded. The light of death, or so she had thought. "That light was the energy transferral. Pixelisation, that is the name of the process, breaks down the visceral elements of the *landskapë* of origin and flips the pieces to build up the *landskapë* of arrival. As such, Miss Freja, energy paints the world."

"Like a memory game," said Freja, imagining how pixelisation might look. The light had been too bright to keep her eyes open. She closed them now and visualised the information. If she had understood correctly, it would mean that part of the energy of Vildaell had been moved alongside her, adding it to Ma'zekaï. It seemed like energy was not the same here as at home, where batteries, fuel, and electricity lit up the city, gave it heat, and allowed for machines and vehicles to function.

Impure, Éloyse had called it. That kind of energy was transferrable of course, but had no place in the Network. Hadn't Éloyse said that all energy originated from the Willow? True, the only energy source she had heard spoken of was the tree and there were no sockets in the house. It sounded like magic to her, despite Topster's denial.

She looked at Klobb who had finally stopped eating and was instead listening intently, a piece of parsnip left on his chin. "When can I go back?" she asked.

Topster rose and shook his head with a wistful smile. "Three questions, Miss Freja. I have kept my promise. Curiosity is not a sin here, but neither is it a virtue." He wasn't smug at all, and Freja could only blame herself for being too reckless and too eager with her questions. She knew little more than she had before and now she would have to carry out this favour, whatever it might be. Or refuse to, and bear the consequences. "I must bear my heart to you," he said. "We need your help."

"My help?" she said, frowning. "I don't see what I could do—I didn't even know Ma'zekaï existed until a few days ago."

"That is less important," continued Topster. "All we need from you, all I need from you, is to help collect something."

"Look, I don't want to get involved in any criminal stuff—"

"All in good time. Rest assured it is within what you call law. I also wish to show you one of our deepest secrets, Miss Freja. One that many Masters do not know about and one that must be kept absolutely in the dark. Once the ray of light throws this out to the public, chaos will ensue. We will forget our modesty and emotion will take over. Can you give me your word that you will honour this secret pact? Oh, Klobb knows, Klobb is loyal to the cause. Will you honour it? That is part of your agreement."

"To keep something secret? I can do that." Who would she tell anyway? "And if I help you collect this thing, I can go home?"

"It is essential for it."

It seemed easy, too easy, unless the item was kept safe by dragons or some other beast, but rational thought gave way to a deeper longing for home. There was nothing in his poise or movements that urged her for an answer and she wondered if he had enough human feelings to experience anticipation, anxiety, or despair. And if so, which one was fighting inside him right now. "Then yes," she said at last. "I will collect the thing and not breathe a word to a living soul," she said with as much determination as she could muster. Topster nodded once in confirmation, then moved his chair towards her.

"Forgive me," he said, still smiling. "I must ask you not to tell any *non-living* soul, either."

Freja suddenly felt queasy. "Oh, of course, no soul at all," she said. Masters were one thing, but dead beings? This world appealed less and less to her.

"Thank you, Miss Freja," he said in the most inclusive voice. Freja felt her cheeks burn. "You are doing us a great favour which I shall never forget. It was truly fortuitous that you came here."

"It's my only chance of going home," said Freja, "I should be thanking you." Topster said nothing and went out, leaving her alone with a smirking Klobb who watched her cool her cheeks with the back of her hands. "Oh, shut up," she snapped. "It's the fire."

"The fire, *hooman*," he said with glee, nodding to the burnt-out ashes, "is out."

Through the window she saw Topster cross the garden, cast a glance at the flower bed, and disappear behind a hedge, out of sight.

She spent the rest of the evening in bed, flicking through the books she had taken with her to the Look-Out, but not minding their content. She was busy thinking. Stumbling into that latch wasn't what she had planned for her Thursday evening. There was only one more thing she needed to find out before heading home. As much as she wanted to consider it an accident, she couldn't forget what she had seen, what had made her rush towards the Gravel Dump in the first place. In sleep she revisited the moment often and always woke up as the woman turned around, too soon to see her face again. Still, Freja had convinced herself out of all doubt. She had never been religious and faith had nothing to do with it. Intellectual reason and first-hand perception told all she needed to know. That woman had been her mother, returned somehow from Curfew's claws.

Despite all appearances, she didn't believe in accidents. At least she didn't believe in this one.

CHAPTER 9

DAYS WENT BY, and then some more. Each morning Freja woke up feeling like some forlorn princess in a far-off land waking from a hundred years' sleep—disoriented and wondering where she was. Each morning the closed bedroom door mocked her and laughed because she was trapped, imprisoned, without allies. Each morning, once the first mist of illusion had lifted, Freja leapt out of bed and turned the doorknob in fearful anticipation. Each morning the door was open.

One of these mornings, while she was still in her dreamy state of mind, the door to her room was kicked open with a bang. In her mind, the noise was incorporated into a dream and it wasn't until she felt a sticky finger poke her cheek that she made sense of dream and reality. Disillusioned instantly when a voice called her "sleepy goat" and to "wake up!" Freja sat up in bed. In the doorway was Klobb, or at least a small figure in Klobb's height, for the identity of the poker might have been up for grabs given that most of him was covered by a heap of lumbering stuff. The stuff hurled on the floor, she saw that it was indeed the little hunched-over man, who now tossed her a piece of clothing. She caught it before it hit her face.

"Master says yer to put it on," he growled from the threshold. "Yer going to the valley 'cross the mountains and ye can't go lookin' like that." He eyed the large tattered t-shirt she had been given to sleep in.

"I wasn't going to go out in this," Freja said and tucked the duvet under her chin, glancing towards her own clothes that were thrown in a pile by the side of the bed. Even her jeans were torn at the knees and the t-shirt she had worn to the Look-Out had no longer any recollection of its own whiteness—it was specked with dirt and shredded by thorns. "Wait, we're going to the valley? What valley?"

"Just put the masterform on, *hooman*."

"Masterform?" The garment unfolded to reveal a boiler suit like the Masters wore. This one was in a deep purple shade with studded gems attached to its low collar. Before she knew it Klobb had slammed the door shut and stood before her, impatiently stamping his foot, arms crossed. "Some privacy would be nice," said Freja with raised eyebrows. The last thing she wanted to do was get naked in front of him.

"Oh, dun' be all *hooman*," said Klobb and rolled his eyes. He moved towards her and Freja flinched at his outstretched hands and cowered under the duvet, covering her head.

"I'll put it on myself, thanks," she piped from under the thick fabric. "At least turn around."

Around Klobb's eyes went again as he obeyed her wishes. "You'll need me for the fitting," he said.

Soon Freja understood why. She wriggled like a worm under the cover trying to peel on the tight garment and, after making sure Klobb was facing the opposite direction, crawled out of bed, pulling and tugging at the hems without success. At last she had to ask for help and although he must have felt smug, he didn't say anything. His hands were rough but moved adeptly and within minutes he zipped up the final part in the back and let her know it was ready. Despite the tight fit, the masterform neither looked nor felt uncomfortable at all. It became a second skin, hugging her body in all the right places without constraining any movement and was at the same time loose and comfortable exactly where it needed to be. Freja admired his work in the mirror. "I almost look like a Master, don't I?"

"Don't go get yer head too big," he barked and collected the other items from the floor. They were gardening tools, mostly. He stopped in the doorway. "Yer no more a Master than I am, but at least now ye look less like a goat. But put yer hair up. Only the Trew wear their hair that long."

It struck her that Klobb was human too and that he wasn't concealing himself in masterforms and ponytails. Then again, he didn't leave the cottage much. The image of Klobb squeezing into a tight overall tickled a laughing fit and even though she clutched her fists so tight that the nails cut into the skin of her palms in trying to suppress it, a hiccup escaped her throat. At first Klobb said nothing, only glared at her, but curiosity won in the end and he asked what was so funny.

"A *hooman* joke," she said to his great annoyance.

"Don't be making those outside," he said and shuffled under the weight of his stuff. "*Hooman* en't the best thing to be out there." With that remark he scrambled out of the room and kicked the door again with his right heel, shutting it with a crash.

Left alone, Freja observed the girl in the mirror while tying her hair up in a tight knot. Luckily she had had some hairbands in her backpack. It was definitely her form in the glass and the girl responded to every one of her movements. Still, she was radiant in the bright purple and every curve of her body was accentuated by its fit. Like Éloyse, it gave her an air of grace alien to her human self. Almost like an adult, she thought, though she felt more like a lost child than ever.

She stuffed the jeans and the t-shirt into the backpack, removed her earrings and put them in there as well. But not before she took out the charm, reattached on the chain and replaced it around her neck, making sure it was concealed under the collar. Somehow she suspected jewellery wasn't part of the traditional Master look, but she wanted to take the charm wherever they were going. That way, she figured, the spirit of her mother was with her at all times. When it was as well hidden as she could wish for, she returned to the mirror. She adjusted the masterform where it looked awkward, smoothed out creases so that the fabric became sleek and smart. The gems, amethysts, on the collar glimmered when she moved and she tried to take on the poise Topster and Éloyse managed so well. After a few failed attempts she gave up and went to the kitchen for breakfast.

It was still dark outside, the sun not yet at work and Klobb grudgingly served her at the table despite repeated assurances that there was no need to wait on her. He poured her tea, toasted bread over the fire and chucked it at her when it was ready, though she was often not ready to catch it. She didn't have much of an appetite but ate everything he put in front of her—or threw *at* her—without complaining. When Topster finally arrived, her stomach was bulging and still Klobb was toasting away at the fire like a madman. She wasted no time in discarding the last half-eaten piece of toast when the Master told her that breakfast was over and leapt out of her seat to follow him.

The sun had thrown the sky into an explosion of red and orange when Topster led Freja out to the porch in front of the house. It was hiding behind a blanket of clouds and the first rays were filtered through the white-grey masses, resulting in the fiery red shades that imploded across the horizon. The lingering signs of night cast ominous shadows by every bush and tree—even the cottage seemed less homely and less cheery than it might during daytime. As the porch creaked under their weight, a bird flittered away and flew off into the tense skies, towards the mountains.

"Here," Topster said and handed her a saddle bag identical to the one slung across his shoulder. It was made from a light leather-like fabric and rested comfortably on her back. She shrugged it on and turned to the colours in the sky.

"I've never seen the sun rise," said Freja as the realisation struck her. "Not like this, not like the horizon was on fire." Back home, if the sun rose after the eleventh bell, it sort of snuck up without fuss and without performance.

The bird became smaller and smaller in the distance as it flew towards the fire in the distance. In the midst of the inferno in the sky was the ocean and the strange island. When she turned to Topster he was smiling to himself. She asked what was on the island, in the building.

"It is our Bank," he replied.

"You keep your money on an island?"

Topster chuckled in his low and composed manner. "No, Miss Freja, there is no money in the Bank." As he didn't elaborate further, she didn't ask. She had to be sparse with her questions in case he decided to remember his three-question rule.

When he took a step towards her Freja's whole body tightened. His proximity was even more powerful than his gaze. With gentle hands he removed two of the gems from her collar and pressed them against her skin at her right temple. His hands were cool and she felt the same electric spark in his touch that she did whenever he seemed to read her mind. The third gem he left on the collar and he let his hands drop to her shoulders where they lay light as feathers. The combination of immediacy and scrutiny was paralysing. He was deconstructing her whole being into smaller parts; inspecting them like a scientist might in a laboratory; observing her secrets, fears, longings.

She cleared her throat. "Why do I have to disguise myself? Did I do something wrong?"

He gave a friendly smile. "Not for me, but certain people may not be so understanding." He grew serious and let a concerned frown crease his otherwise smooth forehead. "It is important that you know that." He paused and looked out over the landscape instead. "We are proud of our world. A little too proud, sometimes. Human interaction is a complex and infected issue and for the time being it is better that you should blend in. Do not speak until spoken to and even then keep your answers short."

"Those who speak too much are liars?"

"Klobb taught you something after all. Should they ask, your name is Tiora. You are my niece who is here on leave. It is a common name among my kind so it should not raise any questions. I doubt we shall meet anyone on the route we are taking, but in case we do, that is our story." Freja nodded to show she understood. Content, Topster backed away from her. "And we greet other Masters as such." He made the same gesture that Klobb had used before and Freja replicated the movement, laying a soft hand upon her heart, feeling the bud of the charm underneath the masterform fabric. "That is a nice necklace you have there, Miss Freja. May I see it?" Topster's eyes were focused on the upper part of her collar and the spot where her hand touched.

Freja lifted the drop-shaped charm and let him hold it. "My mother gave it to me before she went missing," she explained. "I'm sorry, I just always wear it." She hesitated. "She missed Curfew."

"When was this?" Freja told him. "I am sorry for your loss, Miss Freja." Intrigued, he observed it without comment. "You better leave it here," he said as he gently let it go. "In case you lose it." He then called for Klobb, who came so quickly Freja could only assume he had been eavesdropping.

Freja hurried inside and tucked the charm into her backpack. Nothing had happened in Topster's eyes when she had mentioned Curfew: perhaps she had been mistaken after all? Perhaps this wasn't it? Then again, Topster had not asked what she meant by it. Unconvinced either way, she bolted back out to catch the conversation between Topster and Klobb. She hovered on the other side of the threshold, out of sight, within earshot.

"… across the mountains," said Topster. "We shall be a couple of days I imagine."

"Understood, Master," said Klobb.

"You will keep at your tasks as usual. If the Élan sends for me you know what to say?"

"Master is out doing his duty for Ma'zekaï."

"Precisely. Should Master Éloyse return, only say I am grateful for her help and that I shall be in contact with her shortly. There is something else I need from her."

"Noted, Master. But she'll a-wonder where the *hooman's* gone."

"You will not tell her."

Not wishing to cause suspicion, Freja decided it was time to return. All settled, Topster and Freja descended the steps from the porch. At the bottom, Topster turned around to his companion again. "And Klobb?"

"Hm-m?"

"The Rainbow Glory is blossoming again. I thought I made it clear the last time? Do make sure it is taken care of before my return."

Klobb's chin dropped and his face made no attempt to conceal the hurt. It surprised Freja who, given the gruff and hostile nature of the man, had assumed he had no heart at all.

Then she remembered the day she had caught him talking to his flowers—to a Glory kind of plant. The word 'Sora' flashed in her mind.

They left Klobb gaping on the porch and followed a gravel path along the side of the cottage, which then came into a sharp turn and linked to the path she had walked with Éloyse. "There is one more thing," Topster said and made a left turn. Freja recognised the path. Soon enough the trunk of the Willow appeared and Topster told Freja to wait at the bottom of the hill while he sprinted effortlessly up towards the tree. After collecting a trio of leaves from a low branch he returned to her. "If you please," he said and handed her a leaf whose shades gleamed in silver and green in the early sun. Topster closed his fingers around hers and the touch instantly sent a surge of shivering through her body, like tiny branches tickling her insides. With a deep breath, Topster locked his eyes in hers. She was trapped, but without desire to break free, and experienced a pulling sensation as the man in front of her gently hooked into her blue irises. His own dark eyes were bottomless, a well of endless comfort and reliance. She knew now that she could trust him. The leaf in her hand began to pulsate and it evaporated heat and steam, making her palm wet. The heat advanced until she wanted to drop the leaf—wanted, but couldn't—and the next moment the heat leapt into her blood stream. Without meaning to she flinched, but soon the initial discomfort was replaced by a calm and warm sensation focalising in her abdomen. When Topster closed his eyes so did she, and all that existed in the world rested in the heat of the Willow leaf. In her. In them.

When she came to, Topster's kind face hovered in front of her like a treacherous candle, always on the verge of extinction, and then held still in its substantial flesh. "What did you do to me?" Strangely, she could feel the gems at her temple pulsate in an even rhythm.

"You now have the Essence," said Topster. "Masters are born with it and it is one of the ways in which we distinguish friend from enemy here. It will take an accomplished member of the Élan to sense your true nature. As long as you do not reveal them by speech, your secrets are safe."

Her hand was still tingling from the sensation and she could see her veins through the purple fabric. They lit up in pale white lines and then disappeared without a trace. To think that the leaf, now crumbled and dead, had given its energy to her gave her a headache. The amethysts held the Essence. It sounded fairylike and about as implausible as fairies too. With no time to ponder for longer, Freja went after Topster, who was already turning the corner.

They turned right at an intersection and came upon a path leading into wilder areas, away from the cottage and away from the Willow. Soon the undergrowth took over and high grass created a wall on either side of the pathway. Overhead, a group of birds passed in a V-shape, heading east, in the opposite direction, towards the sun. Topster looked up at them, but said nothing. Freja, in turn, curiously followed the birds soaring above in a perfect formation. They made it look so simple, so natural. As simple as it would be for her to find another one of these latch-things, and go back to Amérle. If only she knew where to find one. From what Éloyse had said, they didn't seem to exactly dot the landscape, or even be found in obvious places. Perhaps if the Élan knew … But where would she find one of them? And how would she know they would 'understand' her being there, as Topster had put it? She was trapped under the wing of this Master in blue and though she trusted him fully, being stuck was not a pleasant feeling.

A rustling sound interrupted her thoughts and she almost crashed into Topster, who had stopped. For a moment she wondered why, as the road ahead—as far as she could see before it curved off again—was empty. Then she spotted the dot of swaying grass, though there was not as much as a breeze in the air, and felt fear slap her like a sledge hammer. Images of man-eating fenrirs and other more familiar beasts leapt through her mind, clawing at its nerves like a furious cat. She wanted to grab Topster's arm for support, like she would have done with Robin's in another life, but realised that if it was indeed a fenrir, she'd be better off with the Master's right arm free to wield its jaws off her. Would he? Or was this all a scam to get rid of her? To exterminate the horrid *hooman*? She bet it was Klobb's idea …

The swaying came closer to the road and she saw Topster fish a leaf out of a pocket and hide it in his palm. She could almost feel it pulsating, spreading its energy through the veins of his hand, arm, and body. The veins on his arms glimmered white through the blue masterform for less than a second, then faded.

The fear grabbed her by the throat as the grass closest to the path shifted and swayed, as though an evil wind had taken possession of the landscape and disturbed its peace. Topster raised his palm against the sound.

"Peace," he said in a loud yet controlled voice. "Amend yourself."

For a second the grass went still. As another group of birds passed with squawking above, the dense wall of vegetation was broken and a man stepped out with his empty palm stretched out towards the speaker.

Freja's mind was racing.

"Please don't be a Lord. Please, please, please," she mumbled.

The grey fitted boiler suit and black boots did not ring a bell for Freja, and they would not until much later. The man left the field and brushed away stray straws of meadow grass. And said,

"Master Elflock, of the Élan."

CHAPTER 10

ÉLAN. THE PEOPLE who, according to Éloyse, would be less enthused by Freja's presence—who had been sent to interfere. Minions of the Lords. But she was not human right now, she was Tiora of the Flÿght. A common name that would not raise questions. Tiora, who only spoke when spoken to. She did her best to look Master-like but suddenly the masterform felt ill-fitting. The gems in her face itched and she wanted to scratch them, but worried that they would fall off, like the first chips breaking the smooth surface of a false façade. Even the air seemed thicker. Denser. Harder to dissolve into her lungs.

The Master in grey, Elflock, saluted them both and Freja was quick to repeat the gesture. Too quick?

"Master Topster, of the Flÿght," said Topster.

"I know you."

"As part of the Élan, I expect no less."

At this, Elflock let out a snort, or simply a loud exhalation and gestured towards the high grass. "I am searching for Strays across the borders," he said and pulled out a thick piece of what looked like paper from his saddle bag—a similar one to that around Freja's shoulders. She stretched to see what appeared to be a map. "Latches have been stolen, several ones in fact, and Strays are under suspicion."

"Strays have no will," said Topster in a sarcastic tone. "None to which they can act according, at least. To suspect them of such base acts as petty theft is nonsensical."

"Let the Élan decide what makes sense and what does not." There was nothing in Elflock's voice to reveal malice or reproach—he was stating facts, neutral and objective. "Have you seen any around here?"

"Not lately," replied Topster in the same dispassionate tone. "They tend to keep away from the Willow, as you well know."

"We are also considering human action."

"Human?" Freja saw immediately that she had made a mistake. Topster's glare was unforgiving, though it was thinly veiled by a calm expression. It was his eyes alone that told her about her careless move. "There are humans here? I mean, I haven't seen any so … I was just wondering … Are there humans, like, here?" Her clearly failed attempt at a save was met with a frown from Elflock and tense silence between them all.

"She is worried," said Topster at last. "Young ones …"

"Yes," said Elflock, somewhat pondering. "There has been some trouble, as I am sure you have heard, with a couple of the Obbsborn."

"Obbsborn, yes of course," said Freja as though she knew all about it. "Do tell me, Master. What did these *humans* do?" She ignored Topster's furious stare, which he no longer managed to conceal.

"What is your name girl?" asked Elflock, his eye still on Freja. "Rarely have I seen such eyes on a Master."

She put a hand on her hip, hoping that it was something teenage Masters did as well and eyed the Master up and down. He was as handsome as Topster, but in a more obvious way. Where Topster was conspicuous and fierce, this Master was subtle and a shape of silent symmetry. He had a different body type altogether from the slender figure in blue; underneath the grey fabric were muscles bulging in visible curves.

"Tïora," she said with full confidence. "—of the Flÿght."

"A common name," said Elflock, "for an uncommon Master." He took an affirmative step towards her and her heart leapt to her throat, threatening to erupt. Trying to keep breathing steadily, she felt his presence as he came close, far too close for her liking. Masters clearly had no respect for personal space. "May I?"

As her 'uncle' didn't object and neither did she, out of fear she might throw up from sheer nerves, Elflock took her hand and placed two fingers on the either side of her wrist, as if he was feeling her pulse. His hands were warm, she noted, and nothing at all like Topster's. She looked him straight in the eye—she'd decided that it was what Tïora would do—and hoped he wouldn't be able to see through her.

"The Essence is strong within you," he said at last and released her hand. Her skin tingled where he had touched it.

"You were saying about humans?" She had also decided that Tïora of the Flÿght was full of confidence and held less respect for the Lords and their minions in the Élan—much like Topster himself—and she had to play her part in every move, every word, and every action. She had to *be* Tïora. It was called method acting. The theatre camp her mother had forced her to one summer years ago had finally paid off. Tïora raised her eyebrows.

"Some Obbsborn camps have become trading markets, I'm afraid," said Elflock. "They have found each other, the Obbsborn, and the Élan is concerned with closing down this illicit business. It threatens the whole balance. The Lords also believe that it may have something to do with the stolen latches, if the Strays are not involved. It is most peculiar, Master," he said and looked at Topster, "there are no signs of entry or exit in the Bank—and yet several latches have gone missing."

Obbsborn camps? What in the world— Freja was careful not to let her confusion show—she could feel Topster's glances like a low burning fire on her skin.

The problems we see now are mere buds of what is to come if we let it continue." Elflock turned to Topster. "If you would reconsider our offer it would be greatly appreciated by the entire Élan."

"I am sure it would be … appreciated," said Topster with an imperceptible smile.

"We need those latches, Master, and soon. The hour is late, much later than we thought."

"Yes, yes it is late," said Topster with disinterest. "My work is no less in the interest of the Master race than yours, with all due respect, Master. In fact, Tiora and I are undergoing extensive research and I will be sure to you let you know if we are successful with our attempts over the next solar rotations."

"We cannot wait any longer."

"Elflock—" Topster began before the Master in grey interrupted.

"Master Elflock, if you please." He paused as though deciding if to continue speaking. Then: "As one of the Élan, I must insist that you stop whatever it is you are doing together with Master Éloyse. She is distracted and unreliable—two things she has never been before you." His cool was blown away and his eyes had become wild.

It was a good thing Topster remained calm, as Freja imagined Elflock wanted to send murder his way. When Topster finally spoke, his words were, as always, sharp as red currant yet smooth as silk. "Master Elflock," he said, "not in front of my niece."

"Very well," Elflock said and took a step back. "Master Tiora, if you are interested in latchery there are great opportunities ahead ..."

"We best be going," interrupted Topster and took Freja's shoulder. "I shall look out for Strays."

Elflock bowed his head and Topster pushed Freja forward. Her legs felt stiff and uncooperative as they came level with Elflock, whose arm shot out to prevent further advancement. The Master in grey leaned close to the one in blue's ear, but Freja could still hear his words. "Keep your claws into Éloyse and the Élan will take action," he hissed. "We are not—they are not—ignorant. The Élan sees everything, we know—everything. Given the circumstances the Élan cannot let one of its own allies slip and forget her place. I'm sure you understand."

Topster, on the other hand, spoke in a loud clear voice, unafraid of whatever furtive ears might hear him. "Is that the Élan speaking, or Master Elflock?"

"You forget they are one and the same," said Elflock with a slanted smile. "Her own duties are suffering, Topster. Let her be."

"I cannot be responsible for what she chooses to do or chooses not to do, Master."

Elflock threw a glance behind him and then crept even closer to Topster, so close that they shared breathing space. "If I find out you are working against the Élan, they will have to act. There is a situation, and as part of the Élan—"

"—you have the privilege of not getting your hands dirty," countered Topster with his calm voice. "In the Flÿght we have no such privileges." Elflock retreated.

"Take good care of your niece, Master. Strays prowl the mountains these days. They feel it coming."

"As do we all," said Topster, now without the faintest trace of anger. "Master."

Elflock repeated the parting salutation and, with a light bow of the head, dove into the high grass again, the swaying and rustling announcing that he was heading east, away from them. Did Freja imagine it, or did the air become warmer once he was out of sight?

"I was afraid he would notice," she mumbled, half to herself, half out into thin air. "I thought he'd feel I was human, though I don't know how that's possible."

"Like I said, only a skilled Élan could sense a rift in the Essence."

"Elflock isn't?"

"He is not Élan by birth," said Topster and there the subject rested. "And he speaks far too many words."

"I don't think speaking too much makes you a liar: it just makes you annoying, sometimes."

"And yet, the truest of words are the ones never spoken."

"He seemed like a bit of a pretentious twit to me," she continued, imitating the deep voice of the Master who'd just left. "'Master, if you please'—come on, give me a break." Out of the corner of her eye she thought she saw a smile spread on Topster's face, but she couldn't be sure. They walked on in silence.

When the last rays of the sun began to set on the horizon, they were already far up in the mountains. They had continued along the grass-clad pathway for a few hours until it had come to a sudden dead end in the shape of the yellow brick wall. Though a gate, similar to the one Freja had entered through, was visible at a close distance to their right, Topster had led them through a small archway hidden within the grass, unseen from the path. When she asked about it, he said that the gates were overseen by the Élan and he'd had enough of them for one day. It was fair enough, she figured, and followed him into the grass, lowering herself onto all fours and elbowing her way after him through the wooden flap and the short tunnel through the wall.

On the other side was a corridor much like the one Freja had landed in, though leagues away. This one was more spacious and led straight onto a path into the mountains, taking them on a steep climb of slippery gravel and dark tunnels. Once Freja almost lost her footing on a particularly slanting mountain wall, where she had to use hands and feet to grab hold of crevices and narrow ledges in order to stay upright. Thankfully Topster, who insisted on climbing behind her, caught her foot and held on until she found her balance again. Without his support, she would have fallen down, far down, further than she cared to think about. The thought carrying her through was that Tiora was surely not afraid of heights. She was tougher than Freja.

The air became colder and the rock damper the higher they climbed. When Topster finally announced that they would stop for the night, Freja was out of breath and tired. They had stopped in an open plain in the heart of the mountain where they were reasonably protected from the whipping wind and Freja slumped to the ground, grateful for the rest. Her hands were dirty and sweaty, shaking like aspen leaves in the spring, thirst had long since clawed at her throat and her stomach was rumbling.

Klobb had packed the leftovers of the stew and some fruit for her, and she ate both with ravishing appetite. Topster, on the other hand, had nothing, and for once his perfect complexion was spotted by weariness. The mountain air, so refreshing in itself, had taken its toll on him as well. She asked if he was all right.

"You do not feel it? There is significantly less energy here than within the wall," he said, panting in low shallow breaths. "That is the purpose of the wall."

"To keep the energy in?" He confirmed. "How? I mean, it's not that tall."

"It is tall enough," said Topster and leaned back against the wall behind him. He explained that the wall had been built a long time ago when the valleys first started to decay. Valley of Water showed the initial signs and the Lords quickly realised that the other valleys must be protected. With help from the third *landskapë*, the Red World, the wall was constructed around the remaining valleys, shutting Water out. Now the Klockern, the sea, had risen and formed a natural separation. The wall continued underneath the surface, further out than the eye could see. "Then followed Valley of Wild," Topster continued. "The jungle withered and died as the Network was disturbed. Everything green turned brown, and all the water seeped out of each pore, leaving the valley a sheet of waste and tanned decay, scorched to each leaf. The wall protects us from such a fate, for now."

"It clearly didn't work too well," said Freja. "Seeing as those other valleys died too." He opened one eye and gave her a reproachful look. "Sorry," she muttered. "Well, I'm eating, so that's where I get my energy from. You should try it." She watched as he took a sip from a pouch. Leaf tea.

"Masters of the true Essence are part of the Network," he replied and took a deep breath. "The leaves are our nutrition."

"You eat them?"

"We keep them close. But those I have I will need later, so I access the Network through this." He held up the pouch.

"Sounds filling. Try a bit of stew—it'll make you feel better." She offered him a spoonful. His curled lip gave answer enough. "Suit yourself."

They went to sleep without further conversation and night descended upon their bodies. Freja's dreams were haunted by dying valleys and Cecelya and her mother. They were both running towards her along the wall, with Freja on the other side and she was able to see them through the golden surface. They could not see her. There was no way through—no gate and no flap—and the wall stood firm between them. Her mother's face was concealed in the way dreams can obscure what is right in front of you, and Freja, in the dream, wondered if she had forgotten what her own mother looked like.

It was the middle of the night when Freja sat up, wide awake, as though pricked by a dagger. In her dream there had been someone else: another girl whose face had been obscured in darkness in the same way as her mother's. She had been on Freja's side of the wall and their hands had touched before Freja had felt herself falling backwards, away from the tunnel, and into the underground. There had been clicks and spits but nothing had happened—she had kept falling until she woke up.

She looked over to Topster who was sitting in a cross-legged position, eyes closed but definitely awake. As he didn't stir, she lay down again and listened to the night. A grand calm rested over the mountains. Her mind wandered. Who was the mysterious girl in her dream, and where had she come from? The hand had felt real and much more substantial than the ethereal state of dreams. Before long the soft song of the mountain breeze and exhaustion from the day lulled her back to sleep. This time without the interruption of dreams.

When she woke up again it was still early morning and a chilly one at that. Shivering slightly, she sat up and saw that Topster was not there. His spot was empty and as she looked around, he was nowhere to be seen. Even his bag was gone. It didn't take long for her to scan her surroundings—the mountain pocket was only about two by two metres and consisted of nothing but grey rock. Grey dull rock—and then her.

"Topster?" she whispered.

A low sound came from around a corner ahead. It was a spitting sound, like oil in a heated frying pan, but subdued as if by a lid or a tunnel. After whispering the name again without reply, she grabbed her bag and crept closer to the sound.

It could be a fenrir, she thought, if they lived in the mountains and if they had a habit of spitting. Or it could be another animal, or a Stray. She hoped in any case it didn't have fangs or sharp claws.

Peering around the corner, she saw nothing at first. There was just the mountain wall, rocks, and nothing peculiar or spit-worthy at all. Seeing as it appeared safe, she stood up and turned the corner and came into full sight of the source of the sound. As soon as her eyes adjusted to the bright silver light, she realised what it was: a globular shape, not quite part of the surroundings, yet not entirely separate from it either, resting in a bobbing motion in a corner of the small cavity. The shades within it seemed to reflect every colour of the spectrum without ever abandoning the silver in which it mirrored the grey rock behind and around it, by which effect it blended in well and was almost impossible to see unless you looked straight at it. "Is that …," she began, quite in disbelief.

"A latch, yes," said Topster who, she now saw, was standing behind it, partly concealed by its radiant light. She forgot all about being angry with him for leaving her and crept closer to the latch. "Do not touch it. This is what we have come to collect."

The light played tricks on her eyes and in its reflected light she thought she saw flickers of something other than the silver shades. Squinting, she peered closer. Was there … Was there a city behind it? Was it a window showing her where the latch led to?

"The Élan recognises that our energy supply from the Willow is failing," Topster continued. "The Lords believe that there is a chance to save Ma'zekaï, should the Willow fail to provide for the whole Network."

Freja wasn't listening. Ideas spun in her mind fast and uncontrolled. What if there was a way back? What if the city inside this latch was Amérle? What if this latch—right in front of her very eyes—was her way home? "It's so … shiny …"

"Miss Freja." His voice wasn't angry but filled with that subtle power, and just enough to make her listen. "Control yourself." Only then did she realise that she had a hand outstretched towards the light, and retracted it as though she'd been burned. "Latches are natural pathways," he said, staring into the light. "Made by the Network itself, constructed by relations of energy. A mature latch like this one depends on energy flows, where there is a positive correlation in transferral and direction. Do you follow?"

"A positive correlation," said Freja, urging her head to recap high school maths. "By coming here I removed energy from my world, and added it to Ma'zekaï?"

"Just so."

"And when I go back, it'll move in the opposite direction?"

"In theory," said Topster. "But the correlation is not constant. A body travelling back, in opposite direction of the initial transferral, will indeed cause the energy to be relocated again. But latches also require energy to function, and so suck up part of it along the way. The energy requirement may be different in each transferral."

"Where does this one lead?"

"This latch has been used already and is of no use to us in this state," said Topster, ignoring her question. He pointed to a black and scorched patch within the latch where it looked as if it had been set on fire. "We will collect it anyway. Wait here. Do *not* touch it."

While Topster went around the next bend, Freja peered into the globular shape. The shimmering from the latch intensified for a second and Freja felt her whole body respond, urging her to go through. There was a slight, minuscule even, chance that her anxious father was waiting on the other side, one step away, thinking that she was lost for good.

She glanced towards where Topster had gone, then back to the latch. It would only be a little peek, nothing more. Just a look, to see. She edged closer and stretched out her fingers. The surface rippled in waves as she came into contact with the light. She didn't want to fall through though, not without knowing where she'd end up, and so took her hand out of the warming globe. Instead she picked up a rock from the ground, blew dust off it, and tossed it at the bubble. It bounced on the surface of the latch once, twice, three times before falling in and disappearing from sight with a sucking sound. For the fragment of a second Freja saw the outline of a city, a modern city much like her own Amérle, appear in a warped image within. The latch showed her a dark street, perhaps an alley, where dirty dumpsters lined the side, overfull and with black rubbish bags thrown around them. A rat scurried past and came to a halt, interested in the latch on the other side. It scuttled closer and closer, leaping over a crinkled soda can, getting nearer to where Freja was standing. All of a sudden the rat came leaping through the latch and landed right in front of her, as though it simply stepped through a hole in the wall. The globe blurred and constricted somewhat as the rat scuttled off, squeezing into a narrow crevice in the rock wall, and out of sight.

After a second or two, the latch fizzled again and its light faded a little. Freja was still staring at the crevice where the rat had gone.

Topster returned and took from his bag a small glass container which he then handed to Freja. Fortunately for her, he said nothing about the significant loss of size and glow in the latch. She took the tube, unsure what to do with it. "Place it under the latch and let it sink in," Topster said. Freja did as instructed and carefully pushed the container to fit underneath the orb, and watched in fascination as the silver melted into drops that fell into the container. Once the last piece of the latch had been transferred into the tube, the silver reshaped into an orb inside the glass walls, but it was smaller and more concentrated now. She put the lid on. "Put it in your bag," said Topster, who had been watching her with patience. She did as he said.

"That's all? Why can't you do this on your own? Not that I don't like trekking the mountains …"

"Fingerprints," said Topster with a sly look.

"Yeah, right." Freja watched the space where the latch had been bobbing. The immediate area was black like soot, but otherwise there was no sign that, only minutes before, there had been a tunnel out of here into another world. Perhaps to her world. "Who are those humans Elflock talked about? The Obb-something ones?"

"Transgressing humans who have no respect for laws or limits," said Topster with sudden acid in his voice. "But Elflock of the Élan is wrong, though he will not admit it—they are not the ones who stole the latches. The Obbsborn do not have capacity for it."

"People can surprise you when they really want something," pondered Freja, thinking about how close she had been, and how, if it weren't for the rat, she might have been standing in a dark alley in her own world right now. "Besides, humans are pretty smart you know. Not me, don't look at me like that—I meant my Dad. He's one of the cleverest people I know."

Another one of Topster's most mysterious smiles appeared and he paused in front of a steep descent. "Admiration where admiration is due," he said. "We learn to look up to these fathers, respect them, no matter what shape their nature, no matter the darkness, no matter the lies floating in the Essence we inherit."

"That's a bleak take on family. Anyway, if you'd met my

Dad, you'd know what I mean about him being deadly smart. He's got this game …"

She stopped mid-sentence, taken aback at the view now in front of them. They had come out of yet another one of the endless tunnels, slid down a small descent, passed through more tunnels and narrow paths and finally Topster led them through a natural archway out to the other side of the mountain. He presented the open landscape and a subdued light as the grey masses no longer surrounded them in all directions.

"Miss Freja," said Topster and stepped aside to let Freja come to the ledge. "Welcome to Valley of Wind."

CHAPTER 11

FREJA COULD SCARCELY believe her eyes. Despite the bleak days they had experienced at the house, with incessant rain and not so much as a sign of life from the sun, this land was bleaker yet. There was not a tree, bush, animal—not a living thing—in sight as far as the eye could reach. No movement disturbed the complete mellowness of degeneration that reigned over the far-stretched lands. Even the ground was grey, like a vast and empty ocean of ash. The decay was complete, and crippling. From dust to dust, Freja thought grimly as they climbed down the last part of the mountain and landed on the ashen ground. Though not six feet under, the Valley of Wind was definitely dead.

Indeed it was a valley. The area before them dipped down into a bowl surrounded by mountains on one side and curved hills on the rest. It stretched far and wide, but whether it was really larger than the other valley or whether it was simply a trick of the monotonous landscape was hard to tell. Either way, there was no end in either direction: no sea and no wall as protection. All it had was its own desert of death. If the valley had not been so named, perhaps Freja wouldn't have noticed, but because it carried itself with such false epithets, the absence became evident. "There's no wind," she said as she passed a few naked bush-like skeletons, as void of energy as the ground, the sky, and the entire valley itself.

Topster came up to her side, bent down and scraped together a fistful of dust from the ground. He showed it to her. "This is what our future looks like, Miss Freja, for all of us if the Élan continues its course. They are too slow and their solution naïve and riddled by emotion, not facts."

"How is this possible?" she whispered and gazed out over the valley. It went against all logic that just on the other side of the mountain they had crossed in one day, there was no end to the growth and organic life, while here dust had covered it all. She imagined it as it may once have been—alive, radiant, full of movement and laughter. It made the current state all the more devastating. "The other valleys ... Do they look like this as well?"

"Yes," Topster replied. "There used to be six, at first. But before my generation, two of these were either abandoned or added to an adjacent valley." He explained that beyond Valley of Wild, east of Wood, there had been a stretch of land Masters called the Ama'z, a splendid forest where another kind of Masters lived. Now it was gone. Because the two groups of Masters had no or little contact, nobody noticed when the Ama'z tribes started 'perishing' (his exact word) without apparent reason. When the effect reached the attention of the Lords, it was already too late, and any efforts to save Ama'z—an important source of wood for Ma'zekaï—were in vain. Then the same happened to Isen. The residues of what once was an impressive land of crystal white ice were now buried as part of the Klockern Sea. "Far on our left," said Topster and pointed southwards, "are the Uninhabited Lands. It is a plain with no name and no people. And here is Wind." He finished talking and sank down into contemplation with a deep frown. "Piece by piece they break down until there is nothing left. Wood is still alive because of the Willow."

"And the wall," said Freja.

"Yes, and the wall." Topster let the dust fall back on the ground. "Though many of us in the Flÿght believe it was also built to keep us out."

"I don't understand."

He turned to her. "Most of the Flÿght came from Wind. One day we noticed a difference in the air. The world was empty, asleep, and it would not wake up. I was a younger man when the wind became still."

"It became like this," Freja said and gestured to the death around them, "from a lack of wind?"

"Nature works in mysterious ways," said Topster. "We wanted to relocate, as had many before us, but the gates were locked and so many of us never saw greenery again. The mountains claimed many fine Flÿght generations because the Élan refused to offer their precious valley to their own kin."

"But you made it," said Freja. "How?"

"By compromising my very Essence," he said and then walked on in silence.

They trudged through the valley all day, finding abandoned latches of various strengths here and there. Freja had no trouble spotting the silvery latches—they were the only glimmering thing in the midst of everything grey. Though she tried each time, she failed to catch another glimpse of the cities behind the light, mostly because she felt Topster staring at her every time she collected a latch. A particularly strong one, probably unused according to Topster, had flickered and started clicking as though somebody was passing through, but nothing had come out of it and it had just gone back to its normal condition. Disappointed, she had placed the tube under it and let it melt into the glass container.

It was hard work crossing the valley, not only because the gravel and dust was tough ground to walk on, or that the valley curved up and down, then up again, but the thickness in the air made it difficult to breathe. As there was neither wind nor sun breaking through the dense grey fog that rested heavily across the valley like a suffocating blanket, Freja had to stop several times to cough or take deep breaths in order not to faint. At last she took the cloth Klobb had used for her fruit and tied it across her mouth. It was scorching hot and the cloth wasn't perfect but at least the dust didn't get to her nose and breathing got easier.

Late in the day, they had reached about halfway down the main slope of the valley. The sun was still hot, concealed behind the mass of clouds, and showed no signs of setting. The heat saturated the valley and hovered above the dust and gravel like a wall of smothering air, contained as in a casserole—Freja and Topster being the vegetables about to be cooked. The conditions got to Topster as well, and he even knelt down once, clutching his chest. Freja staggered up to him to help but he brushed her off. It was a strange thing to see him so weak, so vulnerable. From the first time his name had been uttered Freja had imagined some kind of superhero, an invincible man of infinite measures. The person himself had suggested nothing to the contrary.

His energy levels must have been running out severely because his steps were short and staggering, his breathing shallow and wheezing. For the third time he refused the cloth offered by Freja. "There is … a collection of latches," he panted and pointed to a shimmering mass on their right. He sat down and handed a glass tube to Freja with shaking hands. "Go."

"If only you'd take the cloth …," tried Freja. "It helps a little. Or eat something."

"I will not condescend to human customs." Another series of dry coughs followed his outburst and he bent over double on the ground, gasping for breath. "Give me … the bag …"

Freja bolted for his bag and plunged her hands into it, digging for the leaves she knew were in there. Her hand touched glass shapes with swirling silver globes inside but she pushed them aside, ignoring the beckoning temptation lingering in the light. She found the leaves in one of the inner pockets and grabbed hold of one. "You'd do better if you weren't so stubborn," she said and pressed the leaf into his hand, holding them still against his weak protests. After a short struggle, where Freja was the stronger, Topster yielded and let himself go, leaving himself in her care. In his open palm, limp and obedient, Freja watched how the leaf withered before her very eyes as the energy transferred into his blood. She took another and did the same. While the second leaf turned brown and dry the colour returned to Topster's face, his frown was smoothened out, and he breathed normally again. The Master was still on his knees, head bent down, but he was no longer struggling for breath.

"I will answer one more question," he said and took a deep breath. With a reluctant hand he accepted the cloth and tied it around his mouth and nose.

"As a thank you?"

"Is that your question?" When he looked at her with his slanted eyes, Freja saw that he was himself again.

"No. Wait, let me think." There were many questions in her mind waiting for an answer. Was this Curfew? Where was her way home? But now another one gnawed more than any other. "Why do you hate us, I mean humans, so much?"

Topster inhaled, exhaled, but never took his eyes off Freja. "I do not hate them. I do not care for their customs, their greed, and their bias."

Bias. That word again. That Master from the village had said it to Éloyse and made her snap at him. "I know it's another question, but it's only small. When you say 'bias' …"

"Love," said Topster. "In your terms, love. Here, it is not recommended."

"You can't choose who or when to love."

"It is a choice when you act upon that love. You let yourself be partial—you choose to be biased."

Though she thought it sounded entirely delusional, Freja saw a kind of morbid sense in his words. Emotion was as much a psychological state of mind as an instinctive response, an uncontrollable force which no human or Master could keep in a cage for too long. Action was a choice; emotion was not. It wasn't just love. How many times had she wanted to hit Klobb in the head for being obnoxious, and not done it? Wanted to stay out after Curfew? Love had made her obey her whole life to eleven bells. At the Look-Out, she hadn't pushed Robin over the fence despite his Curser talk.

"But there are no consequences of love," she said. "Not bad ones. There's nothing to be afraid of."

"It renders you biased," said Topster again and stood up. "It clouds your coherent mind and disables rational thought."

His words sounded like poetry, though she suspected he had no such intent. "Isn't that beautiful?" she said.

"Beautiful? It is an ugly side of humans." He slung the bag over his head and bent his eye on her with some undetectable undertone. "Bias is the reason you are here, Miss Freja." He turned and started walking away from her, down the valley hillside.

Of course it was love that had brought her into the world, she thought as she hurried after him. The story of how her parents met was one she knew by heart. The young Otto Evenson came to Amérle as a rebellion against his conservative family. She had never met her grandparents, nor any cousins or aunts or uncles, and they rarely spoke of them at all. Marja Lotter, as she was called then, helped him to find his way in Vildaell and it was thanks to her kindness that he finally found a place he could call home. That had been her mother—never judging, always believing in people. How could that kind of bias be wicked?

Soon they reached the expansive bottom plain of the valley. It was no more alive than the hillside. Grey dust and rotting trunks were as prevalent here, only the heat was more intense and there was not a latch in sight. As the day became dimmer with the approaching night, Freja asked how much further they were going, but received no reply. Instead, she watched the landscape, scrutinising it for even the slightest sign of life or something other than the grey, grey, grey. It was so quiet that each step they took seemed to echo between the hills. She could almost hear the long gone echoes from its glory days. Dead footsteps sounding in an empty house. Freja hoped that Topster knew where they were headed, because searching for a latch here, where there was nowhere for them to hide, seemed as fruitful as looking for a weed in Nagel's garden.

"What's beyond the valley?" she asked, squinting in an attempt to see any end to the ascending hill far ahead.

"Nothing," said Topster without stopping or turning. He had used up another two leaves since the last time and was starting to look pale again.

"There must be something," Freja insisted. "It can't just end."

"I did not say it ended," he said. "Ma'zekaï has no end. It is infinite, like the sky."

"Fine, don't tell me then," muttered Freja, not in the mood for his riddles.

Another hour passed without as much as a blink of a latch. The air was getting thicker, the heat more concentrated, and darkness descended by degrees over them. Also, Freja's stomach reminded her of its human needs. A quick inventory of her food supplies let her know that she was running out. The stew was finished and there were only a few lonely pieces of browning apple left in her bag. She nibbled on one of them, feeling how it rattled in her empty stomach. If only she could feed on leaves like Topster. She went back to landscape-gazing for distraction.

On her right was a half rotten tree stump, standing lonesome in the desert of dust, breaking off the monotonous dullness, and beyond it there were several more; some toppled over and some barely standing upright. Nothing unusual about it. Except, of course, the silver light.

She froze.

There was a dim glow, ever so faint, escaping from the cracks in the wood of one of the more solid stumps. A flicker of glimmering danced at the back of its interior, so feeble it was mere dumb luck that Freja had seen it. If she had seen it at all. For suddenly it was gone. She kept her eyes steady, forcing herself not to blink even though the dusty air itched in her eyes and made them water. For a few seconds she thought she had imagined it. Then it appeared again. It was a mere flicker, but it was there. It was definitely there.

Ahead, Topster had not yet noticed her absence and she didn't want to bother him if it was nothing. So she marched towards the rotting stump with the gravel crunching under the weight of her feet. Another three steps and she would be able to touch it. The silver shades became more and more visible the closer she got. A light! A latch! A pathway! With her concentration fully focused on the light, she didn't notice how the ground cracked like ice about to break under her feet. Nothing but the dull deafness of the valley filled her ears as the light became stronger. She saw that it didn't come from the wood, but from an obscure source further down its centre. It was strangely reflected in the cylinder shape of the trunk and bounced off its back to the valley. The interior itself led into darkness. The light went out again. Curious, she leaned over it but could discern nothing in the thick dark down there. Not even the source of the light. Yet something seemed to be moving …

Suddenly the soil under her feet gave way and she barely had time to utter a shrill "TOP—" before falling helplessly down the shaft and into the endless darkness below.

CHAPTER 12

THE FALL WAS a rough reminder of her way to Ma'zekaï, except this time she landed in darkness. Luckily for her bones, she had landed on yielding ground. All her limbs seemed intact and her injuries were limited to a scraped elbow and an aching knee, both of which made themselves known from the moment she moved. She had landed in a pile of barren twigs and branches, like an unused bonfire, which shifted as she scrambled around trying to find her footing.

"Miss Freja?" Topster's voice came from above her head. Though the darkness had been too dense from above, day light and the hole through which she had fallen shed some light into the cave, but not much. She saw the outline of Topster like a dim shadow above as he leaned over the gash. Was that concern in his voice? "Is there a latch?"

She couldn't help but laugh. She threw her head back and laughed until her rib cage reminded her that it was no good. A stabbing pain shot through her side and she clutched it like you might with a stitch, but it only made it worse. Definitely not concern, she thought and took a deep breath through the pain. "I thought there was one," she shouted back and looked around for the light she had followed. Even though most of the cave was visible now, she saw no silver orb. "I can't see it now."

"Then find a way up, we need to be moving. We do not want to be out in the plain when night falls."

"Hold on," she said, because now she saw that the cave went further in than she initially had thought. The underground space she had landed in was merely the beginning of a larger cave. The curved space broke off and branched off into several tunnels a little further on. She stood up, not entirely without difficulty, and found the wall to support her. As she ran her hand over the dirt surface, she realised it was far too smooth to be made by Nature, as did the ceiling, and the railings along the side were definitely not carved and screwed there by evolution. She stroked the wooden railing and wandered around the room in awe. The cave, the railings—it was more than a natural cave: it was a habitat, built by people.

She rushed back to the hole. "Topster," she shouted and his shadow came once more leaning over the hole. "What happened to the Masters who didn't make it across? Who didn't even make it to the mountains? When the wind died, did they stay?"

"They perished," he replied. "Now come up, we must go."

"Give me one second."

"This is not like your Vildaell, Miss Freja. Danger lurks here. Come up, now!"

There's plenty of danger in Vildaell, she thought to herself. Or she wouldn't be here at all. But she knew how to buy herself some time. "Um, there's this light further in," she said. "Like a ball or … I'm sure it's nothing." He took the bait and told her to be quick, throwing a quick glance behind him. "That Elflock person isn't following us, is he?" she said.

"Just go."

With a final look up she turned and went deeper into the cave. Was it possible that the Masters had found a refuge, a safe place, underground when the world up there crumbled into the dusty desert of gravel it now was? Down here the air was normal and she felt nothing of the heaviness that made walking such a burden above ground. She kept the cloth on her face, just in case.

She chose the middle path of five which was lit up by a blazing torch attached to the wall. Perhaps some Masters died. That could mean others survived. Would they still be here? Topster had been talking about generations, not specific years, so she had no clue as to how long it was since the wind drew over the valley. Someone had been there recently, she realised with a jolt of mixed excitement and apprehension as she stretched to unhook the flaming torch from its metal hinges. Somebody had had to light that torch. With the heat from the flames licking her cheeks, she continued. If there were indeed people here, the valley was inhabitable and Masters could live happily ever after, underground. Her task would be complete and Topster would let her go back home and everything could return to normal. She only hoped there was still time to talk Robin out of his and his brother's suicide mission to find Cecelya. With this in mind, she hurried onwards. The stabbing pain had dulled to an ache and the adrenaline of anticipation kept her going in spite of it. She was on her way home, she felt it.

Soon she came to another fork and chose the left path. But it was a dead end and she had to trail back, keeping check of her every turn so that she would be able to find her way back. Down the right path she came across a spiral staircase, built into the ground, and it took her down to another large space like the first one.

Except this one was larger, much larger—and it wasn't empty. The cavernous space stretched in a curved arch some forty by thirty metres and was filled with long tables reaching from wall to wall. On these lay tools of all kinds, many of which she recognised: drills, simple hammers, nails, needles, and screws. All abandoned and covered by layers of dust. Like untouched snow it formed a blanket, obscuring the contents to mere outlines. These tables might not have been touched in years, decades even. By the looks of this, any surviving Masters had left a long time ago. Yet, the torches told other stories. They were placed along the wall, all ablaze as though given life mere minutes ago. Someone had been here recently.

She inspected the tables closer. There were about fifty of them, she counted, standing one after the other all across the space. The table closest to Freja was cluttered with sewing appliances and pieces of fabric of various sizes, all spread out on rectangular place mats. Low stools stood on both sides of the flat surface, equally covered by time's dusty hand. Each table had a theme: needlework, carpentry, wood work, pottery … One table must have been meant for appliances of some kind, because several Transporters, the vehicle she had travelled on with Éloyse, stood leaning against the wall. What looked like an incomplete vehicle stood on the table, its silver pieces waiting to be put together. Work places, Freja realised as she pinched the end of a piece of fabric and pulled its ghostly shape from the dust. Flakes of grey rained from it and landed without a sound on the table. She shook the fabric so that all the dust fell off and gasped in recognition of it: the garment and colour was far too familiar. In fact, she was wearing a similar one.

"They were making masterforms," she whispered to the sapphire blue unfinished suit in her hands. Several seams were missing and the gems were yet to be attached to the collar. A swipe on the place mat revealed the glimmering lapis gems with specks of white in its blue. Without knowing why, she blew dust off the gems and put them in her bag.

There was also a distinct smell in the air. Not quite an odour, more like a faint whiff which reminded Freja of the old fishing villages on the coast she had visited as a child. It had been in the air of the first cave as well, though not quite as strong; here, it went through the cloth and layered a corroding sensation in her nose. The moment she realised what it was, her last meal made an appearance again at the back of her mouth. Flesh. Rotting flesh. Decaying organic matter of a living being, just like the dead fish that had made her swear off meat for life. The smell rose deep in her nose, etching the walls with its acid sharpness straight through the protective cloth. Even as she pinched her nostrils shut, she could still feel it in her mouth, nose, on her skin. With fumbling fingers she dug into her bag and pulled out another piece of fabric, also from her diminished food supply, and tied it over the one already on her face. It helped somewhat. The smell was still there, but less sharp now.

Several questions arose in her mind as she wandered alongside the tables, discovering more incomplete pieces under the dust. Had it always been a workshop? If so, the Élan must have known about it and perhaps even known that Masters were hiding there. But Topster said that the Masters left behind had died … and there was not a soul to be found here. They could have run out of food, or leaves rather. Or water. It seemed like an impossible mission to stay alive here, a lesson those Masters must have learnt the hard way. She imagined them, abandoned by their Lords, slowly starving to death in the darkness of the cave. When did survival instinct kick in?

"Who's there?"

The deep voice, a man's, boomed from one of the dark corners and Freja could, to her frantic heart's displeasure, not see its origin. The torches lit up most of the space, but this particular corner was still ghostly dark, lost in the shadows. The question was repeated and she turned in the direction from whence it came. In the gloom, the outline of something—somebody—appeared as faint contours; black on black. Once the echoes of the voice had faded from the walls, a dark silence descended. It was broken by a slithering sound, like a large snake lugging its heavy body over a rough surface; harsh and full as if dragging its prey with it. No steps sounded but the man was definitely coming towards her. Panic grabbed at her mind again and Freja mentally slapped it away, forced it out, pushing and pressing to make it go away. Instead it came closer together with the approaching man and she hurried backwards towards the tunnel, not daring to turn her back to the voice. She held the torch out but it would not light up enough for her to distinguish the person. Good, she thought. As long as she couldn't see him he wasn't close enough. Where was that tunnel?

She put her free hand out behind, waving and searching after the safety of the tunnel opening. What she found, however, was thin air and nothing more. Not able to keep the internal storm at bay any longer, panic overtook her entire body in cold flushes. She turned her head to see where she was going and almost immediately lost her footing. Stumbling backwards she fell to the ground, losing the torch in the fall. It slashed down and was nigh on extinguished when it hit ground, only leaving a faint spark against the ground.

Darkness swallowed the man, veiled him temporarily in shadow, though Freja could still hear him moving, dragging, slithering. Before long he was close enough for her to see that he was short, shorter than Klobb even. The sturdy body became clearer by the second and once he entered the lit area beneath the torches on the wall, it was as if a fist had punched Freja in the stomach. The shuffling sound had not been the sound from dragging a separate thing—it came from the man dragging himself. Under his upper body, the legs were blatantly absent, ending his torso in short stumps like broken bones under his stomach. He supported himself on his knuckles, moving forward by pushing his torso across the ground. He could move faster than one might guess and was now metres away. Only then did Freja see the long object in his hand. The dagger was locked between his thumb and palm and followed his closed fist up and down as he moved forward. But the dagger was secondary. There was another feature that sent Freja into an abyss of fear and relief at the same time. It had been many years, almost a decade, but she would never have forgotten his face, not considering the circumstances around his disappearance.

The flaming red had now faded to a faint ginger hue, and he had lost most of his hair, but the beard was still as it had been then. Longer and thicker than she remembered it, but of course it must have grown since she saw him last. She shuffled backwards and hit the wall. She was trapped. She searched for words, words, any words, the right words, but the sight of the dagger and the magnitude of his identity tied her tongue. As he leapt towards her, dagger raised, Freja lifted a foot and took all his weight by pressing it against his bare chest. His lunge was cut short and the dagger stopped above his head. His brown eyes stared at her, mere centimetres apart now, with a savage fire within. She kept him at bay and searched for recognition in his eyes, praying that he would still know her after all these years. Her breath let go at last and she managed to pull at the cloth around her face so that her features were revealed, then let out a croaking,

"J-Jaspir, it's me—it's Freja Evenson."

CHAPTER 13

THE PRESSURE ON her foot released momentarily as the weight lifted. The next second, Jaspir Nagel had grabbed the torch from the ground and was once more upon her, demanding to know where, where had she heard that name? A reeking smell as pungent and sharp as those decaying fish in the net from her childhood returned stronger than ever and smacked her face as he leaned in, sending a cloud of erosion and putrefaction down on Freja. Slowly, the glow of the torch grew to a flickering flame, and shadows began to dance around her.

"How do you know that name?" he demanded again, hissing and pushing into Freja so that she was forced into the wall with her knee digging into her torso, rubbing up a nice bruise. "Nobody knows that name, nobody! Nobody but Mother."

"Mrs Nagel is here too?" she asked, but was cut off by another heavy push from Jaspir which caused her knee to bash into her windpipe and send any remaining oxygen down into her oesophagus. Choking, she lifted her hands to show she was unarmed and handed her bag over to the red-bearded man, still coughing and fighting for breath. He took it and threw it to the side, then let her go at last. She leaned back into the wall until the coughing went away. Dark spots danced around her and the world came and went in short flickers of images, like a swarm of flies doing an ill-rehearsed routine of a ballet. Of course, she knew there were no flies. Nothing alive was to be found in Valley of Wind. Nothing but Jaspir Nagel.

"Out with it," he said when she had found the oxygen in the air again and sat up with rasping breaths. His dagger was pointing right at her. "Why do you call me that?"

Still her hand resting on her chest, Freja looked at him. He was eight years older than her, but it might as well have been twenty-eight. When she was young and wrecking Mr Nagel's garden with Robin, she had always had a feeling Jaspir knew about it—watched them, even—but let them continue. One late summer morning, they had been at it again and almost got caught. From within the house, Mr Nagel's voice had come screaming, "Ragamuffins! Thieves! Vandals!" followed by the *cloppeti-clopp* of his clogs. He was a younger man then in both spirit and body, and more than capable of running down thieving children if his flowers needed it. Freja had lost sight of Robin who had reached the gate without trouble, and she had been sure she'd get caught when a low *'psst'* found her attention. Jaspir had snuck outside and beckoned for her to come around another corner of the house. He led her out through an opening in the hedge, saving her from the uncontrolled wrath of his father. "As long as you don't take the yellow roses," he had said and neither Robin nor Freja ever laid as much as a finger on those roses after that. There was some decency in their thievery.

That Jaspir who had taken pity on the little children didn't have much in common with the man now standing—sitting?—in front of her. The red beard was there, but Jaspir Nagel of Amérle never wore such a savage look in his face. His features were stripped of all kindness, and all remembrance of such

140

emotion, instead strangled by suspicion, cruelty, and hunger. Indeed, he was skinny, almost starved; his ribs were clearly visible under his naked skin. There were red cuts striped across his stomach and a simple pair of shorts covered what was left from the waist down.

"Answer me!" he shouted, his voice throwing hollow clones of itself between the walls of the cave. His dagger dove towards Freja and she put up a hand to stop him.

"I know you, Jaspir," she said, her voice trembling like the hand with the weapon in front of her. What if he didn't remember? "And you know me, you do. Freja, Freja Evenson? We lived on the same street. You helped me once when we stole flowers from …"

"You stole from me?"

The dagger edged closer, now at a dangerous distance, and Freja pushed herself back into the wall although she was already flat against it. With both her hands up towards him in a gesture she hoped translated into "I-mean-no-harm-please-do-not-do-any-to-me" she lowered her voice so that he had to listen, really listen, to hear her. It was an old trick she had learnt from her mother.

"'As long as you don't touch the yellow roses'. You remember? The yellow roses. We never did; we never took the yellow roses."

He eyed her with a ripping look, raw with suspicion, but was restrained by some distant recollection of the past. Freja urged him mentally to remember. Remember, remember, remember. In his current condition, fight or flight would have become the only options and asking him to communicate, she figured, was equal to forcing him into a tight corner, a grey zone of uncertainty, rarely appreciated by the wild man. She conjured up images in her mind of Mr Nagel and his family, as much as she could recall of her neighbours before they were torn apart, hoping that the mental presence of these memories would somehow transmit to Jaspir's own mind and light up some recollection in there. He had to remember. Not daring to speak or even breathe too loud in case it would aggravate him further, she watched and waited in deafening anticipation with the occasional interruption of his grunting. Then, after a few tense minutes of consideration, Jaspir turned away and shuffled back to the corner from whence he had come.

"Bring a torch," he growled and pointed to the wall.

Freja scrambled to her feet with a sigh of relief, grabbed her bag and a torch from the far wall, and followed.

*

"Miss Freja!" Topster attempted again, but to no avail. The silly girl had vanished from sight and no reply had come from below in a while. He did not want to consider what secrets she was unveiling down there and turned to his other source of concern. The pair were now less than half a league away. The meeting was unavoidable. Surely the taller of them would have spotted him from afar—the plain gave little opportunity for hiding—and perhaps his presence was even the reason for their approach, but if Topster had had a say, he would have sent them in the opposite direction.

He toyed with the thought of following Miss Freja to escape the meeting, but decided that he was not a Master to hide from trouble; he would face it, as he would face the girl's findings when she returned. In the destruction of the valley, he assumed, most sublevelled Obbsborn would have crumbled and died alongside the world above ground, but here was apparently an exception to that rule. This Obbsborn was still intact and he could only hope that there was no evidence down there that would jeopardise the girl's trust in him. If she found out the truth about the caves, who knew what a human-raised teenager riddled with base emotion could do? Impulse was part of the existence that Masters learnt how to handle early. It was one of many characteristics that separated them from the primitive nature of humans. What made them superior.

Footsteps in the valley. Crunching gravel and sand and dust announced the arrival of the two people. While he watched them cross over the last bit of land towards him, a thought slipped into Topster's mind: had he been followed?

He stood up to greet the Master in mellow tangerine master-form and his younger companion in pale yellow. Her gems were glimmering zircons while the Master had smoky quartz stones along his right eyebrow. Ravn had famously refused the grey masterform that was customary for the Seven of the Élan, claiming that orange was just as dignified and suited him better. Always a rebel, Topster thought and touched his own gems, felt the pulsating Essence.

"Master Ravn of the Élan," said the taller man. "This is Lulja of the Trew."

The girl greeted him in the appropriate manner and Topster reciprocated the gesture. As all young Trew, the girl reacted to the word 'Flÿght'. It never failed: a slight flinch and then pity. She had dark hair down to her waist and solemn pale eyes of a rather captivating colour. Ravn had taught her well. If Topster had not had a keen eye from distinguishing Master from human even he could have been fooled by her proud posture and alert expression. But there was no Essence in this girl's body and he suppressed a curled lip to conceal his distaste.

"I am truly sorry for your loss," said the girl, gesturing to show she meant the valley.

She even seemed sincere. Between her eyes was a sorrowful frown and in her face he saw some truth of confusing meas-ures. She owned the zircons, though they were empty of the Essence, and she was at one with the gems. This Masterful tendency clashed with the typical signs of emotions practised by humans. At least Topster had never seen it before.

"Are you travelling alone?" Ravn asked. In his face was no compassion, and Topster silently saluted him for it. Ravn was inferior in many ways, but he had a strong mind. Topster shook his head and nodded to the hole in the ground.

"And you?" He glanced at the girl in yellow.

"Élan business," Ravn said, putting a hand on Lulja's— or whichever name she usually went under—shoulder. "The Lords are keen on emptying the valleys of latches as soon as possible. We could use all the hands we can get."

"Elflock has informed me already," said Topster and Ravn broke out into a wide smile. He was a high-ranked Master of the Élan, and knew well what was going on in the valleys. Though he did not inquire further, Topster was not fooled—he knew Ravn enough to decipher his poor pretence of innocent curiosity. With this Master, an ulterior motive was more a rule than an exception. At least Elflock did not obscure his intentions.

"You met Elflock, eh?" Ravn said with a widening grin. "Lucky you."

Careful not to reveal his thoughts, Topster opened his saddlebag and counted the twelve latches he had collected with Miss Freja so far; in her bag, there were ten more. "Here," he said and took up three of them. "We found them along the way." He handed them to Ravn with added resignation and hurt pride. Masters like Ravn were hard to read but easy to play, and with emotion being such a scarcity in Ma'zekaï, it was a powerful card to have. Ravn took the bait.

"The Élan thanks you, Master," he said and touched his chest. Topster reciprocated. "Lulja, how many does that make for us?" She counted fifteen and Ravn allowed a self-satisfied smirk which Topster did not care for at all.

"Are they all mature?" he asked. "If not, they are useless."

"Stage one requires the raw energy," countered Ravn. "The

Lords have found a technique, quite revolutionary actually, where the energy can be merged between latches and incorporated into the Network."

"Is that so?" said Topster, an itch in his fingers.

"That is so," said Ravn with a smile. "The Lords are remarkable, are they not, Master?"

Topster held his tongue.

"Hold on," said Lulja. "I thought stage one was ages ago?"

"Master," said Ravn in a low voice, though not low enough for exclusivity. "What did we say about speaking?"

"She knows?" It took willpower to prevent his fist from connecting with Ravn's face. He was not a violent Master, he told himself; not one to be enslaved by emotion. Unclenching his fist, he said, "The Lords made it clear we should not speak of the initial stage."

"Ashamed?" said Ravn. "Embarrassed? She knows about all of it, you know."

"I carried out my mission." Topster spoke in a low voice. "I have nothing to be ashamed of." He came nose to nose with Ravn, so close he could feel the heat evaporating from his quartz; he could smell the breath of the other Master, felt his Essence strong and lucid. "Nothing."

"Then why am I one of the Élan, and you are not? How come the Lords denied you? How come they did not choose you as promised?" he asked, then added in a whispering voice, audible only to Topster, "Was she worth it?"

"Master, step away from me," said Topster, stoic, pushing back flows of passion asking permission to proceed from the depths of his Essence. Feeling drunk from the poisonous emotion in his veins, he hissed, "or I shall step over your Essence."

Ravn grinned and leaned out. "Come Lulja," he said as he backed away from the Master in blue. "We cannot delay Élan business, or we shall become like this mortal one here. Learn his lesson—do not get distracted by pretty things."

"Walk, Master," was all Topster could muster in between ebbs and flows of dark within him.

Ravn turned back to him after a few steps only. "I know what you are looking for," he said, "and you can stop whenever you get bored. The Lords have it. Yes, they have it safe in the Bank, safe from thieving hands of the Flÿght."

Topster watched as Ravn and the girl ventured off deeper into the valley where darkness descended quickly. He forced himself to stay calm, though Ravn's words had stirred up a storm inside him. In Ma'zekaï, emotion would betray you sooner than words. "The Lords have it." That's what Ravn had said. It was a lie, surely. To torment him, to mock his efforts. Besides, how did Ravn know he was searching for the latch at all?

His thoughts were dispelled by another sound, barely audible in the thick air of the valley. Still, he felt it rather than heard it. Hurrying to the gaping ground, he called out again for Freja— but received no reply.

In the west he saw them approach. Dark silhouettes connected like a chain of shadows, moving as one being in wave-like motions, gliding across the plain.

Strays.

Chapter 14

Freja followed Jaspir past the workbenches to the other side of the room, where the vastness of the cave crumbled into a sort of sheltered corner with a separating wall—that's why Freja hadn't seen him before.

"Over a decade," Jaspir said as he entered the darkness. In the next moment a torch flared ablaze as Jaspir lit it with help from two stones. "Darkness all around and not a human soul to save ours. Until now."

Freja peered around to see whether 'us' was an actual fact or if loneliness had taken the better part of Jaspir's mind, but saw no one else in the gloomy room. He had spoken of his mother but she didn't seem to be there.

He explained, stumbling on the words at first, that he had been confined to the cave since he first came to Ma'zekaï. "Charming creatures, Masters, aren't they? Proud as fools and stubborn like donkeys. But they didn't die, at least not all. Many fled, leaving us behind—some to other valleys, some through latches. Happy to take Obbsborn to carry their things across the valley, but sharing latches to *our* home, no. Not one of them. They went alone."

Freja gaped at him. "You're saying there are Masters in Vildaell? In Amérle?"

Jaspir laughed in a gruff disturbing kind of way. No humour or mirth was contained within his laugh. "Dear girl, how little you know," he said and turned his head to the dark corner at the side. "Be patient. Yes, I heard you." He glared at Freja. "Mother says she knows you. Yes, I know Mother, I recognise her now. Yes, I know!"

Freja glanced around as he spoke but the space seemed empty. Had he really gone mad from almost a decade of loneliness? Then she realised that Jaspir was speaking directly into a corner devoid of light. If she squinted, she could make out a slim silhouette in there and when she held up the torch towards it, she nearly dropped it again.

"Mother wants to know why you're here," Jaspir said. "Nobody comes this way."

Only then did Freja see that it wasn't a figment of lonely lunacy. In the corner, slouched on a tattered and filthy mattress with grass sticking out like thorns through the thin fabric, sat an old lady who, with a little imagination, could resemble the late Mrs Nagel.

"Mrs Nagel?" Freja said and resisted the urge to pull the cloth up over her face and hide the smell. She spoke softly, as though a stronger voice could cause the frail woman to crack in two pieces. "Mrs Nagel, do you remember me?" Edging closer, Freja now saw the full condition of the woman. She remembered Mrs Nagel's beautiful face smiling at her when she rode her bike for the first time through the neighbourhood, proud as ever, and she was never too busy for a friendly wave. She had always been the complete opposite of her gruff husband who, admittedly, had fallen deeper into his gruffness when she went away. Now, not only had age and weariness claimed her beauty, but gaping wounds dug into her skin, yellow with infection and glaring red around the edges. She still had, unlike Jaspir, two legs but they lay withered and useless below her torso, twisted to the side in what looked like an uncomfortable angle, skinny as sticks. They couldn't have been used in a long while. Her hair was almost entirely white and lost in several patches on her head, revealing the rounded shape of the skull underneath. But that was not the worst part. Her cheeks had fallen into sagging holes, her arms were bony and skeletal, covered in scars, and her tattered dress—one that Freja recognised all too well— hung on her like a draped curtain. It was a wonder she was alive.

Freja pulled up her cloth, partly to push out the smell, but also to conceal her shock from Mrs Nagel. She couldn't trust her face to conceal the repulsion she felt. Mrs Nagel put up a deformed finger, twisted and bent, and ushered Freja to come closer. Freja hesitated.

"Go on," urged Jaspir. "Mother wants to speak to you. Her voice can't reach too far."

In her mind, Freja stressed the old image of Mrs Nagel, the one who owned the name listed all those years ago and whose curved figure had inhabited the fullness of that spotted dress once. This woman, albeit a transformed exterior, was that same person. She had to get close, too close for comfort, to hear Mrs Nagel's voice in weak and torn syllables. Freja closed her eyes.

"Freja Evenson," Mrs Nagel began, then paused to gather more strength. "You must stop them, or many more will be removed. You must stop them."

"This is Curfew, isn't it?" Freja said, her voice shaking. But Mrs Nagel shook her head.

"What is past is no longer an affliction, and you must forget it. It cannot be altered. Look forward. Stop them. It will be the end. *Stop them.*" The old lady had used up all her strength and fell into a heavy silence.

"Who's 'them'?" Freja asked. "Mrs Nagel, if I'm to stop

them I need to know who I'm looking for. Please."

"The F—" she began but the rest of the word was drowned in a shout from the other side of the room, and the old woman whimpered and buried her face behind bony hands.

"Miss Freja?"

A sharp hiss followed the shout and Freja saw Jaspir shuffle to the wall, close to his mother, cowering with his hands over his face. He was rocking from side to side, whispering, "Not him, not them" and Mrs Nagel was equally pressed against the wall, crumbled into a heap of fear and panic. From the tunnel across the cave appeared a man clad in blue.

"Don't worry," said Freja to Jaspir, not quite able to make herself touch him. "We're collecting latches. I saw one down here, do you know anything about that? Have you seen a silver light?"

"*Our* light," said Jaspir and hissed like an angry cat.

"Okay," said Freja. "We don't need the latch. We can leave it. And he's not with the Élan, in fact, he's the good guy."

"Fool," spit Jaspir. "Who do you think brought us here in the first place? Who made Curfew? Masters. All of them. Where do all Transporters and masterforms come from? That's right, little girl—the Obbsborn."

Freja's mind was racing. "No," she stuttered. "Curfew was—Curfew was instated by the President. For radiation." She went over what she knew and an impossible web of ideas formed in her mind, tangled and snared around the missing names on the List through the years, the look of recognition in Mrs Nagel's eyes, her father crouching at the door with a blinking red light. If Jaspir was telling the truth—and here was evidence of it—everything was a lie. She tried to remember the details about how Curfew came about, but her thoughts were muddled …

Jaspir gave up a whimper and when Freja looked up, she saw the reason for his fear. Topster had taken a torch from the wall and was sauntering down the side of the room. "Miss Freja," he said, "we must leave immediately."

"Don't trust him," croaked Jaspir from the wall, now clawing at his mother's body, almost suffocating her. She bore it without complaint. "Humans are second class here; nothing but animals to be used and tamed."

"What happened to your legs?" she asked, her mind making connections she didn't like at all. "Jaspir! How did you—" But she couldn't say it, and didn't have to.

"A wounded animal won't run far," Jaspir replied and cowered once more as Topster reached the separating wall.

"Stop. Is this true?" She stared wildly at Topster, not sure what to believe anymore. "This place—Is it some kind of slavery? Topster?"

The Master sighed and met her gaze straight on. Those deep eyes locked into hers again and Freja felt her head spinning, as though he was hypnotising her. When he shook his head, she just about sensed her own doing the same, such power he held over her. "Come now," he said. "Strays are approaching. We cannot linger another moment." Without waiting for a reply he wrapped his fingers around her arm and began pulling her away. Freja squirmed. She was done being pushed around. "Miss Freja," said Topster impatiently.

"Tell me, what are these latches for?" She held out the strap of her bag. "No, you talk and then I'll consider whether I'm coming with you or not."

"Very well. You are asking for the truth, Miss Freja?"

"Please."

"Whether the Élan succeeds or fails in building their tunnels across the *landskapës*, it will mean the end of Masters. Blending the worlds is the most severe mistake we will have made in our history—and our last. Why are the *landskapës* of the Trinity separated? Because it was necessary. We are ignoring that reason."

"So what's the reason?"

"I do not hold all the answers, Miss Freja. The hand that crafted the *landskapës* and the Universe, whether two different or one in the same, must have had a good reason to do so. In that hand we of the Flÿght trusted. Now the Élan has abandoned all of Ma'zekaï by throwing those promises to nothing. Now, come."

"You didn't answer my question," said Freja. "What is this place?"

A loud noise, like a roaring waterfall filled with stones, sounded from the direction from which Topster and Freja had come, and all four of them became silent at once. Not even Jaspir or his mother let out as much as a whimper. The roar muffled into a lower decibel, but then grew louder by the second. Jaspir buried his face once more in his mother's chest, seeking the comfort of infanthood, and the mother grappled her withering arms best she could around her only son, both of them weak in physique but strong at heart.

"Miss Freja, come now—stop being … human," said Topster and snatched her arm again.

This time Freja let herself be pulled, paralysed by the sound of the approaching Strays. Even though she had no perception of what they were, neither in appearance nor substance, they made her insides go cold and stiff.

Before Topster could drag her into a tunnel at the far end of the room, she remembered the Nagels and broke loose from his grip. Sprinting for more than just her own life, she bolted to the corner where her neighbours were still crouching close together. "Jaspir," she shouted while trying to bend his white fingers free from his mother. "What about you?"

"Strays don't touch us," he said, his voice steady and clear, and reached up a hand to her face. His fingers, rough and bitten by time and circumstance, landed on the amethysts at her temples where the pulsating Essence was vibrant still. "But if they sense that you're a Master they will certainly touch you."

Instantly Freja regretted allowing Topster to infect her with those leaves. Now she had to make a decision and right now, she was in more danger than Jaspir and his mother, if what he said was true. She couldn't leave them to die there in the cave, not when she had found them against all the odds in the world. Heart racing, she closed her eyes and told it to calm down. Calm down. All the buzz and stress died around her: noise, darkness, light. All became one. In an instant she knew what to do. "The silver light," she said. "Your light! You had one, didn't you?" Jaspir frowned and seemed to think. "Quickly now," Freja continued. "Before, you said 'our light'." After an eternity (at least to Freja who had Strays on her mind), he looked up, still without letting go of his mother.

"There's one at the end of that tunnel," he said and pointed to an opening beside the one filled by the furious-looking Topster. "It's bright, it's burning. We don't go there."

Freja's heart leapt. She had seen it after all. If there was a latch, there was a chance it would lead to Amérle, and if Jaspir could manage to move Mrs Nagel that short distance—or bring the latch to her—they could go home. He muttered something about 'filthy Master magic' but when Freja told him what the latch did, he listened. In quick words she explained how to peer through the latch to make sure it didn't lead to danger, and then made him promise to at least try. "But you can go home," she said, hoping that the words meant as much to him as they did to her.

"You better hurry now," said Jaspir.

With a glance back towards the tunnels where dark shadows dressed the walls like dancers in the blaze of the torches, Freja said farewell to the Nagels and hurried to Topster. Without delay, they re-entered the tunnel, but not before the Strays came into the cave, and Freja caught a blurry image in the corner of her eye. Whatever they were made of, Strays were large, dark, and moving fast.

Freja's lack of knowledge hardly helped matters; it made Strays all the more frightful. After a life time of Curfew and all the uncertainties that came with it, she wanted to know what she was up against. Knowledge was power, she figured, and she had none. Topster was rushing ahead of her, every now and then disappearing from sight around another bend in the narrow tunnel, and wouldn't notice if she wasn't following for a moment or two. She stopped. On quiet feet she turned and went the short way back to the entrance of the tunnel and carefully looked around the corner into the workspace. There they were. Now she understood why they were talked of in plural. Strays. Them. They had their own contours but were connected at the head, at the arm, at the foot—different linkage points bound Stray to Stray like children might do when playing a game. Together the dark mass moved in flowing motions as one being. Yet the features were distinguishable in each one, as if they were regular people, and the female front figure was someone she knew well.

Was that—? She lost sight of the Strays as darkness engulfed her vision.

Freja bolted through the tunnel as fast as her legs would carry her, forced on by the firm grip Topster had around her wrist. He had noticed her absence after all and he had not been amused when he had to drag her away from the Strays. Now her chest was aching from the effort of running and although she wanted to shout at him to turn back, her throat thickened and tears welled up in her eyes, and she could not form the words at even a whisper.

Soon the winding rock walls deafened the rushing sound of the Strays and put them at a distance and at last Topster slowed down. As he crept towards the darker path of the fork in front of them, one without torches lighting the way, he let go of Freja's wrist. Obviously, she was to be trusted again. She saw red marks on the skin and felt it burn as she rubbed it, wincing at the raw sensation.

"I saw something," she said, panting, tears standing high in her eyes, and her nostrils flaring. "I have to go back."

"No," said Topster and kept tracing the walls as if searching for a secret door.

"That was Benna Hjalmar, Topster. Benna Hjalmar was in the Strays. She was a right old hag, but she was there."

Topster snatched at her arm, just missing it as Freja pulled back. He glared at her and for a moment his eyes were on fire. So much for containing emotion, Freja thought. The next second, they cooled down and the fire flared instead in his voice as he whispered close to her face so that hot breath wetted her cheeks, "Strays, Miss Freja, have no time for Masters outside of the wall, and they will not stop to make enquiries as to the origin of someone like you. They have no body, as you saw, to contain the fury and rage that is indigenous within them."

"But I'm not a Master," she cried. "And I did see her!"

"Nonsense," Topster replied with infuriating nonchalance. "They are not people and as long as you have the Essence, they will take you for a Master. Go back if you wish, but know that it is at your own peril. I will not save you because I know better. You saw reflected in them what you wanted to see—what they wanted you to see. It is a quality they have, unfortunately."

"If I wanted to see someone, it'd probably be my mother and not old Benna," muttered Freja and glanced back into the tunnel. Perhaps she had imagined it. After all, there were hundreds, thousands even, in that group, and her encounter with Jaspir had raised more questions than she had had before. And hope; despicable hope to see the victims of Curfew again.

To find her mother and Cecelya.

"If you go back," Topster continued, "they will snatch you. Strays like company, it's what they are, and they are always seeking new talent to join them, willingly or otherwise. It is your choice, Miss Freja, and believe me, I could not care less which one you pick. If you choose to end your presence here by uniting with them, I will simply pick another puppet. Do not for one moment delude yourself that you are special, that you are the chosen one, Miss Freja. You are nothing but a tool and like other tools, you can be replaced."

"That's a mouthful," said Freja sarcastically, but turned around to conceal her tears. Topster found what he was looking for and before she had time to consider his hurtful words further, he dragged her along, round a concealed corner and a sharp turn leading upwards and out to open lands. A secret passageway, probably created by the poor humans who had lived and worked there, Freja figured.

Without having to be asked twice, she followed Topster out and squinted as she came into the dim sun and thick air. They came into the valley, not too far from the mountain side, slightly north of where they had crossed the first time.

And they were not alone.

CHAPTER 15

"STRAYS?" THE MASTER who spoke was dressed in tange-rine-coloured masterform with brown gems over his eyebrow. He was accompanied by a dark-haired girl in yellow. Topster confirmed the Master's assumption and they all greeted each other appropriately. "Last time I saw Klobb he was not quite as tall," the Master who was called Ravn continued and turned to Freja. "What is your name, girl?" She told him and he let out a short laugh. "Tiora? How very original! I must suppose you are Topster's unknown niece." He then approached Freja and held out a hand. Remembering what the other Master, Elflock, had done, she twisted her head to offer her ornamented temple. At least Elflock had the decency to ask, she thought and gave a glaring look at the ground. "Strong," said Ravn with a frown. He did not seem as pleased with this fact as Elflock had. "Master, where did you say you found this one? Surely the Lords did not … Because that would be outside of justice."

"Tiora is none of the Lords' concern," said Topster. "We should start moving. The Strays will not be far behind and we must reach the mountains before they realise where we have gone."

"Uh … Uncle is right," said Freja with an unsure glance at Topster, who seemed neither pleased nor disgruntled at her comment. Ravn, on the other hand, rolled his eyes and laughed again.

"Well then, Tiora," he said and slapped her on the shoulder so that she flinched. "Let us go."

The two Masters took the lead, walking side by side in cold silence, and left the two girls trailing behind. Their pace was brisk and swift, more like a powerwalk in the park. Now and then they had to stop to catch their breath in the dense and dry air, but otherwise they had no interruptions. It would take them a few hours to reach the mountains by Freja's calculations. She didn't feel like asking.

"Good thing Strays don't move too fast above ground," said the girl in yellow as she shook Freja's hand. "Lulja Bellamy." Ahead, Topster snuck a hand into his bag and retrieved energy from one of the remaining leaves. "I wish it was that easy for us, huh?" the girl added with a wide smile as she gave Freja a piece of bread. "Here, you look absolutely dreadful. No offence. Anyway, be glad you got to be a relative—Ravn only introduces me if I make a fuss."

Freja turned to her with a frown. "'Got to be a relative'?"

"Well, unless your name is really Tiora, I'd bet a bucket of leaves that you're not even a Master." Freja's mouth fell open. Had Topster fallen into a trap? Suddenly the world seemed to shrink and the gleaming gems on the girl's face became bright and blinding as the sun across the mountains. Her own amethysts chafed like tics.

"How did you know?" she whispered.

Lulja laughed. "Because I'm human too, of course. I'm also collecting latches, but with Ravn. I like your masterform, purple really suits you." She bit off a large chunk of bread and earned a disgusted look from Topster, who had turned around at her laughter. Lulja seemed unfazed and went on talking and chewing.

Freja remembered that the Élan had sent several Masters to collect latches, or something along those lines. Here was one of those Masters, though Ravn was strangely not in grey masterform as the Élan was supposed to be. Elflock had wanted Topster to join this select group and collect latches for the cause, but he had refused. Yet this girl Lulja assumed Freja and Topster were on the same mission as she was. For the time being, perhaps it was best to keep it that way. It would raise questions; questions Freja did not have answers to, and questions she didn't want Topster to answer in front of these people. Instead, she decided to seek answers to the multitude of other queries that Topster had left unaddressed.

As they trudged through the Valley of Wind towards the mountains, Lulja patiently and enthusiastically replied to as many of Freja's questions as she could. She was herself from the peripheral area in Jahran, closest to the Vildaell border, and had been offered a position by a woman on the street. The street was where most of Jahranian business was handled, she explained and, as was also not uncommon, she had been promised a pocket full of money at the end of it. So, as Lulja didn't have another job lined up and needed the money, she had accepted. Her story confirmed what Jaspir had said about Masters living in Heim.

"Did you know that Masters don't actually sleep?" she said and Freja thought back to Topster in the mountains, sitting with his eyes closed, but awake. "Fun fact of the day. No, they're like sharks, always moving. Well, sometimes they rest but mostly they're like sharks. It's so cool." She told Freja about her place in the village. Because Masters moved around so much, they didn't have their own houses or flats—homes—as humans did, but stayed in groups wherever it was suitable for the time being.

Where she had been placed, there were three female Masters and two male, all of the Trew. "And then me, of course," she added and lowered her voice. "I'm the youngest and I know the deal was to send me back, but I'm hoping to stay and become a full Master."

"Can you do that?"

"Well, no," she said with a shrug and a glance at the two Masters ahead. This was clearly not a conversation she wanted Ravn to overhear. "But I've brought it up with Ravn, and he didn't shut me down completely. I'd always be a Trew, of course, but I won't whine about that. The fact that I would get to live here with them is fantastic! Aren't they fascinating? And so kind and clever and … I could easily have been sent with the rest, but here I am collecting latches with one of the Élan!"

Freja thought back to Jaspir in the cave and shuddered. The casual tone in which Lulja spoke about the underground made her hairs stand on end, and she wondered whether the girl was cruel or just ignorant. "Don't you want to go back? To our world, I mean?"

Lulja thought for a while then shook her head. "I don't think so. My father died when I was young and I never knew my mother. Jahran isn't what it used to be," she said with a melancholy click of the tongue. "I've seen pictures … So alive, full of opportunities. Now it's just a dead country for almost-dead people. But I'm not dead yet and I can't live as if I am. Sure, I could go to Buria or Vildaell even, but I haven't got the money for a Burian lifestyle and Curfew is such a drag. Here, you're outside all the time—you're alive all the time."

If Freja didn't have her father and Robin, would she want to go back? Or could she stay here with Topster and Klobb and join the saving of Ma'zekaï? Quietly, she snorted: the thought was ridiculous. It was different for her, but she couldn't say so without revealing too much. Lulja had no family and seemingly no friends waiting for her. "I'd probably end up seeing nothing but the inside of a laundry basket," Freja muttered to herself.

"What was that?"

"Nothing. Um, aren't there fenrirs in the mountains?"

"Don't worry," Lulja said. "I've encountered much worse in Jahran. Drunks and beggars—and not the good kind. A fenrir or two should be nothing." She flexed her skinny arms, showing off a puny bullet of biceps and Freja laughed. Secretly Freja hoped—and believed—that there was more to the girl than she let on, because the mountains now rose before them in ragged silhouettes against the evening sky, and if she tried hard enough, she could hear howling from within the grey walls.

Shrugging off the feeling, Freja turned to scan the plain they had left behind, but could see no trace of Strays pursuing them. Benna entered her mind again and she almost wished she could meet the dark shadows, just to see. Almost. Topster's warning was still etched in her mind.

The closer they got to the mountains, the more 'normal' the weather became. At the foot of the massive elevation, there was evidence of the sleeping sun and the minute they came onto hard ground, off the dusty desert, the veil of thick air ran off them as if they had just left a room full of suffocating cotton. The generous air was rejuvenating and quickly restored their energy. Glad to be able to breathe again, Freja removed her cloth and drew in the fresh mountain air. She glanced back at the Valley of Wind which now lay as a blank canvas, deceptively calm and peaceful. From here, none of its perils showed. Yet although the Strays were out of sight Freja suddenly had an uncomfortable feeling that they were moving underground through winding tunnels running right beneath their feet. She was thankful when Ravn urged them on.

"We need to reach the first cliff stage before the sun leaves us no option but to stop," he said and pushed onwards.

It was a steep climb with thorns and sharp rocks lurking in every corner and precipice, a lot more strenuous than the path Freja and Topster had taken across. Tired bodies squeezed through narrow loops and pulled their weight up with shaking muscles until, at last, they reached the platform. "We stop here for now," said Ravn and slumped on the ground. It was leagues north of the place where Freja had seen her first latch and, too exhausted to even consider the distance they had covered since then, Freja sunk to a sitting position against a wall, resting her head in her palms. Beside her, Lulja crouched down.

"You okay?" she whispered. "We might have to go a little further, not far, but just so we won't be seen from the valley." Freja groaned.

Topster came up to them without a shred of fatigue showing in his face or stance. "Up," he said. "The sun gives us another half hour."

If Freja had to guess, she'd have bet a lot of money on the presence of a crumbled leaf in his closed fist. "It's unfair," she muttered and let Lulja pull her up. She waited until the dizziness had abated before adjusting the strap of her bag and following Ravn and Lulja who were already moving.

But Topster held her back. He took her hand and held it gently. Before she realised what he was doing, Freja snapped, "What are you do—"

It was as if some higher power had blown a fresh breeze of air straight into her blood stream. The energy leapt from finger to finger, branched out through the palm, reunited at the wrist and then surged up to her shoulder, where it divided once more into a mighty river, flowing to resurrect and to revive. Within a minute she felt as if she hadn't walked a single mile that day.

"Better? Then we should catch up with them," said Topster and let the scorched leaf fall to the ground. "Ravn would not be pleased if he knew, so please do keep it quiet, even to the girl."

"I thought that only worked on Masters?" Freja said, staring at her hands. Energy shot through her limbs and she tried a few jumps. Her legs were as light as feathers but held infinite power. "And you've let me trek on rotting apples until now."

"Miss Freja." Topster's voice was stern and she calmed down. "Calm yourself. It can be done on those with the Essence, that is all. Do not tell the girl, I mean it. Ravn cannot know. Now, if you please, come."

With the new energy, it took them no time at all to catch up with the other two, who had found a mountain spring to drink and wash from. With a fair excuse, blaming Freja for their lack of speed, Topster avoided further questions from Master Ravn. Though it was true, Freja couldn't help but feel a sting of insult as both Lulja and Ravn accepted the explanation without question.

After another mile or so in the uneven rocky landscape, Freja felt the effect wear off and she was grateful when Ravn at last announced that they would stop and rest. Even Lulja with her never-ending flow of enthusiasm, had had enough as she shrugged off her bag and let it fall to the ground. She sat down, closed her eyes and drew deep breaths. A howl echoed between the mountain walls and Lulja snapped her eyes open again. She exchanged a glance with Freja, who saw that Lulja's courage was perhaps not as invincible as she had let on. The howl was such a sound that shook rock and bone alike to the core.

"Erm ... Should we really stop here," Freja said, remembering Klobb's admonition. She was clutching her bag for comfort.

"Even if the Strays have not yet lost interest, they will not reach the mountains before tomorrow," said Ravn with a yawn. "Slowest creatures I ever saw. Except that dwarf of yours, Topster." He let out a cold laugh and went on to imitate Klobb in a clumsy way, swinging his arms, shaking his fists, and clutching his leg just like the man himself. "You should set a collar on him, Topster—last time he almost came at me with his tiny fists and claws."

If Freja expected Topster to defend his companion, she was disappointed. Instead he smirked and even chuckled. "Do not let his gait fool you," he said, toying with a leaf, shuffling it between his fingers. "A man is only as feisty as his mind."

"Pretty dumbed down by now, wouldn't you say?" Ravn stretched out his legs and placed his arms behind his head, leaning against the wall. "Although not as much as other Obbsborn. Lucky, lucky that one."

At this Topster glanced at Freja, who in turn was glaring at the two with disgust. Topster cleared his throat and turned to Ravn again. "Perhaps we ought to let them rest," he said and pocketed the leaf. "I will take the first watch."

"Finally," cheered Lulja and stretched out on the blanket she had produced from her pouch. "I could literally sleep for days. Aren't you tired? Oh, you don't have a blanket? Come here, we can share."

Grateful, Freja edged over to where Lulja had made her bed, partly concealed behind a low wall from the two Masters. The privacy was slight, hardly anything at all, but for once it felt good not being in Topster's, or Ravn's for that matter, sight. As she laid beside Lulja, who was already breathing heavily and deeply as one does in sleep, Freja was afraid to close her eyes. If she did, she knew she would see dark shadows; shadows that looked like Benna Hjalmar, 82 years old.

Ultimately she did it anyway, and went over the scene time and time again to determine what she had seen and what had been imagination. It had been dark, sure, and the Strays had been many, so it was impossible to know for certain. In her mind, however, it was always Benna's face in that group. Always and without doubt. But hadn't Topster said that the dark mass reflected what you wanted to see? Perhaps Freja harboured some deep-set longing for Benna, or maybe the old lady had simply been a projected image of her longing for home? That explanation was far too convenient even for Freja to accept, but it was the only one she could come up with. She needed a second opinion. "Lulja?" she whispered, but received nothing but steady breathing in return. Freja decided not to disturb her, and would ask in the morning instead. She allowed her heavy eyelids to close and lead her away from Strays and fenrirs into deep sleep. Across the mountains the howling was still strong, but the beasts made no appearance in her dreams. There was merely darkness and a whispering voice. What was said, she couldn't hear, but it was soothing nonetheless.

It was still dark when she woke up, and in the first moments of limbo between dream and reality she struggled to remember where she was. The hard ground, the sleeping girl next to her, and the chilly breeze were all strange until the facts came looming back. The night was still upon them. She assumed that the voices had woken her up; voices coming from behind the low wall separating the girls from the Masters who were clearly both awake.

Awake—and talking.

CHAPTER 16

CAREFUL NOT TO make herself known, Freja leaned forward as much as her hamstrings allowed and saw past the splitting wall that Topster and Ravn were standing side by side with their backs to her, their masterforms forming opposing poles of the spectrum of shades of blue and orange against the hard grey. If she sat completely still and controlled her breathing, she could make out their conversation. Ravn's voice was dark and agitated; Topster's as cool as ever.

"You are a fool," said Ravn. "It's for the future of all Masters. Why can you not see what every other Master in Ma'zekaï sees?"

"The Trew remain ignorant of the proceedings, so of course they shall support the Élan," Topster replied. "I can assure you that the Flÿght does not see the inclusiveness in this plan. They have long thought they stand outside of the Lords' light."

"They?" Ravn said and snorted. "Elevating ourselves above them, are we now?"

"You left a long time ago."

"As you could have." A pause. "The Lords put you in your prestigious position, Topster—twice. The Willow, our most precious possession, guarded not by a Trew, not by an Élan—

but a Flÿght. Surely that means something?"

"A cheap gift of false pretence," said Topster and paused for a moment. "I am not a fool, though you and the Lords may think me so. Were I human, yes, perhaps my heart would cheat me into believing such mockery in disguise, but I am not, and so I cannot believe it."

"You are utterly impossible," said Ravn with a light sigh. "Utterly, utterly impossible."

"You said the Lords have it," said Topster, a sudden urgency in his voice which still was calm and steady. "Were you taking me for a fool or is this the case? Truthfully, now."

"Now, now, would I ever lie to you?"

"I shall refrain from answering that, Ravn … The night is chilly as it is."

"It is indeed …" Ravn turned to face the other direction and Freja had to pull back so as not to be caught eavesdropping. She could only hear now, but Ravn's voice was animated enough to channel his persistency. "Let it go, Topster. The Trinity Latch is deposited beyond your reach."

"What is its future?"

"Insurance," said Ravn. "If it all falls to parts …"

"When it does," corrected Topster.

"*If* it all falls to parts," said Ravn, "then the Trinity Latch is our way out."

"I see. Perhaps it is, then, time to act." Topster's voice grew faint, as if he turned away again and when Ravn spoke, it was with astonishment.

"Act?" At once he lowered his voice to a whisper and Freja dared a peek around the corner. Once more, the Masters had their backs to her.

"Act," repeated Topster calmly as if he was talking of milk and not going against the Lords. "The Élan wants to bring in another kind, to mix Essences, before it can even grant the

Flÿght the rights they deserve. I will not see it done. I would rather see Ma'zekaï fall—and fall with it—than to make *humans* part of our community."

"Our community," Ravn repeated with some doubt.

"Of course," Topster snapped, now disclosing signs of agitation. "Never doubt my intentions, Ravn. I am not disloyal. But this plan is flawed and I intend to alter it, that is all."

"You are part of this plan, part of the larger Élan, whether you agree or not." As Topster made a motion to turn, Freja leaned back to the wall again.

"Tell that to the Flÿght," Topster said over the low growl of the gravel as he left Ravn to his own musings. "If you wish, you may tell the Lords what I have said tonight—I stand by every word—and if they proceed, then they—you—are establishing an unforgettable and unsurpassable abyss between us."

"Are you threatening the Lords?"

"Oh, no," said Topster in an unusually callous and mocking way, rather suited to Klobb than him. Perhaps company was rubbing off on him, Freja thought. "That would not be allowed. I am merely explaining the facts. Seven Masters of the Élan and three Lords, put up against thousands of Flÿght. A threat, as you call it, is naught but an empty promise and this is no threat, Ravn. It is a declaration."

"You have too many words," said Ravn after a short pause. His voice was hollow and lacked force. "You always did."

"But I put value into them."

"Too many words," said Ravn again.

A dense silence lowered itself over mountains as the Masters said no more. Behind the wall, Freja wormed her way back into bed next to Lulja and closed her eyes. What she had heard was more important than anything she had learnt to date. The rift between Masters had become painful reality, like an infected wound, blazing red and—in this case—blue. It wasn't simply a matter of one nation struggling to keep alive anymore. The way they were headed was civil war—and if all went according to the plan she was currently helping, humans would be in the midst of it. Unless she found a way out. Then there had been that strange thing—the Trinity Latch. What in the world was it? It had sounded important both for the Lords and for Topster, but nothing they said had indicated what exactly might be exceptional about it compared to other latches.

She did not fall asleep until dawn had already begun to break through, and even in the last fragments of incoherent dreams she mulled over the potential consequences of a war. More than anything else, she needed to bounce her ideas off someone, and, not for the first time, she wished Robin had been there to listen and tell her what to do next.

After another day's walk, they reached the brick wall and the Valley of Wood and were about to part when Freja seized the chance as the Masters stepped aside to speak privately. She took Lulja's elbow, pulling her away from the Masters, positioning herself so that she had a clear view of the older two. "Lulja," she said. "What do you know about Strays?"

"Oh," said Lulja and shrugged. "They're kind of spirits, I think, prowling the valleys—mostly dead ones. And they're always together, shackled and free at the same time."

"Shackled and free …?"

"As one mass, they can move freely, but don't touch Masters inside of the wall. Outside … that's another story. That's the gist of what my sister Master told me anyway. They tend to be a bit dramatic at times, don't you think?" She grinned.

"But who are they?" Freja was impatient. "Where do they come from?"

"I honestly don't know. It's like fenrirs, isn't it? Or those rainbow birds—have you seen them? Absolutely amazing creatures! They're just there because they are and always have been.

Ravn told me to stay away, that's all, because they really don't like Masters."

"Yeah, but they don't care about humans," said Freja, remembering what Topster had said in the cave. "They only go after Masters for whatever reason, or those with the Essence. You said spirits? Spirits of old Masters?" No, she thought as soon as she'd said it, because she had seen Benna in there.

Lulja laughed, covering her mouth as she did so. "I'm sorry, but they're more likely to be the souls of stones than that. Do Masters even have souls? I've heard that when they finally die they decompose just like any other organic matter. Like banana skin." She laughed again. "I also heard their bodies break down and grow a new Master all over again, but I'm pretty sure that's a myth or something they said to mess with me. But it makes sense though, right? You know how love is banned here? Or acting on it at least? Well, not banned exactly, but 'ill-advised' which is pretty much the same thing. I guess baby Masters can be made without love, but that seems too clinical even for Masters, don't you think? Besides, it's gross." Freja said nothing, unsure what to think or believe anymore. "Look," continued Lulja and put a hand on Freja's shoulder. "The sooner you go home, the better. You clearly don't like it here and Ma'zekaï is not a place for humans. I'm an exception. There's not even a name for humans like me, who are free. That's how rare it is."

"I noticed," said Freja in a grim voice, raising one eyebrow. "We found one of those underground caves in Wind. Just before we ran into you."

Lulja's rounded mouth revealed she not only knew of them, but also knew exactly what they were. "It's the way here, unfortunately," she said. "Life isn't fair, trust me, I know—I'm from Jahran. People come here for many reasons, but the Obbsborn are criminal, you know. It's a punishment and a second chance in a way. Not that I envy them …"

Behind Lulja, the two Masters had stopped talking and were impatiently waiting to leave. They looked displeased with each other's company. Freja shifted her glance back to Lulja and said, with a smile so that neither Master would suspect anything was the matter, "They are not criminals, Lulja—is that what they tell you? My mother … She disappeared and I know she's here somewhere because I met someone else I know, I knew before, whatever. They're taken, they're innocent people. Curfew victims. Lulja, this is where Curfew takes you."

"What … I—no, no, they're criminals," Lulja stammered. "Bad, bad people. It's got nothing to do with Curfew—that's radiation and stuff. Hey, I might be from a country where people are ignorant, but I went to school, believe it or not. I'm not an idiot just because I happen to be from Jahran. We have a lot of clever people, you know. Maybe not as many as in Vildaell or fancy Buria, but we aren't stupid."

"I never said you were …"

"I've seen pictures on TV. I've seen what radiation does to people and if you're outside when the levels are too high … Man, it's not pretty."

Over her shoulder Freja saw Ravn approach to collect his companion, so she hurried.

"They're lying to you," she said, still smiling and speaking fast. "Don't ask me why because I don't know. Those humans are taken by force, that's all I'm sure of. Listen, I heard them talk last night, Ravn and Topster. The—the, argh, what are they called? The Flÿght, that's it—they're protesting against the Élan for wanting to open the borders. Basically, they don't like it and are going to oppose them."

"That's ridiculous," said Lulja. "Nobody opposes the Lords. Those three people are the most powerful Masters—they're the *Lords*."

"That's what Ravn said, but Topster was pretty insistent.

They also mentioned a thing, like a weapon, and they called it the Trin…"

"What are you girls chit-chatting about?" Ravn's voice was silky smooth and full of sugar-coated suspicion.

"Human food," said Freja with a radiant smile. "Would it interest you?"

Ravn made a face and then rolled his eyes. "I'll never understand the customs of humans," he said with a sigh. "Ready, Lulja?"

"Yeah, sure," she replied and hugged Freja goodbye. While the girls were wrapped in each other's arms, she whispered, "I'll talk to the Masters in my house. One of them takes to me, maybe she'll talk. Send me a message if you find out more."

"Goodbye then," said Freja as they broke apart. "It was nice meeting you."

"You too," said Lulja. "Good luck."

"Come now, come now," said Ravn and pushed Lulja forward. The parting between the Masters was nothing sensational and hardly worth mentioning. Constrained to a light bow on both sides, the Masters turned in opposite directions together with their human companions. Freja craned her neck to see Lulja walk away, almost wishing she could go with her. Instead, she trailed after Topster through the opening in the wall, through the high grass, and into the great shadow cast by the Willow tree.

Klobb was waiting on the porch as if he was expecting them, and even before he spoke, Freja could tell something was awry. The flower bed in front was sagging and dry, its foxgloves bowing in greeting to its Master, and Klobb himself looked more worse for wear than usual. A little furry creature—Pollux, the batsër—was struggling in his hand. "There's a message from *them*, Master."

"And?"

Topster stood perfectly still as he spoke, his facial expression stoic.

"The thing's all set up, but ..." Klobb said and paused. "Ay, you better hear it from Eden yerself."

Freja checked at the name. Eden. She had heard it before, she was sure of it, but she couldn't recall in what context.

Topster snatched the batsër from Klobb's hands with unnecessary force and tickled its chin. He put its mouth to his ear and listened to the repeated message during a few minutes of complete silence during which Freja felt her legs threatening to cave under her tired body. It was late already, and she would not mind sleeping. She could hardly think straight and thoughts of Jaspir and his mother down under ground in Wind flew hand in hand with fenrirs, Strays, the strange thing whose name she could not remember, and Klobb, who eyed her with his usual disdain.

When Topster turned on his heel and walked away, chucking the batsër into Freja's hands, she snapped back. "Um, hello?" He stopped and turned to her, eyes as cold as ice. Whatever the message had been, it had definitely disconcerted him. "I've completed my part of the agreement," Freja continued. "I want to go home now. Like you promised."

"No, we cannot send you back, Miss Freja," said Topster without blinking.

The air seeped out of her like a deflating balloon and she felt faint. The furry batsër was warm in her hands and his pulse beat against her skin, which turned cold and moist from sweat. Of course she had known it was too easy, but some part of her had still trusted Topster.

"We agreed! You have to! You can't do ... You can't ..." Her sentences may have been incomplete in syntax, but they lacked nothing in sentiment. Tears welled up in her eyes and her voice was reduced to a croaking muddle. She heard ugly sounds escape her throat, like a cat working on a fur ball, and was powerless to stop them. Her knees gave way at last and she fell to the ground, wrapping her arms around Pollux and hugging him like a child might a cuddly toy. It was too much, too much. "You can't …," was all she managed. "I'll run …" The tears obstructed her throat and she had to choose—breathing or speaking.

"Klobb, make sure our guest does not go anywhere unauthorised," said Topster in a bored tone. "Or I will ensure that hers is not the only head that will roll for it."

"Right, Master," said Klobb in a hollow voice, his hand moving instinctively to his healthy leg. "O' course."

"Very good." Topster walked away without as much as a second look at Freja. He turned the corner and disappeared from sight.

Freja remained on the ground until the evening became too cold and she started shivering. A hand, two hands, shrivelled and old like paper that's got wet and dried again, pulled her to her feet and helped her inside when her own legs refused to carry her. A soothing voice whispered until she fell asleep, too exhausted to bother about the world, the night, or the future which now looked too bleak and too uncertain to consider.

*

Klobb closed the door to Freja's room and went out into the back garden. The night was cold, colder than most, and even though he was no Master, he had been in Ma'zekaï long enough to understand what such a change in the weather signified. The wall could only hold up against so much destruction before the fate of Wind, Wild, and Water would be the fate of the Valley of Wood as well. To his left stood the great Willow proud and poised in a large shaded contour against the night sky, where the waning moon hung like a tasty biscuit, tempting the weak and the hungry alike. He felt a rumbling appetite all right, but weak he was not. It was not the life he had imagined for himself, he thought with a sad feeling in his heart; not this life at all. Crouching next to the last lonely stalk of Rainbow Glory, its blue shade dark in the gloom, he stroked its petals and whispered his usual goodnight to it. This would be his last.

"Sora, I'm sorry ... I'm so sorry ...," he mumbled over and over as he took the clippers from his pocket.

As if hearing his words of love and longing, knowing their meaning and their finality, and accepting his apologies without blame or resentment, the blue flower bowed in the evening wind, shyly offering its smooth neck to the executioner's rough hands. With one quick movement it was done.

CHAPTER 17

FREJA DRAGGED HERSELF through the next couple of weeks. In the house, Klobb was no more content with their situation than she was, and it gave her some satisfaction to know he was suffering too. Not knowing when or even if Topster was planning to return proved a gnawing concern to both of them. A daily routine soon emerged to cope with the monotony of life: Freja would throw tantrums and issue threats to run away (*"I'd rather be eaten by fenrirs than stay here for another minute!"*) at least twice a day, and these were always followed by Klobb's fruitless reassuring speeches, at times harsh and snappish, sometimes almost bordering on gentle and sincere.

Given Topster's threat of cutting off a rather important third of Klobb's height, he was reluctant to let her out of his sight. No matter how loudly or how passionately Freja tried, he refused to believe her promises not to run away, and would not let her outside. She asked him: where would she go? "The latches are locked up and unless I want to actually be eaten, I have nowhere to run to."

From her perspective, there was nothing she could do, especially with Klobb breathing down her neck every two seconds. She had noticed he kept himself inside a lot more than usual—and not just because of the decreasing sunny weather. With one eye always ready to pop in her direction, he hovered outside her room during the day, joined her in cooking in the evening, and even accompanied her to the Willow on more than one occasion, despite her request to be left alone. She had, in spite of Klobb's suspicions, no plans to run away. No, as dreary as life with Klobb was, it at least left her with a lot of time on her hands; time she spent thinking about Jaspir, her mother, and Curfew. She had drawn countless mind maps that would have made her teachers cry with joy, trying to make sense of it all. The facts were there but she couldn't connect the dots. If only Robin had been there with her.

Later that week, in bed with Pollux sleeping soundly on her pillow, she looked through her notes. The masterform was draped over the back of the chair ever since she had resorted to her own clothes (a change that had sent Klobb into a manic state of fury at first). It felt good to be back in her comfortable jeans, though they were torn, and t-shirt, even if the clothes reminded her a bit too much of the Look-Out and what had been said there. Also, her mother's charm was once again around her neck, a friendly and familiar weight.

With a sigh she pushed away the sheets and rested her forehead on the back of her hands, felt her stomach press against the mattress with every breath. Condensing her thoughts and memories into words and mind maps had only confused her further, but she was convinced that there was a larger image to be discovered within the mess. She only had to find it.

The link between Curfew and the underground caves was clear. 'Removed' meant being sent here to Ma'zekaï to be used in some sort of morbid work camps. Suddenly the Curfew Law had become part of a conspiracy of enormous measures. She sighed. Whatever was going on, her hands were tied anyway.

There was only one other person who would believe her, and Freja had no idea how to find her or even where to look. Lulja had said she stayed in the village but there was no way Klobb would let her go. The idea made her laugh.

"Oh, Pollux," she said and stroked the soft fur of the sleeping batsër, who had been a lot more amicable than Klobb had let on. "What are we going to do?" The batsër offered no solutions. His snores were low and growling in the silence of the room. Outside, the rain had ceased and the grass was specked with left-behind drops of water, the sky blue. Beyond the long stretch of land, far away, was the village ...

Of course! Freja slapped her forehead and pushed herself up, sending the bed into tremors. Pollux opened one eye, annoyed at being disturbed. "Gosh, I'm stupid," she muttered, scooped up the batsër and hurried out into the kitchen where Klobb was attempting his very first meal on his own. It smelled kind of burnt. "I want to send a message," she said and held out Pollux towards Klobb. "I want to ask Lulja to come see me."

He stared at her and then gave up an ugly laugh. "Are you out of yer mind? We dun have visitors here. Usually," he added when she raised an eyebrow.

"Please, Klobb? I'm bored, I'm lonely, and if I could just see someone—someone my own age—I think I could be a bit happier. Wouldn't that make life easier for the both of us? Lulja's a friend and, besides, Topster only said I couldn't leave, which I wouldn't." Without taking his eyes off the pot, Klobb chewed his lip and questioned her thoroughly as to the reason and only agreed once she promised to send it in his presence. Freja, though having no intention of letting him hear the whole message, shook his hand on it. When he had turned away, she wiped the sweat off on her jeans. "You're the best, Klobb," she said with a grin and picked up Pollux who was busy gnawing at his fur. "Do I just say it?" Klobb grunted in assent.

"Hold 'im up to yer mouth so he can take the words. Keep it short, keep it simple. They have tiny stomachs."

Frowning, Freja did as he said. The batsër's tiny jaws opened in front of her as though ready to bite into a piece of flesh, and she uttered her message. Once she had finished, Pollux worked his jaws up and down, as though chewing the words and swallowed them with a choking sound. Once his jaws had snapped shut he returned to his usual miniature walrus vampire state. Under his chin the belly was bulging.

"Bit long," growled Klobb as he noticed the fattened stomach.

"Too long?"

"You'd know if it was too long." He told her to release Pollux on the porch. "He'll repeat it to no one but the *hooman* girl."

"You stay here, or the food will burn," said Freja, not mentioning the fact that the stew had already been scorched beyond repair. "I'll manage. Thanks, Klobb."

"I'm watching ye," said Klobb, waving the wooden spoon as a warning.

"How could I ever forget," muttered Freja before going outside.

She sat down on the steps. With a quick glance back at the door, making sure Klobb was busy with the abomination he called food, Freja lifted Pollux to her face once more. She wasn't sure how it would work, but as the jaws opened again she added a few more sentences to the message already in the batsër's stomach, and then released him down on the ground, where he stood still. He hiccupped and for a second she was afraid the message would come spilling out, but then he settled and seemed content with what he was carrying.

"Off you go," she said. Pollux didn't move. He sat on his

hind-legs, tilted his head to the side, and looked at her with his bulging eyes as if he was asking a question. "That's it," she said. "I'm done, you can go now."

From behind came Klobb's raspy voice. "You've gotta clap twice," he yelled from the kitchen.

Freja did as he said and Pollux shot off, skipping down the steps and, at ground level, put his claws into the grass and dug a hole into which he disappeared, closing the gap behind him as he went.

Freja remained on the porch, gazing out over the landscape, wondering how quickly Pollux would reach Lulja. She wanted to ask, but decided it was better to save questions and Klobb's patience until more important times. She had to hope that Lulja had found out more since their parting, and with the added part of the message, she crossed her fingers that Lulja would be as curious as Freja was, and come see her like she asked.

Outside the window, rain had made a return in bucket loads, flooding the lands, and the skies were as grey as a woolly jumper.

Instead of Klobb's food—which she politely declined, saying she was not hungry, though her stomach was rumbling— she prepared some tea and snuck a carrot into her room. With her tea finished and the carrot vanished in a few bites, she was still hungry and went to get more hot water. In the kitchen she found Klobb, a half-eaten portion of his homemade brown-coloured stew in a bowl next to him and a chunk of wood beside it, so engrossed in his work that he didn't notice her coming in. Only when she went to the blazing fire and took the pot with a slamming noise did he realise her presence and jumped in his seat. His whole body doubled over the paper on the table. Despite the surprisingly quick movement, Freja had time to see that it was a flower—a blue one—pressed to a flat one-dimensional version of itself.

"Dun' sneak up on people," Klobb growled and covered the

flower with the wood. "It en't very lady-like."

"I'm not a lady—I'm a goat, remember?" Freja retorted as she poured the boiled water into her mug. "Besides, you sneak up on me all the time. Is that gentlemanly, would you say?"

Without replying, Klobb got up and put the pressed flower and log away in the cabinet, all the time shooting furtive glances behind him to see if Freja was watching. She focused on her tea but could see from the corner of her eye that he placed it in one of the drawers. She wondered if Topster knew it was there. Though she wouldn't have guessed it from him, Klobb seemed to have a lot going on without the Master's knowledge.

"What's 'Sora'?" she asked, suddenly remembering the night she'd seen him in the garden, talking to himself. She had asked Lulja in the mountains, but she hadn't recognised it as a flower, which was Freja's initial thought. Nor had it been indexed in the biology book from her backpack. Together they had decided that it sounded like a name, but not a Master one. From the expression on Klobb's face, she immediately regretted asking. A red-flushed fury prickled his facial skin into smaller rashes of coloured rage, disfiguring him into some monstrous creature. His eyes flexed in size, now narrowed to mere slits, then opening again into wide disbelief. Freja could imagine smoke coming out of his ears and mouth, like a steam engine about to explode. "Sorry," she spluttered, desperate to calm him down. Not one of her threats or tantrums had sent him into such a fit. "I didn't mean to pry. I just …"

"Where did ye hear that name?" he said in a dangerously calm voice, so calm it frightened Freja more than anything he'd shouted at her before.

"In the garden …"

"You've been spying on me?"

"No! It was an accident, I promise."

Klobb stood with his fists closed and whitening, his chest

raising and falling in heavy breaths. She half expected him to leap at her with the intention to wound, or even kill, but he remained where he was, as still as a statue. The silence was terrifying and grand. At last she couldn't hold her breath anymore and exhaled in controlled measures, worried it might trigger a vicious streak in him. The rush of air flowing out through her mouth was thundering in the room, but Klobb didn't flinch. He kept his stare firm, not quite at her eyes, but next to them where the gems of her masterform were still attached. She'd not bothered to take them off.

"Never mention that name again," he said at last, adjusting his gaze to her eyes. His own were calm and cold like the deep of an ocean during a violent storm. She could almost see the raging waves inside him which must have been difficult to contain.

"I won't, I promise," she said. "I'm sorry."

Klobb nodded and walked past her out of the kitchen. As soon as he had left the room Freja collapsed into a chair, her heart beating hard as if punishing her for being nosy. Topster's words echoed in rhythm to her pulse: *Curiosity is not a sin here, but neither is it a virtue*. Perhaps it was time to adhere to that, she thought. But then she remembered the message to Lulja—an action completely counteracting that admonition. It couldn't be helped, she decided, sipping her tea and feeling strength return like waves of calm water. Desperate times had no room for virtuous behaviour; and these were desperate times indeed.

Through the window she saw the outline of a short man in the midst of the rain, standing in the garden and staring at the place where the colourful Rainbow Glory had once grown.

*

Another quiet evening passed and Freja dared an unauthorised visit to the Willow in the clear afternoon the next day. The rain had ceased and nothing in the blue sky bore a sign of what had invaded it these past few days. Flocks of birds flew this way and that, great eagles and hawks and smaller sparrows and finches. Freja wished she had some wings of her own, so she could fly far, far away, and not suffer further under the absent Topster's power. Her only way out would be Lulja, or if Klobb had a sudden change of heart and presented her with a latch. Even so, the walls were raised around her, quite literally—she could see the top section of the brick wall from the elevation—with solid bars to keep her in, and keep any potential rescuer out.

Under the wide crown of the tree, on the soft grass, none of her worries seemed to matter. She was leaning against one of its roots, which was gently massaging her back with its pulse of energy flows. It forced her heartbeat into synchronised rhythm. It was the rhythm of the Universe and she was part of it. She was part of a larger vision; larger than the cottage and certainly larger than Klobb. Closing her eyes, she almost felt like a branch of the tree itself. A cell in a larger being, a player in a game of survival.

It wasn't entirely untrue. Robin had refused to let her in on his plans to save Cecelya, yet here Freja was, in the midst of it all. If she could, she would have let him in. Without a doubt. He had always been careful when it came to Freja, as though she was made of porcelain and needed to be cushioned so as not to break. Always protective, always taking the blame when Nagel caught them in his flower beds, when Mops came off the leash once and almost ran out into the street, or when they were out too close to Curfew. He was being her friend then, but since her mother was removed Robin had become obsessed with trying to prevent the world from bruising her further. Like a sister. It should have been chivalrous and sweet, but it was annoying more than anything else. Well, she figured, after all of this he'll have to realise that I can take care of myself. The next rational thought was left suspended in the air as she tried to dodge it like an approaching frisbee. Then it hit: if she ever did see him again.

A leaf dwindled down from the crown and landed beside her on the grass. She picked it up and held it towards the sky where it blended in with the shades of blue, itself turning from green to silver to golden blue. Strange. She thought of the Strays, how they altered their appearance to show what you wanted to see. Somehow, this leaf did the same, adjusting to its environment.

Like a chameleon, Freja thought. Like me.

The leaf warmed her palm. With a peculiar sadness she realised she would no longer have the Essence, as Topster had been gone for weeks already and there was nobody else to renew it. Of course, she didn't need it as long as she was kept here, but she missed it nonetheless. With a hand on her temple, she felt the pulse from the root echo in the amethysts without delay, as if they were one and the same, yet different in their tune and strength.

At the same time she had closed her other fist with the leaf inside. Her skin tingled, but it took another moment for Freja to figure out where exactly—or why. Heat erupted from the leaf inside her fist and burned her palm, her fingers, her blood. Instead of dropping the leaf, as one might tear a hand off a hot plate, she forced both her hands to stay where they were: one covering the three gems, the right one closed around the leaf. All of her attention went to the heat in her palm and one by one, the sensation spread into her body just like when Topster had given her the Essence before. The warmth travelled from her hand through her veins and towards her heart where it rested like a drop of alien hot water surrounding the tissues. Next, it continued down to her abdomen and pulsated there for a moment. Her breathing became heavy and strained, more and more so until the leaf imploded in her hand. When she bent her fingers open, the leaf had turned to a scorched pile of brown debris and her hand was covered in burning blisters breaking out in angry red blotches. The intense pain was secondary and Freja only stared at the leaf, now nothing more than ashes. Her hand was stinging and oozing with liquid from the blisters which grew more serious by the minute, but her legs were frozen.

Somehow, she had taken a leaf and accessed the energy.

Once the shock had passed, she scrambled to her feet and grabbed a handful of leaves using her left hand (careful this time not to close her fingers around them in case it happened again) and stuffed them in her pocket. With a final glance up towards the tree above where three hawks circled, nothing more than tiny specks against the enormous dropping crown, she hurried back to the house in the hope that Klobb had not yet noticed her absence. Unfortunately, he had. As soon as she closed the door behind her, he came hobbling out from the kitchen wearing a face of fury.

"Don't start on me," she said and headed for her room, keeping her right hand tucked behind her back. "I'm not in the mood." Klobb didn't give up so easily. When she tried to close her door for some private healing of her hand, he pushed his body in the gap and the wood slammed against his head. He didn't even flinch. "What are you doing?" Freja shouted and slammed the door once more, again hitting Klobb who refused to move.

"Where've ye been?" he asked. "I've been a-lookin' all over for ye. I tell ye to stay put and ye stay put."

"I didn't go far."

"Dun' matter," he barked. "What if someone sees ye, eh? In them clothes it'd be a disaster."

"For who?" she asked and hauled the door open. She was tired and in pain and sick of his premonitions of catastrophe.

"You or me? Or Topster?"

"That's *Master* Topster for ye and dun' think the Lords would think a-twice about where t'send ye if they found ye. It'd be down, down, lass, down to the worst o' places. That I promise ye."

"You worry about me?" she asked coyly, keen to get Klobb out of her room. "How sweet."

"Now listen 'ere, goat," he growled with a finger ready to scold. "I …"

A knock saved her from the rest of the speech. Freja leapt to the front door and opened it without consideration for the warning she received seconds ago. A yellow masterform met her on the other side of the threshold and before she recognised the face, her insides went cold. Why had she been so careless? If a Master spotted her jeans, her game of surviving chameleon would have failed miserably. Then she saw the dark hair and gleaming zircons. But Lulja's smile faltered as she, too, took in the whole of Freja, including her outfit.

"You look … different," she said, eyeing her from top to toe, frowning at what she saw. "Where's your masterform? And *oh my world, what happened to your hand?*"

"It's nothing," said Freja with a grin and placed her right hand behind her back again. "I'm so glad you're here."

"I brought someone as well." A light was glowing in Lulja's eyes as she called for another Master who had been waiting beneath the porch. "Freja, this is—"

They finished the sentence together. The red boiler suit and burgundy hair were more than familiar and Freja couldn't help but break out in a beaming smile. The Master did the same. It was a small world after all, if this was the woman Lulja had been talking about. Master Éloyse forwent the proper greeting and took Freja in her arms.

"Éloyse!"

"Did I not say I'd be back?" she said and Freja hugged her, unable to quench the tears suffused in her eyes.

CHAPTER 18

KLOBB DIDN'T WAIT long before he slammed the door shut with him on the outside, as Freja invited the two guests inside. Nobody mourned his absence for long. It gave them space to speak freely, for which Freja was grateful.

After a quick tour of the cottage, Freja encouraged the glowing ashes into a proper fire in the kitchen and set a kettle to boil. It was slow work as her main hand was incapacitated and Lulja asked if she needed help. "I wish you could tell me what happened," she said and forced Freja to show her wounds. The blisters had gone yellow and all kinds of shades of red, and some had even developed into gaping flesh wounds. "Freja?" Lulja pleaded. Again she repeated it was nothing, but she could tell Lulja was dissatisfied with that answer. Éloyse said nothing, only watched her in silence. "Wow, this is good," Lulja said and took another gulp of the scorching hot tea. "Ouch."

"You never tried it before?"

"It is a privilege for the guardian of the tree," said Éloyse and wafted some of the steam into her face, breathing in the scent. "It is refreshing."

"I sort of feel like a new person," continued Lulja and

swallowed a large gulp of the scolding drink, followed by a painful expression in her face. "Ouch."

"Stop doing that," said Freja and laughed. The blisters tightened and another one popped, oozing out yellow pus from the angry red area. She avoided Lulja's gaze and focused on her tea. "Topster isn't here," she said. Éloyse had been glancing around since they arrived, and Freja had a good idea what she was searching for. Her mouth formed a small 'o' and she, too, turned to her tea. "So," said Freja, feeling that the time for chit-chat and catching up was over; she had to know what Lulja had found out. "Tell me."

"Basically," Lulja began, twirling the mug back and forth between her hands, "you were right. The Flÿght is definitely on the move. They're not only backstabbing the Élan, but want to leave Ma'zekaï altogether, and create their own world …" She hesitated. "In Heim."

A frown creased the skin between Freja's eyebrows as she took in this information. "In Heim? As in, in the human world?"

Lulja nodded, then realised her mug was empty and shot a glance towards the kettle. After the go-ahead from Freja, she refilled her mug to the brim while Éloyse explained further. There were hundreds, thousands, of Flÿght Masters and if all of them went through finite latches, the transferral of energy would be devastating for Ma'zekaï as they would bring all that energy with them to Heim. "The energy conformation is likely to kill at least parts of our *landskapë*," she concluded.

"Can't you stop them?"

"That's what I said," added Lulja, "but they're so many. The Trew are, how many, a few thousand? And most of them don't even know what's going on. The Élan is, well, ten Masters strong which is weak, even if they are powerful individually."

"Besides," said Éloyse, "the Élan refuses to realise what is happening and like Lulja said, most of the Trew do not know either. Half of them are unaware and half of them would be glad to see the Flÿght go. They do not have a good reputation around here. I was hoping to see what Topster knows about it all."

"What about the Lords?" said Freja, only then realising that she only knew them as 'the Lords' and had heard no details about their power, their whereabouts, or even their appearance. "The Lords are the Lords, isn't that what you said, Lulja? Nobody opposes the Lords? Not that I've ever seen them exactly policing the streets …"

"You *have* seen the Lords, Freja," said Éloyse and Freja frowned at her. "In the village, if you recall."

"They wear white," said Lulja.

A chilling memory stroked her mind. The dark damp alley and Éloyse's hand over her mouth, her whispering voice throwing cascades of hot air into her ear. Three Masters mere metres away. Whispering. White masterforms. Her mouth went dry. The proximity of the Masters—the Lords—overpowered her in a delayed reaction, strengthened by the knowledge she had since acquired, even if she had already felt some ominous threat from the trio.

"Those were the Lords?"

"Yes," said Éloyse. "Trozelli and Eden are the son and daughter of the old Élan Lords …"

"Eden?" Freja said, unfortunately out loud, when she remembered where she had first heard that name. Topster was communicating with the Élan Lords! "Sorry," she added when realising that Éloyse and Lulja were both observing her with interest. "Continue."

"Then there's Py," Éloyse said, curiosity at Freja's interjection lingering in her eye. "Py is a Trew Master who has been given lordship on appointment. Usually it is a rank given by birth, and Py is the first Master ever to come from outside the given line of Essence." Then she added, "There was an incident that left one of the lordships available."

"Bias?" Freja asked and Éloyse shrugged almost unnoticeably. It was as good as a yes. It didn't matter. Py's love life was of lesser importance. Suddenly they had names, identities. Trozelli, Eden, Py. Three Masters who Freja both feared and had to hold her hope against; three Master Lords who held the solution to everything in their bare hands, if only they could have faith in the story of two humans. Somehow that recipe didn't spell immediate success.

"Could they help?" Lulja had finished her second mug of tea and gazed longingly to its bottom as she spoke. "Can I …?" She didn't wait for an answer before leaping up to the fire again.

Éloyse cleared her throat and waited for Lulja to return before replying. "We could try," she said, pondering. "But I doubt they will. Admitting that the Flÿght is strong enough would be a dent to their honour. To them it would be like saying that Strays could overthrow the Master race. It's just not possible."

"Except it is possible," said Freja, annoyed. "Right? I'm not imagining things?"

"It is," said Éloyse and glanced at Lulja. "Should you or I?"

Lulja had been jumping in her seat, but Freja had just assumed it was because of her refilled tea. "Can I? Can I?" she said now with excitement bubbling in her every limb. She filled her mouth with tea until her cheeks were extended into round balls and swallowed it in large guzzles until all of it was gone. She stood up and slammed her hands on the table. "Forget the Lords," she said in a dramatic tone. "If we can't trust the Flÿght, and we can't count on the Élan to do what it's kind of supposed to do—who's left?"

Freja thought for a moment and then the answer struck like lightning, as clear as the Willow water. That's why Lulja was barely able to contain her joy; more, that's why she was here and had brought Éloyse with her. "The Trew," Freja said and looked at Éloyse who was smiling. "Would the Trew believe us? I mean, there's no real evidence—but you're here."

"Some of us know already and have done so for a while, despite what the Élan thinks," she said. "That's why we're here now, to take you with us. Some of the Trew are still ignorant, some are in need of convincing, but I'm confident they will get there in the end."

"I'm going with you? Away from here?"

"You can't do a lot being trapped here in the middle of nowhere," said Lulja, now smiling and still flittering from foot to foot. "So we're going central—right into Trew headquarters. From there we can rally them up."

"Klobb will never let me go," Freja said with a sigh, thinking back to the magnitude of the battles she'd had to face to go further than the porch. "But it's not his fault, really. Topster sort of threatened to chop Klobb's head off if he let me escape."

"Bathroom?" asked Lulja suddenly and her jittery behaviour came to an explanation. No wonder, the amount of tea she'd had. Freja pointed to the garden where the, to her, primitive apparatus was placed. "Be right back." Lulja scooted off.

"Do not worry about Klobb," said Éloyse and reached out for her hand. "The other one, silly." Reluctant, Freja gave Éloyse her right hand which was increasingly worse for wear. She took a bucket, filled it with water, and submerged the hand in it. The cool water soothed some of the pain and soon the hand was numbed. With gentle pressure, Éloyse forced Freja to keep her hand down. "It won't take too long to heal. You're lucky to have the brook outside."

"You're not going to ask me how it happened?" said Freja. Éloyse said nothing and before long—Lulja was still out—the Master lifted the hand out of the now cloudy water and Freja opened her mouth in surprise. Though some redness prevailed, the blisters were gone and the skin was sore, but intact. "Thank you," said Freja in earnest.

"Perhaps now you may answer me," said Éloyse when she had emptied the bucket and returned to her seat. "Where is Topster? We ought to warn him."

Curiosity was not a sin, but bias was, Freja thought. Besides, if anyone knew what the Flÿght was doing, it was Topster. He was more likely the brain behind it all; he as much as admitted it to Ravn in the mountains. Perhaps Lulja had not told Éloyse this particular part. Soon enough she would find out, so for the time being Freja decided to keep it to herself. "Some emergency," she said, decided to also leave her suspicions unspoken. "He left suddenly." It was not a straight out lie, but she still felt a twinge of guilt for concealing the true nature of the 'emergency' from Éloyse, who had risked a lot by coming here to help. There was some light in her eyes that seemed as fragile as the flicker of a candle; a brittleness of faith Freja recognised from her own experience when it came to people who were special to her. Topster's dealings with the Lords could have a logical explanation, for all she knew; and yet, the urgency and agitated exhibition of emotion that Eden's message had instilled in Topster did not spell any kind of innocence to Freja.

"I shall ask Klobb to send a batsër to him," said Éloyse. "Did I see Pollux outside?"

"He's exhausted," said Freja quickly, taking consolation in the truth of the matter. "He won't stand another trip for a few days."

The back door banged and Lulja came sauntering in, no longer in jitters and quite capable of sitting still. "Where are we?" she asked and Freja filled her in on Topster's absence. "Oh, don't worry," she said to Éloyse. "I'm sure he's off on some tree business. Leave a message with Klobb and he'll get it the moment he gets back." Éloyse went to find the man out back where he was, according to Lulja, "pottering and muttering about," while Freja and Lulja went out into the front and sat down on the steps.

The sun cast a golden glamour over the landscape as it began to set slowly over the ocean, leaving a humid blanket of heat hovering over the hills and dales of the valley. "You must be wondering why I came back," said Lulja. "I've not changed my mind, you know; I still want to stay here. Jahran isn't the place for me, never was."

"What about your family?"

Lulja shook her head. "I actually found out I have a half-brother about two years ago, but he lives in Buria in his fancy mansion and wants nothing to do with his street urchin sister. Not even when my aunt kicked me out because she couldn't afford to feed me anymore … She told me to get a job and support myself like everyone else, which is fair enough, really. I'm not her kid."

"I never knew Jahran was so poor," said Freja, wishing she had paid more attention in civics. "I knew it was worse off than Vildaell and Buria, of course, but it sounds a lot worse than they tell us."

"You've gotta see it to believe it," Lulja said and broke off a stalk of a light pink foxglove she had taken from the garden. She started picking the petals one by one. Freja asked about the Buria and Lulja snorted. "Buria's worse than rich—it's disgusting. The Queen is one of the people, but only because in Buria, everyone's royalty. If the Queen came to Jahran—" she whistled— "she'd be robbed before she could say 'my goodness gracious me'." Freja laughed at the impression. The Queen of the Buria was often described as a parody of herself and had had to stand repeated satirical impressions throughout the years. Compared to the Queen, Cecelya Aitken seemed almost lifeless and dull, and Jahran was about as much her natural habitat as a colourful cockatoo under water. Lulja might not be a cockatoo of any measure, but for the first time, Freja understood why she could prefer Ma'zekaï, though she could not quite disregard the horrible treatment and perception of humans here. Lulja clearly could. For her the grass was greener on this side but, considering the state of the other valleys, it probably wouldn't be for long.

"So why did you come?" Freja asked, taking comfort in that she knew the answer already; she just wanted Lulja to say it. To re-establish the borders between the *landskapës*.

"The Élan is right," she said instead to Freja's surprise. "I think the borders should be opened and give the people an opportunity to choose, like I have. Ma'zekaï can't survive on its own resources for much longer and it's not right that they should keep stealing energy from Heim. If we open up between the *landskapës,* we can live together and share."

"Wait, they're *stealing* energy?"

"Yeah, I only just found out myself. Something to do with latches and … I don't know."

"But … how?"

Lulja shrugged. "It's done during Curfew, that's all I know."

"Is the nuclear explosion even real?" All the warnings, the stories, the rumours—was any of it true?

"Yes," Lulja said quickly. "Or at least I think so … Maybe they made it up? Is that possible? I'm sorry, Freja, I don't know."

"Let's see if Éloyse is ready," said Freja and stood up, pushing back the wave of confusion and concern that threatened to blow her mind.

In the kitchen Éloyse and Klobb were glaring at each other. After a short but heated argument with Klobb, who finally failed to stand up against the three women, Freja changed into her purple masterform once more—this time without Klobb's assistance—and unclasped her necklace. It was beyond stupid to risk being caught because she was wearing it, and Topster had already noticed it. When it was safely in the inner pocket, she hid the backpack under the bed and left the room, closing the door behind her. She hoped she would have the opportunity to come back later to retrieve it.

Saying goodbye to Klobb was the least of her worries, and yet a lump filled her throat as they decided in mute agreement to leave it at a short nod; which was lucky, because Freja didn't trust herself to speak. Her life seemed to consist of an endless line of goodbyes these days. As she stepped onto one of the Transporters behind Éloyse, she couldn't help but look back at the house where Klobb was still standing on the porch, leaning on his right leg and with his left thigh in a firm grip. The engines came to life and the usual hum filled the air. Freja took a deep breath and prepared for the speed that would take her away, far away, from the place that had, strangely, gone from a house of horror to a place she called a second home.

CHAPTER 19

THE TREW DIDN'T have homes, like Lulja had said, at least not in the way Freja would have defined it. The small square buildings in the village were indeed shops, and above these were rooms—lodging—used by the Trew Masters. "The lodge is a remnant from our more active days," said Éloyse and led them towards the buzzing square. "With four valleys we had a lot more ground to cover, so we rarely stayed in one place two nights in a row."

"I thought you didn't sleep?" Freja could use a good dose of that herself.

"We still need to recharge," said Éloyse and pushed the door open. A bell rang somewhere within. "Klepta," she called. "I am back."

Movement sounded and soon a woman came waddling, like a duck. Her masterform was washed-out blue and matched the watery paleness of her grey-blue eyes. There were no wrinkles in her face other than the small creases that broke through when she smiled, nor did her movements seem strained or difficult at any rate, and she wore the same clothes and gleaming gems—agates that were almost transparent—as any other

Master, except for the apron tied around her waist. Still, there was something about her that suggested that she was old, older than any Master Freja had met so far. She wasn't exactly beautiful but the bumped nose, rather like a hill in style, and cocked eyebrows gave character to her face and proposed a story of a life long lived.

Master Klepta greeted them one by one and stopped when she reached Freja. Her eyes wandered to the amethysts and her smile widened, showing off a sparse row of large teeth in her mouth. "Alas, what has that Master made you do this time, Éloyse?" chuckled Klepta and closed the door behind them. The bell rang again from another room. "Two of them. And there's a message too."

She produced a batsër from the pocket of her apron. This one had thick streaks of grey in its fur and long fangs hanging out like stalactites from the mouth. Klepta laughed as Éloyse snatched after the batsër, unsuccessfully. "*Ka-ka!*" she cackled. "Shall I read it to you? Ragnar and I go way back, dear, so he tells me all his secrets." With deliberate slothful movements, she raised the batsër to her ear, all the while cooing and cackling, before Éloyse finally got hold of the creature.

While Éloyse listened to what Ragnar had to convey, Lulja had a look around the shop. Freja remained where she was, still not enough at ease with the customs of Masters to move freely. Soon enough Lulja had enrolled Klepta in a presentation of the entire shop and its inventory, from bags of dried leaf shreds used for tea to masterforms to jugs of water labelled "Willow".

"It is from Topster," said Éloyse once the batsër had regurgitated the message, "but it is old. Sent before he left for this … emergency."

"*Kuu!*" said Klepta and laughed. "Does the blonde one need help, Master?"

"Do not intercept my messages again."

"No accusations, *pur*-lease," cooed Klepta and retreated, but only after taking the batsër back into her arms. "It was an educated guess, that's all."

"If I find out …"

"Don't get hissy with me, lass," said Klepta and sat down on a chair behind the counter, petting the batsër and mumbling under her breath. "A tickle in the right place behind a batsër ear, all those precious secrets—out! Oh dear, oh dear." Éloyse's glare was murderous.

"What did it say?" asked Freja and stepped in between the women, not feeling in the mood to witness a fist fight between a Trew and a Flÿght. Not yet, anyway.

"Nothing important," said Éloyse and joined Lulja at the shelves.

"Don't be afraid, little one," said Klepta from her corner and Freja thought at first she spoke to the batsër. It took her a moment to realise she was speaking to her. "Belonging was never easy in Ma'zekaï; not before, not after."

"Excuse me?"

"An outsider knows another by smell," she said and tapped her large nose.

"I'm sorry?"

"But your Essence is confusing—it's not quite linked in the chain of the Flÿght, yet Trew does not fit either …" Klepta tilted her head and cocked an eyebrow, as if trying to read something written upside down on Freja's forehead.

Freja glanced at Lulja who was busy showing Éloyse the trinkets on the shelves. How come it was Freja who stood out? Was she that human? Except Klepta used the word 'Essence'. Perhaps her human nature was new to the Master who could not even distinguish that she did not belong in any of the groups of Masters. It must have been frustrating for her, because the way Klepta's body strained so that veins popped and her eyes narrowed to mere slits in her head, she looked as though she was about to fall apart at any moment from the pressure.

"Klepta," said Éloyse, breaking the trance-like state of her watching. "Can I borrow Ragnar?"

"Oh, and to who is Ragnar going, I wonder?" teased Klepta and handed the furry batsër to Éloyse with an evil grin. "Don't let the grey fur fool you, he is the quickest I've got," she added, as Éloyse went to tell the message, gazing after him like a proud mother. "Used to be in service of the Lords, I tell you. Some very important messages have travelled with that little creature. All delivered, I might add." Before Éloyse let Ragnar shoot off, Klepta demanded to peck him on the cheek, at which Éloyse rolled her eyes and Freja and Lulja exchanged amused looks. "Mock me if you like," said Klepta and raised the tip of her magnificent nose into the air. "He is my pride, my *bias*," she added with glee, causing Éloyse to gasp and glance towards the door.

"Klepta, you ought not to say such things out in the open!"

"*Ka-ka!* We're all friends here, Éloyse. We can be honest about such things, surely?"

"Do not mention that word again," Éloyse said and approached Klepta with menacing steps. "I warn you."

"Warn away," said Klepta with a nonchalant wave of her arm. "Did you find something nice, dear?" She went over to Lulja who was still engrossed in the peculiar items.

"What's this?" Lulja held up a curved needle, rather too wide and flat for sewing.

"Good choice," said Klepta with sudden exhilaration. "It is a tool of the latch welders of old. They used it, I believe, to stitch the pieces of the latch together—making it infinite."

Lulja gaped but next to Freja, Éloyse sighed. "Enough, Klepta. Girls, do not believe a word she says," she said. "Klepta, get some drinks ready and we will be upstairs." She turned to

Freja, said "Follow me" and led them through a door in the back, behind which a staircase wound itself to the first floor.

"Klepta's kind of a funny character, isn't she?" said Lulja on the way up. She had snuck the needle into her pocket and was playing with it. "I wonder what her story is. I've never seen a Master so relaxed. Ravn's kind of like that, but not quite as much."

"She fled early," said Éloyse as they reached the top of the stairs. A closed door stood before them. "The day the wind died, she was already across the border. She's lived in the village ever since and is as much part of the Trew as a Flÿght can hope to be. At the same time her own people renounce her because she escaped and because she lives here. So she's stuck in that blue taint forever, because the Élan won't grant her to trade into the colour of the Trew, not even lowly ones like yellow, which is usually worn by young Masters who aren't yet initiated."

"Cheers," said Lulja, but with a grin.

"That's why she called herself an outsider," Freja said. "She's part of the group we're fighting?"

"Like with any group of people, there are good and bad in the Flÿght. Some do not let their past destroy them, while others do." Freja didn't have to ask in which category she would place Topster.

She pushed the door open and a sea of colours in various shades and nuances met them. Green and red were dominant, but here and there a patch of yellow shone through the crowd. At least twenty or thirty Masters were in there, some seated in a circle around a flat wooden plank with symbols and pawns on it, while others stood in close groups, speaking in low voices. It all stopped as soon as the newcomers announced themselves in the doorway. In an instant the room went quiet and Éloyse stepped forward to greet them.

"Mingle," she whispered once all the customary pleasantries

were exchanged. "Be cautious with what you say, but do not worry—we are trusting people."

"Masters?" Freja snorted. A dark look from both Éloyse and Lulja came her way.

"It's good Topster dressed you in a neutral colour," snapped Éloyse. "It will explain your lack of manners." She left them to join a group of Masters and Lulja quickly explained that purple was the colour for Flÿght Masters born in Valley of Wood; not quite part of the Flÿght, but not disdained as much as people like Klepta.

"Try to behave," she added. "You want to try the board game? It's kind of fun." They joined the small crowd of ten or so crammed around the game, and watched as an exciting round was played out by two Masters in soft green. In low whispers Lulja explained the rules and how to best move the red and blue pawns across the playing field, and Freja nodded every now and then to show she understood.

"But no skipping, right?" she said as she sat down opposite Lulja once the Masters in green had finished.

"Exactly, I was just going to say," said Lulja, curious. "How did you know?"

"We have Rhyffle at home," said Freja and considered her first move. "I warn you, I'm pretty good." She moved her first pawn two steps ahead, then four to the right. "That's my signature move."

"Wait, what?" Lulja picked up one of the red pawns and moved it three squares left. "You can't have it at home. And it's pronounced Rhyff-*el*." She spoke with caution as there were several Masters standing around them, listening. "It's a … a local game."

Freja shrugged. "Apparently not. Hop, switch, roll—I win, you lose." Perplexed, Lulja stared at the board where Freja had, indeed, won in two moves. Around them Masters exchanged impressed looks and offered to play next against her. Freja was about to accept the invitation of a nice-looking Master in peridot-green masterform and five miniature stones over each of his eyebrows when Lulja excused them both and dragged her away from the game. Freja gave a slight shrug to the Master who smiled at her.

"Flirting?" hissed Lulja when they were out of earshot. "You'll get us caught for the B-word!"

"Relax," said Freja, glad it had distracted Lulja from asking about the board game. She didn't feel like talking about her father right now. "He was doing it too. Oh, look, our drinks."

Klepta kicked the door open and brought in a tray with three glasses of grimy green liquid. They both took one and Klepta hurried over to Éloyse, then left without a word. Assuming it was another kind of leaf tea, Freja took a huge gulp, hoping it would steady her nerves so she could talk to the Master in green again, but instead of a surge of energy, there was gagging. A taste of mushy sea filled her mouth and slimed around her gums like tiny worms playing hoola-hoops around her teeth. "That's *vile*," she wheezed once she had managed to swallow the slime against her better judgement. "What is it?"

"This?" Lulja said and took a sip. "Yeah, you're right. After your leaf tea, this does seem gross. The Trew make it from seaweed and sea water—it's supposed to be good for you."

"Good for stomach pumping maybe," muttered Freja and discreetly put her glass aside. "What are we doing here anyway? I thought we were going to, how did you put it, 'rally them up'? Not much of a rally going on here, is there?"

"Tone down the whole bitter vibe," Lulja snapped back. "We're going to talk to them, but we need to blend in first. *Not by flirting!*" Freja had sent a glance towards the Master again, who was also looking her way. "They know me, but you're just the awkward cousin who shows up once in a while, and in purple as well. They need to trust you before you inform them that their world is ending. Try smiling, for once—but not at him. No, no, no smiles for him."

Freja rolled her eyes. "Fine."

They returned to the group around the game and Freja did her best to avoid the gaze of the Master in green, though she felt him searching for her. She decided to follow Lulja's advice. She was, after all, a lot more Master than Freja; she knew these people. Wrong, she corrected herself. In this situation, she was a Master too, or so she had to convince herself in order to perform at her best. Today she was Tïora—of the Flÿght, she realised with a sigh. The other kind of outcast in Ma'zekaï.

She introduced herself as Tïora only, leaving the Flÿght part out, and identified some reservation in the Trews' eyes. Secrecy of your heritage was clearly not a great icebreaker here. Her neutral masterform told them she was not of the Trew, but born in Wood, and they wanted to know where she belonged. If she was to gain their trust, she couldn't remain a mystery. Trusting and tolerant or not, it was obvious in their restless weighing from one foot to another, their constant sipping of the disgusting seaweed drink, and the furtive glances exchanged between players and viewers, that their focus was entirely on this enigmatic intruder. Tïora needed a background, and Flÿght was certainly not the answer. She had to reinvent her own alter ego, created by Topster, and she knew exactly how. It was a compromise to unite opinions under one roof and although she hadn't heard of the concept before, she guessed mixing was common.

"I'm half," she said, trying to sound casual, and she spoke out loud so that everyone would hear. "I'm only half Flÿght and I was born here. My mother was of the Trew."

For a moment she thought she had done it, she'd made herself part of the group. A thrill went through her and she felt refreshed, patting herself on the back for being so innovative. The whole room had heard, surely, and all attention was directed at her. No longer a nobody, she thought it sad that Masters were supposed to hide their feelings because she would have liked some other reaction than these neutral faces. She searched for the Master in green, in spite of her promise to Lulja, and found him on the other side of the game, also staring at her with the same blank expression, though there was some trace of bewilderment shown by his twitching eyebrows, sending the peridot gemstones dancing above his dark brown eyes. Almost imperceptibly, he shook his head and a bad feeling settled in her sternum.

She reassessed the situation.

The room had gone quiet. Conversation was dead. Everyone was staring; staring at the self-confessed hybrid who now stood in the spotlight like a cat born with three heads in a world where one was more than enough. She was a beast, a circus freak—and it wasn't even true. But she couldn't correct the mistake because the truth was infinitely worse. Beside her Lulja was boiling—the only person in the room who let her emotions show—and she was glaring at Freja like she wanted to commit murder, which, if looks were capable of such action, would have rendered the seaweed drink discarded on the floor Tiora, the bastard child's, last!

CHAPTER 20

SHE WANTED TO sink through the floor down to Klepta, and run. Run, run, run. Instead she grasped at one of Robin's tactics in the face of humiliation: laughter. She laughed and laughed as if she'd gone insane.

"This is no laughing matter," said a female Master clad in light grey, lighter than Elflock's, almost white, but signifying Élan anyway. Freja had not seen her before. "I should have known the moment you came in—I could smell it. Who brought the crossbreed?" She addressed the whole room, turning this way and that as graceful as a cat. "Attend, Masters. Admit and atone, or leave the oaths unsworn."

Éloyse came forward just as the Élan Master made a small movement towards a pocket Freja suspected held leaves. It was as strong as a threat came in Ma'zekaï. "Forgive us, Master Florin," said Éloyse and came up behind Freja, who wasn't entirely sure it was in the name of good to confess. Florin's hand was hovering over the pocket of her masterform as if waiting for the smallest sign to act. "I hoped it would not be a problem."

"Master Éloyse," Florin replied. She had a slender body with a curvy outline, was pale and blonde and dark grey eyes as chilly and gleaming as the diamonds on her face; she was angelic in appearance, but not in manner. Her skin was perfect except for an ugly scar on her neck, stretching from the ear and down into the collar of her masterform. "Of all people, I expected you to have better judgement. Then again, I hear talk in the Élan, whispers of inappropriate b…" She paused. "Behaviour." Éloyse said nothing, but the increased pressure on Freja's shoulder where Éloyse had rested her hands was enough to tell her that she was well aware of what the Élan was thinking. "I looked the other way for her," Florin continued and gestured down to the floor and, by extension, Klepta. "One Flÿght in the house is one too many, but what are you thinking bringing in crossbreeds?"

"What is one of the Élan doing in a Trew house?" Éloyse asked in a rather transparent deflecting tactic.

"The Lords value the Trew," Florin replied in a proud voice. "You are loyal, you are true, you are the future. Not them." She turned her eyes down to Freja, who instantly held her breath. Behind she felt Éloyse's grip loosen.

"Master Florin," said Éloyse and strolled over to Florin and came close to her face. "The girl was telling stories on my orders. But as we have you here, we might as well tell the truth. She is here to save Ma'zekaï."

"I don't know if *save* is …," Freja began but broke off as Lulja pinched her waist.

Éloyse turned around and spoke up so that all Masters could hear. "She is not a crossbreed or of the Flÿght—she is human."

Florin's mouth dropped open, as did many others in the room. Muted by the shock revelation, she went over to a man in the corner and whispered to him. Éloyse went after her, snatching for Florin's arm, and joined in the conversation. The three Masters conversed in loud whispers while all Freja could do was watch. Every eye except Florin's was on Freja.

"What just happened?" she said in a hollow voice.

"Royal screw-up," said Lulja, unmoved. "We'd better go, right now. Florin is not the forgiving type. That scar … She didn't get it from knitting, if you know what I mean."

"But Éloyse will sort it out, right? I mean, you were talking about staying here and everything—nobody's kicking you out."

"I'm in masterform and on Élan business, remember—can you say the same?"

Freja closed her fists and bit the inside of her lip, hard. "I'm in masterform," she said. "And I've got the Essence, or had anyway—do you? Did Éloyse bother to give it?"

"What does that even mean, 'bother to give it'? Essence is either there or it's not." Lulja shifted her weight and glowered at Freja. "Maybe it's time you told me what you're *really* doing here, huh? It's not for the Élan, I know that, so who are you working for? For all I know you could be helping the Flÿght. After all, you live with the mastermind of the whole clan."

Freja crossed her arms and glared at her. "I told you, I came here by accident. I didn't know this place existed before."

"Oh, okay," said Lulja and snorted. "And the Rhyffle? 'Hop, switch, roll'?"

"I said we have it at home, or at least one that looks exactly the same with the same rules and the same pawns."

"Fine, keep your secrets," said Lulja and shrugged. From the corner Éloyse looked up and gave them a look that contained everything they needed to know. Freja had indeed screwed up, royally.

"Are you helping me or not?" Freja snapped at Lulja.

"What do you want me to do? We can leave but they'll only find us again—you can't hide here, in case you haven't noticed."

Freja held back from saying that she had noticed, thank you very much, let out a sigh, and ran her fingers through her hair.

Even if Lulja was being obnoxious and unnecessarily mean, she had a point. Fleeing would only get them so far before being re-captured by the Masters, who were so close to being magicians as you could be without a pointy hat and a wand. Freja sent Lulja a murderous look. "It's not all my fault," she said. "So help."

Thankfully the three Masters were still occupied in whispers and around them the rest had resumed the game and were perhaps awaiting Florin's verdict before paying any more attention to the human. Or were they talking about her? Were those glances meant for her? She looked from one Master to another, reading lips, interpreting expressions, but nowhere could she determine if she was the topic of conversation or not. Not even the Master in peridot green would look at her now. Her heart sank. She was about to say something callous to Lulja when a hand landed on her shoulder.

"What—" Lulja said as they were both pulled backwards by a hand accompanied by a silky voice.

"Come, come," the voice said and hauled them through the door, out of the room, before anyone noticed. The door shut soundlessly in front of them and they disappeared from the room like ghosts. In the gloom of the staircase, their saviour remained obscured, and led them through a back door into an alley, similar to the one Éloyse and Freja had stood in once before.

"Where are you taking us?" Freja asked while scanning the open street they came into for Masters in white or grey. Every colour was potential danger now.

"*Ka!* Where you belong."

*

In the room, Éloyse had enlightened Florin and the male Master of the situation. They were not convinced.

"Opening the borders is not necessarily the solution," said Florin and knitted her hands behind her back, adjusting her poise. "Those Masters have already forgotten what it means to wear a masterform—I hear some have taken to the habit of *eating*." She took a sip from the seaweed tea and paused to savour its tangy saltiness.

The man, Skylar, was striking and tall, his brown skin standing in radiant contrast to the light red of his masterform.

"So you refuse to stop the mass movement of Flÿght across to Heim—" Éloyse said.

"It is not going to happen," interjected Skylar.

"—and will merely watch our valley—our *landskapë*—fall because of pride?" Éloyse's voice grew louder as both Skylar and Florin tried to speak over her. "Perhaps the Red World was right in signing the treaty. Perhaps the Trinity is infected and doomed to fall. If the Élan is anything to go by, it certainly is." The other two were silenced. "Attend and amend, Masters, while you can. Soon there will be nothing to attend to."

"You speak too much, Éloyse," said Florin with a sniff, then turned to address Skylar alone. "Master, what action do we take towards the human?"

He touched the pink crystals above his right eyebrow and looked over Florin's blonde head.

"Nothing," he said and Florin's mouth fell open again.

"Nothing, Master? But surely …" He took her shoulder, at which she froze mid-sentence, and turned her around to see what he meant.

"We can do nothing," he said again, "seeing as she and her friend are gone."

PART II

OBBSBORN

Obbsborn

n. Perpetrators of the Curfew Restriction Legislation (§34.2:1) who fall under Master care, regardless of race, rank or other variable. The Élan acts as primary custodian for all Obbsborn and retains the right to assimilate, integrate and terminate any Obbsborn affiliation at any given time without notice.

Signed,
Mr. Fiende,
Honourable President of Vildaell

Chapter 21

Once the over-ground was a thing of the past, the rescuer had no reservations about revealing her identity, though Freja had already taken a not-so-wild guess. So far she had only met one Master who cackled like a hen.

"I'm ever so sorry to break up the party, girls," Klepta said as the dingy steps down which she had led them came to a murky end. "That Florin is a real piece of work. *Ka!* Come now, come now, and let's not stand in the hallway like burglars."

"Where are we?" Lulja asked, repeating the question nagging at Freja's mind as well. They had been pushed into the hidden entrance, where dark and slippery steps had taken them down to the damp underground. A smell of earth filled their nostrils as they left daylight behind.

"Obbsborn Z," said Klepta and turned the next corner.

And as the heart of Obbsborn Z opened up before Freja's eyes, courtesy of the torches, it struck her. Obbsborn. She had been here before, but in another place.

Unlike Jaspir Nagel's abode sharing the same first name, however, this Obbsborn was bustling with activity and low chattering. The great hall, with torches situated along the wall casting eerie shadows and illuminating the entire space, was by and large the same as in Wind. The long workbenches were also similar—long and flat—but instead of dusty surfaces long since touched, these were in constant use with men and women, boys and girls, of all ages seated or standing next to them, hands full of fabric, plastic, or other textures, busy at work. A low humming danced in the air, and soon Freja realised that they were singing. The harmony of the room struck her as one big melody: heavy hammering on metal echoed by lighter nibbling of soft textiles, the sing-song vocals leaping between the cavernous corners; footsteps moving …

In an instant the enchanting symmetry distorted and bent into a threatening tune of dread. Suddenly sorely aware of her and Lulja's masterforms, Freja watched how a group of workers—Obbsborn, she assumed—in tattered clothes dropped their work and came to inspect the newcomers. The chatter from the hall died down and heads, plenty of heads, turned in their direction.

"We come in peace?" Lulja said and shrugged. "That's what they say in the movies," she added at Klepta's reproachful look.

"Peace?" she said. "These are Obbsborn, they don't know the meaning of the word. *Ka!* They're nothing but humans, like you."

A small crowd gathered before them. They were of varying ages, from young children to white-haired stooping ladies and men with wrinkled skin and tired expressions. They all looked weary, their clothes were worn and often too large, hanging limp on tiny bony bodies which, Freja now noticed, was another common feature. It was a far cry from the proud poise of Masters above ground, and quite a fitting image at that. The skeletal figures eyed them with large curious eyes. She scanned their faces, one by one, searching for something other than the suspicion and hatred blazing in each without end. Beyond the weariness it was all she could see: anger. Anger that was without doubt directed at the three Master-clad women who had crashed and entered their premises.

"Yo, what you want … Master?" said a ginger-headed boy at the front, only adding the last word after a pause and even then in a sarcastic tone of voice accompanied by a defiant flick of the neck. A smirk edged across his mouth. Around him, the Obbsborn snickered in unison.

"Little boy Pojk," said Klepta with surprising softness, causing the boy who had spoken to raise his eyebrows and purse his lips, much like Freja had seen Cecelya do so many times to her mother when she threw fits at home. "We do not hiss to each other."

"If you say so," he replied and gave her a slanted semi-smile. Freja couldn't swear it was all amicable, nor entirely evil. "I've trusted your word enough before though, and it's getting worn out. As you can see there is something—someone—missing from amongst us."

Klepta cleared her throat and gave the girls beside her an uneasy glance. Klepta, nervous? That was a first, Freja thought.

"A mistake," Klepta said, not quite meeting the boy's eye. "I apologised and it is best to be forgotten. There."

Pojk laughed, and this time it certainly wasn't a friendly laugh. He crossed his arms and craned his neck back towards the group, first left, then right. If the situation hadn't been the way it was, Freja might have laughed at his theatrical gesture. The way the Obbsborn nodded put a big lump in her throat, bottling the laughter, reducing it to a nervous reaction cut short. His fierce green eyes were still on Klepta, who straightened up slightly but didn't move. "They haven't forgotten, Klepta. Have you, Obbsborn?" A low murmur of assent came from the crowd.

"Look here, young Pojk," Klepta said, shaking a finger in

the air. "I've owned up for that mistake. Don't forget I could snap my fingers—" she did it— "and there'd be Masters, Élan Masters, I might add, running here, running Obbsborn Z altogether. So think twice before you threaten me, boy!" Glares as sharp as nails were thrown between them and there was a long silence with room only for the exhausted breathing of some of the older members of the crowd. Wheezing and sighing filled the silence between Pojk and Klepta. "You have nothing to say? Ka!" said Klepta at last. "Nothing at all, son?"

Pojk's eyebrows flew together and his nostrils flared. "Obbsborn," he said and turned his head halfway back so that his chin might have been a swinging door attached to the shoulder. "Give us a moment."

Freja watched how the crowd moved away, mumbling as they went with reluctant steps, and were soon back at the benches giving furtive glances in the direction of their leader. If he was their leader, that is, and not just an audacious boy wanting to give Masters some hell. He was young, perhaps seventeen or eighteen, and almost as tall as Topster by her estimation.

"I must assume you have something to say?" Pojk said. "And you brought friends of the Trew. You will forgive me for not *bowing* to your masterful grace."

"There's no need for that," said Freja with narrowed eyes. She didn't like this boy's arrogance, Obbsborn or not.

"Didn't I tell you to shut your mouth until spoken to?" snapped Klepta with acidity.

"I was spoken to," said Freja without taking her eyes off Pojk whose eyes were scrutinising her. She could feel his judgment and took some amusement in how wrong he was. Pojk struck her as someone who wasn't used to being wrong, and who didn't like it when he was. She wondered where he had come from. After all, she'd heard of several cases where people from outside of Vildaell had been removed because of Curfew.

It couldn't be Buria, because nobody had such bad and crooked teeth there. On the other hand he was far too composed and uninjured to have grown up in Jahran; those children were often covered by scabs or scars or both, and a lot more hostile than this. The rest of the world was mostly a mystery to Freja—she knew the names of distant countries but had no idea what they were like, it was so far away from her own home. Could he be from her very own Vildaell? She'd never heard the name 'Pojk' before, but that didn't mean it couldn't be old-fashioned or one of the new trendy ones. Yet, he didn't strike her as a Vildaell boy (a stereotype she, instinctively, based on Robin). There was a growling savageness in his manner that jarred with the tranquil mentality of her kinsmen.

They kept hold of each other's eyes for what seemed like a long time before Pojk snorted and gave her a slanted smirk, and turned away. "Come on, Klepta," said Pojk. "We have work to do."

"Correct that attitude of yours first," she snapped back. "That is no way to treat a guardian—a mother."

Lulja's mouth fell open, as did Freja's. Not one single feature in their appearances made them look alike. Klepta was a Master. She was round in comparison to Pojk's Obbsborn frame and he had, in complete opposition to her bloated face and hooked nose, a straight nose bridge and thin mouth. Besides, there was not a strand of ginger in Klepta's hair.

Pojk's face curled into a cruel grin and he gave up a heartless laugh. "Oh, I see. These are your new rescues? How endearing." He turned to Freja and Lulja. "Careful, girls—listen to your real mothers and don't go with strangers. They might steal you away and lock you up until your existence is a tattered memory as alive as ashes. Until you have nothing left to be called human." His eyes returned to on Klepta, calm fury thundering inside the pale green retina. "'Mother'," he said with a snort.

"We didn't exactly follow," said Freja slowly, unsure whether she was defending Klepta or herself. "She saved us from … from a situation."

"You're chasing them in real dangers now? Brave." Pojk was unforgiving.

"I don't chase people," Klepta said and crossed her arms. "Like she said, I saved them."

"Like you saved me?" He took a step closer to them and pulled up his sleeve to reveal ugly tearing scars on his lower arms. At least ten of them had cut deep into his skin, leaving a nauseating irregular surface like a rocky mountain chain.

Klepta didn't move. "You'd be as dead as the wind, boy," she said in a low voice. "You mean nothing to the Élan, no more than the Flÿght."

"Bo-hoo," said Pojk. "There it is—the self-interest. You're like a bloody broken parrot, you are. On behalf of all the Obbsborn, we feel so sorry for you. Sincerely." Behind, the eavesdropping Obbsborn cheered and loud 'hoorays' bounced from wall to wall.

"You'd be dead as the wind," said Klepta again.

Pojk sauntered up and pressed his face close to hers. Klepta stood strong against his tall frame and only Freja noticed the lingering tremor in her right fingers. "I hear your words," he said, taking care to articulate well, "but they mean nothing."

The raw savagery in his eyes suggested he might take a physical course of action, so Freja did what she thought she had to do in order to prevent a confrontation. As soon as her fingers closed around Klepta's upper arm, however, the Master tore her limb free. Likewise Lulja, who tried to come to her aid, was quickly shoved aside by a surprisingly strong arm as Klepta squirmed out of yet another attempt to save her from a black eye. There was no way she could overpower Pojk in a fight except with leaf power. Fierce as she was, Pojk was both

219

stronger and bigger than she, and he kept his stare intense and unrelenting. Despite the clear disadvantage, Klepta leapt and threw herself at Pojk, who had a fearful look in his eyes. His nostrils flared again as the blue-clad Master stretched her arms around his neck—and fell into a tight embrace. Pojk let his arms, stretched and ready for defence, relax and fall on Klepta's back as he returned the hug. He rested his chin on her shoulder and though Freja couldn't hear the exact words, she understood that the woman was murmuring sweet lyrics into her boy's ear, at which Pojk nodded fervently.

The two were still whispering to each other when, from the other side of the hall, came the sound of hurried steps, their echo travelling the room at great speed.

"Great," muttered Lulja under her breath. "There's more of them."

It was a girl. She came rushing from the shadows and came to a stop a few metres behind the small gathering, panting from the run and poor stamina.

"Pojk, darling, what in the world is going—FREJA?!"

The voice was familiar, unmistakable even, but Freja still didn't react to its smooth singing tune until she saw the girl's face protruding from the shadows. Now she understood how baffled Jaspir must have been to see her in Valley of Wind, to hear her call him by his name. Obbsborn was not the place you expected or hoped to meet a friend. A booming sensation of relief, or perhaps simply the heart-warming feeling of seeing a familiar face, spread like hot water sprinklers inside her. Before she even met the dark blue eyes with specks of brown, her own filled with tears.

"Oh, Freja, darling," Cecelya Aitken croaked. "You're here! Thank heavens!"

CHAPTER 22

CECELYA RUSHED FORWARD, her noble airs forgotten, and collapsed into Freja's arms, embracing her so hard that Freja struggled to breathe. But it didn't matter; oxygen was secondary. She held Cecelya, that fragile figure of grace and youth, just as tightly, and they stood that way, listening to each other's breathing and beating hearts, until Pojk cleared his throat and put the moment to an end.

"I can't believe it," Cecelya said before her voice faltered as the implications of 'being here' sank in. "You're here. But what are you wearing, darling?"

"It's a long story," Freja mumbled in reply.

Only when Cecelya stepped back to join Pojk did Freja notice that there was something different about her. It wasn't that her hair was shorter, or that it was tied back instead of flowing free in curls around her face as it always had in Amérle. Nor was it her bare skin, free from make-up and revealing the natural beauty she possessed, though it was tainted now by the same weariness as seemed prevalent in these quarters. The clothes she wore were large and baggy, again in order with the local custom, but the deep-felt alteration in her persona did not lay in the change of fashion sense. No, it was none of that, and still there was something that was odd. Freja couldn't quite place it. Not until she had reached halfway to Pojk, who met Cecelya halfway, did she see it. Her steps were uneven. His gait was spastic. In paroxysmal strides they approached each other and Freja realised at last—both of them were limping. One of the legs was dragging behind (much like another human she had met). Also, when Cecelya dragged Pojk with her to introduce him to Freja he greeted her with his scarred arm, the hand limp and damaged.

"You did this to them?" Freja asked Klepta. She thought back to the legless Jaspir and his ageing mother in the cave in Wind, no longer able to move. 'A wounded animal does not run far,' he had said.

"Don't look at me," Klepta said, holding up her arms.

"Then who? Who did it?"

"Let's not quarrel," said Cecelya and took Freja's hand in her right palm. Then Freja saw that three of the fingers were hanging useless. The girl was holding on with her ring finger and thumb alone. Her right hand. Her violin hand. The hand that had played such beautiful music for Freja through the years.

"Oh, Cecelya …," she started but was interrupted.

"It's nothing," she said. "I was lucky. In Ground Division we need most of our body unlike some others." She glanced at Pojk and fought a brave smile. "I was lucky."

"Ground Division?" Freja asked, looking from one disability to the next.

Suddenly she realised that every single person seated at the benches probably had one. Hadn't the mob earlier been stooping? Hadn't they limped back? Caught in the suspense of the anticipated fist fight between the Master and the boy, she hadn't paid attention. Klobb had been right about Ma'zekaï being a dangerous place, but right now it appeared to Freja that the

Masters were the danger in this world, not fenrirs or batsërs.

"I've done my bit," said Klepta with a sigh and before anyone could say a word, she had sulked off and disappeared into the darkness from where they had come without as much as a last look at Pojk.

He shrugged and said it was typical. "She comes and she goes," he said.

"Good riddance," Freja said and squeezed Cecelya's hand. "Now tell me everything."

There were numerous Obbsborn locations, Cecelya explained as she led Freja and Lulja into another area, the Turf, on the other side of the work hall. One place for work, one for leisure. Whether other Obbsborn communities had similar ones, Cecelya didn't know. How many there were, she couldn't say either. All they knew from hearsay was that Ma'zekaï—all of its valleys—were peppered with underground Obbsborn caves invisible to the eye above ground. The entrances were concealed and known only to Masters involved in the work. These were usually of the Trew, but Klepta had managed to sneak her way into the system with Obbsborn Z and acted as its protector and guardian.

"She's right about one thing," said Pojk. "Without her we'd have Masters intruding around here like thistles. What little freedom we have would be impossible."

He explained about the system, where there was Ground, Craft, and Energy Division. Ground worked with geological tasks: digging, exploring, building; Craft was innovative and technologically-minded, using human expertise to develop technology adapted for Masters; Energy was usually considered the best division and handled the big Question—how to prevent Valley of Wood from dying.

"Why is it the best one?" Lulja asked.

"Because the energy is up there," said Pojk and pointed

to the ceiling, beyond that even, and added that no one from Obbsborn Z was involved in the Energy squad.

"They're above ground?" said Lulja, eyes wide.

"We don't even know how many of 'them' there are," said Pojk as they approached the entrance to the Turf. "There might be a hundred or there might be just one soul wandering around up there, alone."

Cecelya was, as she had said, in the Ground Division; Pojk was in Craft. In there they made Transporters among other things. Pojk pointed to a boy as he passed the opening of the cave and said he was also part of Craft, but a deeper circle where they had recently reached some sort of break-through. What it was, he didn't know. "That division is so secret that they take their voices," he explained as the boy waved to them. "That's Tryll and he won't tell you a single word about it. He can't. They took our legs, and they took his voice."

"That's—" Lulja, who had stopped and whose eyes lingered on Tryll as he and his gleaming smile were engulfed by the shadows of the tunnel, didn't finish the sentence. "Where is he from?"

Pojk replied, "Down here, we're all Obbsborn."

"Curfew does this?" Freja looked around, searching among the faces.

"All Obbsborn," said Pojk again.

Silence ensued. The echo of hammers clashing with steel, drilling nails into wood, and other noises from the work hall travelled into the room. It lasted until Cecelya found her voice again.

"Tell me, darling," she said. "How are mum and dad? Robin, Enton? They're all okay?" In short and with as few depressing details as possible, still retaining a sense of truth, Freja told her about the last day she'd seen them. She left out the part about Robin and Enton's plans. A few people had joined them in the

Turf, and she felt it was too personal. Besides, there was no need for Cecelya to contemplate on the potential consequences of such a quest, which must be apparent to her as well at this point. When she was done Cecelya hugged her and whispered a low 'thank you.' "There's something I haven't asked you," she said then with a frown and a peculiar look at Freja.

"What's that?"

"What on earth are you doing here?"

The ridiculousness of it all made her burst out laughing. Shortly Freja and Lulja followed suit and they all lost themselves in the liberating mirth echoing across the bare walls. Pojk, on the other hand, restrained himself to a smile.

*

The laughter would echo until late into the night when the Obbsborn began welling into the Turf as the day's work was concluded. They had arrived on a fortunate day, Cecelya said, as it was the day of dispatch and on a free night, there was no work until the morning and little risk of a Master's supervisory visit. Most Obbsborn would take the time to bathe in the underground springs, play games, or some other recreational activity. During the day there was no time for such amusements. Despite Klepta's best efforts some Trew Master stopped by occasionally to ensure nothing was awry, she explained. "They're scared we're going to rebel—but how could we? Look at us."

She was right, of course, but Freja didn't have the heart to agree with her. The Turf filled with limping Obbsborn, so the little group relocated to one of the sleeping cabins. Cecelya brought bread and cheese—"courtesy of the agricultural branch, that's part of Ground"—a rarity if you were to believe her. "Only on dispatch days," Cecelya explained as she tore the bread into small pieces and shared with the group. The protruding collar bones and row of visible ribs on most of the Obbsborn gave Freja no reason to doubt this claim.

Already they had decided to stay the night and they were seated in a corner of the girls' sleeping cabins. They had no idea what the Trew Masters had in mind for the intruders and Freja had no inclination to find out what Florin was scheming. Whatever her underlying motive, Klepta had been sensible in bringing them down here; all they could hope for was that it wasn't simply to keep them in custody until Florin could get her hands on them. When they told Cecelya and Pojk about their Master encounter, they stared with wide eyes. The thought of a human hiding in Ma'zekaï, fooling them to believe they were indeed Masters, was inconceivable.

"What about the Essence?" Pojk, who was well-versed in Master lingo, asked.

Lulja shrugged. "Nobody tested me—I guess the word of an Élan Master was good enough."

Freja didn't reply. It didn't matter now that Topster had given her the Essence—it would be faded long ago. Besides, she wasn't sure she could explain it because she didn't understand it herself.

"Tell me once more," said Cecelya, who was now recuperating more into her gracious self after a full meal and the presence of Freja. "The Élan plans to open the borders—?"

"—and allow pretty much free influx of humans to Ma'zekaï," Lulja filled in. "The idea is that the positive energy insertion will help the valley stay alive and that cooperation across *landskapës* will result in other sources of energy."

"Do you know about the *landskapës*?" Freja asked as Cecelya dressed in a confused expression. How much information would the Obbsborn be privy to down here?

"We're not stupid," Pojk shot in and raised his eyebrows. "Just because we're Obbsborn doesn't mean we're ignorant."

"I didn't mean—"

"We know about them," said Cecelya. "Pojk knows a lot

since he was … Anyway, I know some too. So they open the borders—what's the problem? If everyone can live together and both *landskapës* stay alive, what's wrong with that?"

Freja ignored the glaring look from Pojk. "Besides the politics of such an opening, the problem is the Flÿght," she said. "They're treated as badly as you are—well, not exactly as bad," she quickly added, "but badly enough to be resentful."

"Exactly," continued Lulja. "Instead of opening the borders, the Flÿght want to go into Heim, and keep them closed. Move there, kind of."

"Considering the energy transferral in latches, it's likely to kill Ma'zekaï," Freja finished. "And everyone in it." She threw a glance at Lulja. "We're not sure what would happen to Heim."

"They want to merge the *landskapës*?" said Pojk, but from his tone of voice Freja could tell that he had heard, understood even. He just couldn't grasp the concept.

"Not only that," Lulja said. "Masters are already there, some of them of the Flÿght."

At this, Pojk snorted. Whether his self-asserted arrogance had taken a dent at new information or because he simply couldn't believe that it was news at all, no one could be sure.

They wanted to control the energy balance, right?" Freja said, seeking confirmation in Lulja. "The Network—something …"

"Energy Harmonisation Network," said Pojk and rolled his eyes.

"So the Masters are spies?" Cecelya said.

"Sort of, except that sounds a lot more dramatic than it is." Lulja gave the history in brief, with a little help from Freja on the details: Masters seeking alternative energy sources in Heim back in the year of the Lion, the Curfew Law was set up to cover up their dealings—and now energy supplies are waning, time is scarce, and Masters are getting desperate. "It all started falling to pieces when the Masters sent to control humans started to sympathise with them—siding with them against the Élan. As far as I've heard, these Masters are split in two—those who want to open the borders, and those who'd rather see them stay as they are or even close altogether."

"Together with the Flÿght that makes three contrasting opinions," said Freja. "All battling each other."

The weight of this piece of information sunk in with silence like an iron hammer. It had become more and more apparent to them that the problem with moving into Heim was not confined to politics alone. With the energy flows already disrupted, such a large twang on the string of balance could be fatal. Of course they couldn't know for sure, but until an expert came along, their judgement was all they had to go on.

"But," started Cecelya after a moment's silence in which the distant sounds of the other Obbsborn jingled through the room. Laughter, shouting, bare feet on dull ground. "But what on earth can we do about it?"

Freja and Lulja looked at each other. They had discussed it on the way from the cottage to the village, together with Éloyse. It wasn't a fool proof plan by any measure, it couldn't even be called solid—but it was an idea. "For a start, if we can get hold of the latches to Heim we can send everyone back," Freja said, feeling the same rush of excitement as she had when the words had first been spoken. They were in the area of the Latch Bank, and she explained that if they could access the entrance somehow, they could steal the latches, leaving Masters stranded in their own world. The more she spoke, the more detail she handled and digested, the more the magnitude of the project ate into her mind. "Every single person removed by Curfew can go home."

"You're out of your mind," said Pojk with a snort.

"Shush you," said Cecelya gently and placed a hand on his

arm. "What about the energy transferral?"

Then Pojk, "The Élan will simply find new latches."

"It's not a solution," admitted Lulja, "but it'll buy us time at least. By the time the Élan have gathered enough latches again, we will have warned the authorities."

"I don't see what choice we have unless we want to sit back and watch them destroy each other—and us in the process," said Freja. "Masters are clever," she added, a new thought coming to life in her mind, "but we have technology—we have weapons."

Another intermittent moment of silence ensued in complete stillness as if the Obbsborn had all reacted to the presence of the word 'weapon' and ceased to stir, to talk, to breathe.

"You're declaring war," Cecelya said, more a statement than a question, and Freja couldn't determine neither from tone of voice nor the expression on Cecelya's face whether she said the words in agreement or opposition, and decided it didn't matter. Though Freja hadn't used those exact words in her mind, when spoken out loud she realised that they were true. Whatever fancy costume you dressed their plans in, it was war. The strangest thing was that she didn't mind them being true either. All the pain and anxiety from her own life and from Mrs Aitken's and Nagel's—it could all be undone if they succeeded. Whatever happened after seemed irrelevant if only they could send the Curfew victims back.

Because among those, somewhere, she'd find that face she'd been searching for—her mother.

If they wanted to call it war, then it was war. Freja raised her eyebrow in response, hoping that the ambiguity of the gesture would dampen the severity of its confirmation. Cecelya and Pojk shifted in their seats, though not out of discomfort. They shuffled so as to turn their backs to Freja and Lulja and huddled together, whispering. In hurried hisses they conversed and Pojk was soon agitated, raising his voice so that Cecelya had to tell him off and throw a meaningful nod towards the two girls behind. He pouted and lowered his voice after a particularly distressed, "It's not that simple, Ceci," escaped from their private sphere and past the invisible barrier.

Beside, Lulja looked about as exasperated as Freja felt.

"'Ceci,'" Freja said in a low voice to respect the barriers. "That's what Robin used to call her." Calls her, she reminded herself. What he calls her, and would call her as soon as they got back.

"What do you think?" Lulja asked. "Will they help?"

"I'm surprised they even have to talk about it."

"Well, put yourself in their shoes," Lulja whispered with a small shrug and edged closer to Freja so as to limit the audience of their conversation. "Your friend has been here, what, a few weeks, and is already hesitating. Remember what Pojk said? Down here, everyone's Obbsborn. While back home they've been buried and grieved for."

"Hm," said Freja and wondered if her own father had moved on already. If he'd given up on ever seeing her again.

"In practice they're lost," Lulja continued. "Only imagine how Masters have treated them. Going home doesn't mean safety, not with the forces still at work there. You can't just turn the clock back. They want reassurance."

"We can't give them that."

"No."

Freja started drawing in the dust while Lulja bit into another piece of bread and chewed, her mind clearly somewhere else. There was no reassurance, but there could be hope. Hope of going home. She observed Lulja from the corner of her eye and wondered what would happen to her if they succeeded. Would she stay? Would she try and find her own family in Heim? She froze. Heim. She was already referring to her home in Master terminology.

"Why are you looking at me like that?" Lulja asked without taking her eyes off the bread.

"I …"

Before she had time to come up with a lie, Cecelya and Pojk swung around to face them again. The embarrassment of having been caught staring subsided in Freja and was replace by a thrilling acceleration of her heart beat. This was it. Cecelya maintained a patient expression. Only the brownish tints in her eyes spoke of the emotion in there. It was a vivaciousness that Freja had always admired in the young girl, but now felt strangely uncomfortable with. She spoke slowly.

"We will help you …" She paused and raised a hand to prevent an outburst from the two girls. "If you help us."

CHAPTER 23

"Us?" Freja repeated, confused. "You mean us?" She waved her arms in a wide circle including all four of them. Cecelya shook her head.

"I mean the Obbsborn," she said, her face still not revealing an ounce of unrestrained emotion. "We don't agree with the Élan or the Flÿght and even though I don't want to speak on behalf of the others without consulting them, I can't imagine we would condone either of those options. We have a plot too—we agree, ironically, with some of the converted Masters." She paused. "We want to close the border completely."

Never had Freja even considered that Cecelya's loyalties may not lie where they used to. That she'd have switched sides. It had been weeks—mere weeks—but she already seemed so at ease with her new (dare she say it) family. The thought of the Aitkens, agonised over the loss of their daughter bumped and bruised her insides, and she had to force the feeling away. The Aitkens were not part of this world. Left behind in the shallows of the violent tremor was a strong determination to make Cecelya see straight. This was all Pojk's doing, she decided and sent a glaring look at the ginger boy hand-locking her best friend's little sister. She was a prisoner here, though she couldn't see so for herself.

"Before you say anything," continued Cecelya, obviously sensing the coming outburst in Freja's mind. "Let me show you something." She moved to stand up and within seconds Pojk had thrust an arm around her waist as support. It was so quick and automatic it must have been habit. In return Cecelya gave Pojk a small smile before offering her hand to the seated Freja. Lulja was already on her feet.

With Pojk and Cecelya leading the way, they soon came out of the sleeping cabins and through the work space. The benches were empty now as all the Obbsborn had begun enjoying their free night which, as soon as they passed through another arched portal on the opposite side of the space, through a short tunnel leading west, became apparent. Already in the tunnel they could hear laughter and sounds echoing between the walls, bouncing through the rock surface. During their first visit to the Turf it had been empty, but now there were at least a hundred people crammed inside, all busy talking, playing, or chasing each other across the area. It was as grey and damp as the other spaces in the cave, dull rock and dry soil being the only two elements. However, the walls here wore patches of dye in various colours, as if a wild paint fight had occurred, and it gave the room a new light. It was almost cosy.

Scanning the bustling crowd, Freja noticed that all of them shared one common feature. While some of the Obbsborn would use only one of their hands to toss the ball to their friend, the other staying unnaturally still along the side of their body, others leaned on one leg and often held on to their useless one with cramping fingers. Freja saw one girl who wore an eye patch who was speaking to a boy who might have been semi-deaf because the girl was shouting into his ear. Everywhere she saw the reality of the Obbsborn. All maimed, all injured.

It didn't take long before the Obbsborn noticed the movement and succumbed leisure to curiosity. The bustle died down as though someone had flicked a switch and all eyes turned towards Freja and Lulja. Before, the masterform had been a comfort; now it made them stand out more than ever. A rock came flying from the crowd and almost hit Freja. It would have as well, if Cecelya had not reached out a hand (her healthy one) and caught it. "Stop," she said, not quite shouting but with undeniable authority in her voice. "They are not Masters."

"They look like Masters," shouted someone, a boy, and rest of the crowd agreed in low grunts. "They have no business here!"

"They are human," said Cecelya. "Taken here by force, like us." At this Lulja and Freja exchanged glances but neither amended the statement. "The masterform is nothing but a clever disguise for these two, and what's more—they have come to help." The crowd calmed down and no more rocks were thrown. The Obbsborn had really started listening when she mentioned 'help' and were now stretching to get a good look at the intruders. Cecelya introduced them by name. "They're my friends," she said. "I hope they can be yours too. Please listen, just listen."

"'Attend', you mean?" said a girl in the front, her face immobile. The Master word came as a slap and Cecelya didn't say anything at first. Once the bustle of the crowd, agreeing, sniggering, cheering, had calmed down again, she gestured for Freja and Lulja to begin.

"They'll savage us," Freja hissed, but before she could finish the sentence Lulja was one step ahead, addressing the Obbsborn.

"There is a plan to open the borders between Heim and Ma'zekaï," she said. "To make latches of it all and tear down the walls. This is very much happening right now. Freja and I," she gave Freja a demanding look to join her, which she did, "we want to stop it."

When none of the Obbsborn threw rocks or uttered as much as an obscenity, Freja felt her courage return by small drops of white in an ocean of dark flight instincts. "We want the same as you," she said and the drops increased as the Obbsborn turned their attention to her—curious rather than murderous. This new attention made her voice steadier and she continued to explain about latches, how if they could break into the Latch Bank and take them all, there would be no way for Masters to cross themselves. "Anyone who wants to," she said, "can come back with us."

"If you don't want to, you stay," Cecelya continued. "You stay and fight for your rights here."

"But we need your help," said Freja as a pleading finish. She'd read somewhere that to make people do what you want them to, you have to make them think it's their own decision and make them feel superior. It wasn't a bold guess to think that the Obbsborn neither had ample experience of free will nor self-possessed authority.

Silence filled the room and Freja couldn't decide if their message had hit home or not. Doubt was the only emotion she could read in the faces before her. Doubt and fear. They were glancing at each other, casting furtive looks, as though trying to read their friends' minds too, afraid to make a decision that would upset the group. Without meaning to, the question had threatened the collective, Freja realised. It was such a forbidden thought—perhaps like the one she had posed to Robin at the Great Square a lifetime ago: *what if we could stay out?* Curfew and Obbsborn had that in common: they were both prisons.

"Come back," she said, telepathically reaching out to each of their invisible souls, tugging at their wandering thoughts. "Come back and we can try and stop Curfew together."

"Will the police not arrest me?" came a voice from the back of the crowd.

"The guy gave up on finding me?" said another.

"What if they found her?" cried another one and trailed off into a whimper.

"They'll kill me for sure," muttered a boy at the front with black curly hair. There was a scar across his face and he stroked it as he spoke.

Freja stared at them at a loss for words. She bit her lip and scanned the crowd, hoping, trying to find at least one sympathetic face in there. Not a single one appeared. It was a miscalculation on a grand scale. Hot dizziness crept over her. She had to take a step back to prevent a swaying tumble. Her head was spinning. Breathing became difficult. Shallow breaths gave no oxygen. Oxygen that was scarce down here anyway. Down here. Obbsborn. Refusing. Not wanting. "Oh god," she whispered to herself.

"I—" Cecelya was glancing from the Obbsborn to Freja and back again. "I'm so sorry, I thought—"

"No, I'm sorry," Freja said with a slight tremble in her voice which she hoped would be absorbed in the walls. "Um … If we can stay here until we figure out what to do, we'd be grateful." She turned and walked out of the Turf. Feeling everyone's eyes, including Lulja's, follow her as she left the room, she went back to the sleeping cabins. Without the Obbsborn they were doomed to fail. It had been their way into the Bank. It wasn't herself she needed to give strength to. The Obbsborn wanted something she couldn't give. It was as simple as that.

As if all the strength seeped out of her body she fell down onto the nearest mattress, made from light fabric and dried grass, ignoring the prickling that came from the dead straws. She buried her head in the pillow and drew in a pleasant scent of lavender. It must be stuffed with dried flowers. For once she let her emotions run free and fill her entire body with a hot conglomeration of all the disappointment, all the longing for home, and the deep unquenchable sense of loss together with all the forgotten emotions she had suppressed since she came to this world.

It was over.

She realised this undeniable fact as new tears burned in her eyes and drew patterns on her cheek before falling into the lavender meadow below her dripping chin. All was done and soon the war between Masters and humans would undo this world or hers, or both, because she had failed. Not she alone, but the Obbsborn too.

She swore into the fabric, cursing the Obbsborn for being selfish. As much as she tried she could not comprehend the reasoning, and a thought was sent particularly to Cecelya. If she had one thought left for her family, surely she would have reconsidered? One lonely piece of recollection from when her uncle disappeared should have been enough to send her running back on bare feet. But it didn't. She wanted to stay with that awful boy.

An image of her father and a blinking red Signaller box started another series of sobs and she curled into a ball, pushing her knees as far as she could into her chest, hoping it would relieve the pressure, hoping it'd make her so small she would disappear into herself altogether and never see the world again. With her head buried into her knees she let the sobs pass without constraint and then fell asleep from sheer exhaustion.

In sleep she wouldn't have to worry. In sleep, the goblins and trolls fled at the first sight of sunlight back into the darker woods. In sleep, all the bad things were only nightmares and would eventually pass with no tangible harm done.

In the waking world, however, they would not.

*

She was woken up by a gentle nudge on her shoulder. Lulja's face was stern and unmoved. She was seated at the end of the bed, waiting for Freja to wake up, which she did eventually, still disgruntled. It felt like sleep had done more damage than good. "If you're here to tell me the world's ended," she said with a yawn, "I'm going back to bed."

"Your little pity party is over now," said Lulja, stood up and reached out a hand. "We have lots to do."

"No," said Freja, stretching her aching muscles. "I'm going home. If you want to stay and play Master, you can, but I'm going."

While drifting between wet reality and dry sleep, an idea had come to Freja—an epiphany of sorts. A new determination. She had had enough. Somehow she would leave Obbsborn, find a latch, and go home to her father. This charade had gone on long enough and whatever happened next was no longer in her hands. The fate of the Obbsborn was not her responsibility. She had given them a chance and they refused it.

Strangely, this resolution felt at once like all the weight lifted off her shoulders and as if another was put in its place. Failure is never pretty, she thought, but at least I tried.

"Funny stuff—you should take that show on the road," said Lulja.

Yawning again, Freja frowned at her. Didn't Lulja see how serious she was about going home? She was about to insist when Lulja continued, pulling her arm, "Get up, now. The Obbsborn have been conferencing all night. You'll go and hear them out right now."

Freja groaned and let herself be pulled out of bed. Whatever they had to say, she decided to leave on that same day. She couldn't stand being underground any longer and longed for sunlight. It was dark and gloomy down here and her skin had become dotted with blemishes. And she needed a good wash.

She packed up her bag and slung it across her chest. As soon as she'd talked with Cecelya, tried to convince her one last time, she would leave, with or without her.

To find a latch—her way home at last.

CHAPTER 24

SHE FOLLOWED LULJA into the Turf, through the work hall where Obbsborn were again at their seats and producing the cacophony of noises echoing from wall to wall. In a corner sat Cecelya and Pojk with their heads close together, but they moved apart as soon as Lulja made her and Freja's presence known.

"Are you okay?" Cecelya asked and Freja felt her cheeks flush, murmuring that she was fine. She hadn't meant to fall apart quite as much last night and could only imagine what they had been thinking. What difference did it make now, anyway? She was leaving.

"We will help you," said Cecelya once they were seated.

"What?" All of Freja's home-bound plans waved goodbye and vanished into thin air.

"We will help you."

"I don't get it."

"They will help us get all the latches," said Lulja and knocked playfully on Freja's skull. "Anyone at home at all?"

Cecelya cleared her throat. "We have convinced the others. As we said before, we will only help if you return the favour."

A short silence in which nods were exchanged. "As it happens, we have also been collecting latches—directly from the Bank."

So it wasn't the Strays, Freja thought. It was the Obbsborn. She wondered if Flflock and the Élan had considered that possibility as a real option, or dismissed it as preposterous.

"That's amazing," said Lulja, clearly impressed. "How is that even possible? The way Éloyse spoke about it and the guards, it sounded pretty bullet proof."

Obviously flattered by the compliment, Cecelya tucked a stray hair behind her ear and smiled. "It's Pojk you should ask. He's the one who started it long before I came. You want to explain?"

"All you need to know right now," said Pojk, "is that we found a way in there, a way which I'll show you if we pursue this agreement. First, let me explain under what conditions we will co-operate." He cleared his throat. "You need something, and so do we. And this is not just me speaking, remember, but the entire community down here. You will have our expertise— which you will need—at your hands to enter the Bank, and also in stealing the latches to Heim."

"What's the catch?" Freja asked. She was getting spasms in her stomach, whether from hunger or nerves she didn't know.

"There is something else in there that we can use in our fight once you're gone. Bring it to us, to me, and we have an agreement."

"What is—" Lulja began but Freja cut in.

"Once 'we're' gone?" she said to Cecelya. "You're not coming with us?"

"He's speaking for the Obbsborn, darling," Cecelya said quickly, not quite meeting the eye of either Freja or Pojk. She turned to Lulja. "It is also a latch. More and more latches have been moved to the island. For some reason the Élan don't want latches just lying around. Including this particular one."

Pojk continued, "It's called the Trinity Latch and in our possession, it will not only be safe from cloning and misuse, but it'll work as leverage when we make our demands. It's as simple as this: bring us the latch and we will show you the way in—and out."

"Ravn spoke of it," Freja said, thinking back to the conversation she'd overheard between Ravn and Topster. "He said it was insurance in case things went badly for the Élan."

"They are clearly worried if they resort to sending the seven of the Élan out on a treasure hunt," said Pojk with reference to what Lulja had told them about her mission with Ravn. Freja asked what he meant. "I mean," said Pojk, slowly and with care, "that they are the Élan, the Lords' pets and gems. You don't send a gem out to be tarnished for no good reason. Especially not in Wind."

"You seem to know an awful lot," said Freja.

"I do?" he said with a smirk.

"He does know a lot," said Cecelya and took his hand with a beaming smile.

Lulja cleared her throat. "So what's the deal with the Trinity Latch? Why is it special?"

"It opens up to the Red World," said Pojk. "None of the silver ones do that."

"It's the only way there?" asked Freja.

"As far as I know," said Pojk. "Now, about the Bank …"

They continued to map out the Master movement. With Lulja's information from Ravn and the Trew and Freja's observations on the Flÿght, they had quite a good overview. It was lucky for them that the Trew and Élan were gathering latches in one place: not only did that exclude the Flÿght from accessing them, but it allowed easy contact for the Obbsborn. One attack could be enough. There was only one party that was still off radar: the Lords.

"Well, they are the Lords," said Lulja. "It's not like they wander into the local café and ask for a tall skinny latte, is it?"

The three girls laughed but Pojk sat quiet, rubbing his chin with his thumb.

"Oh, come on," said Freja. "It's a joke."

"Right," he said and went back to his chin.

"Where are they then?" asked Freja. "The Lords, where do they stay, or whatever it is that Masters do?"

"Nobody knows," said Lulja and Pojk nodded in agreement. "The three Lords are as evasive as fenrirs, if not more." The Lords went about their business in secret, Lulja continued to explain. Where they moved and why they moved was nobody's business outside of the Élan. Ravn, though one of the seven Masters more commonly known as the Seven of the Élan, or simply Élan, wouldn't be able to tell where the Lords were to be found. "Or he wouldn't tell," she concluded with a shrug. "Either way, it's not something people on the street know."

"As we can't know, we can't waste time on them," said Pojk. "Will you bring us this latch?"

This distinction between 'us' and 'them'—as necessary as it was—felt like it stretched the gap between with every use. An unsettling nagging was stirring in Freja's stomach and despite how casual Cecelya seemed about it, no matter how much she tried to deny this gradual separation of the entities, she didn't like it.

"Of course," said Lulja. "Freja?"

"If that's what it takes."

"It is," said Pojk, ignoring Freja's glaring look. "Also, you better change. Masterforms don't look too good underground. Hey, Tryll?"

The boy they had seen before with black locks and dark skin was passing the entry tunnel between the work hall and the Turf when Pojk called. At his request Tryll went away and soon came back carrying clothes for them in true Obbsborn fashion—worn-out tattered t-shirts and ripped jeans.

"I'll go change into this," Lulja said when Freja didn't move or even look away from Cecelya. "Tryll, will you show me the way?" Tryll smiled and made a sign for her to follow. Lulja hesitated. "Pojk, you too, maybe?"

"Why do I—?" Pojk started, but Lulja widened her eyes and snapped her neck. "Oh, fine."

The three headed off towards the cabins, leaving Freja and Cecelya alone in the Turf.

Freja held on to the clothes, barely feeling the damp smell oozing from them. The girl in front of her was a stranger; a negative photo image of the girl she'd known in Amérle. All the dazzle and glamour was replaced by a sober realism with a surface as hard as metal, refusing to budge to even the softest of prods. Similar to Jaspir, Freja realised. "Your parents are devastated," Freja said with a solemn resignation she didn't have to feign.

"I know," Cecelya replied in a frosty voice. Only the constant wetting of her lips revealed that there was indeed some recognition of home left in her.

Fury flared in Freja again as she recalled the taint of realisation in Mrs Aitken's face where hope had been hanging on like a gargoyle. Those who had met Curfew before knew, and she had known then, before the List. The silence that had filled the room and Robin's shaking hands as they had read the name together at the Look-Out. The brothers' plan to save the sister who, it turns out, didn't want to be saved. She'd rather stay with the dragon. "I wasn't going to tell you," Freja said at last. "I wasn't going to say anything, but Robin and Enton are planning to look for you." She nodded as Cecelya's head snapped up and she made a grimace. "That's right. They're going to risk their lives for you, and you choose to stay. For what?" Cecelya's eyes wandered straight to Pojk, who was hovering further off, at the entrance. He was conversing with a group of Obbsborn but was only semi-listening to what they were saying. His attention was placed elsewhere. "A boy?!"

"It's different here, Freja," Cecelya said with a contemplative frown. "It sounds silly to you, I know, but nobody here has even dreamt of going home. You do for the first few days, then you get it: there is no going home. For some, most even, there's not even a home left to go to."

"There is for you."

"Look at that girl," she said and pointed to a dark-haired girl standing in the group with Pojk. She was wearing a red t-shirt that was torn in several places, and carried glaring scars on her throat. "She was attacked on the street on her way home. It was close to the border and the guy dragged her into the woods between Buria and Vildaell right before Curfew. He knew what he was doing. Her attacker made it back, she was sent here. Do you think she'll ever feel safe again?"

Freja didn't say anything, mostly because, as reluctantly as she admitted it, Cecelya had a point. Still not convinced though, Freja shook her head. "That's an exception, surely?"

"Sadly, it's not," Cecelya said. "You know how Curfew works. People in Vildaell are careful to the extent of ridiculousness, and those from across the borders aren't stupid either. Some are victims. Others have killed, Freja. Some of these people here are murderers, by accident or otherwise. They can't go back. Few people disappear due to sheer recklessness."

That made Freja remember something else. "Is Kale here too? Robin told me you were travelling with him."

Cecelya shook her head.

"No, I imagine he's in Vildaell, hopefully drowning himself in a cocktail of nuclear waste but, more likely, he's cosy in the hotel in Jahran, enjoying the freedom and trouble free mind.

We didn't separate on good terms," she explained.

There was a hint of evasion, which Freja picked up. Didn't Cecelya's eyes also glaze over for just a second? Perhaps she had imagined it, but she still felt sure that there was more to the story than a simple argument.

Besides, there was another question she needed to ask that had been gnawing at her since her encounter with Jaspir. The clue to Curfew was only partially solved, but now at least she knew where the disappeared had gone to. Curfew only covered Vildaell and, though there were plenty of victims from other countries, there was a small chance that her mother was here. She asked, heart flapping with anticipation, only to be sorely disappointed once again.

"I'm sorry. I know most of the Vildaell people and your mother is not one of them. Don't be dismayed, she might be somewhere else. It was more than two years ago, right? This is Obbsborn Z, it's relatively new, and I think they go double digits too. There was a woman, Benna Hjalmar, who came a day before me …"

"Her name was on your List."

"Yes, we would have been on the same. But she's—she's not here anymore."

"What happened?"

"Let's not talk about it, darling. It's not a pretty story."

Cecelya had always preferred beautiful things. At least something remained unchanged. Yet so many things about her had indeed transformed, and Freja wanted to know why. She asked what had happened on the border to Jahran.

"It's a long story."

"Make it less long then."

Cecelya sighed. "Why, what does it matter now?"

"I'd say it matters a great deal. I've never known you to be so secretive, Cecelya. What on earth happened?"

"Fine," she said with another sigh. "We got to the border about two hours before Curfew, and the guard wouldn't let us through. He was there, reeking of alcohol, and Kale started arguing, of course, but to no avail. The gate was closed, and that was that." She started tapping her fingernails. They had gone to a dingy hotel in Rim, the border village, and decided to stay there during Curfew and go through in the morning. Kale had still been upset and angry and wouldn't leave her alone to sleep. So she left the hotel. She'd rushed out past the shouting doorman wearing nothing but a bath robe, and kept running as far as her legs would carry her. One moment she had been sitting down on the ground; the next a strange light came over her. "I must have left the hotel after the tenth bell because I don't remember hearing it at all. Then this light came and everything sort of broke apart around me, like snowflakes, and it was so bright I had to close my eyes. Next I know, I'm here. Like that—" she snapped her fingers—"I'm an Obbsborn. There was never any question about it. The moment you set foot on these grounds, you're one of us. We may not look alike, but we're a family. Truly."

"And Benna?"

Cecelya sighed. "Okay. Benna Hjalmar was a lovely lady, but too old to work with the physical tasks we do here. Unfortunately for her, Obbsborn Z is all physical. Other Obbsborn might not be, but her mind wasn't too clear either. To Masters, she was useless. And what do you do with a useless thing? Here, you throw it away."

"They killed her?"

"Benna begged and pleaded with Pojk, and me, and Klepta— even with the two Trew who came down to get her. They were so cold and heartless. All pragmatic, but that's what they are, Masters. Cold and heartless, not an emotion in sight. Benna is gone, god knows where. If she's alive at all … Perhaps it is better not to be, alive I mean. I don't know." She paused and drew a strand of hair back. "So you see why we need the latch? It's been a topic of conversation for a while and we believe that your arrival is a sign, Freja." She took Freja's hand and squeezed it. "A sign that the time has come to act. God doesn't cover this world, or we wouldn't be here, so we are left to sort it out for ourselves. There are many Obbsborn communities across Ma'zekaï but every effort we have made at communicating with them has been unsuccessful. If we get that latch, we don't need them. It cannot be stressed enough—we need the Trinity Latch. Or we are all lost."

"Including my mother," said Freja. Cecelya nodded.

At that moment Lulja came back into the Turf, pulling her shirt with a crinkled nose.

"These don't smell right," she said. "Everything okay here?"

"Yes," said Cecelya and stood up after which she helped Freja to her feet as well. "It's good that you came. Freja, you go and change too. Then we must sit down and decide how to get to those latches, or, rather, how to get to them—all of them—without Masters finding out."

*

The planning took most of the working day. The group had seated themselves in an offside part of the Turf, commonly used by couples seeking privacy, Cecelya said. Did she blush? Maybe, Freja couldn't be sure in the dim flickering light from the torches.

With no sun to guide the passing of time down in the cave, the Obbsborn had worked out a system to separate night from day and to know when Master inspections came or deliveries were due. "Obbsborn use time in their own way," Pojk concluded after explaining the rather complex structure of Obbsborn time. "In our truth it's three-ten and we need to keep going."

With Tryll, who had been added to their group, they were a small assembly of five. Tryll was in his twenties and quite handsome with dark skin, high cheekbones and sparkling white teeth. If Freja had to guess, she'd say he'd come straight from the palaces of Buria. He had that aura of nobility around him, although now it was tainted and cracked by Obbsborn dampness. He didn't speak, but smiled a lot instead, and while she at first found the muteness a discomfort, his kind demeanour and gentle conduct—never running, never shouting (obviously), always smiling—made her realise that he was just the same as anyone else. Only he didn't have words. Tryll's muteness did not stop him from being helpful. Instead of speaking he communicated with complex signs that only Pojk seemed to understand, and Cecelya to some extent. His fingers moved quickly and confidently and Pojk interpreted the signs as he went along. It had taken them ages to work out the system, they explained. They had no access to pens or paper, which would have been infinitely easier.

Accessing the Latch Bank would be no trouble with the secret pathway of the Obbsborn (of which they still didn't want to reveal more until the time came to use it), but the island would be guarded by at least four Masters and if they were to collect every single latch they needed a plan to distract the guards. Pojk estimated they would need at least half an hour to do this. A long time to keep a Master preoccupied, he pointed out. Once the latches were in their possession, the Flÿght would automatically be prevented from continuing their plan.

"The Élan will be trickier," said Lulja thoughtfully. "But I guess the latch thing stops them too? If only I could talk to Éloyse … She'd know what to do."

"I thought she's of the Trew?" said Cecelya, referring back to what Lulja had told them earlier.

"She is," said Lulja. "But the Trew are far from coherent in opinion. I saw them arguing about it all the time. Not this, per se, but human-Master relationship, that kind of thing. Éloyse is pretty open-minded, I'd say."

"Can we contact her?" asked Freja.

"No way out of here," said Pojk and sucked in his cheeks. "As sealed as the third *landskapë*."

"We came in," Freja pointed out and raised her eyebrows. "If you come in, you can come out."

"You're welcome to try," he said. "At your own risk, of course."

He exchanged a look with Tryll who tried to conceal his smile but failed miserably. Mocking her, was he? Suddenly Freja felt less inclined to like him, or Pojk for that matter, who was about as likeable as a slug. "Maybe I will," she said in defiance.

"Oh, don't, darling," said Cecelya and grabbed both of Freja's hands. "Don't. It's not—just don't. Promise you won't?" Her pleading and begging was so sincere that a small fear came to life in Freja. Was this real, or was it another version of Klobb's admonitions that each and every living thing in Ma'zekaï was out to get her? That paranoia had faded in power rather quickly, but Cecelya wasn't exactly the fearful type.

"Fine, I won't," said Freja, but only changing the subject because she had something else she needed to include in their plan. "There's another thing—my mother. She's in one of the other Obbsborn so we need to get to her first. We should find her before we enter the Bank, that way she can come and help as well, and we don't know what'll happen after, do we?" Four pairs of eyes told her what she didn't want to hear, or see for that matter. Even Tryll had input in this conversation. "She's in one of the other Obbsborn," she repeated, hoping that they simply hadn't heard her. "I'll go find her before we set out, you won't have to do a thing."

"There's no time, Freja," Cecelya said in a low and cautious voice, almost a whisper. "We need to move within two days and we've already tried to contact the other Obbsborn, remember? It's endlessly difficult."

"Batsërs?" suggested Freja, making grander and grander hand gestures. "It'd take what, a day?" There was no end to her verbal diatribe; she knew that once she stopped, the inevitable verdict would come, and she couldn't—wouldn't—face that.

"Freja …"

"No! We're dismissing my mother because it might be difficult?" she spluttered and then broke out laughing. "Or are we part of the 'community' now as well? Because it's so welcoming."

"That's not fair." Hurt shone all over Cecelya's face and it glossed her words as well.

"Look," said Lulja, "I know it's difficult, but maybe we can find her afterwards?"

"Maybe it'll be too late afterwards," shouted Freja, only then realising she had attracted quite the crowd at the entrance of the Turf. Pojk shooed them off and the cave went back to silence.

"I don't mean to butt in—" Pojk began.

"Then don't," Freja snapped. "Cecelya, come on." She grabbed Cecelya's hands. "Remember me. Remember your family—remember Robin for god's sake."

Cecelya bit her lower lip and chewed on it, her eyes glazing over. "You think I've forgotten about them?" Freja returned that it sure seemed like it, the way she was acting. "You're unbelievable, Freja." Cecelya reclaimed her hands with a jerk.

Freja shook her head. "Where's that girl who would draw and play and be kind to everyone? Who would do anything in the world for her brothers and her parents?" She got to her feet. "I don't know this new you, but I don't like her. Maybe it's better if you do stay here." She stomped out of the room and waited for the guilt to set in. As she turned in to the tunnel, she heard loud sobs. Guilt set in all right.

With blurring vision from the tears in her own eyes, Freja left the Turf, hurried through the tunnel, and crossed the hall where the many eyes of working Obbsborn followed her every step. She couldn't care less about them right now. All she needed was to get out, to get away.

CHAPTER 25

CECELYA'S WORDS WERE hurting, not so much for the sake of the Aitkens, but a more selfish reason that she hadn't quite figured out yet.

Having ensured that nobody was following her, she slouched down against the rough rock wall, waiting for her eyes to adjust to the dark. The curved contours of the archways soon appeared as if by magic and she could see more of her surroundings. It wasn't completely dark, of course, but with no torches as source of light, it was truly underground. Through a crevice came small cascades of dim silver light and she focused her gaze on it, thoughts swirling in her mind, making a messy knot of incomprehension. She imagined her brain nerves like little wheels and forced them into motion. It was slow at first.

Exhaustion clamped her body in a suffocating, yet releasing, way. All that tension from worry, fear and longing were released and allowed her soul temporary liberation. For once she didn't want to think about what to do next, where to go, who to trust. She just wanted to be.

In a feverish dream she was running along a cliff edge, seemingly unafraid of the steep drop beside her. The path was narrow, barely wide enough for two young feet, where one faulty step would send her down quicker than food in sight of Klobb, but she kept on running and never looked down. As if on cue he appeared in her vision like a ghoul, beheaded and holding on to his foul face in one hand, a steaming cup clutched in the other. He was grinning in his incredulous way. Klobb disappeared and Jaspir Nagel took his place. He was bleeding from invisible wounds and he reached out for Freja, but she couldn't reach him no matter how hard she tried. Whenever she got close, he was further way again. All the time she was running alongside the mountain wall. A hand came from behind and before she had the chance to cry out in warning, the hand shoved him down the side of the mountain and Freja let out a soundless scream. For the first time she looked down and saw the ragdoll body of Jaspir tumble and recoil against the hard surface until he vanished into the distance. When the head belonging to the murderous arm materialised from around a corner she tried her vocals again, but failed. A wall of blue devoured her entire visual field from one end of the spectrum to the other. All she could see was endless blue, but whether sky or ocean she couldn't tell. It was all the same.

A hand woke her up with a gentle shake and she stirred in a violent spasm. The dream had subsided but she still felt cold clammy sweat all over her body and here and there pecks of dust from the ground had got glued into the stickiness. She peeled her eyes open and the darkness around was strange at first, until she remembered. She sat up. A rough-skinned palm rested itself on her forehead and she saw that it belonged to Tryll, who had a frown on his face. He was checking for a fever. He thought she had passed out, not merely fallen asleep in the comfortable silence and gloom. She felt no need to correct him. In a genuinely croaking voice she asked if she was warm, which she apparently wasn't, as Tryll shook his head and left her forehead alone to offer the same hand to help her to her feet. She accepted it, muttering something about feeling a little feverish after all.

Together they walked back to the sleeping cabins where some of the Obbsborn had gathered. The work hall was empty so it must be after working hours. The chattering and laughter from the Turf jingled in the distance. In the cabins, there were several groups huddled together, whispering and talking to each other, though when Freja and Tryll entered to room, all conversation died down. It wasn't a comfortable silence.

"You decided to return? Or did you just fail to find the way out?" Pojk was the first one to speak, and it was with unconcealed hostility.

"I wasn't leaving," said Freja and explained she may or may not have passed out from a fever. She could tell from the glances and the rolling eyes that they didn't believe her. "I wouldn't leave," she added.

"We finished the plan," said Lulja.

Freja sat down and waited for Lulja to continue. When she didn't, Cecelya crept up next to her on the mattress and began explaining the wittily named 'Master Plan', explaining in detail each step of the way. There was a chilled hesitation between them, but she was glad Cecelya had forgiven her enough to still speak to her. Later, they would have to talk, but right now the plan was priority. Freja asked a few questions to clarify the points she didn't understand and soon enough the whole operation became clear to her.

"It sounds dangerous," she said. "Many things could go wrong."

"You got a better suggestion?" Pojk was unnecessarily unforgiving, she thought and decided to ignore him. "All right then," he said when Freja offered no alternative solution. "We'll head off tomorrow evening." He helped Cecelya up from Freja's

bed. "Everyone get some rest tonight—you'll need it. Ceci?."
The two left the cabin, leaving Lulja and Freja behind.

With a quick goodnight to Lulja, who wanted to stay up a bit
longer, Freja turned to face the wall. The questions popped up
like weeds inside her head, each demanding immediate attention. She wondered where Éloyse was, and if she had got into
trouble with those Masters, Skylar and Florin, or not? Had
Topster returned yet, only to find an empty house? Would he
let Klobb's head roll, like in her dream, for her absence? Had
she signed his death warrant by leaving?

She was still wide awake but pretended to be asleep when
Cecelya and Lulja returned a while later. Whispering, the two
girls soon crawled into their beds and the cabin came to rest as
the Obbsborn went to sleep. After a while, Freja gathered from
the heavy breathing that she was the only one awake. Turning
as quietly as she could, she peered around the room. All the
girls' bodies were heaving and sinking in a slow rhythm. With
careful movements she slipped off her mattress and to her feet
and left the cabin.

Sleep seemed too far off to be expected anytime soon.
Better she collected her thoughts so that she would be ready
for tomorrow. She wandered aimlessly around Obbsborn Z,
past the boys' cabin where the snoring was loud and rattling.
All asleep. There was an eerie quiet about the place now. The
abandonment reminded her too much of Wind where Jaspir
and his mother were confined. A shudder made her dispel the
thought, not quite ready to deal with the difficult questions at
this time of night.

For some reason she found herself walking across the hall
and back to the tunnel in which she had dozed off earlier in the
day (which was probably why she couldn't sleep now). She felt
the walls and found that same corridor where they had walked
with Klepta on their way in and where Pojk had confronted

them. One thought filled her head. To her right was the place where Tryll had found her, and she once more spotted the sliver of light she had seen before but not taken particular notice of. Only memory could lead you here, she realised. Only if you'd been here before, conscious and perceiving, could you find your way, or the darkness would capture you like a hungry beast. Following the light, she turned another corner and her hand touched something cold, wet—and soft. Grass. She followed the steps upwards and saw patches of grass, slippery steps wet from dew, and the moon hanging in the night sky.

One thought: if there was a way in, there had to be a way out—and here it was: the exit from Obbsborn Z.

CHAPTER 26

OBBSBORN Z WAS a bustle of movement the next morning. In the cabins were people talking in excited voices, leaping from one bed to another, munching on whatever scrap of food they had left from the week's ration, until Pojk came in and said that it was time to be seated. The cabin in which Freja lay, still under the thin duvet, was girls only, but because of the lack of doors in the cave, she could hear similar voices from the boys' sleeping room. A small tunnel and a sharp bend separated the two.

"It's like Curfew all over again," muttered Freja and turned to see if Lulja was awake. She had also been observing the morning ritual that was happening around them. Unlike Freja, though, whose concern of the slave like conditions might as well have been written on her forehead, Lulja, rather than show outrage, was fascinated. The last girl leapt over her legs and rushed out of the room. The cabin became silent and there was an intermittent vacuum until the tools started sounding from the hall.

"What do you reckon happens if you're late?" Freja said with a yawn. "Sacrifice a lock of hair? A toe?"

"Please don't speak," said Lulja and threw her pillow at Freja, who ducked under it. "You've gone snappish again."

"I'm serious."

"I know."

With the Obbsborn at work they had nothing else to do but stay put during the day and wait for evening to come. The group would set out for the Bank as soon as the day's work concluded for Cecelya and Pojk, and there was no risk of Masters visiting. "I guess we'll stay here?" said Lulja. "Everyone else will be working."

But Freja wasn't listening to a word she said. She was preoccupied, twirling her hair around her fingers and thinking about her discovery last night. The way out of Obbsborn Z was not merely a possible escape route, but a potential communications path as well. If they were to infiltrate the Bank they needed inside help—Master help—whether the others liked it or not. Whatever this secret help was that they had obtained it would count for nothing compared to an alliance with the enemy itself. There was but one Master she trusted enough to seek help from and she was definitely above ground.

"Hello?" Lulja was waving a hand in front of Freja's face, searching for her attention. "Anyone at home?"

"Not yet," said Freja, seeing an opportunity to discuss another delicate matter. "But we could be by tomorrow, touch—well, rock lacking other options." She thumped the ground three times with her knuckles. "Gosh, it's a dull place. So—have you decided?"

"No," Lulja replied without hesitation. "But I'll go with you to Vildaell to try and sort this mess out." She sat upright and pulled her hair back, showing off her features. Round cheeks with roses like natural ornaments and lucid eyes made her pretty in a non-obvious way. "Why can't people just get along?"

"Somehow I struggle to picture Topster in the local co-op,"

said Freja and Lulja sniggered.

"Can our differences really live side by side?" she asked but Freja had no answer.

The energy question was likely never to allow full reconciliation between the *landskapës* and perhaps closing the borders was the right choice after all? The least bad one in the bunch? Then again, as long as latches existed there was a way across, and some day another cycle of the same history would begin. It always did when given the opportunity, or a loophole. The borders would never be fully closed.

That reminded her. "Where's the third *landskapë*? I hear it mentioned by name, the Red World, but no one ever talks about it in more detail. I mean, who lives there? What do they do?" Lulja shrugged and said she didn't know. On their journeys Ravn had mentioned it, as Freja said, by name a few times, but he didn't seem willing or able to talk more about it so Lulja hadn't asked. Wherever they were, she pondered, they were probably better off than the other two.

"I'll go crazy if we just sit here all day," Lulja said and jumped off the bed, stretching her arms into the air. "But it's not like we can go anywhere."

"Maybe we can," said Freja with a smirk. She didn't blame Lulja for the confusion sent her way. Before she could start asking questions, Freja patted the mattress and had Lulja sit down again. She told her about the path she found and her concerns about the plan. Master interaction was perhaps not the safest route, but it might be a necessary risk. "Four guards on that island," she said and held up fingers to illustrate. "We will need someone to help us—and I know just the person." When she uttered the name, Lulja lit up at once in excitement.

Though she was hesitant to leave Obbsborn Z, even for a short while, she shared Freja's concern. While twiddling with her thumbs she admitted that the secret ally that Cecelya and

Pojk had managed to get on their side was none other than Klepta. "I wanted to tell you, Freja, but I couldn't. Not with them there. That guy does not trust you. Not Tryll, he does I think, but Pojk is such a tool."

"Klepta?" said Freja. "That's a joke. She's just as likely to sell us out."

"I agree. Last night I had no better suggestions so I kept my mouth shut. Sometimes I think Tryll's got the best way of things … Anyway, do you really think it'll work? Do you think she'll do it?"

"Do we have a choice?" Freja asked.

"There's always a choice."

"Either way we'll get into trouble."

Lulja rested her chin on the back of her hand and sighed. "When are we leaving?"

By the time Pojk signalled lunch break for the Obbsborn, Freja and Lulja were ready. Their masterforms were stuffed into their bags, the bags themselves hidden just outside the cabins for easy access, and the two girls were making sure they were seen by as many as possible, mingling around, chatting with Cecelya about the plan and how ready they felt. Lulja even had a signed conversation with Tryll. The only person they avoided contact with was Pojk, who kept to himself anyway, content with glaring at them from a corner of the Turf. As soon as Cecelya joined him they left together, and Freja and Lulja could relax.

Half an hour later, Pojk returned and it was time for the Obbsborn to return to the benches. In the hustle of hurry-ing feet, moving inside the crowd, Freja and Lulja retrieved the bags, followed it to the work hall and then snuck out into a dark corridor on the opposite side from the sleeping cabins, unseen by the rest. They stood in the damp darkness until the familiar sounds of hammering and slamming echoed through the open space. Freja gestured for Lulja to follow and before long she found the steps, now dry and dazzling in the light of day.

"Pretty neat, right?" she whispered to Lulja who had gone to the light like a moth and was now warming her face in the sunlight.

Just as they were about to begin the ascent, voices sounded from the top of the steps. With panicked looks at each other, Freja and Lulja leapt into a shaded spot beside the steps, almost behind them, and pressed their bodies tight against the uneven walls. Crevices and small dents scraped against the thin fabric of their t-shirts (they hadn't had time to change into master-forms yet), but moving was no longer an option. The voices were descending, coming towards them. Beside her Freja heard Lulja's heavy breathing and she wished she could tell her to be quiet. Or was it her own? All she could do was hope that it wasn't loud enough to expose them. Visitors in Obbsborn were of two kinds: Klepta or other Masters. Neither kind would be happy to see the false Obbsborn by the exit.

Boots met rock in dense thuds as the visitors climbed down the steps. There was more than one, perhaps more than two. Low voices kept murmuring, but then fell silent as the first Master landed on Obbsborn ground. Her blonde hair and pale masterform were her signature: Florin, the Master from the Trew house. A Master of the Élan—one of the seven. After her followed the Master in red, Skylar. He carried something over his shoulders—the body of a teenage boy, Freja real-ised with a shudder. "Obbsborn?" she mouthed to Lulja, who nodded with knitted eyebrows. Another victim, Freja thought.

But the third person made her leave all thoughts about the Élan and the seemingly unconscious boy behind. Red and burgundy blended together in the darkness but she would have recognised this Master anywhere. A small twitch next to her let her know that Lulja had seen her as well. Éloyse crept down the steps with obvious caution, holding on to straws of grass on the side and taking care with each step, constantly glancing sideways for each time her foot touched another step, as if pre-empting an attack or sensing what was hiding in the shadows of the Obbsborn. Skylar waited for her to leave the last step and set foot on solid ground and then showed his open palm to this last member of the group. He told her to wait and she gave him a small nod, and Florin and the Trew Master disappeared into the connecting tunnel, leaving Éloyse alone in the last dash of sunlight to touch the underground. It glimmered down on the Master like a halo of light.

Their luck was astonishing. Freja took it as a sign from some higher force. But they didn't have much time. She wriggled out from the spacious crevice in which Lulja and she were hiding and approached Éloyse from behind. She had found that the best way to stop people from crying out in surprise was to surprise them before they had the chance to even consider that option. Besides, hadn't Éloyse done it to her? With quick feet and a strong arm she locked Éloyse's arms and covered her mouth, but not before a faint cry escaped her, and Freja froze in motion. No movement came and the dark tunnels lay as still as before.

*

Inside the work hall, great commotion broke out at the sight of the Masters: gasps and curious gawking followed Florin and Skylar's entrance. Inspections were rare thanks to Klepta, but they did occasionally happen—and when they did, they were as always unannounced like this one. Still, there had been one not too long ago where two of the Élan had brought new Obbsborn in and that had lulled the community into what was now proven to be false certitude that another one was still weeks away.

Pojk, who was seated at his station close to where the

Masters entered, stood up. As self-proclaimed leader he had the responsibility of dealing with intruders, Masters included. The way he spoke to them was a far cry from his usual manner of speech: silky smooth and friendly on the border of fawning. In another setting, with other people, the blandishing sweet-talk might be punished for its blatant transparency, but self-satisfaction hardly knew any limits when it came to Masters. Skylar allowed himself a smirk; Florin, on the other hand, did no such thing. She stomped past the benches and slammed her hand on each one as she passed it.

"Attend," she said in her composed forthright way which still offered enough tension for every single Obbsborn to drop their work and follow orders. A domino sonata of clattering followed as, bench by bench, a hundred Obbsborn let needles, hammers, fabric, and nails fall to the ground. Then, once they had all put down their tools, a new kind of quiet filled the hall; a quiet only Florin could conjure. "Little working bees," she said softly with a wry smile. "You know we protect you. You know we would not do anything to harm you." The room was throbbing with tense silence. Not one Obbsborn dared speak or even breathe or clear their throat, though the cave dust oftentimes forced them to. Everyone knew Florin. You didn't have to stand eye to eye with her to fathom the cruelty. She had been down there before and the particular individuals who had then come in confrontation with her stood trembling, holding a firm gaze at a spot far, far away. When she sauntered past one of them, she paused a moment before continuing. Perhaps she didn't even know it was them, perhaps she was simply selecting new victims. At last she returned to her companion who was a new face to the Obbsborn.

He nodded as Pojk approached him to take the limp body from his arms. A boy, he saw, with reddish hair and fair skin. Another Curfew victim added to the Obbsborn population.

While Skylar remained where he was, Florin demanded that a blonde girl sitting next to Cecelya should accompany her. After an encouraging nod from Ceci, the girl, visibly trembling, went up to Florin's side. The Master grabbed her arm and pushed her ahead of her, so hard that the girl almost stumbled over her bad leg, however she managed to stay balanced and led the way to the girls' sleeping cabin. A total of three long minutes went by before Florin came out and shoved the girl back into her seat. The girl looked as surprised as Florin looked fuming. She crossed the room with composed steps, slow but determined, tucked loose strands of hair behind her ears, lips pursed and cheeks somewhat sucked in.

"Nothing," was all she said as she walked through the length of the hall, sending vicious glares to each Obbsborn. "We can go."

Master Skylar scanned the room once more and placed his hands behind his back. Before leaving, he faced them and said, "Obbsborn Z, you are one of the most productive Obbsborn in Ma'zekaï. You should be proud of your commitment. The Élan salutes you." He exchanged a look with Pojk and sought Florin's attention.

"As long as you perform," added Florin and turned on her heel to follow Skylar out.

The next moment they were both gone. The Obbsborn stood motionless for a moment, just in case either Master would return for some reason, but, when this seemed unlikely, exhaled and slumped down on the chairs as if their legs had failed them after a long run.

While Pojk kneeled by the newcomer, who was still out of it, Cecelya pushed out her chair with a loud screech echoing through the hall, and hurried into the cabin. Empty. There was no Freja or Lulja and, what was worse, their bags were gone. Not a sign remained that the girls had been there at all.

"They're gone," she said to herself as she returned with slow steps to the hall, shaking her head. "My goodness me … They actually left." A hand closed around her shoulder and she allowed it to, even put her own hand on top of it. He was still there. "They left," she said again, hoping that Pojk would contradict her. But he didn't.

*

For the same reason as the Obbsborn, Freja and Lulja remained in the shadows for almost an hour after seeing Éloyse, Florin, and Skylar—the latter two coming out of the hall with disgruntled looks on their faces—leave the underground.

"I still don't believe she said that," said Lulja with a vacant stare. "I mean he's one of them."

"So's she though," Freja added and pulled her knees closer. It was getting cold now that the sun had rotated and no longer reached down to the mouth of the underground. The halo of light had slowly seeped away, step by step, up towards where it belonged, leaving those down here with nothing but the constant damp dusk that they saw every day. "Anyway, we won't know until … until later."

"But Ravn?" said Lulja and made a face. "He barely says two words."

"To you," said Freja and grinned.

"You're one to speak—Tiora."

Freja laughed at the name, her old Master identity. "It's pretty," she said. "Why didn't Ravn change yours?" Lulja shrugged.

"I guess he deemed 'Lulja' to be of such noble nature that it suited a Master of the Trew." She feigned a dramatic swoon.

"Yeah, that must have been it," said Freja and stood up. "I think the coast is clear, let's go back."

"I'm hungry," Lulja muttered as they traversed the maze of dark tunnels, following nothing but their instincts and memory.

"You reckon they will have dinner on the table when we get back?"

"I wouldn't count on it," Freja mumbled in reply as she felt the wall slither to the right, then turn left, then lead right again. She couldn't believe their luck. The odds that Éloyse of all people would come to Obbsborn Z were definitely not in their favour and everything that had happened next had been a chain effect of good fortune for them.

According to Éloyse, Florin and Skylar had used the new Obbsborn boy as a cover to search for them; for the humans. Though Éloyse hadn't been explicit in her accusation, Freja sensed from her words that Klepta had something to do with the Masters finding out where they were hiding. It was, after all, she who had put them in their cage. Then again, the Obbsborn trusted Klepta. Freja decided not to assign blame until she was sure. And definitely not mention her reservations about Klepta to Cecelya or Pojk, or she suspected she would get a good old scolding from the latter. But she would be careful with Klepta from now on, and she would make sure that the Obbsborn were too.

Another forked intersection appeared, and Freja turned right. Two more tunnel pathways and they would be inside again. Behind her she heard Lulja's steady breathing. Would they still be breathing at the end of tonight? If Éloyse could keep her word, it wasn't entirely unlikely.

The heat of blazing torches ate into the chill from the gloomy dark as soon as they stepped into the antechamber of the great hall, and the cold faded away. Like amphibious creatures they had adapted to the Obbsborn temperature and any outlying conditions were out of the ordinary; even the loose and ill-fitting clothes now seemed more comfortable than the masterforms—or regular jeans, for that matter. First, they noticed this—the heat and the familiarity of the Obbsborn cave—and then they noticed something else: the silence.

"Something's off," said Lulja.

"Definitely off," said Freja.

"It's very quiet."

"It's too quiet."

"Is that …? No. I thought I heard something."

"Someone's speaking. Come on," said Freja and tugged at Lulja's hem. Careful not to make a sound, they tiptoed through to the empty hall and towards the sound of the voice. It came from the Turf, and it was Pojk who was talking. Before making their presence known, Freja and Lulja hovered in the tunnel.

"Whatever we choose to do next, we must do without them. Also …" Pojk paused. "We can't rule out that they have sided with the Élan."

Outrage broke out among the listeners who, given the emptiness of the place, must be the other Obbsborn, Freja concluded. "'They'?" she mouthed to Lulja.

"They're talking about us!" Lulja pointed to her ear and to the Turf.

Listen.

CHAPTER 27

"I TOLD YOU," shouted someone. "Didn't I say?"

"You did say— " Pojk's voice. "I didn't listen."

"Maybe you should next time," said the voice, a boy Freja saw as she dared a peek around the corner into the Turf. "We're all thinking it, you know."

"What?" said Pojk, the humility all vaporised. "What are you all thinking, Alfons?"

"Our leader. Ha!" Alfons said, gathered spit in his mouth and released it to the ground on his left. Someone yelled at him to 'watch it' but Alfons didn't apologise. "It's all filth down here anyway," he said.

"There's no use in arguing," came a voice Freja recognised as Cecelya's. "Don't let this cause us to fight amongst ourselves. If anyone's to blame it's me. I convinced Pojk, if you want to be mad at anyone, be mad at me."

She peered around the corner again. There were all the Obbsborn and Cecelya and Pojk were standing in front of them like the President and the First Lady about to give a speech. The new member was lying in the arms of a brown-haired boy in the front, still not conscious. Freja saw his chest was moving, so he was breathing at least.

"What's going on?" came Lulja's voice from behind her.

Freja shrugged and waited.

The boy Alfons didn't say anything more. His cheeks were flaming red, like blossoms on a white canvas for the rest of him was pale as a sheet. He was young, probably no older than twelve or thirteen, and had piercing blue eyes, almost as pale as the whites surrounding them. His clothes were quite well-fitted for an Obbsborn attire, and it revealed the thin body of the child underneath; he might even be older, but with a body that didn't match his age. The area around the eyes was sunken in, making them look skull-like and hollow, and his arms were bony, sinewy, and fragile. Scars covered his neck and left side of the face; even from a distance the missing teeth were black holes among the remaining white squares. Clearly Jahranian, Freja thought. Native Jahran people had three common features in Freja's small experience: missing teeth, too many scars, and a starving frame. Maybe Lulja knew him. She had no idea if Alfons was a common name in Jahran and she would remember to ask later.

Having watched the meeting for about ten minutes, she started feeling bad for eavesdropping and turned to Lulja. "We should go in," Freja mouthed. Lulja shook her head. Freja nodded with a frown and hissed. "We can't be eavesdropping. It's rude!"

"Just a little more," Lulja whispered back.

As another girl joined in the conversation, Freja gave in with a sigh and closed her eyes to listen.

"We need a Master," said the new girl in a deep, somewhat nasal voice. "What abou' that?"

"Perhaps Klepta …" Cecelya did not have time to finish.

"Klepta will do no such thing," said the girl and got a murmur of agreement from the group. "Ye know that."

She was Burian. The Queen's speeches had made sure everyone knew and recognised the Burian accent; everyone watched the Queen's talks on television. They pronounced 'O' in a funny way, as if there was an E at the end of each word—*oe*. It was distinguishable and eloquent if you asked them; incomprehensible and up-nosed, if you asked outside the border. Yet, people loved the accent. It sounded like an ancient language, spoken in the forests of the old world, or so Freja thought. Robin was excellent at imitating it, but she had never got the hang of it.

"Laren, please," pleaded Cecelya.

"*Noe*," said the Burian girl Laren in her ancient accent. "I will not 'please'—what are we going to *doe* now they've gone?"

"Yeah," shouted Alfons. "What now?"

"Everyone just shut up!" Pojk's fuse had blown and he was screaming uncontrollably. "We'll find a way. We always find a way—we're Obbsborn Z! Right?"

"Right," chanted part of the group.

"If we need a Master hand tonight, I will cut it off and carry it there myself."

The crowd cheered and Freja opened her eyes as the penny dropped. "They think we left," she said, staring into the dark. About three hours had passed since they had vacated the room, but not once had she considered this possibility.

"Still want to go in?" asked Lulja.

"We have to." She turned her head. Lulja was standing like her, flat against the wall, eyes staring into nothingness.

"Yeah … I just hope they won't cut off my arm …"

"Don't be silly," said Freja in an attempt to muster up courage for both of them. "They said they needed a Master hand, right? So we're good."

"We're good …," said Lulja after a pause, and it was far from convincing.

Freja tugged at Lulja's arm. "We won't let them know we

heard a single word, okay?" Lulja nodded in assent. "Okay, let's go then."

Alfons was the first to spot them. His mouth fell open and he managed to raise a finger pointing straight at their chests, accusatory and blind with condemnation. One by one the Obbsborn turned their heads towards the entrance where Freja and Lulja had entered. The Obbsborn watched them in silence, with Alfons as the voice of the group, shouting "There! There!" over and over like a record on repeat. His childish voice, seemingly yet untouched by puberty, echoed in the quiet room, bouncing against the walls back and forth, until eventually it was absorbed by the many bodies in there, upon which he threw out another one, and the cycle started again. Like a flipper game, the word surged around the room like beams of noisy light as the two girls crossed to join the Obbsborn, feigning ignorance about the conversation that had just taken place in there.

"Do something." Alfons's finger was relentless.

Nobody did anything and even if they had, Freja wouldn't have noticed. She had her eyes on Cecelya all this time and followed a wave of emotion from wide-eyed shock, gaping disbelief, all the way to glazed-over relief at which point she exhaled loudly and rushed into Freja's arms.

"I thought you were gone, darling," she sobbed into Freja's shoulder. "You were gone. Your bags ... But you're here now. Oh, when that horrid woman went to look ... Oh, darling, darling, darling, darling, don't ever leave like that again."

Freja promised she wouldn't and hugged her back. They were, after all, in this together now and in this embrace Freja saw a glimpse of hope that she might be taking Cecelya back to Vildaell.

As expected, Pojk was not as enthused at their return. He demanded to know where they had been and what they had been doing. Every single Obbsborn was observing and listening with critical eyes and ears as Lulja began telling them that their intention had been to recruit Éloyse to the cause, what had happened at the arrival of Florin and Skylar, and lastly what Éloyse had said. It wasn't the conversation or the promise, however, that Alfons caught up on.

"You were going to go outside?" he said, frowning. "That's like impossible."

"Like, totally impossible," filled the Burian girl in.

"Of course they weren't," said Pojk before Freja could answer. "They were going to try and find a batsër, weren't you?" He turned to Freja and blinked. There was no chance of missing the message in his eyes. "Weren't you going to find a batsër and send it to this Éloyse when the Masters entered?"

"Yes," said Lulja when Freja failed at finding the words. "Yes, that's it. It was sheer luck that they came so we could speak with her directly."

Well, it wasn't an outright lie, but Freja didn't like the way the conversation happened. She pursed her lips and forced the smallest of nods, obviously enough to satisfy both Alfons and Laren who relaxed and exchanged suspicion for astonishment.

"That is so stupid," said Alfons. "A batsër is a Master's minion."

"We know that now," said Lulja through clenched teeth. To compensate the harsh tone, she gave Alfons a strained smile. "We're not used to this world," she said. "Not like you."

"Sure, you're the experts." Lulja gave Freja a glaring look. Deserved as well, she thought; now was not the time for sarcastic remarks.

Alfons weighed from one foot to the other, as though wavering between accepting this offered token of goodwill and discarding it and return to hostility. He crossed his arms, landed on his right foot and an evil smirk stretched across his face. Freja knew they had appeased him. That kind of smirk was a limited edition for people who thought they had won. She had seen it before: Robin, despite his gentle nature, often dressed himself in one at the finish line of one of their competitions. "That's right," said Alfons and blew up his chest as if an invisible pump added air to his chest cavity. "We're the experts. Don't think you know more than we do. You wander off and risk getting seen outside Obbsborn grounds. Who would suffer for it? We would, that's who! Tell them, Pojk."

Pojk seemed taken aback by this sudden order from the boy and glanced at the Obbsborn, excited and enthused by the argument, before speaking. He also took a step back to stand in line with Alfons and Laren and Cecelya, cutting Freja and Lulja out of the circle. "It was infinitely thoughtless," he said flatly. "It doesn't matter how well we have this mission planned if you two go and sabotage the whole thing." Momentum caught him and his speech grew faster and harsher. "There is a plan in place—an actual plan that is done in each and every detail and you decide, what? That it's not good enough for you?"

"Pojk …," said Cecelya but he brushed her off and raised a warning finger to Freja's face. And he came close, so close she felt his body heat. His breath smelt stale.

"Disobey me again and we will personally hand you over to the Élan and accept our reward in return. Understood?"

"Aye, Cap'n," said Freja and made a sailor's greeting. Pojk glared at her and she rolled her eyes. "Yes, Pojk, we will do no such thing. We will stay here until it's time to leave—with you. Satisfied?"

"I'll be satisfied when I see it done."

Pojk turned his back to her and she had to make an effort not to grimace or show even the slightest sliver of her thoughts. Instead she pulled her face into neutral disinterest, impossible to interpret as defiance or any of its derivatives. It worked and soon the Obbsborn were scattering again; those who weren't finished with the day's work went back to the hall, others engaged in leisurely activities with anyone who would join in.

"I'm so glad you're here," said Cecelya and hugged Freja once more. She gave Lulja a pat on the shoulder before disappearing to complete an appliance she'd been working on. It was to be sent to Tech Division that same day and she needed to make sure it was working. Pojk went with her, without a word.

"Freja …? Freja Evenson?" came a small voice from their left. The woman had come on silent feet and was only a metre or so away when she spoke the name.

"Yes?" said Freja, wondering where she had seen the woman before. Because she had most definitely seen her face. It was a memorable one, even if it now carried the same signs as the other Obbsborn. She was perhaps in her late thirties, had deep black hair, and a pale complexion; she was skinny in a natural way and didn't look as unhealthy as many other Obbsborn. Her eyes were slanted, her nose straight and cute, giving her face symmetry and a roundness that suited her. Large shadows hung under her eyes like cocoons holding all the loss and longing in her body in an external pouch for everyone to see. She was limping—her left leg.

"You don't recognise me?" she said in a voice not untouched by tremor. When she smiled her charming crow's feet added another dimension to her facial features; as if there was more story than could be told. "I guess I have changed quite a bit …"

"Tessandra?" said Freja, not sure where the name had come from. "You're Tessandra Wilkins."

The woman smiled and her eyes filled with tears. "I do look like me, then," she said and joined her palms at her mouth. "And you remember."

Freja did remember. Tessandra was the aunt of one of Freja's friends at school and she had met her years ago at a birthday event. Already then, at a young age, Freja had been set on one day owning a motorcycle, and Tessandra knew a lot about the different models and editions. Thunderball X450 was the best according to Tessandra, Freja recalled, but she had been drooling over the latest Huzula 60-R in metallic blue—even though she was years away from being allowed to drive one.

"I got the Thunderball," was all she could think of saying. "Just like you said. For my eighteenth birthday, Dad took me there and I chose the Thunderball X770. It's like flying."

"There's a 770 now?" Tessandra asked and laughed. "I've been gone for a while." Freja asked how long. "My day was the fourth of June, you remember the year, when Curfew numbers were higher than ever? That year."

Freja calculated that it meant Tessandra had been in Obbsborn for at least three years. Though she couldn't remember ever hearing about Tessandra's disappearance, or reading about it in the List, she and many others had lost touch with Leah, Freja's friend, about three years ago. After months of cold encounters, Leah had moved town, changed schools, and wasn't heard from again. So when Tessandra wanted to know how her niece was doing, Freja had no answers. "I'm sorry," she mumbled after explaining what had happened.

"Typical Leah to pick up everything and leave," Tessandra said, smiling through the tears. "Never mind. It was nice seeing you, Freja."

"You too."

As Tessandra walked away she stopped suddenly and turned back. "Freja," she said, lowering her voice, "if you're going back, let me know. I want to come with you."

Freja nodded and Tessandra went back to her friends.

"That was intense," said Lulja, following Freja's gaze after the woman.

Freja said nothing. Jitters and angst tangoed in her every

limb and the meeting with Tessandra Wilkins left her shaken. She was the closest person, besides her mother, she had lost to Curfew, but that wasn't what bothered her. Not really. It was the fact that her mother had disappeared two years ago, Tessandra three—but only one of them was here, in this Obbsborn.

She was preoccupied with these thoughts as she followed Lulja towards the cabins, and didn't see who the person approaching from the opposite side was; not until he had his elbow at her throat and her whole body pinned against the wall.

"Hey," shouted Lulja, because Freja had no longer access to her windpipe.

The tunnel linking the hall and the Turf was a few shades darker than the other spaces, and colder, because of the single torch on the wall, and in the dim light, his face had a spooky pallor.

"Keep moving," he hissed with so much fervour that Lulja had no choice but to leave the two alone. Once she was gone, Pojk released the pressure of his arm somewhat and Freja drew in air, spluttering and coughing. "Let's talk," he said.

"Let me breathe, first of all," said Freja with obvious effort and moved her eyes to his arm, tense and stiff against her throat. It was as if he had forgotten it was there and he immediately released it. Freja put her hands on her head and filled her lungs with air. "That was not necessary," she said.

"Whatever," he said in a low voice and glanced sideways to see that nobody was coming. "Don't cry about it."

"I won't. What's your problem with me anyway?"

"You know why I yelled at you before." It wasn't a question. "Without me, the Obbsborn would fall apart—hey, no, don't smile, don't laugh. It's true. I've seen it." She asked what he meant, and Pojk told her he was born in Ma'zekaï, one of the few—perhaps the only one, now—Obbsborn who were; certainly the only one in Z. His mother and father were both

Curfew victims from the southern parts of Vildaell and both taken at an early age. They didn't know each other, they lived in different cities, but found each other in Obbsborn 4—one of the earlier ones where they used numbers—and eventually had a child. Him. A first generation Obbsborn native, Pojk grew up to be, as strange as it sounds, envied by newcomers. Maybe it was because he was different, or because he knew the Obbsborn system inside out and they felt inferior to his knowledge, but the new Obbsborn wouldn't be associated with him and he suffered physical and psychological bullying for years. When his parents died, Pojk was twelve years old. He had nobody left. "Then the valley fell and I got left behind."

"What valley?" Freja asked.

"Wind," said Pojk and Freja's mouth fell open. "Yeah, and all the Obbsborn were left, abandoned. I wasn't just going to sit back and watch it fall to pieces like the others did."

"So you knew Jaspir Nagel?"

Pojk's mouth twitched. "Yeah, I knew him. He stayed."

"He's alive," Freja said and told him about her encounter with Jaspir in Wind. She left out the part about his severe condition and the fact that he was likely to die within a near future. "How did you get here?"

"I wanted to live, so I lived. Klepta found me wandering the mountains and brought me here when it was already populated with the first newcomers. Everything was a mess because they had stuffed a bunch of semi-criminals in a confined area to starve and work under their own responsibility. I got here, I was thirteen, and I took charge. I sorted it all out. Look at us now—one of the best Obbsborn and we laugh sometimes, too. I'm not sure they do elsewhere. They didn't in Wind, anyway."

There was nothing insincere in his voice, nothing hidden under the thick hide of self-protection covering his words. Freja could see the source of his anger now, at least in part.

Confined to an underground world for life, she would probably not feel too keen on pitying the kind who imprisoned her there in the first place, oppressed or not. Then again, where had Klepta, the individual, stopped being a saviour and become the bad guy? She asked.

"You choose," said Pojk calmly. "When she sold me like a piece of junk to the Trew for a place in their house, or when she didn't stop them from shoving me down here?" He laughed a hollow laugh and pulled on a mocking tone, "'For my own good'. Or when she sent Benna Hjalmar to her death."

Freja said nothing. What could she say?

"You know about the way out," she said then. "That's why you were talking batsërs before. The others don't know about it?" This conclusion had slowly dawned on her since the awkward situation earlier.

"Of course," he said. "I know a lot of things the others don't. I know Benna was a Master." Freja gaped. "Sure, she was one of the Masters in Heim and the Élan was upset with her so they took her away. One of their own, and they cast her away, shoved her down here with the rest of the vermin. I know about the path because I was conscious when I walked down it, I possess the memory. But I can control myself. I know that we're safer down here than up there, at least for now. I'm not so sure the others would be as convinced, are you?"

Freja didn't reply, but she agreed. Hadn't she herself been on her way up the steps mere hours ago?

His eyes were different shades of green, she saw now when he stood so close; nuances dancing into each other and apart again as the pupils moved from her eyes to her nose to her lips and back up again. He was studying her face.

"What happened to your arm?" His eyes shifted as if by instinct to the exposed scars, nothing more than light hacks in the dim light, but broad and ragged enough to speak of a violent background.

"Fenrirs," he said. "They would have killed me if Klepta hadn't come." He sighed. "I'm forever in her debt."

"I'm sorry."

"And I'm sorry about your mother."

The earnestness of his voice surprised Freja and for the first time she saw him as something other than the cold, harsh leader he had been to her before. He was born here, this was his home, and all he was doing was protecting it. Just like she was preparing to protect her own home, Vildaell. There was no way she could blame him for that. "Thanks," she said with a smile. "Maybe you're not so bad after all."

"I do my best," he replied and Freja felt a flutter in her stomach which caught her off guard.

She frowned. She had waited for this moment to ask him. "So maybe there's hope still."

"Hope?" he asked, pulling back. He knew, she could tell, what she was going to say.

"You have to let her go," she whispered as the contour of another being approached in the far end of the tunnel. "Whatever it is you're feeling, you have to be selfless and let her go."

Pojk frowned for a moment, then relaxed as he understood what she was talking about. At the same time came Cecelya's voice soaring in the tunnel in five versions of itself as the echo travelled back and forth.

"Pojk?" she said in that exquisite voice which had regained some of its nobility since Freja arrived. "Oh, Freja, hi." She looked from one to the other. "Everything all right here?"

"Fine," they both said in chorus without breaking eye contact. It was as much a promise from Pojk to Freja as reassurance to Cecelya.

"I'll go see what Lulja's doing," said Freja with a smile and left them, hurrying through the tunnel and to the cabins where Florin's work had been cleaned up and everything was in order again. Lulja gave her an inquisitive look but Freja shook her head. There were other Obbsborn in the cabin as well, and she felt no need to share her conversation with Pojk with them. "Later," she mouthed and Lulja nodded.

With his promise, a fragile calm had spread its feathery wings and chased the previous anxiety away. There was a plan, a schedule, according to which they could be heading towards Vildaell, towards home, in a few days' time. Tessandra would come with them, Cecelya too if Pojk kept his word.

Freja allowed herself a smile where she lay, the quiet breathing of the Obbsborn and Lulja around her. It would all be all right.

CHAPTER 28

THE MOVEMENT BEGAN when the Obbsborn cage became quiet and the rattling of work had long since stopped; the jail birds wouldn't sing until morning.

If there would be another morning in Ma'zekaï, thought Freja. She was walking as the second to last member in their group of four through a long winding tunnel, her saddle bag across her chest, heavy from its content: rocks, and plenty of them. They clashed against each other in the bag, creating a gravitational force with which it thumped with a dull sound at her leg each time she placed one foot in front of the other.

She had hoped that Tryll, being in the Tech Division, would have been able to conjure up some more potent way of protection, but his hands were as tied as his tongue. There was a reason the secret Tech Obbsborn worked elsewhere and were so carefully and ruthlessly maimed. Thorough checks at each entry and exit in the Tech workspace ensured that the secrets of the Division remained within its walls. Before they left he had tried to sign something about guns, and Freja's heart had leapt in her chest, hoping that he had managed to get hold of some. With guns Masters wouldn't stand a chance with their precious leaves. Then Pojk had killed the moment and told them that there weren't weapons in Ma'zekaï—they simply didn't exist. Sure, there were hammers and nails that could technically be used, but they also required body contact and while he was sure we were vicious enough to use them—at this point he had smiled at Freja, who grinned in return—it would be suicide to come so close to a Master of the Élan. "Leaves," he had said and held out a flat palm. Nobody asked any more questions.

The absence of weapons in Ma'zekaï was of course in their best interest but she would have felt better carrying some kind of bat or even a gun, though she'd never held one in her life. At the same time as it set them at a clear disadvantage, having nothing but dusty rocks, sharp as they were, to attack any enemy they came across, it also meant they knew what kind of weapons they would be facing in such a situation. Leaves were lethal in the hands of the right Master, but required close body contact, Freja had learned. She had had enough experience with the dual power of the leaves to know this already. So tonight, if faced with a leaf, run like mad. That was the plan.

The noise of the bag was loud enough to get on her nerves, already tense like guitar strings, and she adjusted the strap while walking, pulling the bag to her front, where the sharp edges chafed against her thigh instead. She sighed and winced at the pain at first, but decided it was better than the rhythmic war drum. It set her hair-on-end and right now she needed to keep her nerves in place. This was not the time for second thoughts.

She was back in masterform, as was Lulja who was walking in front of her, second of their group. Leading them through the rough underpass was Tryll, who had taken a quickly sewn masterform from Craft, a deep yellow one, which, though it had been a rushed job, fitted him well. It was quite the upgrade from his tattered Obbsborn clothes. Last in their little assembly was a late addition to the mission: Alfons. The boy had been determined to come despite many admonitions of the danger, the deadliness, and the dead end nature of the task. These had only seemed to spur him on and at last there had been no more time to argue. But he refused to go in masterform. Said it was beneath him, that he would not be caught dead in one. Guessing from the look he received from Pojk as he gave voice to his dignity, Freja wouldn't be surprised if Pojk wanted him to be found dead in his own clothes.

The torch in Tryll's hand cast tall shadows on the walls and ceilings ahead and more than once Freja jumped as she thought someone appeared in the darkness. Lulja turned around and laughed silently. "Like you didn't jump too," wheezed Freja and Tryll had to signal for them to be quiet. They were still under ground, and quite shallow, too.

The passage itself was engulfed in darkness. It was nothing like the other Obbsborn spaces—smooth curves and hand-crafted railings did not exist in this one. This tunnel had been dug by Craft Obbsborn, and originated from a concealed cleft in the boys' sleeping cabin. In other words, it wasn't for Masters to find and seal. And it didn't lead straight to the world up there either. Eventually, yes, but first it slithered like a furtive snake underneath the sea itself and ended up in the one place more vulnerable than the Willow: the Latch Bank. It was through this tunnel, which the Obbsborn had worked on for years before finding the way, that the latches had been stolen directly from within the Bank. Like ghosts, the Obbsborn had moved in and out, taking a few latches each time so that it might not be noticed. Like now, they had moved in small groups and left the other Obbsborn at work just in case another inspection came along. This time the risk was higher, because Tryll would be missing from Tech and when the time came, so would Pojk, the most prominent of them all. It couldn't be helped; they needed both of them for their knowledge of the plan. Or, down here at least, Tryll's. Pojk had insisted on accompanying the girl who was to cause a diversion above ground. It was easy to guess who that girl was.

Thud, thud, thud. The bag slipped around Freja's back and returned to its pounding. "Sorry," she mouthed to Tryll who sent a glaring look back at her. Fine, be quiet, I get it, she thought. They were all on edge tonight.

To steady her mind and prevent her thoughts from rushing off to other possible frightening endings and complications, she looked around the hacked tunnel walls and floor. The torch threw intermittent cascades of light and in these short intervals, Freja saw that across the walls were carvings and paintings of various kind. Some simple drawings depicted people and beasts, mostly fighting, sometimes together, sometimes alone. The vast majority of scribbles were, however, names; rows and rows of names up and down the walls, all in different handwriting. She hadn't seen them before because there were so many of them that they melted into the grey surface of the wall and appeared like blemishes in the rock. The walls were probably smooth underneath it all. There were simple ones like Janok, Ia, and even the male form of her own, Frej; others were more exotic and foreign-sounding. A few she recognised from history books. Jahranian and Burian names mixed with those of Vildaell. All together in this forsaken passageway. As the monumental significance of these names struck her, she stopped abruptly and Alfons, who had been uncharacteristically quiet, walked straight into her from behind.

"Watch it," he hissed.

She mumbled 'sorry' and forced herself to carry on, now trying hard not to look at the walls. Try as she might, the names on the wall of past Obbsborn followed her every move. She couldn't help herself and continued to glance left and right, catching unfamiliar names of unfamiliar people in unfamiliar lands that still managed to put a small dagger in her heart. Thankfully, except for a surname or two that were common enough, none of the names were recognisable to her. All these names put up there to last forever; immortalising the victims who were, as Lulja had said, buried and grieved for in their homelands. Quite the opposite of what she was trying to do. Long ago had these people played their part and this was their legacy: letters carved with a shaking hand in a tunnel far beneath the surface of a foreign world.

Out of the four of them, she was the only one who wanted to leave this place. Tryll and Lulja and Alfons fought for continued survival while all Freja wanted was out. Was that even an option? The complexity of the pathway system gave her way too much time to think and she decided to focus on the task instead, to go over the plan again.

They would enter the Bank on the west side of the island, collect all the latches including the particular one as named price for Obbsborn assistance, then get out as soon as they possibly could. That part was simple in itself, but depended wholly on Pojk and Cecelya and the diversion, a plan whose constituents she had not quite grasped herself. She only knew it involved a boat and a "secret weapon" as Cecelya had put it with a mysterious smile. What it was more specifically, she didn't want to say. "You'll know when you—You'll know," she'd said.

She crouched as they passed through an extremely low tunnel where not even Klobb could've walked upright.

Given that the collecting of latches was successful, they would come back this same way and use a side path out to a spot close to the shore, lately ploughed, in secret, as an escape route in case the Obbsborn needed one. There, Éloyse would place Transporters—her promise to them—on which they'd all, Pojk and Cecelya included, travel back to Topster's cottage and the Willow. If Topster had returned to Ma'zekaï there was a chance they could stop him there and then, but in any case they would move on to Heim and—

—that's where the plan ended.

For thus far, Freja had no idea what to do once she got home. Warn the authorities? How long would it take for them to lock her up for hallucinations and mental disorder? You didn't simply waltz into a police station with stories of parallel worlds and a superior race about to take over the world. If Éloyse came with her, or Klepta, they might believe her story. And then what? Well, it didn't matter at the moment. They needed to get into the Bank and out again safely before worrying about what to do next.

"Lulja," she whispered. "How far are we?"

"Almost there," she whispered back.

Tryll cleared his throat and Freja fell silent. She looked up, imagining the ocean waves above, crashing in the night. A cold chill rushed through the tunnel as if somebody had opened a door. Tryll turned to them with a concerned frown and bit the inside of his lower lip, but continued.

After another series of short winding passages, one of which they had to walk sideways through, Tryll stopped again.

"You'd think they'd dig them wide enough for a person," said Lulja as they exited the last one. She brushed dirt off her masterform.

Freja ignored her whining. In front of them was a round portal, barely visible and about two metres across. Its lines were so thin and delicate that it might easily be missed by any random passer-by.

But she saw it clearly.

She went up to it, ran her fingers against its body, the carved lines. A metal taste licked her tongue as her fingertips ran over the chilly surface.

"This is it?" she asked Tryll, a new light in her eyes and fresh energy surging through her veins as if fed by a Willow leaf.

Tryll confirmed with a nod and a smile. At last, they had reached the entrance to the Bank.

CHAPTER 29

ABOVE GROUND, THE moon was up; a shard of dangerous light in the sky, like the precarious eye that never sleeps and is a constant watch over the resting lands. A lonely shadow moved across a smaller plain and onto the sand strip which made up the western banks of the Klockern sea in Ma'zekaï. On the right, some leagues away, was the village, now submerged in darkness and stilled by the late hours of the night that would all too soon transform into early morning.

Cecelya made sure no one was around, then drew in the night breeze which was cool and refreshing and a nice change from the musty Obbsborn air she had been breathing lately. She was hovering behind a wall of lilac shrubs where cascades of fluffy purple—like clouds on earth—concealed her to the main path. Pojk had gone off to pick up a batsër at the agreed place and left Cecelya crouching in the bushes like a fugitive. In a way, she was. They both were. He had been gone a while, though, and her legs started hurting. The shrub wasn't tall enough for her to stand up behind while still retaining her concealment, and she had no mind for sitting down on the damp ground, moist from the chill of the night and heavens knew what passing animals.

She scanned the surface of the sea. It was still and glazed like a carrot cake. Her stomach rumbled. No carrot cake for an Obbsborn, she thought. Her knee started aching and she adjusted her position.

Freja had asked her to go back to Amérle with her. How could she explain why she couldn't? That if she did, life would not go back to its normal rhythm and she would never forget what had been. Not a day had gone by without her thinking about her family and Amérle, the life she had had there—the life she had loved. Beautiful memories floated in her mind like fragile roses on a pond, but that was all they had been—memories—and soon the petals had begun to fall off and the roses started withering one after the other. Soon enough there would be nothing left but a soggy pond with the scattered remnants of what had been. There wasn't a life to simply pick up again, at least not for Cecelya. Despite her parents, her brothers. What could they do for their daughter and sister now? She was lost, dropped like a rag doll; she had been picked up and put in the wrong lost-and-found box. So she had volunteered as soon as Pojk had voiced the need for a group to distract the security on the island, and something small, like the sad sparkle in the eye of an injured bird, had entered his eyes when she put her hand up. There was no helping it—she had to participate in the plan, flawed and uncertain as it was. Unless she did, there was no going back for anyone. If they succeeded tonight there would be enough latches to send people home to their countries as well as leverage to pressure the Lords.

She touched the lapis gems at her temples, the ones Freja had given to her to go with the light yellow masterform. They were cool and still, like the night itself.

Her pulse was high, and it increased further as she saw Pojk approach in the near distance. There was no doubt it was him—not many people wore such clothes up here. He should have put on a masterform as well, like Cecelya, but had refused with fervour. She wondered if he had been above ground much in his life besides the time he fled from Wind. He'd squinted in the moonlight, as if its glow hurt him, so perhaps visits out of Obbsborn had been scarce even for Klepta's favourite. If there was one subject they didn't cover much in their conversations, it was above ground. Maybe he thought Cecelya needed to adjust to the fact that she'd never see it again, or so she had thought. Yet here she was.

She crept out of the shrubs, pushing delicate lilacs aside so that a few flowers broke from their stems and fell towards the ground, and ran towards the beach strip. The sand was dense and wet from the falling tide and she could rush across it without trouble, while a salty tang from the sea entered her nostrils and stung pleasantly in there. She drew it in, relishing the tingling force of the salt crystals. She got to the boat moorings where, like she thought, the rowing boats were up-side-down straight on the sand, unchained. The trust Masters invested in each other, that building block of their community they took such pride in according to Pojk, would, ironically, be their downfall tonight. She chose the smallest of the three boats, large enough to hold only the two of them and which had a small motor as well, and dragged it out from its holding. A faint 'T' scratched on the side let her know it had been made in Obbsborn T, most likely by the Craft Division. She smiled at the small act of rebellion; Obbsborn were supposed not to be seen or heard, even heard *of*, yet here was concrete evidence above ground that there was another community in the valley.

Getting it out of the holding and turning the boat around was no problem, but the sand was too unrelenting to drag it any further. Her arms were weak; any muscle she had had in them once had been eaten up by the rest of her body, greedy for the life supporting energy she was no longer getting from food.

Pojk had reached the beach now and was walking towards her. She gave him a smile but couldn't tell if he returned it. Hopefully the batsër had been carrying good news.

While she waited for him to reach her, she looked out at sea and the island. Somewhere under the surface, deep under there, were Freja and the others moving towards the Bank, relying completely on their diversion up here for time. Since the Obbsborn started stealing latches, the security system had doubled and there were now four guards on the island: two Élan and two Trew. Collecting the latches would be a noisy business and so the guards needed something else to think about during that half hour. The plan was based on a lot of guesswork, some inside information, and plenty of what-ifs, but once Cecelya and Pojk did their part at least two of the guards—the Trew, probably—would be sent out to find the source of the disturbance, leaving two Élan in position. The Trew shouldn't be able to see them in the dark boat, as long as they kept a safe distance, and would have to call the Élan guards as well. That would give Freja and the others enough time to enter the Bank from below, collect the latches, and leave before anyone noticed.

If the guards didn't react as Klepta had said … No, Cecelya didn't want to think about it. Lost in thought, she didn't notice Pojk's return and it made her jump. "Sorry," she said. "Just a bit nervous."

"We should be," said Pojk but with an encouraging smile. "Éloyse sent Ragnar." He was grinning and Cecelya gave him a curious look. He shrugged. "I like batsërs, okay? Whatever, shut up. Anyway, she says that there will be five guards tonight—three Élan, two Trew."

"Five?" whispered Cecelya, still hearing her voice like thunder in the silent night. "Five guards, three Élan? Heavens, how are we going to handle five of them?"

"Let's hope we don't have to. I'm not very good with a bow."
He gestured to the arrows and bow slung across his back—a
safety measure only which they hoped they wouldn't have to
use. "And I don't like you in that," he said, nodding to the
masterform.

"It's all for show, remember," said Cecelya and squeezed his
hand. She didn't worry about the bow, or the masterform; she
had another part to play. "Do you have it?"

Pojk crouched down and zipped open his bag. He pulled
out an eight-shaped object with six strings running across its
body, just like she had ordered. After handing it to Cecelya, he
also drew out a long stick, this one also ordained with a tight
string. It was the smallest and ugliest violin she had ever seen,
barely worth carrying that noble name, but as long as it made
sounds, it would work. The Craft Division had done as well as
they could with the tools and short time at hand. She returned
it and put the bag gently in the boat. They needed no accidents.

Together they managed to push the boat across the shore
and down to the waterline, where it waddled in the shallow
water. Pojk held it still while Cecelya climbed on board, pushed
her out until the water came to his knees, and then climbed
in himself. He sat at the oars while Cecelya was in the front,
checking the water so that they didn't run aground. They rowed
out, or Pojk did, until the boat was bobbing about half a mile
from the island. From their position the sound would travel all
the way, certainly, and they would have a good head start on any
attackers to flee if needed. Both of them hoped there would be
no need for such action, but felt more comfortable at a distance
anyway.

The current rocked the boat to and fro, the cold quiet night
singing its lullaby to the creatures of the dark. Despite the chill
they sat as still as they could, ignoring the shivering urging to
break out in legs and arms; neither of them wanted to fall into

the water, especially not without life jackets. Ahead, basking in moonlight, the Bank held its square poise proud and cold in the glimmering shine. Nothing moved around it at the present time, but soon, soon it would. It was the calm before the storm.

"How long?" Cecelya asked, feeling the shivers shoot through her wrists and into her hands. She blew hot air into them, sadly noting the loss of sensation in her injured fingers. She blew harder. Her hands had important work to do tonight.

"We're early." Pojk looked at the position of the moon. "I'd say we give them another few minutes to reach the portal."

Cecelya nodded and turned to the island. Where were they now, the others? The tunnel was several miles long and they would be travelling mostly in darkness, although the torch would help some. Tryll would lead them straight. At the end of the path was the entrance, the secret passageway that led straight into the Bank, which Cecelya herself had helped construct in her very first days in Obbsborn Z. It had been a joyous moment for everyone, she remembered with a smile, and she had felt strangely part of the celebration, despite the novelty of it all. Pojk had made sure of that.

"Are you thinking of home?" asked Pojk and Cecelya turned back to him, smiling.

"Just about our friends," she replied. "I hope they find the way."

"Tryll knows it well enough," he said, echoing Cecelya's own thoughts.

They had known each other a few weeks, but she already felt as though he could see right through her. He had taken her under his wing from day one, cared for her, initiated her into Obbsborn life, made her into one of their own. He had made her forget, at times, where she had come from. Neither of them mentioned the topic, but the fatal question was their third passenger. Of course it was on both of their minds, although it remained unspoken for now. Pojk opened his mouth and Cecelya knew that he was about to speak the forbidden, so she leaned in and silenced him with a kiss. Lips pressed together hard, as if to crush or confuse the most painful thought of all. When they broke apart, she couldn't decide what it had meant, or what she had thought it meant.

"Let's not talk about it," she said with tearful eyes. She blinked over and over. The tears were relentless. "We have to focus on this now or there will be nothing to talk about at all."

"Got it," he said and the night filled with silence, interrupted only by their harmonious breathing and the crashing waves. It lasted a minute. "But just so you know ..."

"Don't."

"... if you have a life to go back to, I must let you. You must go. Don't let me hold you back."

"I'm not listening," said Cecelya.

"I'm not like you. I don't have anyone who misses me." There was a reason Pojk didn't trust easily. The ghost of his dead sister passed by as a cold breeze and reminded Cecelya of what he had told her.

"It was an accident," said Cecelya when Pojk sunk into some trance-like state, clearly reliving moments from Wind, the past he had left behind until recently.

His sister had died in Wind, under peculiar circumstances because of which Pojk had been pointed out as a murderer and a traitor—him, a traitor! It hadn't mattered in the end because the valley had fallen and most of the Obbsborn died. Cecelya was the only one in Obbsborn Z who knew about it; not even Klepta had been invited to share his dark secret. He had managed to stand up straight again after he told her, something he had failed to do in many years. And now his back was hunched, his hands covering his face, and he saw the terrible events all over again. The ghost had set her claws into him and all Cecelya wanted to do was scream at it to leave him alone.

A desperate flame clutched her, one that would kill the ghost, burn it to ashes. She gave voice to the hot opportunity: he could come with her, leave Ma'zekaï and Obbsborn and live with her in Vildaell. To herself she added silently, *the ghost won't find you there.*

"Yeah," said Pojk with a sad smile when the spectre had left the boat, swimming off to new distances. "The low profile as a Curfew returnee slash run away from the law. Shouldn't cause any curiosity."

"Except you'd not be a returned Curfew person," corrected Cecelya, but she saw that he hadn't been talking about himself.

"Me, I'm not even sure the sun won't burn my eyes off," said Pojk with a kind smile. "It's been a long time since I tried."

"I mean it." She was squeezing his hands, not caring about betraying her innermost thoughts. "It'll be fine. You could live with us, I'm sure Mum wouldn't mind. My brothers can be tools, but they're lovely, really. Enton's a solicitor and has a little baby, a son, and Robin, oh, I think you and Robin would get along just fine—and Freja is friends with him too so you can all spend time together being … being …"

When he stroked her hair she knew he was still blind to the possibility. "It's a fantasy, Ceci," he whispered, his face so close to hers she could feel the hot breath accompanied by the words. He brought her forehead to his, a hand gently placed on the back of her head, and their bodies touched. "But I'll live in that fantasy for now. I don't want to feel like we're saying goodbye."

Cecelya closed her eyes and joined him in the dream. Her lower lip quivered, but not from the cold.

Silence once more claimed the night and fell over the small boat in the vast sea. The cradling moon was still high in the sky, whisking light over the still surface; the village in the bay was quiet and calm, and so it would hopefully remain; and across on the island, the lights were still off. The two sat leaning against each other until Pojk mumbled that it was time. As they broke apart Pojk dried the wetness on Cecelya's cheeks with his thumbs and held her face in his hands afterwards. No words were spoken now, because none were needed.

Cecelya unzipped the bag with a sharp rasping sound and brought out the violin and the fiddle-stick and precariously stood up in the boat, which rocked in the opposite direction to her movements and made it all one big bold balancing act. With only one good leg it was nigh on impossible to sway the bobbing boat, despite Pojk's best efforts to keep it still. Then, as suddenly as it had started, the rocking stopped and the boat became still as though some creature of the sea had heard their plight and reached up to still her stage. She breathed in, breathed out. It was show time. The tunes leapt off the strings as they should and she found, despite the clumsy composition from her damaged and soon aching fingers, the right rhythm after a few sour notes. It was the last piece she had written in Vildaell. The notes were part of her; grown into the cells of her brain and hands like nerve ends of her own, and the melody came out in her fingers as naturally as breathing to her lungs. It was as though the whole landscape inhaled and listened, afraid to break the stride of harmonious notes flowing from the instrument—and why wouldn't it? No violin had ever played before in Ma'zekaï. This was the birth of music to a world of silence.

She saw nothing but the stretched-out blanket of the sea and the tunes she imagined soaring out from the body of the violin as the fiddle-stick skipped and drew over the strings; pale and transparent, the notes bobbed in the air and floated out towards the island, towards their goal, like floating bombs with nothing but good power within. Almost in synchronicity with her visualisation, in the moment her imaginary notes reached the island, which was not even a minute after she started playing, a light appeared.

"Here we go," whispered Pojk, whom she had almost forgotten was there as well. One light after the other appeared on the southern side of the Bank like glow worms close to water. He picked up binoculars, also courtesy of Craft, and peered towards the island. "Three Masters on the shore facing sort of south, south-west," he said as he observed the evolving scene. "I can't tell if they've seen us or not, they're probably following the sound."

Cecelya was still playing, but less controlled now as the flow had been broken. All she needed to do now was make sounds, any sounds. A few sour notes breached the melody, but she didn't care. "Élan?" she asked and kept her fingers moving. "Pojk, talk to me!"

"Oh, there's the fourth … I think there's one Élan missing, only two of those on the shore are wearing grey. The other two are in green, which must be Trew colours, right? No, no, keep playing, they're still trying to figure out where it's coming from." He swore. "Still no fifth guard. We want all of them out."

"Maybe they're spreading? Across the island, I mean?" Pojk didn't reply instantly, and kept the binoculars pressed against his face. Then he lowered them and Cecelya could see a touch of something fearful in his eyes. It scared her witless because she had never seen him afraid, ever. "What?" she asked again. "*What?*"

"Didn't we say that there wouldn't be a boat on the island?"

"Except when latches have been delivered, that's what Klepta said. And she said that's only at full moon so no, no, there isn't a boat there." She nodded up towards the shard in the sky that was several nights away from the full body of the moon.

"Oh, but there is," said Pojk and threw the binoculars into the open zip bag. "And it's coming this way. Turn the boat."

Cecelya stopped playing and let the violin drop to the bag, no longer concerned with drawing more attention. They had had enough of that.

"Go towards the shore," Pojk continued, "and let's take them as far away from the Bank as possible."

"What if they catch up with us?"

"It's all we can do right now." Pojk pulled a string and the engine came to life. A mechanism inside ran on leaf energy and it rendered the noise to a minimum; it gave out almost nothing compared to the sound of human engines. Of course, this rule applied to the Masters as well.

As Pojk steered away from the island, gliding silently across the water surface, Cecelya grabbed the binoculars and watched the Master boat. Like Pojk had said, two green-clad guards were travelling in it. Their faces were partly concealed in the shadow of moonlight, and it gave them a ghoulish appearance. She could see that there was one man and one woman, both wearing similar expressions of menace and meanness: sharp cheekbones, chins, and angry eyebrows were their common features. They didn't seem to be talking, all their focus directed ahead at what they must be thinking were the latch-stealers of late. They weren't too far off.

She wondered how the other group was doing underground, if they had reached the Bank, if they had any better luck. Her throbbing heart certainly hoped so. "Will we make it?" She asked the question without wanting an answer. Perhaps Pojk didn't want to give one, because he ignored her.

"You know," he said instead. "I've heard you speak of music, I've heard you illustrate it with rocks and wooden sticks." He paused with a small laugh. "You didn't do it justice. That … That was fantastic."

She was going to offer something along the lines of modesty when it happened.

An ear-shattering sound rattled across the sea and Cecelya frantically turned this way and that, scanning across the Klockern with the binoculars. The lights on the island were now far off and didn't provide enough illumination anymore. They were maybe two-hundred metres from the shore. Amidst the dimness she discerned something that was moving and realised with a jerk at her chest that the Masters had changed course and that the sound came from their boat—and that the boat was coming straight towards her and Pojk. If that arrow of fear hit a nerve, then the next crashed through skin and bone. When she saw what had caused the rattling her breath left her body.

She whispered the word, barely audible to even herself and Pojk asked over and over what it was she saw. An invisible bullet wheezed past her ear, missing by millimetres. It woke her up from the paralysis of fear and the severity of the situation smacked her across the cheek. She was shouting now, fear working through her voice, offering it both strength to carry through and, like a fiddle-stick on a string, distressing it into an unmistakable tremor.

"Guns. Since when do Masters have *guns*?"

CHAPTER 30

THE HOLLOW RATTLING sound from outside was the first thing Freja noticed when she had followed Tryll through the portal leading straight into the central hall of the Latch Bank. She stared at companions, asking, but received no reply. They had decided not to speak since they had no idea about the situation outside.

Freja looked around the room. It was a great hall superimposing the entire cavity of the square building, its walls reaching all four corners of the island. Not much land was left for other activities and the dot in the sea existed merely for the sole purpose of the Bank. The walls were solid and unrelenting without windows and the room would've been completely dark if it wasn't for the hundreds—thousands—of crystals that were suspended from the ceiling at various heights. Some hung dangerously low so that a man like Klobb might be safe, but a tall Master would have to watch his head; others were out of arm's reach, hovering in the air like giant stars. Every single one of the crystals was shimmering within with a tender light that shrouded the room in a blurry haze. Without asking Freja knew what they contained.

Latches.

Lulja and Tryll were already at work releasing the lowest-hanging latches from their strings and placing them with careful hands into the bags. As worried as she was, there was no time to dwell on what might or might not be going on outside. Masters didn't have weapons, she remembered. She shook off the ill-boding feeling growing inside her and collected five latches that hung at head-level.

Like Tryll had signed, voiced by Lulja, earlier, Alfons would have been too short for this task and it was just as well that he wanted to keep watch.

Soon their bags were bulging with latches and the room was significantly darker. Freja reacted to a 'psst!' from Lulja and turned to see her and Tryll in the middle of the room, standing on what looked like a trap door in the ground, ornamented with a tree—the Willow—and some unintelligible scribbling. When she reached them, Tryll pointed up towards the ceiling, or rather a crystal. It was smaller than the others, diamond-shaped, with a faint purple glow rather than the usual silver. This crystal was the only of its kind, Freja realised as she quickly scanned the remaining bulbs of silver light hanging higher than they could reach.

"The Trinity Latch," said Freja with a small gasp and without needing Tryll's confirming nod, she knew that she was right. The only latch in Master possession leading to the third *landskapë*, still unknown to all of them. The one hope the Obbsborn had left. Leverage, Cecelya had said. Freja certainly saw the potential leverage in the delicate purple latch.

Tryll made a climbing motion, his hands cycling up and down as if grabbing on to invisible shafts.

"Ladders," said Lulja and followed Tryll to the other side of the room.

"Craft Division?" Freja asked with obvious effort as they set down the heavy metal double-step ladder. Tryll nodded in reply. "How in the world did you smuggle this in here?"

"They didn't," said Lulja. "The Élan need to reach the latches too, right?"

"Élan put it here?" Freja couldn't quite picture the Lords, though she hadn't met them, climbing a ladder.

Lulja nodded. "It's funny—Masters are funny people," she said and then frowned. "Horrible, but funny too."

There were three smaller ladders as well and they placed these across the room to reach the higher-placed crystals. Soon they were picking latches like common apple thieves and Freja suffered some memory flashbacks from childhood when she and Robin had been roaming Mr Nagel's trees. Even then she had kept to the ground, catching the fruit picked by Robin, just like she now remained on the floor and took latches collected by Lulja and put them in the bags. It was highly efficient work. Before, the Obbsborn had only had time to take one or two latches at a time, but now, thanks to the diversion which seemed successful, Freja had already lost count and estimated that there were at least a hundred small crystals in her bag, and as many in the others'.

After fifteen minutes the room was drawn into darkness and the light was centred on the purple latch and a few glowing silver crystals around it, just bright enough for them to work in. From the threshold, Alfons had turned and was holding the torch like a dwarf guarding some ancient treasure. He was eyeing them with mixed thrill and fear; he knew what would happen next.

It was time to get the final prize. The three stood straight below the Trinity Latch, gazing up towards the gleaming light. The tallest ladder had been placed underneath and all one of them had to do was climb up and hope their arms were long enough to reach the precious crystal and that the Obbsborn calculations had been accurate. From the ground it was impossible to tell whether it was high enough or not. Nervous eyes glanced at each other. Freja knew as well as the others that without this latch the Obbsborn would not let them go: it was the agreed price for the help and co-operation, and if it wasn't paid Freja and Lulja would have breached the agreement. In this latch lay a multifaceted ticket to freedom and flight as well as fight. Freja dispelled these thoughts and looked to Lulja and Tryll, who were both equally entranced by its shimmering surface. She knew that they saw it too—every possibility, every chance and opportunity contained within that washed-out purple light.

"I'll go?" said Lulja somewhat unconvincingly and grabbed hold of one of the side bars, placing one trembling foot on the first step. "Here, take the rocks so I don't smash it." She froze. "Wow, what if I smash it?"

"You won't smash it," said Freja with an encouraging smile, eager to let Lulja take the high mission. "Give me those."

But when Lulja opened her bag to empty its contents, Tryll's hand flew out and held her back. He shook his head and placed his deep dark eyes on Freja; his pointed finger needed no verbal instruction, no words—words he didn't have anyway—as it selected the girl in purple as its target. In an unnecessary clarifying gesture he then turned this pointed finger from Freja and up to the crystal with the same shade of lilac.

"She should do it?" Lulja didn't quite manage to conceal the tone of relief and let out a small whimper when Tryll confirmed in a slow nod, never taking his eyes off Freja, who was now knitting her eyebrows and swallowing hard. "Well," continued Lulja and snatched back the rocks from Freja's frozen hands, "I won't argue with an Obbsborn." She wasted no time in leaving the ladder, which shook with a hollow rattle as she jumped off.

It stilled and was free for the next climber, but Freja wasn't too keen on clambering some thirty metres up—one hundred steps, according to Tryll—in the air on a simple metal ladder made by disgruntled Obbsborn without a safety net below to catch her if she fell. The world swayed for a moment, spun in her head, and Freja had to shift her right foot to stabilise the imbalance.

They were already wasting precious time. Though she had managed to suppress the fearsome ideas of the concealed actions outside, Cecelya and Pojk could only hold off the guards for a limited period. Already, they had taken a long time. "How much more time?" she asked while emptying her bag of the dirty rocks, handing them over to Lulja who greedily accepted the token of safety. In that moment Freja felt some annoyance directed at her supposed friend; but then again, had Freja offered to take Lulja's place? No. Tryll held up five fingers: ten minutes according to the system they'd worked out beforehand. She turned to the ladder. "You sure?" she said but didn't look to see Tryll nod once more.

The ladder was hardly exemplary in terms of Health & Safety, something Freja found out when she grabbed the sides a bit too violently, resulting in the ladder shifting a centimetre or two to the left. Tryll was quick to steady it and he gestured for Lulja to hold on to the other side, which she happily did. Anything not to be on it. Freja suppressed the urge to make a face at her. "Catch me if … you know," she said.

"Don't be silly," said Lulja. "You're gonna … you know."

"Yeah."

Focusing her mind on steadying the tremor in her hands, Freja began the ascent. The lower parts of the ladder were easy enough but the further up she went, the shakier the journey became. With every step she mumbled, "don't look down, don't look down" until her mind skipped the first word and she looked down, and she nearly swayed off the step and the ladder altogether. Only halfway up, the ground already seemed miles away. Fifty steps lay below her feet, fifty remained. After a deep breath, fresh air rejuvenating her lungs, she continued. Counting the steps helped soothing the violent waves crashing and roaring inside her like the worst of sea storms. Thirty-two, thirty-one, thirty … Or was it forty? From below Lulja stage-whispered something she couldn't hear. With the crystal coming closer, she decided it could wait and increased her pace, hoping that her sweaty hands wouldn't slip and leave her falling helplessly to a certain bone crushing death.

All of a sudden she was at the top.

The fantasies of falling had distracted her enough to lose count and lose all track of progression, and she only realised she had reached the top when there were no more side bars to grab.

Unfortunately, she realised with a sinking heart, the crystal was even further up. The Obbsborn had miscalculated the height. She saw that the only way to reach it would be to stand on the top platform and reach out for it—without anything to hold on to. Don't look down, don't look down. A trembling breath later she had pulled herself up to the platform and settled onto her knees, knuckles white and muscles screaming from the effort. Cold sweat was trickling down her back, and her hands were slippery. She wiped them on the masterform, eyes straight ahead. She forced herself not to look down, fearing how her head might react if she did. Fainting now was not an option.

Instead she focused up towards the ceiling where the last crystal hung, glimmering like a lustrous fish diving into dark waters. Its purple shimmer was faint and delicate, like a candle that might go out at a mere breath too many in its presence. That something so small and fragile could carry such magnitude as this dainty crystal did was beyond comprehension, and for a moment Freja was lost in its mystical centre where, for a second, she thought she could discern the other *landskapë* just beyond the glass …

"Just take it," yelled Lulja, the pressure of time clinging to her voice like an imprint.

Freja snapped back to the present and pushed herself up to a crouching position, causing the ladder to sway precariously along with her, and a cold shudder travelled through her body. With one final effort, Freja stood up and reached out for the crystal, momentarily forgetting all about height and distances; a thick silence forced out everything else and pressed like cotton to her consciousness. A whimper erupted from her throat as she felt her fingers close around the glass shape, felt its warmth and purring life vibrate against her skin. With a swift jerk of the wrist it came loose from its string and Freja fell down to her knees again, safe on the platform. Once her furious heart had slowed to a decent rhythm, she dared a look downwards and waved the crystal in triumph.

The descent was easy and fuelled by the comfort of success. Both Lulja and Tryll stared at the crystal in disbelief as Freja came to the last step. She held it up in the dark and even Alfons had braved his way in from the portal into the Bank and stood a few metres away, admiring their treasure.

Freja could only imagine what it must mean to Tryll, who was marvelling at it, wide eyed. The ideas that were floating in his head now that they had the ultimate weapon; that dream they had barely dared to conjure up in their minds. It was far from worthless for her, of course. With the latch in her hand she felt comfortable disarming the safety measures and the fences she had put up in her mind, just for a brief moment. This crystal was her way home—the way for anyone amongst the Curfew victims who wanted to go back. For Cecelya. There was no way she would leave without her; the idea of facing

Robin, telling him that she had found his sister, but left her—impossible. Cecelya would come, and Pojk too if it couldn't be helped, and someone else as well …

Since their stay in Obbsborn, Freja had devised a plan. It all depended on timing and the progress of the Flÿght. Without the latches, the Élan couldn't proceed with the border opening and the Flÿght could hardly intrude on Heim. Keeping the borders closed was crucial in order to give her time, time to warn the authorities and do what she needed to do. It wasn't just Cecelya she needed to bring back. If Curfew was equal to Obbsborn, then her mother was somewhere underground in Ma'zekaï. First, however, Freja would go back to Amérle, find her father and tell him everything was all right—and Robin too. There were so many possible endings, and all of them contained within this tiny purple crystal.

A fearful squeal from Alfons shifted her attention in an instant. He screeched and bolted at the first sound, leaving the fading torch dropped on the ground where it turned to ashes. Then the voice,

"Attend!"

It echoed through the dark room and Freja felt the ladder lurch as her two companions jerked in surprise and she stepped down from it, quickly shoving her hand into her bag, hiding the latch. Nobody would take it from her, not after what she had gone through to get it. Her heart sank to undiscovered depths when the person came closer, a torch in his hand, and she saw the grey masterform. Élan.

They had missed their chance. Thick dizziness filled her head, making the world blurry and unstable while burning hot failure sizzled faint in her chest, scorching and harsh, bringing tears to her eyes. All the plans, all the opportunities she had allowed herself to feel—gone. They had been so close, so close. If she had climbed faster, reached quicker, not jumped to conclusions and happy endings in her mind before completing their mission …

The Élan Master didn't say anything else, just stared at the four of them. Freja felt the Master's eyes fix on her and she tightened her grip on the latch inside the bag. She moved her gaze from the floor to the black boots, up to the sombre grey of the masterform and the black hair with streaks of silver in it—and recognised him. At the same time, the Master's puzzled expression straightened out into full recognition as well and there was no need for either of them to attest to their identity, as Lulja now ordered the Master to do. He took no notice of the order. Lulja shouted again. But the Master was watching Freja, and Freja was watching the Master as though floating outside her own body. "Attend, Master," Freja said in a low voice.

"You know who I am," he said without expression. "But I will tell your friends, who might not be privy to the information." He reached around his back and brought out an object Freja had not expected to see in the natural world of Masters. The gun glistened in the flickering light of the torch, its silver exterior and open barrel glaring directly at Freja. "I am Elflock of the Élan."

*

Outside the fort, about a mile outside the island shore, the Masters in green approached the two bodies lying face down in the water beside the abandoned rowing boat with a 'T' at its head. No visible wounds penetrated the skin nor did any blood discolour the clear water, but there was no life left in the young humans. The Tech Division had exceeded themselves in combining the natural power of the leaves with machinery to create a hybrid weapon which allowed the carrier to aim the destructive energy from a distance.

"Obbsborn and one false masterform," said the Master

in the front of the boat and poked at the bobbing bodies in the water. No response came in return. "Perished." Grabbing the girl by the collar, the Master pulled her up and stripped her temples of the bright lapis gems. She held them up in the moonlight. "Flÿght. Klepta will see Essence spill for this."

"Unless it is her Essence that spills first," said the other as he turned the boat and sped soundlessly back towards the island. There was no need to waste precious energy on the corpses; soon enough the tide would wash them ashore and wild animals would take care of the rest.

CHAPTER 31

IT WAS AS if the world had frozen in time and space. In those seconds of complete and utter stillness the quietude of the night announced its presence and Freja's stomach lurched, making her flinch and she was glad she had her feet firmly on the ground again. There was a gun, cold and unforgiving, and she was a mere press of a finger away from being shot. Of dying.

Her hand was still in the bag, clutching the Trinity Latch. The bag. Rocks. They weren't entirely defenceless. She risked a glance at Tryll who he gave her an almost imperceptible nod and then threw his first rock. Freja had let go of the latch only to remember that she had given her rocks to Lulja. She was unarmed.

The rocks landed on the ground with a loud echo, forcing Elflock of the Élan to back away and duck under the shower of stones. Another one from Tryll spun in the air, had better aim, and was surging towards Elflock's head—where it would have hit, had the Master not managed to raise a hand just in time and prevent it from smacking into his eye. In the commotion, the gun went off. A loud echoing rapid-fire cracking filled the space, bore into every crevice and every bit of the hollow; ear deafening and hollow like cotton pads, forceful and relentless; one, two shots whistled round the building.

Out of the corner of her eye Freja saw Tryll grab on to Lulja's arm and pull her back towards the portal. She would follow them. Only she couldn't. A white searing pain was tearing through her flesh in her left arm. Kneeling on the floor, she touched the painful area, expecting blood and gore, but found nothing but a pale white line in the fabric, barely visible. Still, the pain remained. Though it sent electrified shocks through her entire arm, she angled it so that she could see the spot where the bullet had hit, but couldn't find it. There was nothing physically wrong with her arm, but the ripping sensation inside, as though her muscles were clipped one by one from the bone, was real enough. She heard her name being called but couldn't reply. Everything was black and white dots around her, no contours or contrasts, just a world of polka dots dancing in a frenzy. She leaned over, buried her face in her knees, and held on to the arm, screaming inside—or was it out loud?—until the voices came nearer. One voice. A deep soothing calm voice speaking words that were healing, at least to her mind, or her head was shutting down from the pain. She had read that somewhere, that when the pain got too severe the body would flick the off switch until it was ready to cope with it. Switch off, Freja thought. Switch off!

But instead of moving further into darkness, Freja felt herself return and the polka dots popped one by one. Slowly, like venom sucked out from a vein, the pain floated down her arm to the elbow and then vanished into thin air. The sounds around her emerged as though from below water and became clear. It was Lulja, yelling at Tryll.

"He had a gun," she shouted. "A gun!"

"I did not intend to fire," said another voice—the voice, the soothing deep voice she had heard before.

"Shut up," said Lulja with acidity. "Tryll, what were you thinking?"

Obviously no reply came from Tryll and Freja thought it was rather unfair to scream at somebody who couldn't scream back, and was about to say so when the words stuck in her throat like a jammed car queue and she started coughing.

"She's back." Lulja's face came into view as Freja peeled her eyes open and blinked away the dryness in her eyes. "Freja?"

"Move," said the deep voice and Lulja shifted to the side. Freja's body tensed when Elflock leaned over her, a frown creating a deep furrow between his eyebrows just like her father. "Are you feeling all right?"

A laugh bubbled up inside Freja, a harsh cold laugh, and she was about to let it out and give a snarky reply referring to the fact that he had shot her when she stopped herself. The words weren't stuck anymore, but she hindered them herself. Because she was feeling all right. The pain had vaporised, she could move her arm as usual and her head was clear. Nothing ached, seared, or even itched; a minute tingle at what would have been the entrance wound jingled like nothing more than a tickle. It was impossible. She had felt the bullet hit, felt the wound being torn open like a rock cleaves the water surface. She was about to ask when, as if on cue, from Elflock's hand fell the residues of a charred leaf.

Of power and destruction; of power and creation.

"Yes," she said, confused. "Yes, I'm fine."

"Good," said Elflock and let Lulja push forward again, this time with Tryll close by. "Forgive me, it was not my intention to harm you. In fact, Éloyse sent me."

All three of them stared at him in various kinds of disbelief—from scepticism to wonder.

"How do we know you're not lying?" Lulja was clearly, and

unsurprisingly, the sceptic. "You just shot Freja."

"For which I am deeply sorry," Elflock said again.

"Don't worry about it," said Freja and sat up. She had learned that Éloyse was full of surprises and she sincerely hoped this was one of them. Elflock had, after all, been hostile to Topster. She had seen it herself.

"Where are the other guards?" Lulja had her arms crossed and tilted her head in anticipation of the reply. She was determined to find fault. "What's going on outside?"

"There was noise from the sea," Elflock said and fell into a thoughtful stance. "Strange noise, like crickets singing, only ... different. I've never heard crickets sing in such a manner."

Freja thought of Cecelya struggling with her damaged hands to find the notes she harboured inside like a second heartbeat. "That wasn't crickets, that was music," she said. "It's beautiful, isn't it?" Elflock hummed in affirmation. Freja searched for his gaze. "What happened?"

When they heard the noise, said Elflock, two guards of the Trew had been sent to sea to find the source of the sound while the Élan Masters protected the island. The other two were stationed at the south side for now, awaiting the return of the Trew Masters.

"Sent to sea?" Freja's blood froze and nausea filled the back of her throat, making her gasp for air. The absent sounds—the same sound that had erupted from the gun in Elflock's hands—became suffocating; the silence was too much but she found no words with which to fill it. Thankfully, Lulja did.

"You're Élan," she said. "You're directly under the Lords, I know this. Ravn told me. He said that you must carry out the work of the three Lords, no matter what, like a contract. I think this situation seems 'no matter what' inclusive, wouldn't you say?"

"The Lords are intent on continuing on their path," Elflock

said, carefully and consciously choosing his words all the while glancing upwards as though listening to the sounds from the outside. "Unless we find evidence of the Flÿght's intentions, they will not set aside time or effort to stop them." He paused. "There are a number of ways in which they may be convinced, some bad and some worse. The Élan is divided, as is the Trew. Only the Flÿght seem united—and that is the most precarious thing of all." He stopped and the let the message sink in.

"You believe us?" Freja asked, her voice spotted with equal parts suspicion and pleading. "You believe the Flÿght is taking over Heim?" Elflock looked at her, sincerely regarded her, and she felt that tingling sensation again like she did whenever Topster watched her like that; as if he could see right through her.

"Tiora," Elflock said as if he just remembered. "Of the Flÿght."

"Actually, it's Freja. Freja Evenson, of nothing." She felt Tryll's and Lulja's asking looks but didn't take her eyes off the Master. "Topster is not my uncle."

"Evenson?" Elflock said in a neutral tone with some underlying tension that Freja could not place. When she confirmed he observed her in such a peculiar manner, deeply and thoroughly as though searching through every corner of her face, like you might with someone you've met before but cannot place. He was dissecting her features like a pathologist, categorising, severing, adjusting.

"This is that Master? The one you met on the fields?" said Lulja and Tryll nudged her arm again with a kind smile. "Sorry, carry on."

Instantly Elflock seemed to exit from his trance and he took a moment to link back to the conversation. "What was I saying …? Yes, Éloyse was speaking fast so I did not understand it all, but this explains it," he said. "I understood she had done something she was not proud of, something that would compromise her situation here and that could have consequences for the entire valley, though she did not know so at the time. She did not act with destruction in mind." He paused as if to ensure this fact was accepted. "She placed the latch in Heim, Freja. She took you to Topster, on his command of course."

A tension so profound and all-powering took over Freja that she thought her heart had stopped. She hiccupped. Inhaled. Exhaled. Bit her lip to stop the tears from falling. She had cried enough for a life time already. But the sensation only intensified. Éloyse, her one friend and ally here. Éloyse, of all people. Sure, it was before they met but if what Elflock said was true … Éloyse! It was not possible and yet the truth at the same time. The equation failed to register in her mind. No.

"When I met you two in the village I thought she was providing him with more crops or seeds for Klobb, she has done so in the past. Only now do I see, understand, that it was you under the cover, on the Transporter."

"You were the Master in grey," Freja said with a loud inhalation which got caught in her blocked throat, causing her to choke a little on it. She went back to that first day in Ma'zekaï, tried to remember what had happened. She had gone through the gate with nothing but woods and open field ahead, when— "Éloyse was waiting for me to come through? She wasn't just passing by, was she?" Elflock sighed and that was answer enough. With a large portion of irony, Freja laughed. "And the thing on the street? Was that like a—a magical shadow or something?" It was clear from Elflock's frown that he did not understand what she was talking about. Neither did Lulja, nor Tryll, because they asked what she meant by 'shadow'. "The shadow. The—the thing that I went after before I fell into the latch at the Dump. The shadow!" She found no words to better describe it. If she said it had looked like her mother, they'd all think her crazy, or crazier at least. Given the puzzled looks aimed her way, they already thought she was. She waved it off. "Whatever. No shadow."

"Okay, no shadow," said Lulja, patting Freja on the shoulder in such an undignified way that it made Freja snatch her arm back, stretching her tongue out in jest. "Elflock, why would Éloyse go and escort a human across the valley on Topster's orders?" she then asked with reproach.

"Do not ask me why," said Elflock, adding a small smile that stretched his mouth and revealed a row of straight white gleaming teeth. He had a hypnotising smile, Freja thought. "She has helped Topster with much before, crops and the like, although not this extreme. Again, I cannot answer your question."

Freja suspected she could. The meeting at the village came back to her in full now, like a recorded video that played in her head. She remembered it all. He had even said the abhorred word himself and made Éloyse furious at the very idea. Perhaps she knew that there was some truth in it, perhaps she was denying it to herself. To be biased was no virtue neither here nor in the human world.

"What do we do now?" Freja asked, pushing the love drama aside. That was for the involved to sort out.

The answer came from Tryll who might have been thinking it for a while. He was gesturing towards the portal.

"Tryll's right," said Lulja who gave him voice. "Before anything else, we need to get out of here. Those guards will be coming soon."

"There is still time," said Elflock. "The guards will not act until I return. But I agree, we ought to leave. I suppose you have an alternative way in?" At this Tryll and Lulja exchanged looks, suspicion still ripe. "My duty with the Lords is hereby finished," Elflock said with reverence as he stood up. "From now on we are the same, you and I."

"We'll see about that," muttered Lulja as Tryll led them to the portal.

Before she trod down the small steps on the other side of the round exit Freja turned back to the Bank, now abandoned in the dark, ladders placed across the room. It was now nothing but a crime scene where the gorgeous play of light on the walls and on the ceiling was relinquished to mere shadows veiled in more ghostly shapes of darkness, the lonely strings lacking their most precious property. She crouched through the portal and let Tryll close it behind her. It melted into the wall as if it had never been there in the first place.

The journey back felt longer and darker—and heavier, given the large number of latches clucking against each other in their saddle bags, but they soon emerged back into Obbsborn were the large crowd gathered around them asking how it had gone, what would happen next, and how could they help? They let Elflock sneak towards the exit without being seen and he was hiding in an adjacent tunnel in where the others would meet him as soon as they had soothed the crowd and informed them of the latest plan. Incessant chatter continued until Tryll leapt up on a chair and held out his hands, miraculously silencing the prattle altogether. The Obbsborn watched him with intense curiosity, a light glimmering in their eyes that Freja had not seen before. The information was met with loud protestations and insults being thrown their way. The Obbsborn didn't want to be left behind at all.

"We will come back for you," Lulja tried, but to no avail.

The Obbsborn yelled about being abandoned, about being left behind, saying that it was a plot to kill them all. Someone asked what Masters had given them to sell out their friends, their family. Not until Alfons stepped up next to Tryll on the chair, balancing with some difficulty, did they quiet down. "We have all risked a lot tonight," he said. "Everyone in here, but especially these guys and Cecelya and Pojk, who are waiting to meet up above ground. Trust them. If for nothing else, then for that fact alone. If they say they'll come back, they will. I trust they will." He turned to Tryll. "Is there anything we can do?"

"Try to act as normal as possible," said Lulja. "We don't know how long it'll take, but we will return as soon as we can."

"As soon as we can," repeated Freja with an extra push at the 'soon'. In the crowd she saw Tessandra Wilkins' face, inquiring, hopeful, eager.

"You hear that? As soon as they can." Alfons jumped down from the platform. He was grinning. "Now we act as if delivery day was tomorrow, which means—" he tapped an invisible watch on his wrist— "we have a lot to do." Muttering, but less discontent than before, the Obbsborn scattered and returned to work.

Alfons lingered behind. "You are coming back, right?" He was still grinning and watching the Obbsborn pick up their work as if it was a regular day without surprises.

"Yes," said Freja. "But we have to see what's going on before you start your revolution." Alfons looked at her. "We're coming back," she said again, hoping it was true, sensing that he could hear the sliver of doubt in her voice. Who could promise anything now?

"Tell Pojk I'll be happy to see him," said Alfons with a cheeky grin. He had dimples, Freja realised, like Robin.

"You tell him yourself," said Freja with a smile. Before she could bid him goodbye, he had hurried off to his bench and was measuring fabric for a masterform.

They left Obbsborn Z through the tunnel where Klepta had taken them on that first day. The steps were moist from the chill of the night and the moon shone a clear light right down the opening. Dawn was still hours away. The night was clear and cold but all four of them relished the fresh air as they climbed out of the underground. Following Elflock, the expert of these lands, they headed out from the village like thieves, through winding alleys cast in shadows, avoiding the open paths in case some late night wanderer would come upon them. He led them north-west, towards the sea and in the direction of the Willow tree. Somewhere close to the shore, Éloyse would have hidden the Transporters.

They had decided that Topster's cottage was the place to go; nobody would look for them there. When Freja had, impatient and eager to set foot on Vildaell soil again, asked why they couldn't just use the latches here, Elflock had explained that whenever a latch was used it sent out vibrations into any nearby Essence—it was part of the same network and linked by invisible threads, like nerves. When the energy balance in a latch was disrupted by transferral of a body, the threads, or nerves, contracted as they would in a muscle, and the carrier of the Essence would feel it. There was too much Essence around the village to risk stepping through, but if they went to the cottage it was highly unlikely that the vibrations would reach all that way. Besides, Cecelya and Pojk would be waiting for them there. She couldn't spot the boat that had been involved in the plan, so she hoped they were already at the cottage, bantering with Klobb. The thought made her smile.

"Won't the Élan know you've helped us? When they see you're gone?" Freja asked as soon as they had reached a concealed patch of trees where they sat down to rest and to decide what route to take.

"We are beyond loyalty now. Some of the Élan, not including the guards, have also seen what the Flÿght is doing and we have brought it to the attention of the Lords. They will not listen. They will not recognise such power in their hearts," he said with a grim expression. "It is the most dangerous thing not to acknowledge great passion. But the Lords are not unfair—if they see evidence, real proof, they will act." He concluded that with the latches in their possession, they had leverage.

"So we go tell them," said Freja.

Elflock shook his head. "It's too late," he said. "The Lords are far away, I happen to know, and the Flÿght is getting closer by the minute. If I had to guess, I would say that they are moving as we speak and that we may not have much time to stop them."

"Until morning," said Freja, realising what was about to happen.

"What?"

The pattern dawned on Freja. "I know what they're planning," she said and made a quick calculation. "Curfew." She explained her suspicions and stood up. It was clear now: they had to reach Heim before the eleventh bell.

Elflock followed suit and scanned the landscape. "I see a safe route."

"Let's get the Transporters," said Lulja and leapt up. "Cecelya and Pojk are waiting." Together they left the hiding place and walked another few minutes closer to the sea and the curved beach until they reached the agreed place.

There was nothing but grass and dirt.

They plunged through every bush and shrub in the vicinity, shoved their hands into the dirt by the root of the trees, all the while knowing that had there been Transporters there, they would have seen them. Had Éloyse failed them?

Freja felt her heart tighten again, thinking about the arranged latch, placed by Éloyse, that had led her here. Was it so impossible to think that Éloyse was on Topster's side after all? That she had tricked them? A voice inside, an evil one, hissed that it wasn't—Masters were deceitful, experts at hiding emotion and feigning whatever state of mind was necessary for manipulation. She glanced at Elflock. Was he doing the same? His face was contorted into a rare expression of concern that didn't look fake to her. He was on their side, she decided. This conclusion didn't help soothe the constriction in her chest that amplified swiftly as the realisation sunk in: there were no Transporters there.

Dread flowed over her like rippling waves and she looked out to sea. The island was lit up by torches and stood shrouded in calmness, basking in the moonlight. It gave the Bank building an eerie ghost-like look, like a haunted castle in a gothic novel; rattling chains and forgotten secrets. For a moment she felt as if she was a character in such a story and let it quash the frantic whirlwind inside her. Didn't romantic stories usually have happy endings? Somewhere in her blurred consciousness she heard Lulja's voice, though the sound was warped and distorted into complex noises like bird twitter and Freja shut her eyes tight. She tried to think. Think! How would they get to the cottage and the rest of the latches hidden there? Walking would take forever. If only she'd had her motorcycle, it would've taken them there in no time. But she didn't have it. In her bag was the one item that could save everything—everyone!—and they would fail on logistics.

A warm hand landed on her back and spread some heat in the cold fit of panic while a body crouched beside her. Elflock's kind eyes gave her comfort and he helped her up, asking what was wrong. She told him. "Nothing more?" he said with a frown. "Dry your tears, Freja Evenson. I did not become part of the Élan because of my good looks."

He pursed his lips and gave sound to a loud but clear whistle. A minute passed.

Then the howling began.

CHAPTER 32

THE WHISTLE ECHOED through the landscape and over the fields. It lasted longer than one would imagine a human whistle could. Of course, this was no human whistling. When it faded away into the night and left them alone again, the roar of the sea against the sand banks and the dense silence of the night took over once more; the whistle was out to hunt down its recipient.

"What—" Freja began but Elflock lifted a finger to his mouth and she said no more.

Time passed and there was nothing. Then: howling. Howling from the mountains. Though she didn't know all the nooks and corners of Ma'zekaï, she understood howling and she saw in Lulja's and Tryll's faces that they had reached the same conclusion: fenrirs. 'They'll eat ye alive!' Klobb's words ran through her head and down her spine in a cold shudder.

"Do we run?" she asked, feeling hot stuff build inside again. She put a fist on her chest and the pressure helped, well, a little at least. "Do we run?" She searched for Elflock's attention but his gaze was intent on the distance from which the howling originated; Lulja was staring in the same manner, seemingly frozen in her place; Tryll was looking out towards the sea. It was he who shook his head in reply to her question. No, they would not be running tonight. With two fingers he signed running legs and then crossed his arms like an 'X'. They would not and could not run from the galloping fenrirs. "We're about to be eaten," Freja said with increased urgency. "Some sort of reaction would be nice."

"Let them come," said Lulja in a low voice.

"Come again?" Lulja's sudden death wish was completely new to Freja, and she let her know as much.

"There is no need to be alarmed," said Elflock. "I summoned them." Freja opened her mouth to protest, but he held up a hand and continued, "But I advise you to refrain from speaking or they will recognise that you are human. Fenrirs are excellent listeners, and they do not have a taste for humans … or, rather, they do, depending on how you see it."

Jokes felt sorely out of place, but Freja still found herself smiling.

"It's a Master spell." Lulja edged closer to Freja as Elflock wandered off to keep watch. Tryll sat down with them, facing the waterline, and nodding as Lulja spoke. "Ravn told me about it. Under special circumstances Masters may ask for help from fenrirs—like they do with batsërs. Otherwise Masters are supposed to live independently from all living beings, except the leaves. It's bad karma or whatever. Yes, Tryll, I understand they hardly have religion like we do, so don't give me that look like I'm some airhead. You get the gist." Tryll raised his hands, pretending he had done no such thing and the two exchanged sly smiles.

With a sigh Freja turned to landscape gazing, hoping it would soothe her wild soul, all the while feeling the stress well up inside. A second ago they barely had time to stop for a breath and now she was looking at trees while waiting for fenrirs to find them? Masters made little sense to her, but she had learned to trust Elflock's instinct. They were entirely in his hands now, and there was no turning back on the trust they had instilled in him. He was the reason they were out in the open; why they managed to escape the Bank unharmed. The reason she would see Cecelya again and take her home to her family.

When she looked over to her friends again she saw that Tryll and Lulja's hands were knitted together, resting on the wet grass. She caught Lulja's eye and raised one eyebrow. Lulja's cheeks flushed red and she took hold of Freja's hand too, squeezing it tight with cold sweat.

"Tell me we'll be okay?" she said.

Freja replied by squeezing her hand with a smile, as convincingly as she could muster through fatigue and mental exhaustion. "We'll be okay," she said, mostly because it was something she needed to hear as well, and if Lulja wouldn't speak the words, at least she could do it and hope that they rang true. It helped, but not much. The howling was still distant and came in waves, sometimes lost behind a mountain top. "How long until they get here?" Freja asked, but none of the other two knew.

Elflock replied in their stead. "The den in the mountains is almost ten leagues away, and across the wall. Fenrirs are swift on their feet, but it may be a little while. Use the time to rest." He watched the distant mountains framing the valley as he spoke.

Freja imagined the wolf-like creatures with white cheeks roaming the rocky mountains, cliffs and caves, climbing closer to their caller.

"Yes, Tryll, I'll ask," said Lulja and watched Tryll sign for a minute or so. "A-ha, okay. So Tryll wants to know, and me too, really, what exactly we're doing once we get to Vildaell?"

Elflock showed no hesitation. "We are not the only ones moving tonight," he said and explained that several Trew and some Élan were already in Heim, hunting for old members of the clan who now lived in the human world, trying to regain their loyalty and remind them of old times. "Including one of our old Lords," he continued in elation. "If he will join us again, there is a chance we can make the current Lords listen. He was a subject of admiration and sympathy in his day." Éloyse had gone with Ravn and Neese, both of the Élan, and a fresh Trew Master to find him. A legend of his time, Elflock explained, he was by far the most popular Lord through history, and it had come as a shock when he refused his position after a visit to Heim. It had been a routine check about three generations ago; the Lord had travelled through to see that Masters in Heim were following regulations when collecting energy and sourcing it back to Ma'zekaï the way they should. Every now and then, perhaps three-four times per generation, a Lord went out; otherwise it was usually one of the Élan. On one of these visits he came across a Master who had lived in Heim most of her life. "He became biased," Elflock concluded with raw wretchedness tainting his voice. "And left."

"He abandoned the Lords for a human life?" Lulja exclaimed. "For love?"

"Yes. He found a world where love, or bias, was not a vice and that was worth a lot to him. He left the Master race and settled with her in a different place. She was of the Trew," he concluded almost to himself.

This Lord sounded like a soft one, Freja thought. Very much unlike the cold and emotionally disturbed Masters she had met, who refused to view emotion as anything other than pure evil and mind-crippling waste. Bonds of nature were chains to them, not strings of guidance; affection was weakness; virtue was being obstinate. Here was one Master who had been of stronger earth and been brave enough to author his own life. She decided that she liked this Lord. She asked his name.

"Lord Tej," said Elflock with reverence. "A role model for

many of us. Lord Py, as strong as she is, never quite managed to fill his shoes." He fell silent and a ghost-like shadow of Lord Tej passed, making him inhale the air as if it was the Lord himself, take in his absent aura, letting it give him strength and encouragement. Freja recognised it, because she did the same with the idea of her father.

The water was still, as was the ongoing night. The moon had journeyed in the sky and left the Bank in shadows, throwing its light instead on the shoreline. In a few hours it would leave the sky for the sun to paint it golden and bright, but Freja would not be here to see it. She would be home. The cataracts of dim light cast long shadows across the beach, at times reaching all the way to the waterline. She could easily distinguish the trees thrown flat across the sand like cloned paper cuts of themselves, and there was a mooring for small boats, thick and clumsy like a lump of clay without any visible detail.

But there were another two shapes resting on the plain as well, thicker and more sprawling than tree trunks. She had not seen them before. They weren't shadows, that much she could tell. There was more substance, heaviness, to the way the shapes broke through other, paler, shadows on the sand. Could they be washed-up shafts from the Klockern? She narrowed her eyes and sought to peer through the gloomy light, focusing all her attention on the figures. If they were shafts, they were peculiar ones indeed: one of them had a small sprawling crown while the other had a smooth top, as if it had been cut off. The ivy one almost had the impression of—hair. The instant her brain connected the dots her blood froze up and seemed to hit pause for all bodily activity. It all shut down.

"Freja, are you okay?"

The words were distant and Freja ignored them. She stood up and was breathing heavily, though no oxygen filled her lungs; she began to feel faint; the world spun in a circle, with only the beach standing painfully still, the scene echoing itself over and over; she found her voice.

"Cecelya," she cried out, slapping away Lulja's hand. "Ceci … Pojk … What—?" In Tryll's clenched jaw she saw that he already knew: her worst case scenario—real. She pushed forward, but was held back.

"There is no time, Freja," said Elflock with his hand on her shoulder.

The same words had come out of Cecelya's mouth before but hurt just as bad this time around. There was no time for her mother; no time for Freja—and no more time for Cecelya. When had time become so scarce? Weren't they young enough not to consider it an enemy? One sharp thought after the other battled in her mind, pricking and tearing whatever matter was held in there, and she didn't know whether these thoughts were on her side or not. The world had narrowed to a telescopic view of the two bodies on the shore: one delicate and graceful, the other mature and masculine. She could see them clearly now, at least in her mind. Their faces calm, hair spread out in the sand, fingertips touching. The lapis gems in Cecelya's face. Pojk's ginger hair spotted with sand. Their hands pulled apart once and for all. How would she tell Robin? With the question came a bubble of grief, unfolding and pounding, threatening to burst its potent content and intoxicate her entire being. Maybe it was better if she never went back? No, she decided instantly, it couldn't be. It wasn't true.

She pushed the hand from her shoulder and ran, ran, ran towards the shore on shaking legs that would barely keep her upright. Every step was hollow and void of strength, but some other force had taken over and urged her forward. Before long Elflock caught up with her and grabbed her around the waist mid-step, pulling her back. She squirmed, fighting to escape his arms, but he was too strong. "Your friends did well," he murmured in her ear and, eventually, she stopped struggling and felt her limbs relax, any remaining strength leaving her like evaporating water on a hot day.

Without Elflock she would have fallen to the ground, but he held her up. A violent wave of emotion shook from her core and overflowed her being: shaking her bones; sending bile up her throat and making her gag; causing convulsions. Elflock held her, murmuring in her ear, and she felt less free-falling than she would have done without him. The ground did not quite leave her feet and the attachment to another body anchored her to this world, despite its horrifying content. "There is nothing you can do for them now," the voice whispered in her ear. Perhaps it was Elflock's—it sounded like it—or maybe it was her own inner voice, she didn't know. She blinked and looked towards the dark shore again. For a second she thought one of them moved, ever so slightly, but as hard as she stared afterwards, they lay as still as before. Both their faces were turned away from her and hidden in darkness. It was just as well.

The last time she had seen Cecelya, she had been full of energy and excitement, just like she always was. She had taken Freja aside on the day of the mission—yesterday, though it felt like an eternity ago—with a sly grin on her face. Freja had asked what was up and she'd peered around the corner and glanced sideways to make sure nobody was listening before whispering in hurried and excited sentences, "I'm coming with you. I've decided. I'm going to ask Pojk to come too and we can all go back to Amérle. No, don't say anything—and don't tell anyone." She had been smiling with every feature. "Goodness gracious, Freja, I'm going home!"

Memories have the most peculiar effect on people. For the duration of this one, Freja forgot reality; for the brief interval between dream and past reality and present, she eliminated the terrible fate right in front of her. They were going home. Once the memory passed into history again, it all returned and she saw what had become of that smiling face, now stripped of all emotion; past, present, and future.

"I never answered her question," Freja mumbled, but she was cut short by a loud howling. Close. Elflock twisted her arm and pulled her close. She flinched but didn't find the strength to fight.

"Listen to me now," he said. "Listen with all the Essence in your body."

"I don't—"

"Freja!"

"You killed them!" she burst out, tears springing to her eyes. "Your Master friends ... it's their fault she won't—"

"Listen!" Elflock shot a glance towards the other two who were busy with each other. "There is a chance the Flÿght will have advanced further than we think. No, do not tell your friends, it will only cause them grief and they have had enough of that already, as have you. I am telling you, Freja, because if Topster has done more harm than we can imagine, if we meet him on the streets of Vildaell, if, by some means, he has acquired latches we are unaware of—there is but one place to go. Are you listening? Freja, this is important. In case we get separated, in case it is too late for us to act, you must go to the Red World." Freja frowned at him. "The Red World," he repeated. "The third *landskapë*."

Behind them Tryll and Lulja were seated on the grass, hands braided and quietly watching each other, exploring every feature. Cecelya and Pojk had looked at each other in the same way. Had.

"Are you listening?"

"Yes, Red World," Freja repeated without enthusiasm, as if her brain simply regurgitated its last impressions. She felt like nothing mattered anymore. With Cecelya lost—for sure this time—and her own mother equally lost in this world, what else was there for her to do? To fight for? Topster would take over the *landskapës* and be the villainous dictator and all would live unhappily ever after. All the energy rushed out of her like a tap left open. Elflock kept talking, but his words were dull and uninteresting.

"They are called the Duo, the rulers of the Red World. Twins, brothers. Freja, *listen to me*." He took her shoulders again and shook her like he was a berating parent. But he wasn't her father, she thought. Her father was in Vildaell. Her father, and—

The howling brought her back. It was closer. Louder. Behind, Tryll reacted too and pulled Lulja to her feet, hesitating. He must have seen that the conversation between Elflock and Freja was a private one, and waited. Elflock held still, searching Freja's eyes like Robin once did. Like then, Elflock made her promise to pursue the Duo and plead to them to break the pledge, the ancient pledge signed by all three *landskapës* to protect the Red World from any interaction or flow of information from their neighbours. "The pledge was signed the same year as Masters entered Vildaell," Elflock said. "The Duo wanted nothing to do with such business and the border was closed. You need to bring them back."

"Why don't you tell them yourself?" asked Freja, tired of all the hassle and the rushing around to different worlds. Couldn't someone else do it for a change?

"Because the Trinity Latch is in your bag," said Elflock in a solemn voice.

"Then take it!" she said and offered her bag without removing it from her shoulders. The weight fell back on her with multiplied force when he pushed it back.

"You have picked it, Freja. It is yours."

Freja's hand went instinctively to the flap of her saddle bag under which the purple Trinity Latch rested among the silver crystals. A strange sense of ownership fell over her in line with Elflock's words. The latch was in her bag. She had picked it. Though she was a bit old for playing Finder's-Keeper's, that's what it felt like. It was her latch now. "Okay," she said, drying her cheeks with the palms of her hands.

"Are—are they coming?" Lulja's voice was trembling uncontrollably as she came rushing over, Tryll trailing behind with an apologetic sign. He had not managed to keep her back. Even he seemed shaken by the approaching fenrirs. It was none the better for Elflock's silent confirmation. They were coming.

Not only could they hear low growling—there was galloping. Elflock reminded them to stay quiet, no matter what. But nothing could have made Freja form words when she watched them climb over the last hill and come into full view in the glaring moon. Her voice was locked along with her body. Locked in fear and awe.

The white cheeks announced their arrival: glowing in the darkness like tiny half-moons beckoning across the ground, driven on by some invisible force. The crescent gave their eyes a peculiar and eerie luminosity from below and it created dark tailed shadows leading up towards the ears. The paws, the size of frying pans, were ornamented with substantial, sharp claws, also glimmering white, like the cheeks. As the fenrirs trotted down the slope, their massive bodies gradually became apparent like gliding spectres in the night. Furry and dark-coated ghosts, sleek and shiny, a long tail wagging to and fro with every step. The blood band to wolves was evident, only these were like morphed copies, upgraded doubles, zoomed in for effect. With long effortless strides the pack of fenrirs clawed their way down the small hill towards them. They were graceful creatures despite their body mass, and made almost no interruption to the silent canvas of the night with their luminous paws.

They stopped some three metres away from the Master and lined up one next to the other in front of the little group. There were four of them: one for each of the humans and one for the Master. The smaller of the fenrirs took a step forward the leader. Elflock showed his empty palm and the fenrir bowed its head slightly. The greeting was complete and trust had been established. "Asuka," said Elflock with a warm smile. "I thank you." The fenrir growled in reply and Elflock laughed as if Asuka had said something amusing. He turned to his humans. "They will have to bite you," he said and they stared at him as if he'd made another grim joke. "Trust them, I am a good friend of Asuka, the alpha female. They will not harm you. The bite drains you of energy. Temporarily," he added quickly. "A hollow box is lighter than a full one. Trust me, trust Asuka."

When nobody protested, at least not in words, Elflock gestured to the fenrirs that they were ready. Still half-heartedly hoping that she would go to sleep and never wake up, Freja offered to go first. She held up her open palm to show she was unarmed and her fenrir, a fat one with the lightest fur in the pack, named Yna, bowed. Instructed by Elflock, she held out her arm.

"Please be quick," she said before she was able to stop herself. She slapped a hand over her mouth and waited for the fenrir to react. But Yna just smirked, if fenrirs could smirk at all, and Freja closed her eyes, waiting for the pain. But it didn't come. Instead, she felt soft edges like foam rubber close around her wrist and a seeping sensation appeared where the fenrir sunk her teeth into her arm.

"Next," said a voice far away.

Before she could sense anything else—

CHAPTER 33

"GOAT—WAKE UP," said a gruff voice and a sticky finger dug into her soft cheek once, twice. "No time to sleep."

Peeling her eyes open, Freja saw nothing at first. The world was blurry and nauseous. Wet grass told her she was outside, below a dark canopy of bushes, and the sticky finger poking her could belong to nobody else. There was only one person who referred to her as a 'goat'.

"Klobb, where are the others?" she asked and used all her effort to raise her heavy body and sit up, her head touching the towering lilac bushes, still in bloom. She was in the front garden patch of Topster's cottage.

She stretched out weak limbs and accepted a cup of steaming tea from his dirty and gnarled hands. With the first sip she felt her strength return.

"Still asleep." He pointed left and right and Freja saw her friends lying still on the ground. Chests heaving and sinking, she noted with a sigh of relief. The tea returned heat into her cold body and the recent events came flying back, as though contained in the light grey smoke swirling from the mug to her nose. That Elflock was nowhere to be seen did not yet cross her mind.

"We need to get to Vildaell," she said with sudden urgency and tried to stand, only to find it was severely detrimental to her still spinning head. As long as she sat down, it was fine, so she slumped back onto the grass "As soon as possible."

"There, there, sit yerself down again." Klobb hushed and forced her down, patting the top of her head a bit too roughly for endearment. "I'll a-wake the others. Drink yer tea."

Unable to convince her body to move, Freja relaxed and sat back on the moist ground, sipping her tea while Klobb hobbled from Tryll to Lulja, prodding them both with his finger. Tryll came to in an instant and leapt up, ready to attack while Lulja was slower and had to be poked several times until her cheek showed a red stain from where the little man's finger had probed her skin. Both up and alert, with a mug of tea forced into their hands, Klobb abandoned his guests and proceeded to pick weeds from the flower bed, not minding or commenting on their presence.

"What happened?" Lulja asked, still looking somewhat confused. In short summary, Freja recapped everything she could remember. "Thanks, fenrirs," Lulja said with a shrug and lifted her mug in salutation.

"If it wasn't for Elflock ..." Freja turned to Tryll. "You okay, Tryll?" He nodded, either oblivious or ignoring the seeping blood coming from a hole in his masterform sleeve. Lulja pointed it out to him and crawled over to inspect the wound. It turned out to be nothing but a scratch, but, as he pointed out himself, it must have been a sharp tear if it got through the tough fabric of the masterform. He made a series of signs to Lulja which Freja didn't understand and finished by pointing to Freja's arm.

"Oh yeah—" Lulja's mouth stayed open in an unspoken 'how'—"you were shot."

Freja had forgotten about that. There was no residual

damage from Elflock's accidental shot—not even a tear in the fabric. The tingling sensation had disappeared altogether, leaving the arm as good as new. "Are you sure?" she said. When Lulja couldn't say for certain either, they fell silent. It was like waking from a dream and not being able to tell its content from reality; had it happened, or was it a construction of fantasy? Here were three people remembering an accidental shot, but with no evidence of it occurring at all. Freja saw the scene so clearly: the staring contest with the barrel, the idea to throw rocks at an armed man, Tryll throwing that first rock, Elflock ducking, pressing the trigger ... She dispelled the question because it made her head hurt. There was no sign of shooting, period.

"Klobb," she said instead and pushed herself up to a crouching position, from which she managed to stand up and limp over to him. Her body was not quite recovered yet. "Where's Elflock?"

"Where's a-who now?" Klobb didn't take his eyes off the weeds and pulled out a nasty one with thorns, not even flinching. "

"You heard me." She followed him around the front garden and each time she came close to facing him, the little man spun on his good leg and hobbled in the opposite direction, in which Freja followed like a tail. "And where's Topster? This is important, Klobb!"

Suddenly Klobb stopped in his step and Freja nearly walked into him from behind. She took one, two steps back for safety—his fists would not reach that far—and met a surprisingly sombre face when he turned, chewing his lip with his few good teeth. His eyes darted from Freja to Tryll to Lulja, and back to Freja. Then quickly down to the grassy ground. "Lie down, *hooman*," he said and brought out a clipper and turned to his recovered foxgloves. "Great shock, just lie down, that's right. Someone will come, maybe, yes."

"Klobb, I swear I will—"

"Listen, goat!" A whopping metal *kla-klack* whooshed in front of Freja's face and she jerked back at the threat of Klobb's giant clippers. A regular sized man might have clipped her nose if he was careless; thankfully Klobb did not reach up that far. "Topster never wanted to send ye back to your *hooman* world. He tricked ye. He got that red Master t' get ye here for keeps."

"For keeps?" A frown dug furrows between Freja's eyebrows, deeper and deeper as the full extent of what Klobb was saying sunk in. "But he said—"

"He says many things," said Klobb and lowered his clippers. "He says ye'll be a great man and then he makes ye smaller. Didn' I tell ye? Eh? About those who speak too much?"

"They're liars," Freja said, remembering what she had been told.

"Exactly," said Klobb and clipped off a dry stem from a nearby bush. "So sit yerself down."

Without having to be asked again or forced, Freja sat down on the ground, stunned. Topster was her protector. He had brought her here intentionally but she had figured it had been for a reason, a reason she did not yet know. He would let her go back as promised. Her presence had nothing to do with the plans of the Flÿght. Right?

The cottage door squeaked and Elflock came out from the house, bearing a grim expression. "Good, you are awake." He sensed the tension, saw Freja slumped in incomprehension on the ground and gave Klobb a tired glare. "You talked?"

Instead of answering, Klobb made a series of faces, shrugged, and shuffled over to a spot close to Freja—but still at a safe distance—and sat down with a loud huff, rubbing his bad leg and muttering to himself.

Over by the lilac shrubs, Lulja was resting her head on Tryll's shoulder and they sat quietly watching the scene.

"I am here now," Elflock said with a sigh and put his hands behind his back. He was addressing Klobb. "Speak."

The man sighed, playing with his tattered t-shirt. "I dun want t' tell ye anything," he said. "Ye'll go there, and that's what he wants ye to do. Topster's got a plan for y'all and it'll all become clear soon."

Freja believed him, she saw that he meant every word he said—Klobb was not a good liar. But it didn't matter. "Klobb, if you know something, you have to tell us. We're going back anyway, but your information can help us once we're there."

"It'll end with murder, Freja." The sincerity in his voice was crushing. At another time she might have appreciated the full meaning of his using her real name, but under the circumstances it only spoke of the dangers waiting.

"Where is he?" Elflock asked, calm but with thinly veiled force.

"I won't be the one to send ye to yer death." He found a stray weed in the grass and pulled it up from the roots. Freja came over and crouched next to him.

"You will be the one if you don't tell me what you know." It was to no avail. Klobb made as if zipping his mouth shut, locking it with an imaginary key which he then 'threw' away. "Fine, suit yourself. We're going then." She stood up.

Klobb's hand flew up and grabbed onto her bag. The latches clinked against each other and she saw that Klobb instantly recognised the sound. His eyes widened and he got a wild streak in them. "Fools and goats, that's all y'are," he snapped, pulled himself up and proceeded to walk in a large circle around them, gesturing wildly. Freja followed him with every step. "As empty in yer heads as the Lords. Aye, aye aye … Ask the Flÿght to live with humans? Ha! I laugh, I laugh, but it en't funny. Ye might as well ask the Strays t' team up with the Obbsborn. Ha! I laugh!

338

You know why I laugh tho' it en't funny? Because they think it will happen."

"Who?" asked Freja. "Who thinks it'll happen? The Flÿght?"

"Ah, everyone! The Lords, the Flÿght, the Strays … The Flÿght will never let humans in here. Not as long as they're treated as donkeys themselves."

"He is right," said Elflock. "Jealousy is powerful, so is fear."

"Pfft, jealousy," huffed Klobb in return and stopped with his hands behind his back, facing the Master like a projected miniature of the proud figure. "You Élan dun know what yer talking about. Jealousy? Ha!"

"You have a better name for it?" Elflock asked in a mocking yet kind voice.

"I got one for ye if ye want one!" Spit spewed out of his mouth like hail.

"Stop it," said Freja sharply and made both of them snap their mouths shut, evidently with more insults in store. "Klobb, can I speak to Elflock alone, please? We won't leave yet." With a suspicious nod Klobb scuffled up the porch and past the Master into the house. A moment later Freja could see his snout in the round window, but then the curtains fluttered and he disappeared from sight. "Fenrirs?" It was the first word that came to mind, and perhaps not the most pertinent one. Elflock smiled.

"They have a reputation, I admit, but I have always been loyal to those who are loyal to me. Kindness can go a long way with a feared enemy."

"Don't suppose kindness will help us with the Flÿght, do you?"

"It might have, a long time ago. But Master Topster is beyond that, I am afraid."

He told her, in short, the story of a young Master who wished above all to become part of the Élan, of the seven Masters. He almost succeeded, too. Granted a prestigious task in stage one of the energy re-balance of the Network, Topster went towards a bright future and the award of the grey master-form when he entered Vildaell one night some generations ago. But it had gone wrong. Though the young Master of the Flÿght had not been to blame in any way for the untimely explosion of the power plant, the aftermath had seen some questionable behaviour from him. The President was replaced with a Master of the Trew, the moustached man known to Vildaell as new leader Mr Fiende, but Topster disappeared from sight.

"Topster was close, so very close that night and he did in a way complete his task. But there was one fatal flaw for him, one that he was unable to suppress." Elflock paused but did not avert his gaze. If anything, it became steadier. "The President had a daughter. Sofia. Believe it or not, Topster became biased and he could never forgive himself for it."

Upon his return to Ma'zekaï he had forfeited his reward from the Élan and thrown a great tantrum over the entire valley, claiming that the Flÿght were treated with injustice. He insulted the Lords and made himself an enemy to them and the Élan. In an attempt to silence him the Lords placed him as guardian of the Willow, hoping it would manage his wrath and establish some kind of loyalty to the Élan again. "He is complicated," Elflock had said. "It is his dream to become part of the Élan, and has always been, though he hates it. Yet he could not deny his bias for Sofia. It could drive the most relentless Essence to madness."

"Love?" said Freja, not believing what she was hearing. "Topster—the one I've met—failed for love?"

"Why do you think he resents humans so much?" Elflock smiled. "We do not lack emotion, Freja, but we learn to master it. What Sofia did was unforgivable to Topster. She made him weak, made him not the author of himself any longer, but forsworn and melted. She proved he was not of stronger earth than any other Master—than the Masters who abandoned our cause, whom he begrudged strongly even before." He shook his head. "Even though Topster technically achieved what he was supposed to, the Lords chose Master Ravn for the Élan position instead and the two have never been able to see eye to eye after that."

"And after this, the Curfew Law was set up?" Elflock nodded. "Is the radiation threat even real?"

"The accident happened," said Elflock, "but it was not, as you think, a plan by the Lords. Though I will not pretend it was not fortuitous as a veil to their movements within Amérle."

"Your movements," Freja corrected. "While the people are imprisoned in their own homes."

Elflock was silent for a while and observed her with his penetrating gaze. His eyes were also grey, she noticed, as if he was born to be of the Élan, they glimmered like pure silver.

"There is a time for truth and there is a time for redemption," he said at last. "The movements happening now are a thousand times more dangerous—for all of us. May I?" He gestured towards her bag and she let him take out one of the silver crystals. Holding it up, he observed the swirling silver smoke inside. "This is what we fight for," he said. "Latches are energy. We have fought for the balance of the Network our entire lives, and it is about to be disturbed once more." He gave her the crystal which felt cold to her skin. As if its life was fading. "The borders must stand, Freja. They must."

She could almost hear the clock ticking. "We need to leave, don't we?"

Elflock confirmed with a small nod. "Get the other two ready. I'll find the latches."

"Give me one minute." She leapt up the small steps to the porch and went inside the familiar house that had been her home for a short while. It seemed desolate now, void of life—

and a strange place. The floor where she had been eavesdropping on Éloyse and Klobb in her first days, the window she had cleaned countless times … She cast a glance into her old bedroom, now spotless and tidy as if she had never been in there at all. Klobb had kept busy. In the kitchen, everything looked the same. A fire was crackling in the stove and the kettle stood beside it, still steaming. She ran a finger over the rough kitchen table, thinking back to when she had met Topster for the first time, smiling to herself at the awkwardness of it all. Through the window she saw the back garden and the trunk of the Willow tree, reaching up towards the sky.

It didn't take long before she found what she was looking for. Topster had left in a hurry. The tubes she had been collecting with him were still there, in an open cupboard in the far corner of the kitchen, a silvery light revealing the treasure. She counted twelve latches of various strengths. Together with the ones from the Bank, they had more than they could carry around for too long. They would have to figure out what to do with the rest. Destroy them? Give them to the Obbsborn? Considering her own plans, she took one of the brighter ones in the Master's bag and placed it in her own. She needed all the ways back she could spare; back to find her mother.

A dry cough made her blood freeze. She stopped what she was doing and swore under her breath. In the midst of all the excitement, she had forgotten all about him.

CHAPTER 34

"WHAT D'YE THINK yer doing?" said Klobb's growling voice as she turned around. Their eyes met and Freja felt her heart sink. Then, scowling, Klobb shuffled over to a box in the corner Freja hadn't seen before. On opening the lid, a glowing silver light shot up and blinded her. "There's another eight in 'ere," said Klobb and let the lid drop to the floor with a thud. "Do what ye want with 'em."

"Thank you," Freja said, surprised. She took the crystals and put them carefully among the others. "We're leaving for Vildaell now. These will help."

"Dun waste the energy of that Network," he said and waved for her to follow. "There's a better way."

He kicked the lid away from his patch and hobbled out from the room, one hand firmly on his left leg. Freja followed, curious as to what he meant by 'another way'.

Outside, from the back garden patch, she called to the others who soon came hurrying through a wall of lilac flowers. A white flower caught in Lulja's hair and Freja was about to let her know when Tryll reached out and plucked it out. Lulja repaid him with a smile that only widened when she saw that

Freja had noticed.

With Elflock by her side, Freja followed Klobb to the end of the garden and out through an archway of elderflower bush, angled so as to be invisible from the house. She asked where they were headed, but received mere muttering in reply. Behind the bush was a smaller trail, curling like a wreathe along the outside border of the garden, leading to a small trio of steps which took them below ground level and onto a small platform below. "In ye go," Klobb barked and poked Freja in the back so that she stumbled and almost lost her footing.

"Careful," she snapped and straightened up. "I won't be moving so quickly on broken legs."

"In there?" said Lulja and looked sceptically at the dark entrance.

"Quit jabbering. Go!"

Once in the cave, Freja looked around her and considered their location. The cleft had led them into a cavernous space with high ceiling and walls, and tunnels leading off deeper into the ground and off into an intangible distance. The air was murky and damp as though the sun had never touched the ground in here.

Suddenly she knew where they were. The curved elderflower had concealed the shape of the tree outside, which is why she had been confused. They were in front of the Willow, inside the hill on which it stood.

"Tryll says this is part of the Obbsborn," said Lulja.

"Your translation skills are certainly improving," teased Freja and made Lulja blush in the dark.

"Come," growled Klobb and shuffled onwards. "I dun have time to stand around a-whis-telin'."

"Is it really an Obbsborn?" Freja said as she hurried after him, the rest trailing behind.

"One o' the early ones," said Klobb.

"The very first one, in fact," said Elflock behind Freja. "I thought they were out of use."

"You hear any other feet than ours?" snapped Klobb and Elflock didn't reply.

A minute later Klobb came to a stop and let the rest catch up. He waited around the next corner, and Freja suspected he had gathered them for effect. And what an effect! The silver globe was free and hovering just above ground, brighter than any other Freja had seen. She had to hold up her hand to protect her eyes from the bright light. Lulja and Tryll did the same. Elflock, however, crept closer.

"An infinite latch?" he whispered, a mix of ire and excitement battling in his voice, ill-concealed. "You keep an infinite latch in an abandoned Obbsborn? When the Élan finds out about this—"

"'Tis very likely that Ma'zekaï is already *kaput*," said Klobb, shooting a stern glare the Master's way. "Off, off."

"What's an infinite latch?" Freja asked.

"They're, like, infinite," said Lulja in awe.

"Wow, so helpful." Freja received a scowl in return.

"Incredible," said Elflock, his eye intent on the silver swirl, in constant motion like a paint brush with a life of its own, diving into its own creation then out again, ceaseless and eternal. The irises of his eyes glimmered along with the latch. "The energy block in these latches is endless," he said. "There is no scarcity, no limit—they have an infinite life span. The energy is contained rather than transferred." He pointed to the light. "It does not break and build in the same way as regular latches, but acts instead like a permanent tunnel." Though many stories had been told about infinite latches, no one had found proof of their existence; a myth of latch welders and tunnels between the *landskapës* proliferated among young Masters, and a few old Masters partook in the legend as well. "We never thought they existed. Where does it lead?"

"My auntie's kitchen drawer," said Klobb and rolled his eyes. "To Vildaell o'course—that's where ye going, en't it?"

"And they're permanent, they can't be destroyed?" asked Freja, the realisation sinking in. "All these latches, everything we risked—and there are latches like this lying around?"

"They can be destroyed," said Elflock, a matting darkness passing his grey eyes. "Used in an extracting manner. But it is difficult and there is not time for it now."

Tryll poked Freja and signalled to an invisible watch on his wrist. "Tryll's right," Lulja translated, "we'd better move."

"Even I could've guessed that one," said Freja with a teasing grin. "Come on."

Tryll went first, then Lulja who also reached out for the light and was pulled into the whirling silver—and disappeared. Elflock walked into the latch without hesitation. Only Freja was left.

She turned to Klobb. "It's not goodbye, you know," she said. "I'll come back."

"Goat, this en't the place for ye. This is yer way out—take it."

"My—"

"Yer mother, I know. W'ass her name again? I'll ask the Obbsborn if they know of 'er. I got sum friends down there still."

"Marja," said Freja. "Marja Evenson."

"Evenson?" Klobb's mouth fell open. "Aye, aye, aye … I will ask, *hooman*, but I—I will ask."

Freja could not help but smile, and thanked him. It was a strangely affectionate moment. A dark voice inside her whispered that she would never meet the foul, grimacing, insulting creature again. It also told her she would miss him. Obviously uncomfortable with the softness in the murky air, Klobb fingered his tattered t-shirt, made knots with the fabric and untied them over again, as he chewed his lower lip. All of a sudden he flung his finger up in the air, above his head, opened his mouth as if to sound an '*ah!*' and rushed out of the tunnel from where they had come. Just when Freja thought he had abandoned her, he returned holding a green bulk in his arms—her backpack.

"I held on to them books of yers," he said, hurling it to her. "Thought you might like 'em back."

Excited and touched to be reunited with an item of familiarity, Freja hugged the backpack, took in its smell—now more of Klobb and Ma'zekaï than her own world—and unzipped it. The books, her wallet, and that infernal List with Cecelya's name were all in there.

"I might've borrowed one or two," said Klobb. "I en't seen books since—well, since a long time."

"Since you came here."

"Since I was taken here." His emphasis required no more clarification and for the first time Freja saw the underlying humanity in the gruff little man. He was a victim, just like the others.

"Was there one you liked in particular?" She passed the open backpack over to him. He thought for a moment, then stuck his head inside and fished out the biology book—*Arborary Arbitraries*. Freja laughed. "Have it," she said.

Klobb's face lit up. He hugged the book and stroked its back gently with his withered hands. "I used t' teach," he said thoughtfully, his hand still patting the cover. "Before, I was teachin' and now I dun teach."

"Yes, you do, Klobb," said Freja and reached out a hand, unsure of where to put it. She decided on the shoulder, placed it there, feeling the roughness of his shirt against her smooth skin. "You taught me how to be less of a goat," she said with a smile. "Look at me—I even fooled Elflock with your work."

"Elflock is an airy-fairy," Klobb replied, but smiling. "Maybe if Miss Freja—if Miss Freja wins, I can return home. It en't far from here, y'know."

"Where is home for you?"

"Muspeldal," he replied and smiled at Freja's reaction. "Yes, Miss Freja, I am *hooman* too—but a different kind."

The ticking clock crept into the unfilled spaces of silence.

"I'd better go, I—" Freja said at last as she searched for the familiar shape around her neck, out of habit, and found that it was missing. She dove into her bag again. In an inner pocket she found it. As soon as her fingers clasped around it, she took comfort in the chill drop-shape of the charm. Her mother's only memory gave her strength, strength that she needed to step through that latch and into an unknown world to face whatever lay behind it. She had sorely missed it since she had left the cottage and held it up to view. Busy observing it with a smile, she didn't notice her companion's reaction: Klobb's chin had fallen to the ground and he twitched to reach for the charm, but managed to restrain himself.

"Miss—Miss Freja?" he stammered and stumbled forward a step or two. "Aye, aye aye ..."

"Klobb, what's wrong?" she asked and crouched down where he had fallen flat on his back on to the cold ground. The silver shuddered beside them, reminding her that time was scarce. The others were waiting. Her hand closed around the charm in silent prayer that there was a little time left, just a little. "Klobb, are you okay?"

"The leaf ...," he mumbled. "The leaf ... Let me see." He stretched out a crooked and trembling hand towards Freja and she let him bend open her fingers like petals to reveal the precious flower within. His eyes glittered in the gloom of the cave as he stared at the little glass shape. "Where did you get this, Miss Freja?"

"My mother gave it to me. But it's not a leaf, it's a drop, see?" She held it up so that it caught the light of the latch. It swept across the surface of the glass crystal and leapt within to mix with the swirl inside. To her surprise Klobb began to laugh. The laugh went over to a wheezing cough that echoed in the cave and Freja, afraid that someone might hear them—as unlikely as a passer-by was—she pleaded with him to be quiet. The infinite latch shuddered and she thought she saw Elflock's face in there, searching for her, but nothing stirred further.

Soon Klobb composed himself and wiped the tears from his eyes. "That is no drop of water, Miss Freja," he said, jumping up from his collapsed position and dragging her up as well. "I'm curious that you en't recognise it. Hold it up again."

She did as he said and observed the charm she had owned for as long she could remember, in the glimmering light from the infinite latch. It spun on its chain, moving in shades of yellow and white—and silver. Flakes, dust, of silver fell inside the charm like the fake snow inside a snow crystal, and although she knew what it reminded her of, the thought was ridiculous. She looked at Klobb, who was wearing a wide smile and at once knew it was, as impossible as it seemed, true.

"That's right, my dear goat," he said and stretched out a hand into which she gently transferred the chain, making sure the charm hung still in the air. "This is no drop, it's a leaf, and what's more—it's a latch."

PART III
AFTER CURFEW

CONFIDENTIAL

MAY 4, —th Year of the Lion. The Élan takes upon it to administer and maintain balance of the Energy Harmonisation Network at all times. Should the balance shift to a level regarded as "high-risk" (see §34.2:6 for criteria), no notice need be given before restoring the balance in whatever way necessary.

Signed,
Mr. Fiende,
Honourable President of Vildaell

CHAPTER 35

Seven hours until bell eleven.

ONE BY ONE, the four latches fizzled out and faded to dark when the Masters, three men and one woman, stepped through and onto Amérle ground. The sun had left the sky several hours ago and the tenth bell had already herded the human sheep into safer grazing fields. All that was left behind were empty streets and dark houses with blinds pulled down, doors locked, and fear expelled for the night. Despite the calmness, they chose to steal away like ghostly shadows through the gardens, away from the streets and the open areas. More so than any other night after Curfew, there were movements in the dark, movements that these Masters would rather not encounter without warning.

The taller of the four crept forward, then turned around to the other three and signalled that it was safe to continue. It was likely that they would sense any energy fields, should they come close—half of them were of the Élan after all—but the tall Master saw no room for error. They had one chance only. The figures turned around a corner, ducked and disappeared into the shadows under a hydrangea bush, bowing in sight of this unnatural habitat. Masters were creatures of Nature and did not belong in Vildaell, this land of steel and coal—of unclean energy.

The stench was almost unbearable.

A well-groomed hedge led them into a narrow street in the residential area, which was situated in the northern part of the city. Amérle. It was an ordinary name of a city in Heim, plain enough to go by without particular notice. Not tonight. Tonight it was the one place the Masters needed to access—to find one whose name they had rarely spoken at all in years, decades. Until this day, the name of the man they were seeking had been a mere shadow of recollection, a memory of disappointment and a word tainted with a slight foul taste. Tej, the name of the old Élan Lord was as forbidden as a word became in Ma'zekaï. Tonight was different; tonight it was perhaps the most important name of all.

Next, a lavish garden gave them temporary relief from the stench and they stopped for a moment to take in the green energy from a bed of flowering roses. This area was far enough out to still allow organic growth. The female Master clipped one of the yellow ones, careful not to touch the thorns, and felt its gentle pulse synchronise with her own. She closed her eyes and felt smooth energy transfer into her bloodstream. It wasn't as strong as the Willow leaves, but still subdued the raw sting of human energy. Besides, she needed the precious leaves in her pocket for other things. Behind her, the other Masters did the same, rendering the rose bush maimed and leaving only a few buds behind. Without as much as a glance towards the house where the owner slept blissfully unaware, the Masters hurried onwards without guilt. Nature was not anyone's property – it belonged to the Network.

A moment later they reached their destination. The two-storey villa was no different from any other on its street: its shutters closed, blinds pulled down, doors secured with the tripartite lock that was custom in Vildaell.. At the bottom of the steps connecting the path to the door, three of the Masters waited while the last one left to inspect the back of the house. They could leave no escape route, no matter what.

In the open garage stood two vehicles—one for each person who called this place home. The female Master passed them without further thought and felt soft grass under her boots. There was no door in the back, only large windows, all covered by the blinds and shutters. Éloyse pulled out a leaf from her pocket. Its silver shade glowed slightly in the dim moonlight, casting reflective shades on her face. Her eyes closed and in the darkness she thought she heard noises from the other side of the house. The Masters had made their move.

With the burning energy from the leaf, Éloyse made a small hole in the shutter, making sure it reached through the blinds as well. A faint light came from the interior of the house. She leaned in to see it more clearly. A lamp lit up the sitting room where an unfinished board game stood to the right, in front of a cushioned sofa, a mahogany table scattered with magazines and empty glasses with dark stains from a coloured liquid left too long to dry, and a box she knew was called television or "TV" in the far left corner. Elflock, who knew a lot more about humans than she, had told her about them once, but she had never seen one in the flesh. Moving pictures were sent through the air and appeared on a screen, he had said, and she had not quite believed him, but there it was, right in front of her.

The night was a quiet one, quieter than in Ma'zekaï, but she knew there were movements in the shadows; movements that would become apparent when the sun cast its rays over the city. The only question was in what light the humans would wake up? Topster had latches, and they weren't from the Bank. She had not told Elflock—how could she, without also uncovering her part in the scheme?

Her heart was fluttering, although it should not. This visit was not quite pleasant, but not entirely disagreeable either. It would all come down to how the Lord answered their question. She was sure that he would accept their request. He was one of them, and had always been fiercely loyal—except that one time. Bias could be reversed (so she had been told), but whether it worked in real life or not, she wasn't sure. There was only one way to find out; one way to reverse the damage she had done by helping Topster; for yielding to her weakness. Only, Topster did not yet know of her treachery and it gave her stomach ache to think about it. When he found out … Suppose—

A crashing sound from within the house broke her thoughts and she leaned forward again, peering through the hole. A man with a familiar face came rushing in from the open door leading to the hallway. He was older, more weathered, but every bit as handsome. In his face was no fear, no trepidation—only determination. Éloyse allowed herself a smile. Stumbling and almost falling in the process, Tej leapt towards the lamp and at once the room tumbled into darkness, though she could still hear the front door hinges move and she knew it was time. She headed to the front where the Masters had unlocked the door and three crumbled leaves lay scorched on the ground below the handle.

The eerie quiet of the night echoed from the inside, despite the man of the house being present somewhere in the darkness. A faint scent of heat and sweetness lingered in the hallway, which led straight into the kitchen on the left. Éloyse and the younger Master searched through the downstairs area while the taller of the group, Neese, and the fourth member went upstairs. Passing a bureau where family photos were lined up, she headed straight to the sitting room.

Although she knew it would be empty—Tej had rushed out

again after killing the lights—she wanted to see it from the inside. The only sign of disturbance was a knocked over glass on the mahogany table. Otherwise all was calm as before. Smiling, she went up to the board game and played with one of the pieces on the red winning team. He remembered his old friends yet. She wondered if he had told anyone what the colours stood for. Red and blue. The old grudge between Trew and Flÿght, immortalised in a trivial board game. Did his friends know? His human friends? How could they? He could not reveal his past to them. None of it; not his excellent reputation, his high rank, his peers. Her name would not have passed his lips in a long time. With idle fingers she pushed the pawn forward one step, two steps—a move that closed the game. Red, Trew, wins. She could only hope that the game could predict the future.

"Nothing," said Neese when he returned downstairs while Ravn came stalking behind, having reached the same conclusion, and the young Master by name of Tomsom came from the kitchen and shrugged, tossing his unused leaf on the table.

"Still knows his tricks, old fox," Tomsom said and lunged down on the sofa, stroking his goatee.

He wore the dark green masterform and was a future member of the Élan. Being the cousin of Lord Py, he was next in line for lordship in absence of her children. A Lord not by blood, but by association. Éloyse would not have chosen to bring him on this particular task, but Neese had insisted. Especially in light of the old Lord, this youngster was arrogant, nonchalant and greedy.

"I heard about him of course," Tomsom continued, his boots making marks on the shiny surface of the table as he rested them there and leaned back against the cushion, inspecting his fingernails. "I figured it was all glorified rumours. You know, like when someone croaks they are suddenly praised left and right."

"Not at all," said Éloyse. She remained standing. "He was one of the most accomplished Masters of his generation. You'd do well to learn from him."

"Except he wasn't accomplished enough to resist bias, was he?" Tomsom smirked with raised eyebrows. His grin faded into a pout as he met the eyes of Neese, the oldest Élan.

"It is easier to speak, than to do," Neese said, somewhat thoughtfully. "Tej was in a difficult position—the human world is different. Even the best of Masters can fall, evidently."

"Bias is for the weak," muttered Tomsom under his breath so that Neese did not hear. But Éloyse heard, and she saw that Ravn did too. He grabbed Tomsom by the jaw and bent to his level. His eyes were livid.

"Ravn—don't," Éloyse tried, but Ravn ignored her.

"Listen," he said, his face so close to Tomsom's that the young man received a shower of spit with every word. "This man was one of the Lords—a concept you should be familiar with, but clearly aren't—and he would never have let us get into this situation, had he still been among them. Bias is a weakness, but I can think of ten others that are worse. Tej is not weak, not like you. What can you say for yourself?" Ravn let go of him but continued to scowl at Tomsom, who sat quiet, rubbing the sore spot. Éloyse guessed that more than his jaw had been bruised.

"Never did I think I'd hear you defend me, Ravn."

They jumped at the voice shooting out from the darkness and failed to locate it at first. When the man came out from the corner by the bookshelf, there was no longer any doubt. This was their old friend, Lord Tej. Neither was there any doubt about the gun in his hands. He patted its long body. "I've learnt a few human tricks as well through the years. Let me tell you that you're in an awfully delicate situation here. Don't you dare." Tomsom had reached for the discarded leaf on the table but only came halfway before he had the barrel of the gun pointed at him. He stopped in the motion and put his hands forward, palms open and empty. Ravn gave him a sour look and then turned back to the man with the gun.

"Master Tej," he said and touched his heart.

"That is not my name anymore."

"Not even going to greet us properly?" Ravn said with feigned disappointment. "Tut-tut."

"Get out of my house."

"Tej," said Neese, "you of all know that we do not speak in vain. At least listen." He took a cautious step forward with both his palms open, but froze as Tej pointed the gun at him and pulled the safety hack.

"Stop, unless you want a hole in your head. I will do it, I promise—I *attest*."

"Don't be stupid," said Ravn and rolled his eyes. "Is this human behaviour? What happened to reason?"

"Yeah, what happened to reason?" said Tomsom with a snort.

"You," said Ravn and pointed at Tomsom's chest. "Consider yourself an Obbsborn—a quiet Obbsborn."

With the gun still pointed at Neese, Tej was watching the exchange and Éloyse saw his mouth twitch. There was her old friend, the one who had such fervour for the Master cause.

"Tej," she said and her eyes met his.

"That's not my name," he repeated and kept the gun steady. "Of all people I thought you'd respect my decision." The fierce darkness glazing his eyes stung, but she ignored the feeling and continued, daring a step forward. At once the gun shifted from Neese to her. "Don't tempt me," Tej said. "I could just pull the trigger, you know."

"I think we all know you won't," said Ravn and let out a little laugh. "You've had enough opportunity to do so, yet here we are, still standing."

"The Flÿght is rebelling," Éloyse said, grasping the brief recess. It was strange to see the stoic Lord so ridden with emotion, not even trying to conceal it. "Unless we stop them, Ma'zekaï—the whole Network!—could perish."

"Why would I care?" Suspicion had no hiding place in his face and he asked the question with narrowed eyes. "I've left that battle behind me."

"Look, the guy clearly doesn't want to come," said Tomsom and stood up. "Let's not waste more time here."

"I could kill you—I don't know you," said Tej and aimed the gun, causing an outburst of shouting from all four Masters.

"Whoah," yelped Tomsom and sought cover behind Ravn.

"Braveheart," Ravn said and rolled his eyes, but didn't move. Perhaps he didn't trust Tej's self-control after all. His finger lingered on the trigger. Ravn held out his hand to show his palm held a surreptitious leaf. "Nobody's dying tonight, Tej, or whatever you call yourself these days. The Flÿght are moving into Heim tonight and the Lords want to open the borders. One venture will kill Ma'zekaï, one will potentially save it—but both entail open Master presence in your precious human *landskapë*. You cannot run anymore, Master."

"The only question is what relationship you will have with us," continued Neese.

Tej was still clutching his gun, but was not quite as white around the fingers anymore. The finger wrapped around the trigger let go and now rested on the side of the gun, and his eyebrows knitted and stretched out. His face grew desperate, then fell into resignation and he shook his head as though he couldn't believe his ears. Éloyse could almost see how his mind processed this information. At last he lowered the gun, still suspicious, but attentive. "I'm listening," he said.

Ravn and Neese exchanged a look. Neese explained the situation. "Masters are visiting old friends as we speak. The Lords want to open the borders and old relations will be invited to come back."

"Become Masters again," Éloyse filled in, hoping that the words would mean as much to Tej as they meant to her. "It could be like the old days." Tej kept his gaze firm on the ground. "All will be forgotten, you could be someone again—"

He finally looked up, but not with the excitement she had hoped for. Disdain was thrown in her face and he frowned. "I am someone, Éloyse. Your values are not my values. I am someone. I have a family and a career."

"I didn't mean …"

"Of course you did." He looked to each and every one of them. He laughed. "I'm happy." He paused. "Or I was … Your lot has cost me everything. Was it not enough to take my wife from me? Two years, Éloyse, two years I have been looking for her. And now my daughter?" One step closer, gun itching but still pointing to the floor. "For how long will you keep punishing me for my choices?"

Inside Éloyse's chest her heart beat in furious rhythms. Try as she might, she could not steady her breathing and felt burning behind her eyes. The first time she had felt it was when she was a young disciple of the Trew and saw a batsër die from exhaustion. She had been scolded by her mentor and never let another tear touch her cheek. Except once, and it wasn't all too different from this situation. The people were the same. He had been such a hero in his time, and the day he left had changed all of them forever. Hearing that one of her closest friends had decided to leave them for good, without as much as a goodbye to her, had been harder than Éloyse cared to think about. Tears were not at the level of bias, but a weakness not to be admitted to in public. But right now there was nowhere to go.

She wanted to assure him that the Élan had nothing to do

with his wife's disappearance, nor his daughter's, but some itch inside told her that it was not the truth. Therefore she was glad when Neese spoke again.

"We need your support," he said. "The Lords want equality, the Flÿght dictatorship. You can be part of creating a new world where we live in harmony, not conflict."

"You're asking me to wage war against the Flÿght," said Tej. "Remember I was one of you. I know when pretty words carry ugly meanings."

"Fine," said Ravn and held up a hand when Neese tried to contradict him. "No, we might as well be honest when we're at it, Neese. Tej, it's war, it is. It's war to quash the one power that's trying to upset the balance."

"It seems it is the responsibility of the young to destroy the past," Neese conceded with a glance at Tomsom, who was still pouting, "but it is equally our duty as Élan to protect the future. The Flÿght are out of control."

Tej fingered the gun and for a second it looked like he might pick it up again, but he didn't. Instead he polished an invisible spot over and over. Éloyse felt time go by too quickly, but didn't want to stress him. He was coming around, she felt it. He had to.

"What if I decline?" he asked, not looking away from the gun. "What if I don't come?"

"Granted that we manage to stop the Flÿght, which is by no means a given," said Neese, "the Lords will open the borders. A system of latches will be placed—a structure is already drawn up. Whether you like it or not Masters will live in this world. You could be treated with the respect deserved by an old Lord ... or not."

"I never cared for you," said Ravn and a grin appeared on Tej's face. "But you're one of us. End of story."

"Please," said Éloyse, coaxing that smile out of him. "You

can be all you are now plus everything you were in Ma'zekaï. Don't you see? You don't have to choose, you could have it all." In the briefest of moments, their eyes met, and she saw that he would fold. While she waited for him to come to that conclusion, she glanced at the other Masters, who looked less confident. Tomsom was clever for once and kept quiet, only watching and listening from the sofa. Ravn had crossed his arms, tapping his foot, and Neese stared at Tej, as if sending telepathic messages. The minutes dragged by.

Tej was rubbing the gun, turning this way and the other, not standing still for longer than a few moments before shifting again. At one point he left the room and they let him. He would not run, not now. It would be an insult to his intelligence to think that he saw himself as anything other than cornered. The choice was really no choice at all, and he would realise as much soon enough. Éloyse saw years of anguish over his wife being played back in his mind all at once, and she perceived it tear him from the inside. That's why he would come with them—to start over. At last, after another turn in the kitchen, he came back, mouth open and ready to speak.

"On one condition," he said.

"Name it," said Neese.

"My daughter. She went missing and people only go missing for one reason here. Find her and I will join you. Find her and bring her back, and I'm yours."

Éloyse pushed back a whimper of joy and swallowed all the emotions swirling around inside. When did she become so soft?

From Neese, "If she has indeed come into Élan hands, we will of course do all we can to return her to you."

"Unharmed," Tej said.

Neese repeated his statement. "We will do our best."

"Your best is not enough," said Tej and shook his head. "I need a promise."

"In that case, I promise," said Neese without taking his eyes off him, without as much as a moment's hesitation. "Now, old friend—come greet us." He placed his right hand on his heart and the whole room held its breath in waiting for Tej to repeat the gesture. When he did, Éloyse exhaled with a smile, a flush of chill relief tingling on her skin. Tej mimicked the gesture and broke out in a smile as well. Tomsom rose from the sofa and brought out a grey masterform which he handed over to the old Master. He received a courteous nod in return and Éloyse suppressed a smile. Tej had always been subtle, but effective.

"Back in grey," said Ravn as an explanation to Tej's questioning look. "The Lords approve, don't worry."

"Put it on, friend," said Neese with a proud smile.

Tej eyed the masterform with ambiguous feelings. Éloyse saw how he struggled between joy and the ghosts of the past. She thought it better to get moving, get his mind focused on the matter at hand. "Do you remember Topster?" she asked. "Of the Flÿght?"

He tore away from the masterform, thinking.

"He's not much to remember," said Ravn. "Snotty little kid obsessed with glory and becoming a Lord?"

The story of Topster was not well known except to those close to him. Éloyse knew it better than anyone else. But word had spread since the incident, and recognition now lit up Tej's face. He said he remembered a young man with ideas of grandeur unusual for a Flÿght.

"Those ideas are the same," said Neese gravely. "We need to keep an eye on him. He is most likely the source behind the Flÿght's coup."

"How do we stop him?" asked Tej, meeting three beaming faces. "What?"

"It's good to have you back," answered Ravn. "Even if I still don't care for you."

Once Tej was changed into the masterform, Éloyse felt like no time had passed at all since their last meeting. Back in grey, Master Tej had found his place again and it was by her side. She caught Ravn observing her and frowned to form an enquiry as to the reason. She received a grin in return. It didn't matter. Tej was back and together they would save Ma'zekaï.

"Your daughter," said Éloyse as they left the house behind and ventured into the dark night again. "What's her name? We should notify the Trew immediately so they can search the Obbsborn."

"She'd be in one of the recent ones," said Tej and glanced around the corner before stepping into the road. Not as much as a rat was stirring in the neighbourhood.

The implosion of his next words happened only in Éloyse's mind.

"Her name is Freja—Freja Evenson."

CHAPTER 36

Six hours until bell eleven.

FREJA KEPT HER eyes open as she half-walked, half-fell through the tunnel of the infinite latch. The walls were bulging and were in constant movement, as though threatening to collapse into little square pieces at the lightest touch. She had wrapped her arms around her torso, careful not to tempt them. The swirling rush of light and spectra of rainbow colours, reflected in invisible mirrors made it all the more difficult, as she tumbled through the beams of light which occasionally struck her skin and left a stinging mark. The walls remained intact, to her great relief. She did not need to be trapped in another place right now; not when she was about to go home.

As expected she soon fell out of the latch and stumbled in the change from fluid to hard ground. She braced her fall with both arms, but still couldn't stop her lower body from slamming into the ground and winced. The bag thankfully remained on her back, and no crushing sound escaped from within.

Lulja came rushing towards her and Freja let herself be pulled up, ignoring the pain surging from her hip. "You okay? What took you so long? We were getting worried."

Freja groaned and leaned over, rubbing her shoulder as the world spun inside her head. She must have underestimated the effect of the latch. Dizziness and nausea spread like snakes inside her and she gagged a few times before at least the disorientation faded away. The world became clearer as her vision returned and Lulja's face appeared in front of her as Freja opened her eyes. A concerned frown knitted her eyebrows into one.

"Are you hurt?"

Freja shook her head, grimacing. She stood up to see where they were. Every movement caused a stab of pain in one limb or the other, and nausea still growled in her stomach. It didn't matter, she thought as she tied her hair back only to receive an angry crack in her right shoulder. The pain would have to wait: tonight was busy enough. She brushed the dust off her masterform and saw that all of her friends seemed unharmed although Lulja had a cut across her cheek, as if a cat had scratched her, and Tryll's dark hair was messy. Elflock was as polished as ever—he didn't have as much as a stain on his grey masterform.

The infinite latch had led them to a city of monochrome. It was night, but not too dark to distinguish the shapes and silhouettes of the surroundings, and the full moon cast its light on the low buildings, making them throw long shadows into the darkness. The night cut the dimensions of the city short, minimising its depth, making it smaller and intrusive. Freja shuddered. Their immediate surroundings were indeed abandoned and had a lonesome feel to them, as if nobody had been there for a long time. They were standing behind a pattern of cumbersome box constructions, dirty although they probably had been white once. These 'boxes' were dotted here and there as far as she could see in the area ahead of them. Some had objects sticking up from the top, which led Freja to believe they were dumpsters for waste. A curved cylinder stood at a distance, in the middle of the site. It reached up towards the sky, jagged at the once smooth corners, as though some giant beast had taken a bite out of its body. It was grey, as everything else around it. The square pattern of constructions created a maze of buildings, winding pipelines, and overflowing dumpsters. A crossing created an intersection between lanes and a large warehouse building stood on the other side, a few alleys off while four solid chimney pieces emerged from the roof of the warehouse, but no smoke erupted from them now. A fence ran all the way on their right and behind, and between the dumpsters on the far left, which meant they were inside a closed-off area. Dusty, grey, and abandoned.

"Is this really Vildaell?" asked Elflock in a low voice. "It looks rather abandoned."

"I know this place," said Lulja and wandered a few steps. "I've … I've been here before. Well not here-here, but over there." Lulja was pointing to the far right and to somewhere beyond the fence. She saw something Freja didn't and took slow steps towards it. Not until she was too close did the buzzing become apparent. They all heard it, but Lulja felt it and leapt back, retracting her outstretched arms in fear. "That's Jahran," she said, backing away from the electric fence separating Vildaell from her homeland. "Tryll, that's Jahran!" Tryll joined her and squinted to see across the fence to what was visible of the broken land. It had taken the worst hit in the disaster. The site lay so close to the border that the explosion had wiped out the nearest city and left nothing but toxic soil for the people to live on.

Freja followed their gaze. If that was Jahran, then there was no doubt about where they were. The one closed-off area in Amérle. She had never seen it in real life before, only in tattered photographs and blurry and shaky film images on TV.

The nuclear power plant.

As the realisation dawned on her, its hollowness descended and wrapped itself around her being like a cold towel. Whisperings appeared in the air; whisperings of ghosts of what it once must have been. The pride of the once wealthy nation of Vildaell—a development that had made the royalty of Buria see red and the Jahranian to issue warning campaigns. The countries of Muspeldal had refused to get involved. She had read it all in school. Nobody believed the Jahranian scientific reports, all unanimous: it was dangerous, too dangerous. But nobody listened, not until it was all too late and Jahran took the worst hit.

That's when people usually listen, Freja considered and thought of the Élan Lords. Why is it that people don't listen until it's too late?

Not a soul was moving around them. The night was dead silent. A chill tasted the insides of Freja as she realised why that was. The reason she had never seen Amérle in this state was quite simply because she had never been outside at this hour. Although she wasn't sure of the time relationship between *landskapës*, it had been evening when they left Ma'zekaï. The darkness, the moon, the emptiness—they had arrived after the tenth bell, which meant both that they had yet time to fight the Flÿght, but also that they were in severe danger. "We need to get out of here," she said, now seeing the site in a new light altogether. "If it's true the radiation will be high, especially here."

"I already feel my skin crawl," said Lulja and scratched her hand so that red marks appeared. "It's getting at me. I'm radiated!"

"Calm down," said Elflock, but looking all but calm himself. He addressed Freja. "Will it harm us?"

"I don't know," Freja confessed. It wasn't a lie. Annual reports—all asserting the continued necessity for Curfew—

were given on the levels of radiation but, as far as she knew, it could all be made up. It did not, however, change the fact that they needed to leave—soon.

That large hangar across the site must be the nuclear reactor itself, she realised. Once square, not entirely unlike the Latch Bank, it stood in ruins like a tooth attacked by unfixed cavities. Its roof was ragged and only mended with temporary tarps. The nuclear site was usually cut off from visitors at all times— which was probably the reason why it was a good place to keep an infinite latch. There was no risk of humans wandering into it. Plans to restore the plant had been made and scrapped several times over. The result stood before them. This place was an echo of Amérle in every way. It was its evil twin, abandoned by friends and family and utterly lost and unattached. Much like Valley of the Wind compared to Wood in Ma'zekaï. This place was the lost voice of a city once alive.

"Please?" pleaded Lulja and cowered close to Tryll. "I'm not making it up. I don't want to ruin this. She gestured to her face and Freja couldn't help but smile.

"It's after Curfew," she said. "Every door in Amérle will be locked and shut by now. Nobody will let anyone in under any circumstances. Not … not even family." She silenced. Sometimes she thought she remembered banging on the door, but she couldn't be sure. True or not, there would have been no way for her father to open it and she knew that. It still hurt. Such were the rules of Curfew. Therefore, all homes were out of the question as refuge, but they certainly couldn't stay where they were. She looked towards the city. It would have been easier to hide in Ma'zekaï where there were forests and caves, but in Amérle there was nothing but flat concrete and locked doors. She hadn't thought this far. None of them had. Every effort had been focused on getting back and in the rush of excitement, she had forgotten about the task at hand.

"Is there a plan?" asked Lulja, still making red streaks on her hand. "Ugh, it's itching."

Tryll gently grabbed her hand, relieving her already rosy skin from more injury. Freja couldn't help but smile. They were sweet together, but she wondered whether they realised it themselves. Tryll was good-natured and Lulja seemed to understand his non-verbal communication better than anyone else. As she was musing upon their relationship she gazed out in the distance of the city, feeling desperation claw its way closer to her senses. Amérle, the place where her own life was anchored, was depending on her help. She felt dangerously close to sinking it. Tallest of the buildings was the TV tower, which Freja now spotted on the skyline. It stood at a close distance, poking the sky, darker and bleaker than she had ever seen it before; ominous and mean, like an approaching enemy. All of a sudden it seemed evident; so evident that she did not see how she hadn't thought of it before. "The tower," she said and turned to Elflock. "Will the Ringer be there?" She still had many questions about the mysterious Ringer of the bells— their prison guard—and she hoped to get them answered.

"Not until the morning," said Elflock, nodding in agreement. "That is a good thing, Freja." She asked why. "His identity is secret—not even the Élan knows it. We cannot count on his loyalty yet."

"And the others?" said Lulja. "Tryll's asking." She blushed and interpreted the signs, too quick for Freja to follow. "The other Masters?"

"I will follow you to the tower, then find our friends," said Elflock.

"Do you think that Lord will come back?" Freja asked.

"There is no way of knowing," Elflock answered with a shrug. "He is a loyal man, but where his loyalties lie now, I am not sure."

"Pfft," said Lulja. "Doesn't sound too loyal to me."

"He was biased," said Elflock without judgement.

"He was loyal to himself, to his bias," said Freja and nodded. "That sounds like a noble thing to me."

"Whatever," said Lulja and shrugged. "Can we please move? This place is creepy. It's too empty."

Freja jumped as she felt something poke her shoulder, but calmed down when she realised it was only Tryll. He gave her an apologetic look and then pointed towards the empty square and the hangar. With quick glances to the sides he communicated his concern so that even Freja could understand. "There's something out there," she said in a low voice and gestured for Elflock and Lulja to come behind the sealed container. The stench of waste was tangy and sour up close, but there was no remedy. They needed to get out of the area. It seemed indeed too quiet, too calm to be real. Tryll had felt it, and now Freja could sense it too. The grey foundation lay motionless like a beast asleep, cast in selective shadows, hiding who knew what monsters? There was a breathing though; an invisible voice whispering that the city was alive under the surface, even though its inhabitants had gone into hiding. Wherever Freja looked, she seemed to be a second too late to catch the moving shadows that disappeared from sight every time she shifted her gaze towards the old nuclear reactor. What if someone was in there? Freja wasn't sure what had given birth to the thought, but this breathing she felt—that Tryll felt—seemed to originate from the warehouse where once vast power had been generated. There was power there still, but of a different kind. One she had felt before.

Using the TV tower as direction, keeping it steady on her left, Freja guided them through the narrow lanes. The nuclear site was a square plain kept in by the electric fence so, with quick glances around every corner, she led them towards the warehouse, hoping that that's where the gate out from the site would be located.

Crouching under a rusty handle protruding from another grimy dumpster, from which a strong stench of waste erupted, she leapt over a pile of debris and stopped behind the rusty carcass of what was once a van for the site workers. Nobody had cleaned up in thirty years, and she had a distinct feeling that nobody would either. Once Lulja, Tryll, and Elflock were all safe behind the hollow shell of the van, she peered around the corner. The power plant hangar was now three or four lanes ahead, slightly left, and the energy she had felt earlier became stronger with every step. She could see in Elflock's wandering eyes that he felt it too.

"Wait, I saw something," whispered Lulja on Freja's right, making her freeze mid-step. A sinking sensation dragged at her heart, pulling it down to the depths of despair. Again, the shadow had evaded her keen eyes, but clearly not Lulja's. She asked what it was. Lulja shook her head and picked at her scratched cheek. "It was only for a second …"

"Maybe you imagined it?" It wasn't right to accuse her of making things up, but Freja preferred it to have been imagination.

"No, she did not," said Elflock and crept up to them. "Someone else is here." His eyes were fixed on the reactor now.

The soiled exterior glared at them in the dim light. If Freja put her mind to it, she could imagine sounds coming from within the heart of the power plant, but she didn't want to—and that was the problem. Because she could still hear the noises, the thundering murmurs like the sing-song melody of an approaching storm on the horizon. By all appearances, this heart was still beating.

The sky gave her no comfort in its bright canvas of stars. It was such a big world; bigger than she had ever known. Freja felt her senses give in to the song, embracing it, welcoming the storm. Let them come, she thought as she closed her eyes and let it fill her. Let the storm come and sweep it all away: Vildaell, Ma'zekaï, Masters, Obbsborn let it all fall.

"We should go before they, whoever they are, realise that we are here," Elflock said and she nodded in agreement.

The main reactor was slightly left of their position and on its right side was an open area filled with debris of various kinds: toppled over vans, lonely pipes with gaping holes where gravel and bits of concrete had slipped in by natural forces, and broken glass lay scattered across the plain. If they headed right, back the way they'd just come, and aimed for the dumpster standing closest to the fence, they could avoid going right by the large reactor. She pointed out the place and Elflock agreed it was the best path. Seeking the shadows, they hurried east as far as the site allowed them.

"One last run to the gate," Freja whispered and put all her faith into hoping that there was indeed a gate, and that it was open. A hundred metres separated them from its supposed location, but it was still hidden behind the corner of the hangar. "Watch out for stuff on the ground." On the count of three, after having made sure that the reactor was still quiet, Freja leapt forward and the others followed behind her. All that filled her head was to move as fast as possible, while avoiding the thick pipes and pieces of broken glass. When she saw the gate, she let out a small sigh of relief. It was open. With a final push, they exited the site and stopped behind a container to catch their breath. The fence was growling only two metres away.

"It smells," said Elflock and crinkled his nose. "Plenty of unnatural energy inside."

"It's called nuclear power," Freja said and smiled at the Master's reaction to this 'new' type of force. "Comes from, well, *came* from in there." She pointed to the reactor. She regurgitated the process in words she learnt at school. The reactor used uranium and water to split the mineral into smaller parts, from which energy is derived.

"Splitting natural elements by force?" said Elflock. "It sounds perilous."

Freja gestured towards the wasteland around them. "Well …"

It was quiet now, the murmur swept up by whatever came next. When all words were spoken, wasn't action the logical step in the sequence? The thought was terrifying.

"I feel funny," said Lulja. "Tryll, what are you doing?" A slapping sound came from behind them, where Tryll had been crouching. He was standing now, pale-faced and fear written all over him. Red blotches covered his arm where he had pulled up his masterform and continued to slap, tear, and bite at his own skin. Not a nerve twitched in his face, not even when blood seeped out from the consequential wounds, staining the yellow fabric. Lulja flew at him and tore his hands away, but fell back the next moment, her wide eyes instilling a chilling fear in Freja.

"I can't feel my arm," cried Lulja, tearing up. "Freja, why can't I feel my arm?"

"Lulja, take it easy," Freja said, grabbing her face, begging her to be quiet. They were so close to the reactor. The sounds were still in the air, louder now. Lulja started convulsing, completely out of control of her body. Beside them Tryll had stopped biting himself and just stared into the sky, not seeing anything. Freja begged them both to be quiet as Lulja dropped to her knees, hugging her body as though cold.

"I can't see anything," she cried, loud enough to make Freja glance back at the reactor. The screams echoed between the buildings and she could only hope they were swallowed up as well. "Freja!"

"It's okay," she cooed, trying to soothe her agony. Jaspir had not embraced panic in his dehumanised state, but she saw the same signs as she saw then. The loss of sense, the empty gaze. "Elflock, do something," she said, but the Master kept watching the reactor.

"I can't hear you," Lulja cried out. "I can't …!"

Freja's eyes met Tryll's before he fell to the ground, the dust swirling for a moment around the body, but she didn't see the boy who loved Lulja in there—only emptiness. His mouth was open, as though trying to scream. No scream came. Then Lulja's body stopped seizing and went unnaturally still. Her deer-like eyes were huge and glazed, pupils small and unresponsive, staring at Freja and at the same time not at her, but a point beyond her physical being. The next moment she, too, collapsed. "Elflock," Freja said, gently lowering Lulja's limp body to the ground. She looked so peaceful now that the seizing stopped. "She's breathing. Tryll too. What's going on?"

"The effect will wear off eventually," said Elflock and at last Freja put the pieces together. She shot a wild look at the reactor and swallowed hard. There was somebody inside that hangar and they were not human. In fact, they never had been.

The next moment, the massive gateway of the hangar screeched and folded inwards. The Strays were coming out.

CHAPTER 37

BEFORE FREJA COULD wonder what business Strays had in an abandoned nuclear power plant in Vildaell or how they had travelled from Ma'zekaï, Elflock snapped his fingers and brought her back to his attention. They had to move—and quick.

He went over to Tryll and lifted him from the ground by the shoulders like it was the easiest thing in the world. Freja on the other hand groaned as she dragged Lulja's relatively small frame from the open street. Once Tryll was slouched against the back of the container, Elflock helped put Lulja in a sitting position beside him. All hidden, they peered towards the hangar. The door was fully up now, revealing the dark interior. Nothing was moving yet, but something—someone—had opened the gateway and the murmuring song had been taken up once more. It was more subdued now, not as sinister. Behind them Lulja and Tryll had coiled into tense balls on the ground, their bones shaking with every tune of the melody from within the reactor.

"This is peculiar," said Elflock, crouching next to Freja with the reactor in his field of vision.

He saw the shadow first, and stiffened. Only when it came

out in the moonlight did Freja see the full body of them. More accurately: all three bodies. When she realised who she was looking at, a heavy weight like lead sunk inside her. The nuclear reactor might as well have exploded in front of her and she would not have noticed. It was unfathomable, but no doubt about it: the white masterforms glimmered in the light, black onyx gem stones glistening on their faces.

"Are those …?" Freja whispered, knuckles whitening from the firm grip on Elflock's shoulder. If she was hurting him, he did not notice. She could only imagine what was going through his mind.

"The Lords," he confirmed as the three Élan Lords reached the path right where Elflock and Freja were hiding. In fearful anticipation, Freja leaned into the container and held her breath.

"Some foul business, this," said a light voice with a hint of disgust. If Freja interpreted Elflock's mouthing correctly, it was Py who spoke. "It is pure extortion."

"I would expect nothing less from a Flÿght. Just hope to your Essences that we locate that latch soon," said another female voice, this one deeper than the first. Eden. "Everything depends on it."

"That, and the Strays," agreed Py.

"The latch is irrelevant," added a third voice, Trozelli. "The only way we could lose power here is if we willingly let go of it." Eden expressed her reservations but Trozelli insisted. "Once they are absorbed by the Network we will control the Trinity borders, not him."

Who 'they' were became obvious once Freja saw what followed behind the backs of the Lords' white masterforms: a cluster of Strays, then another. Moving like one being, there were clearly several—about four in each—following the path where the Lords had gone before, murmuring the song as they did so. Freja counted fourteen groups of Strays before the last of the melodies faded away and the surroundings returned to silence. Elflock went to make sure that the hangar was empty and came back announcing that they had all gone. Adrenaline was pumping through Freja's veins and she considered her two friends, still paralysed by the Strays. Strangely, now as well as in Wind, Freja only experienced a dull internal tickle, not more.

As they waited for Tryll and Lulja to recover, Elflock told Freja about the Strays. It turned out Lulja had been right: Masters didn't simply die. No written records existed of course, so nobody could know for sure how long it took for a Master to break down all the physical energy within and forego his body. The transition time was known as Strays —the collective energy of deceased Masters. "They are a pure energy field capable of obscene destruction if not contained," he said. "The first generation of Lords made a treaty assigning them to Masters. They belong to us. 'Once a Master, always a Stray,' is what they said." He laughed, but not with mirth. "I think they underestimated how slow time seems when forced to endure it."

"I don't understand."

"Some of the old Masters of my first generation are still part of the Strays," Elflock said and Freja started to see where the problem was. "Always moving together, never knowing when the darkness will come to an end. We are not like humans, Freja. This world is mortal and all beings within it. It is destructive—and finite. A Master in Ma'zekaï will live to see many generations of Obbsborn if allowed the full span of his life. Even more as a Stray."

Freja contemplated this and wondered how old he was. Elflock's smooth skin and muscular body carried no indication of being impaired by age. If her human perception had to guess, she'd say about thirty, or at least late twenties.

"I have seen five generations," he said with a slight smile, as if reading her mind. "Five generations, that is my age. Topster has seen fewer, perhaps three or four."

"And the Lords?"

He shrugged. "I cannot say for sure, but more than I have."

She turned towards the reactor. There was something about the Strays that had seemed odd, but she couldn't put her finger on what it was exactly. Fourteen groups of four had exited the reactor. In Wind, they had been hundreds in one. She pointed this out to Elflock.

"Yes, these Strays are independent," he mused. "They are set free. Do not ask me how that is done or even what it means. I do not dare think about it."

The answer struck her a moment later and she clasped a hand to her mouth. The words from physics class repeated themselves like they had when she put pen to paper barely a year ago in her exams. The words she had told Elflock only minutes earlier: nuclear fission is the process where the nucleus of a particle is split into smaller entities. "It's the reactor," she said and received a dumb look in return. She clarified. "They divided the Strays here," she pointed to the hangar. "That's what they used the reactor for. The Lords must have found a way to use fission to separate them, but why?"

Elflock scratched his chin. Suddenly all colour drained from his face. "What does Ma'zekaï need more than anything else?" he asked. Freja frowned. "Energy," he continued, more impatient with each sentence. "Ma'zekaï needs energy. That is why we have been taking it from Heim for generations. But now the Lords are desperate; desperate enough to want to open the borders, but what if that is not enough?" He spoke in a pitch she had not heard from any Master before. It frightened her, but she forced herself to listen. "Think about it. What are Strays?"

"Collective energy," she said and her mouth fell open as

she realised. "That's why they don't want to close the borders. They need the reactor. They're splitting the Strays to generate energy?"

"Of the foulest kind," he said. "It will contaminate the Network in the most irreparable way." Elflock hissed and a flush of colour painted his cheeks. He glared towards the reactor. "Lord Tej would not have seen this done, not over his perished Essence."

Freja sent a thought to the other Masters, hoping that they had managed to convince their old friend to return.

"Who's doing what?" said a feeble voice behind them. Lulja had opened her eyes and turned to Tryll, who was also withdrawing from whatever land of dreams the Strays had committed him. With apparent effort their hands found each other and gave each other strength so that, soon enough, both of them were shuffling to sit up properly.

"How do you feel?" Freja asked and got a weak thumbs-up from Tryll and a stiff smile from Lulja.

"Are we still here?" Lulja asked as she shook off the last of the daze. In no time at all, both of them were back.

"We're going now," whispered Freja and patted her hair back into place, picking out pieces of dirt. It had been dishevelled from her writhing. She turned to Elflock. "If we're right, they'll be back soon. Are you listening?" He was facing the reactor, hands behind his back and a grim expression on his face. Nothing in his poise suggested he had heard. "Elflock." He turned, gave her a curt nod, and helped an inquisitive Tryll to his feet. "I'll tell you later," Freja muttered as she pulled Lulja up. "Let's go."

It took them half an hour to reach the small Linden Plaza, named after its circle of planted linden trees at its west point. The square itself was surrounded by a low granite wall, assumed to be for decorative purpose, and consisted mostly of a plain cobble stone area and benches lining the contour of the space. The centrepiece, a fountain, stood eerily quiet, as the night itself.

Nothing had disturbed their way there, not even a disconcerting caw. The bells of Curfew had emptied the city; even the birds had gone into hiding. None of the Curfew guards, believed to police the streets of Vildaell at night, were in sight anywhere and, judging by what Freja knew of the ill-reputed guards, if there were any around they would have captured the illegal streetwalkers already. Though it did make their journey across the city a whole lot easier, it did nothing to soothe her state of mind. There was a numbing ache in her body, not quite like the effect of the Strays, but dull and deep. Her friends were pale and worn out as well. Dark bags sagged under their eyes and only Elflock maintained a straight poise. Being out in the open like this, Curfew guards or no Curfew guards, was nigh on reckless. The others agreed and they climbed over the stone wall, into the square, all of them praying that the Ringer would indeed be gone until the eleventh bell.

The tower stood at the midpoint of the arboreal circle, surrounded by trees dressed in seasonal green leaves. Freja could not remember having observed the tower at such close range before and now saw its complex steel structure in detail. Its side was spotted with small round windows so that whoever was inside could see the city without being seen himself. Its body rested on four platforms and stretched up like a narrow pyramid with the entrance in the centre. Stripped by its connotations, Freja considered it quite beautiful.

Elflock managed the lock with help from a leaf and the tinted glass door swung open to reveal a dark lobby. "I'll leave you here for now," he said and crumbled the leaf ashes to the ground where they were whisked away by a breeze. "I shall find Éloyse and the others. Stay here."

In his face Freja saw the weight laid there by the Lords. His supposed leaders were betraying their own kind, and in a most horrific way. While Lulja and Tryll entered the tower, Freja waited a moment and watched Elflock walk away until he slipped behind a corner of the tower's west pillar and disappeared from sight.

She followed her friends into the tower lobby. It was beautifully decorated with thick carpets of various shades of grey and with cushioned sofas lined along one of the walls. She had assumed that the tower contained nothing but the Ringer of the bells, but this looked like the lobby of an office building. A sign told them that there were conference rooms to the left, and a reception—now abandoned—to the right. In the middle, just beyond the reception, was the staircase leading up through the interior of the tower. There was no elevator, as Lulja pointed out with a groan. "Better start climbing," she muttered and took the lead.

The staircase was steep and strenuous, even Freja had to admit to that. Every fifty steps—she counted—led to a small platform with a door. None of the first three would budge, but the fourth door obeyed Lulja's push and they entered a square room with bare walls, bare floor, and only a window to break the monotone white of its interior. A single light bulb hung from the ceiling, but did not work, as Tryll found when clicking the switch. It only sputtered out a low growl before giving up completely. Luckily the window was on the side of the moon and a faint light entered the room. Through it, they could see the plaza with its benches and the fountain. All empty. Right now, at least. Freja had an ominous feeling that they had been spotted. The Lords didn't feel like the kind of people who would overlook three humans and one of their own kin spying behind a dumpster.

"Did you figure out what the Strays were doing?" Lulja

asked on Tryll's behalf. Freja kept her gaze on the empty plaza. She told them no. "Weird," continued Lulja. "Well, I'm just glad they didn't catch us."

"They don't mean ill," said Freja, remembering what Elflock had said about the perished Masters. "They're just stuck. Like us." She sat down on the floor, leaning against the wall. She closed her eyes and pretended that she was at home, waiting for the bell. The vision changed and she was back on the stairs watching her father slump to the floor as a red light changed their lives forever. "I just hope they won't come after us," she murmured and opened one eye. She gave no remark to Lulja's tilted head resting on Tryll's shoulder. It didn't seem important anymore. Like old news in the midst of a new catastrophe. The Strays were probably tracking them right now, she thought. Maybe. Or would they be too busy to concern themselves with a few sleepwalkers?

"His face," said Lulja after a moment's silence. "Elflock's face when he came into the Bank." She gave a very life-like imitation of the Master's absolute bafflement as he had discovered the three humans reaching for latch crystals like common apple thieves. Tryll gave a soundless laugh. "It's the only time I've seen him speechless." She wiped tears away from her eyes as her laughter filled the hollow box of the room.

It wasn't the only time Freja had seen him at a loss for words, but neither Lulja nor Tryll knew that and she decided to keep it secret for now and just smiled. She told them about the Lords at the nuclear site, only leaving out the part with Elflock's reaction. He deserved to keep his dignity and reputation as a stoic Master. At least one of them could remain the strong one.

"There's going to be a war, isn't there?" said Lulja biting her lip.

Freja nodded. "I think we're already in it," she said, sighed and covered her face.

Tryll signed something to Lulja and she translated it in words for Freja's benefit. "He asks what we should do? Now, I mean."

As she finished the question Tryll looked up towards the ceiling. Freja guessed he wasn't particularly interested in the flailing paint. There was one place in the tower they had yet to explore; one that may hold many answers. Again he bobbed his head upwards, causing his dark locks to dance with it. Freja had always thought words were important, that language was the key component of their perception of the world, and had never considered a life without them. Tryll showed that sometimes words were unnecessary.

He wanted to go to the Ringer's room.

CHAPTER 38

Four hours until bell eleven

FOR THEIR OWN sakes she hoped that Elflock was right, that the Ringer would be gone until the morning, but it wasn't without a fluttering stroke of disappointment that she entered the most mythical place in Amérle and found it empty. All her questions about this person and still no answers.

It was a room about halfway up the neck of the tower and as far as the staircase went. With its rounded shape it stretched across the full length and depth of the walls and it had panoramic windows—tinted from the outside—giving whoever was looking a full view of the city. The Look-Out wasn't the only place that saw everything, Freja thought grimly. On the desk were papers, pens, and files ordered in delicate and impeccable rows and piles, and ten TV screens hovered on the south wall, just above the windows. Freja guessed that one of the many buttons on the keyboard sitting at the edge of the desk controlled the bells. "It's a monitor," she said as she took in every piece of technology in there. The equipment, including the screens, was designed for one thing: surveillance. "He's watching us."

"Or she," added Lulja and joined Tryll who brought their attention to the screens, which Freja now saw covered various parts of the city. "You recognise any of it?" Lulja asked.

Freja stepped closer, even though she didn't have to. She recognised all of it. The images were in a greenish hue—night mode, she guessed—and seemed to move from east to west, from left to right, starting with the highway over the bridge leading in from the suburbs to the nuclear site at the far end. Every single screen showed empty streets and locked-down houses, as would be expected. There was the main shopping street at the Queen's Parade, a few other locations in residential areas, and Linden Plaza itself was on the sixth screen, as vacant as the others. She went through the screens one by one and was surprised to find that the Look-Out was not among the covered areas. To her it seemed the perfect place for a CCTV camera, but whoever installed them clearly did not share that opinion. There was a residential area she didn't recognise on the ninth screen and the black and white power plant showed on the tenth and final one. Nothing moved in the shadows. The Strays had left the compound. A shudder travelled from Freja's toes upwards as she thought of the dark creatures prowling the city below them—and in whose hands they were. Elflock's expression as he witnessed the Lords at the scene of the crime was etched into her memory and would not let go.

"What is it, Tryll?" Lulja's voice brought Freja back to the present, away from Strays and Lords, yet still not as far away as she would wish. Tryll was pointing again towards the screens or, more specifically, the eighth one. The Great Square. "I don't see anything," said Lulja and Freja had to agree. It looked like usual to her. The camera was attached to one of the light poles on the pedestrian path, and the square itself was a dark blotch below. A few bikes stood left behind, leaning against the metal railing, carelessly left unlocked.

Then she saw it. They weren't bikes. "Transporters!"

Tryll sighed and clapped his hands. Freja made a face but berated herself for not having noticed the vehicles earlier. Given the angle they stood at, the wheels looked twisted and almost straight, like on a bicycle. Still, she shouldn't have been so oblivious.

"If Transporters are here …," Lulja began, and Freja finished the sentence for her.

"Then so are Masters."

"Can we at least hope that they belong to Elflock or Éloyse?" Lulja was pleading without conviction.

Tryll shook his head and Freja had to admit there was a minimal chance—if any at all—that Éloyse would be so careless as to leave something so obvious behind. She only knew of one Master who was arrogant enough to be so unconcerned and irresponsible.

The next moment a woman came into the picture and the three onlookers went quiet at once. They followed her in silence as she leaned over the railing, said something they couldn't hear, and walked out of the image again. The poor quality lent itself to few details but her blonde hair gleamed through the night filter, her slender body and sharp features made her stand out in the midst of the urban landscape. She was a creature of Nature, not city, and every move she made suggested an awareness of this particular fact. It was as if she made an effort to be uncomfortable and out of place. Even to Freja, who had met her in one brief moment, Florin wore her haughtiness and superiority on her sleeve.

"How did they even get here?" Lulja said. "We have all the latch—Oh, that evil little thing!" Another woman had come into the screen together with Florin and they were conversing by the Transporters. Again, the figure was unmistakable. The stooping poise and old-but-not-old appearance could belong to nobody else. Klepta was carrying a saddle bag and handed it to Florin, said something, then left again. Florin glared after her for a long time.

"Can we switch on the sound?" Freja asked and scanned the keyboard. "No sound button …?"

Tryll pushed her aside and sat down in the chair, shoving some papers to reveal the full keyboard. He considered the myriad of buttons and scratched his head. The first button he pressed did nothing.

"Quickly now," said Freja and received a sour look from Tryll in return. "Sorry, it's just … you know, kind of urgent." With a sequence of quick waltzing on the keyboard, Tryll managed to find a settings menu. A few more presses found the sound on the first screen, offering nothing but the silence of the empty highway and the low hum of the camera. "Screen eight," said Freja, hoping that she sounded more helpful than irritated. It wasn't his fault that the complex keyboard was, well, complex, but she couldn't help the pressing time frame. The very air carried with it a virus of tension, of threatening impact; like an aerosol of thick and sticky pull which glued the atoms of the world together, making them inaccessible to the people moving among them. Freja felt this density around her as if the world could—and would—explode at any moment.

The sound came on with a press of Tryll's finger. Crackling, at first, then clear as if they were standing right next to Klepta. She was speaking to someone outside of the frame.

"*Ka-ka*," she said in her idiosyncratic way. "Are they coming?"

Tryll shifted in his seat when she spoke, as if her voice caused him agony. Lulja noticed this too and sat down on the arm support of the chair, holding herself still by help of Tryll's shoulder. How many times had the cackling woman been proof of the Obbsborn's safety? Pojk's very existence had guaranteed their relative well-being, but the moment Klepta stepped into the greenish image on screen eight, the walls of protection had come crashing down like an avalanche. Such deceit did not go by unnoticed.

"I bet it was that snake who took the Transporters," said Lulja in a low voice, glaring at the small blue form on the screen.

"How would she have known?" Freja asked, not revealing that the thought had struck her as well. Few people would have had the opportunity, and here was one who clearly had the incentive. Whatever it was.

"She knew," Lulja replied. "Remember we wanted her as an ally?"

"Great choice that," said Freja but instantly bit her tongue. It didn't matter now—that part was over.

"All is well," said Florin. "It is a rich world, is it not?"

"*Ka*, indeed," replied Klepta. "But the smell, Master Florin—it's rich in the obscene way."

Florin closed her eyes and drew it in like it was the most expensive perfume. It took a moment or two before she exhaled. "Obscenity, Klepta, is not a sin," she said with a grim smile. "All the best of things are obscene, after all."

"Whatever do you mean by that?" Klepta was torn between being shocked at the profanities spoken out loud, while she was evidently curious to hear more, probing her partner for more, more, more. "You are not speaking of … Surely, not?"

"Too long have we condemned it," said Florin in a calm voice. Klepta took a step back, wide eyed. "Is it truly as detrimental as we have been taught to believe? Could it not be, and this is just a thought, beneficial?"

"Now, Master, if I were you I'd keep my opinions to myself," said Klepta, a finger waving in the air. "Don't let Topster hear you. *Ka-ka!*"

"What are they talking about?" whispered Lulja, frowning. Tryll shrugged in the chair and Freja said nothing. She needed to hear more to be sure, but if her hunch was right then this conversation was astonishing. Of all people she had not expected Florin to defend a weakening quality of mind.

"I am not speaking as if it were true," continued Florin, incredulous. "But times are changing." She gestured out towards the square as she spoke. "And we have much to learn from this world. Have we not already adopted some of their advantages?" Technology had given them Transporters and other tools in Ma'zekaï—technology directly taken from Heim. "Is it too obscene to reconsider some of our values as well?"

Freja couldn't believe her ears. Was this really Florin speaking? She wondered what had happened to change her mind so radically.

"It's this *landskapë*," said Klepta, casting a glance out of the camera's reach. "Its energy has intoxicated you."

Florin gave up a laugh and drew another deep breath. "If it has, my dear, I thank it for it."

"Master Florin!" said Klepta. "If Topster …"

As though his ears had been burning, the man himself stepped into the frame and all three of them leaned forward. If Freja had hoped to see him strained, his hair out of order and a flair of distress in his eyes because his plan was all but satisfactory, she was sorely disappointed. Not a single hair was askew and his usual expression of complete composure was as it always had been, perhaps spiced with a hint of complacency, which only made Freja tense up even more. When his voice sounded through the sound system it was as if time stood still. Her whole concentration was focused on the screen and what was said. Nothing else penetrated Freja's delimited sensual field.

"Beautiful night, is it not?" he said in the same silky distanced voice as had been lingering in Florin's speech. He, too, drew in air through his nostrils and let out a chuckle.

"Beautiful," said Florin and—*batted her eye lashes?*

Freja exchanged an amused glance with Lulja. This was a different kind of Florin from what they had seen before. What's more, Topster did not oppose her; rather, he stepped closer.

"Or it's all this foul—" Klepta sniffed and then pinched her nose— "I can't, *ka!*"

A voice out of frame called Topster's name, and he left together with Florin, leaving a distraught Klepta clutching her hair and squeezing her nostrils shut.

As Freja's attention shifted back to the world around her, she heard voices—voices approaching the door. Gathering from the alarmed look on Lulja's face and Tryll's quick press at the mute button, she assumed they had heard them as well. They had all been too focused on the screen to hear the steps. With no other option available, they remained where they were, waiting.

"You promised she'd be safe," said one of the voices, a man. "You made a Master promise."

"Calm yourself," said another, also male. "She is safe."

The door was pushed open in a painful slow-motion and a body-less hand reached inside. A leaf was wedged between thumb and palm and it hovered there for a moment before revealing the Master to whom the hand belonged.

Lulja gave up a small shriek of joy and shot up when Elflock came in, followed by Éloyse, then Ravn, then two Masters who Freja didn't recognise, while she remained seated until the last member stepped through the door. She had recognised the voice without aid from visual confirmation. It was the voice she had heard her whole life, so how could she not? But it wasn't until her father came in behind Master Ravn that she dared to think that she was right. Their eyes met and the next second she flung herself into his arms, wrapping her arms around his back. "Thank heavens you're all right," he whispered into her ear and she felt her eyes well up. She buried her face in his chest, expecting to be submerged in the familiar scent of flour and a heated oven that was his natural perfume. When she realised that it was lacking and that the material pressed against her nose wasn't flannel or even regular fabric, she released him and stepped back, frowning. She tried to connect the face to the body in front of her, and failed. At first she thought she had hugged the wrong man and felt heat travel to her cheeks. Then she saw.

The sound reappeared from the monitors behind them as Tryll showed the Masters what they had found. None of that registered in Freja's mind.

Both father and daughter distorted into confused frowns as the one realised what the other was wearing. The grey masterform washed out her father's colourful self into an image of the dirty thawing snow in the city. Even his face looked different. It was harder now; washed-out and pale as if the masterform shade had seeped into his blood stream and taken over the pigment of his skin. Gleaming gems in a clouded ashen hue sat above one of his eyebrows, just like her own amethysts ornamented her temples. They could only stare at each other, perplexed.

Éloyse had to call three times before Freja heard. Elflock and others had gathered in front of the monitors, and they were all staring at screen eight again, from whence new voices were coming. "Come on, you probably want to hear this," she said. "You too, Lord Tej."

Freja looked around the room. Her gaze stuck on the two, to her, unknown Masters. One of them was younger, but if she had to guess she'd say that the older one was the famous Lord so well spoken of, who gave up his title for bias. For love. Neither of them reacted to the name, however, and Lulja was still addressing Freja and her father. Not until Otto Evenson lowered his gaze and mumbled that 'Lord' wasn't necessary did the truth sink in. It was as gentle as a nail against a wall of glass and as sharp when it hit. Black spots pricked her eyes, causing her to blink frenetically.

"I'm Lulja," said a muffled voice beside her and greeted Freja's father the way a Master would greet another. "That's Tryll, he's a quiet one."

Ordinarily Freja would have been bothered by Lulja's constant attempts at behaving like something she wasn't—especially when it wasn't needed anymore—but clearly Lulja wasn't the only one doing so. "Tej?" she managed, surprised that there was enough control in her left for her to speak. "Lord Tej?"

Without allowing her father room to reply, she turned to the monitor where more people had entered the frame, and pretended to listen, though her head was spinning and her chest tightening so much it felt as if it was holding a small bird in its cavity and it was fluttering in desperation to escape.

CHAPTER 39

NOBODY SPOKE UNTIL the screen was abandoned again and Tryll killed the sound. The conversation that had just ended had thrown the small group into contemplation and no one said anything for a long time.

"What's a Champion?" Lulja asked at last, breaking the silence before it sunk over them again.

Nothing in the conversation between Florin and Topster had given any clue as to what exactly this 'Champion' was; only that it would be instrumental in the process—and that it would arrive soon. There had been a certain weight in Topster's voice when he spoke of it: a richness, a power, and a terrifying confidence. Florin had probed him to tell her more but Topster refused. Nobody was to know more before the time came. Such were the orders. It was his card of triumph, he had said, and the presence of the 'Champion' was essential to the coming events.

"Is it a weapon?" Lulja tried. "Freja?"

Freja shook her head. Topster hadn't mentioned it to her or to Klobb as far as she could remember. She glanced at Ravn, thinking back to his conversation with Topster in the mountains. Had they mentioned a Champion then? She couldn't remember. She couldn't remember anything beyond the wall of grey pressed against her cheeks only moments ago. Everything was suppressed by it, concealed behind its bewildering mass.

"Without the latches they can do nothing," said the old Master, Neese. "No matter how many of the Flÿght are involved."

He spoke in a drawling voice, slightly moist, and Freja couldn't help but wonder how much time he had left in life. How many generations had he seen? Had he known her father when he was a Lord? She forced herself not to look at him, not trusting her body to obey her resolution to suppress the fact that her whole life was a lie and focus on the task ahead instead. She would not be biased, she thought fiercely, then flinched at the thought. Had she fallen to the Master norm? The idea didn't quite leave her, not even when she caught herself noticing the anxious glances cast her way from the Master, the Lord, in grey, and felt a swirl of knotted emotion in her stomach.

"What if they have latches?" said Éloyse. "How else would they get here?"

"The Bank is empty," said Elflock with pride. "These young ones made sure of that."

Lulja gave a short account of what had happened in the Bank and afterwards, resulting in impressed gasps and encouraging smiles. Éloyse was outraged to hear what Klepta had done with the Transporters.

"The snake," she said with force and glared at the screen where nothing was stirring.

"Clearly the job was not done properly," came from the back where the young Master had sat quiet and observed the scene. He pointed to the screens. "They're here." Though he received a couple of angry glares, Tomsom was right. Somehow the Flÿght had acquired latches, although they didn't know how many.

"Infinite latches?" suggested Lulja on behalf of Tryll.

"It's possible," said Elflock, scratching his chin. "They are real, Neese," he added as the Master began protesting. "I saw it with my own eyes."

"I know where I would turn for latches," muttered Tomsom. Ravn asked if he had anything useful to say. He cleared his throat and spoke up. "Latch welders …"

"Nothing but a myth," interrupted Ravn. "A tale told a long time ago."

"I have sources that say otherwise."

"They are wrong," said Ravn. "The welders were expelled generations ago. There are none left in Ma'zekaï."

"Maybe not in Ma'zekaï," Tomsom spat back but silenced as Ravn shot him a furious look of exasperation. The young Master leaned back against the wall, pouting.

"Ravn," said Elflock, pondering. "Until hours ago, I did not believe in infinite latches. Could the welders have returned?"

"Thank you," said Tomsom and sent a daggering look at Ravn.

"I agree with Ravn," Neese broke in. "That welders were to be involved is exceptionally unlikely. Nevertheless, we must assume that the Flÿght have enough latches, whatever number that may be and in whatever manner they have acquired them. Tomsom, you come with me. We must see the Lords."

"Remember to tell them the good news," said Éloyse with a broad smile towards Freja's father. Her eyes glimmered—or perhaps it was just the light from the screens throwing shadows. Freja rolled her eyes and picked up conversation with Lulja instead. Still, Éloyse's words drowned out her own. "That the old Lord has returned."

"If anyone can stop this madness, it is the Lords," said Neese with a slight bow towards Otto, or Tej. He squirmed in his seat, not quite returning the bow. "Can we trust the infinite latches?" Neese continued.

"Use this," said Lulja and handed him a crystal from the Bank. Neese observed it closely, watched the silver swirl, but didn't make any further inquiries. He thanked her and wrapped his fingers around it.

"Lord Eden is your best chance," continued Éloyse. "She saw the first rebellion of the Flÿght. It's in her Essence to understand."

Elflock bereaved Freja of her attention to Neese's reply. His eyes burned into her side and she had to shoot him a reproachful glance, at which he focused on Neese instead. They had not yet told the rest that the Lords were in Vildaell as well tonight. Freja wasn't sure why, but didn't feel it was her place to tell. Elflock was one of them. To Freja it seemed nothing but appropriate that he shared the news. Except he didn't. Perhaps he was waiting for the opportune moment, but surely that was sooner rather than later?

Before she could bring it up, Neese was on the staircase with Tomsom sulking behind, now speaking in a loud voice to his mentor all the things he dared not speak inside the Ringer's room with Ravn hawking at his every syllable.

"Peace and quiet at last," said Ravn with a smirk. "Lulja, are you still set on Master life? Tomsom isn't rare, I'm afraid. These young ones seem to be made of similar stuff."

"I've seen the worst of humanity," said Lulja, her fingers braiding themselves with Tryll's, "I'm from Jahran, remember?" She turned back to the screens, where Tryll had kept his attention all the time. Nothing had moved. Whatever Topster and the others were doing, they were doing it out of sight of the cameras.

"As I understand," said Éloyse, now addressing Lulja and Tryll, "the Obbsborn are moving tonight as well? Is there any way we can persuade them not to?"

"Oh, they won't," said Lulja before Tryll had a chance to respond. "Not yet."

"And why is that?" asked Ravn with narrowed eyes. "The Obbsborn have never shown proof of patience before."

"I'm glad you realise that," said Lulja with acidity. "Living in misery serving a totalitarian superior isn't as constructive as you think for building character. Another thing I picked up back home."

"The Obbsborn promised to wait," said Freja to Éloyse. "They understand that their future is at stake tonight as well." Also, and this she kept to herself, the Trinity Latch was still in her bag.

"We're relying on a human promise?" snorted Ravn. "Excellent."

"Don't be condescending," snapped Freja. "It's not because of humans we are here, is it?"

Ravn glowered at her as Elflock put an arm between them, as if he feared they would leap at each other. "Where is it?" Ravn addressed Elflock.

"Safe," he said and, thankfully, did not look at Freja.

Without asking, she knew what Ravn was referring to. She could almost feel the purple latch burn through the fabric of her bag. The Trinity Latch. There were too many secrets buried. These Masters were the trustworthy ones, and still she watched and heard one lie after the other slip out. Yet, she said nothing of it herself. She participated in the lies—worse, she carried one of them. Every secret had her name signed at the bottom. All but one: her father's. She caught his eye but looked away again. Something was distinctly wrong about his appearance and she didn't like him at all in that masterform. She had imagined their reunion countless times in the past weeks and in her imaginations it was always happy and joyful, not saturated with burden and deceit. None of her fantasies ended in a cold war of averted glances. As soon as she found the words she would ask the big questions, but something was stopping her. A nugget, a gnawing nugget of irritation probed the decision-making part of her brain: shouldn't he be the one explaining?

"There are bound to be Flÿght in Ma'zekaï waiting to enter Heim. Can we stop them?" Elflock had positioned himself between Ravn and Freja, as a precaution, she imagined. He didn't have to worry. She knew well what the slip of green sticking out from Ravn's palm was, and she had no inclination to leafy suicide today.

"You and Ravn should go to Ma'zekaï," said Éloyse without taking her eyes of the screens. "Two Élan will be a lot more persuasive than a Trew. It looks like we can't do much here so we need to stop them before entering. I wish I could come, but I will be needed elsewhere."

"Persuasion has not soothed them before," said Elflock with a sigh. "I doubt it will this time."

"The Flÿght are too self-biased to see beyond the blue cloud around them," said Ravn. "You'd have to promise them eternal glory to have the slightest chance at changing their minds."

"So do it," said Éloyse. "Play to their greatest weakness. Promise them lordship if you have to. If they will not listen to reason, you use any means necessary. Any means." Elflock and Ravn nodded, taking in the weight of what Éloyse had just said. Freja wondered what authority she had to issue *ad nauseam* on methods of influence as a Trew. As neither Elflock nor Ravn opposed her, however, she assumed it was either authority she possessed or authority she claimed when necessary.

"And you?" asked Elflock with something soft added to his usual tone.

Éloyse hesitated a moment, wetting her lips, before speaking. Her eyes wandered to the CCTV screen number eight, where Topster had entered the image, alone. He was standing by the railing watching over the lands he expected to be in his possession soon. Tryll hit the sound button. The droning sound of camera could be heard.

Elflock was the first one to catch on. "No," he said and stood up. "Not a chance."

"I have to," Éloyse said with softness.

"You're going to him?" said Ravn and laughed. "I knew you were crazy, but never this crazy."

"He counts on me to be there," said Éloyse again.

"Éloyse, reconsider," said Freja's father, who had been mute until now. "It'll be like last time."

"That was a long time ago," said Éloyse. "You haven't been here." Éloyse's remark, as fair as it was, hit hard and he said no more.

"But we have," said Elflock in his stead. "I have." He paused and let the words sink in, before continuing. "Éloyse, we have reason to believe that Topster, together with the Lords, are behind the Flÿght's efforts." Something wild took possession of Éloyse's face and she flinched. Elflock stood stoic but Freja detected the slightest tremble in his voice, only at the very first syllables, after which it took on firmness again. "Before he left Ma'zekaï he received a message from Eden. We can't trust her either." Though she had shared that with Elflock in confidence, Freja could see that Éloyse needed to hear it. Her nostrils were flaring, her breathing became heavier, and there was something glassy about her absent stare, still focused on Elflock and yet not. She saw someone else entirely.

"So why did you let Neese and Tomsom leave?" she said. "Never mind …" She swallowed a few times and not once did Elflock take his eyes off her. Patiently, he waited for her to continue. "He wouldn't …," she managed at last, concealing a sniff poorly in a low laugh. "He loathes humans."

"He was biased towards Sofia," said Ravn as Éloyse's

expression broke down brick by brick, baring her, to Masters, shameful emotion inside. It was painful to watch. Perhaps she had been more biased than she knew herself. "Good job on getting the kid out of here by the way," he added to Elflock with a curt nod.

Elflock knitted his hands as if feeling a need to keep them in check. "Éloyse," he said and she lifted her head to face him. "Ravn is right. This is Topster's way of punishing Sofia and her kind."

"Who's Sofia?" Lulja mumbled to Freja, who remained silent though she certainly knew the answer as Elflock had whispered the story to her earlier. She noticed her father shifting in his seat and wondered what he was thinking.

"I'm still going," Éloyse said and stood up. "You know I should be there."

"She's right," conceded Freja's father in a low voice and Éloyse gave him a small smile. A pathetic way to restore her confidence, thought Freja. "Besides, it would be good to have someone on our side in the midst of it, wouldn't it?"

Nobody opposed this truth.

"What about you, Tej?" said Elflock.

"I want to stay here," he said straight away and glanced at Freja. "I will stay here and try to find this Champion."

"So will we," said Lulja with Tryll nodding beside her. "Right, Freja?"

It was strange, wanting to put as much distance between her and her father when they had been separated for so long, but she did. Every look, every fretting frown, every movement he made caused a surge of agitation within her. She should let him explain, of course, but his words were as dark and hateful as the gems above his eyebrow. She felt betrayed to the very core. Every cell in her body—half of which were derived from him—was personally offended and would not let go of this resentment so easily. Yet there was nothing for her to do in Ma'zekaï right now. There would be later, but she needed to stay in Vildaell. For the first time that evening she looked straight at him and she saw him crumble under the coldness in her eyes. The wall of strength she imagined in him had tumbled down once before in her life and now she witnessed it again, but with less sympathy. She didn't like to see him weak. The cold silence became more and more unbearable, but it was he who broke it.

"Sweetheart, you must have questions," he said slowly.

"I can think of a few," she replied while trying to control the tremble threatening to enter her voice. Tears welled up but she forced them back. She would not be biased, not now. "But we have something to do first." There would be a time for him explain once it was all over. "We have to find the Champion."

"I—" Another voice interrupted him. It came from the eighth screen where the noise of the camera was overpowered by a fierce voice belonging to a squat and gruffly man.

"You are not mistaken?" said Topster in reply to Klobb's statement. "You saw them?"

"Four of 'em, Master—the Master with white teeth and grey 'form and the three *hoomans*." Florin and Klepta were there as well, listening to Klobb's witness account of how he had seen Freja, Lulja, Tryll, and Elflock into the infinite latch behind the tree. He conveniently left out his own part in their departure, something Topster put into question. Klobb mumbled some excuse.

"Florin," said Topster. "What do you make of this news?"

Florin took a step forward and straightened her back. "It is a ploy, Master," she said with a haughty glance at Klobb. "It cannot be true."

Topster sighed. "As usual you are wrong," he said, bored, and Florin's mouth twitched. "A weak mind is a weak body, Florin. Remember that." He knitted his hands behind his back and began pacing back and forth, sometimes looking at something that was outside the frame, smiling. Could it be the Champion, already in place? Were they too late?

"Shall we send the Strays, Master?" asked Florin.

Topster said it wouldn't be necessary. Not yet. "The Strays are on limited favours," he said, gazing out of frame again.

"I do wonder how she got those scars," said Lulja, referring to the jarred lines on Florin's neck.

"Élan is not all fun and games," came Ravn's voice from behind. "Never cross a Lord's path."

Lulja spun around to face him. "Really?" A raised eyebrow was all the confirmation she needed.

"Everything is falling apart," Éloyse said with a hollow absence.

On the screen, Topster was once more giving orders to Klobb. He then told Florin and Klepta to leave him and turned to face straight into the camera. He knew it was there, Freja realised with a twinge of undefined emotion. He knew they were watching.

Then he spoke to them.

"Attention. I would like to call upon a special person who I know is listening. Come see your dear old friends—we have missed you. Be a darling and spare me the trip to Linden Plaza, will you? We will be waiting for you, Miss Freja."

CHAPTER 40

Three hours until bell eleven.

LITTLE DISCUSSION TOOK place—if any at all—in the short lapse between the end of Topster's speech and when Freja reached for her bag, slung it across her chest, and scrambled to the door. With her fingers wrapped around the cold handle she found one eye blink's worth of hesitation, enough to stir the others behind. A hand fell on her shoulder in the same instance; a welcome weight added to the one just dumped on her from the Great Square.

Turning around, she saw that it was Elflock who had come to her aid. Even now her father had not chosen to act. "Be reasonable," Elflock said. "You will not go alone."

She shrugged him off, imagining the stinging disappointment take wings and lift along with this Master's hand. "Yes, I will," she replied. "He called my name. Not any of yours, but mine." In his eyes she saw that Elflock thought it was bravery that spoke. Though it was the opposite of the truth, she didn't correct him. She didn't tug away from their little group out of bravery or any of its cousins. Like the young child realising her own identity for the first time, a feeling had begun stirring in

Freja; a feeling that not only forced her to view her father in new light, but also herself. Whatever stuff her being was made from had changed—the stuff had gone from solid to fluid or the other way around, depending on its original form. Nothing was solid anymore, so perhaps it didn't matter. It wasn't bravery, it was quite different—a form of selfish affirmation, perhaps—but it wasn't bravery.

Her hand was still on the door handle. All that was left was to exit the Ringer's Room. That's all it was. But nothing happened. She stayed where she was, her back to the screens and the rest.

"At least let me go first," said Éloyse and came up between Elflock and Freja. "He's waiting for me too."

From the corner of her eye Freja saw Elflock shift his gaze, but no more revelation of emotion came from him. Had she not been glancing at him that very moment, she might have missed it. The next second he retained his usual expression. Masters of disguise, she thought.

"We'll go with you," said Lulja and stood up, dragging a less than willing Tryll to his feet. In spite of his obvious discontent, he nodded in an assuring manner. "When I get my hands on Klepta …"

"Then what?" Éloyse raised an eyebrow as Lulja squirmed under her demand for detail.

"Well," she said, glancing at Tryll for support, who shrugged and seemed to enjoy her brief humiliation. "Oh, I don't know," she said at last and lashed out with her arms. "But I'll be very upset with her. I'll give her a few carefully selected words."

"Fierce," said Éloyse. She gave them a kind smile as she continued. "Freja is right—Topster called only her name. If we are in any luck, he does not know about all of us yet. Let's keep it that way if we can. Let's also be effective. Lulja, Tryll, you go together with Tej back to the house—they won't expect you there. It's obvious, but I'll say it anyway: stay out of the monitored areas. Stay in the house until you receive further instructions from any of our allies." She turned to Elflock. "Anything to add?"

He shook his head and failed to conceal a stroke of pride across his face. "All very clever," he said and cleared his throat. "A clever mind is a strong mind, is that not what we say?"

"And a biased mind is a weak mind," Éloyse echoed.

Suddenly Freja felt as though she was intruding on an exceptionally private moment. She wondered whether Lulja and Tryll could sense it too, but saw no signs of it in their faces. Then again, they didn't seem to be listening at all. They only had eyes and ears for each other. Her father was staring at the screens. Something told Freja that he was aware of what was going on in the room. Once upon a time they would've have exchanged a glance, perhaps a suppressed smile. Not this time.

It was decided that Elflock would return to Ma'zekaï to oversee the gathering of the Obbsborn and preventing the Flÿght from going forward. There was nothing left to do in Vildaell, he concluded, except find out what Topster had in store for Freja. "Do not allow him inside your head," he said. "Topster is a skilled manipulator of minds." Something told Freja the words were not, at least entirely, meant for her, though Elflock had addressed them to her alone. She only nodded and accepted the 'good lucks' with complacency. Luck had seldom anything to do with anything, she had learned. Power and knowledge and the ability to disregard any emotion were a lot more important when dealing with Masters.

Though she had promised herself not to, she threw a look towards her father as she stepped over the threshold and left the Ringer's Room with Éloyse. He was staring at a point to the right of her, surely focusing on her in secret. Despite this, she saw the concern in his eyes. It was the same depth of apprehension and fear that she had perceived every day since her mother disappeared; the fear that he would never see her again. Depending on what happened at the square, this time it might be true. The door narrowed the visual scope gradually until it closed altogether. The barrier was strong as if an abstract force field had materialised; like a ghost stepping out of the pages of a horror tale right in front of your eyes. In a way she was glad to leave. It still wasn't bravery.

"What does he want with me?" she asked, not quite sure if she asked with apprehension or simple curiosity. "Klobb said he never intended for me to come back here."

"I have an idea but I hope I'm wrong," replied Éloyse quizzically. "This 'Champion' … I have heard of it before." She said no more for a while. From within the room came low voices, but what they were saying was impossible to tell. The barrier swallowed all meaning. Éloyse frowned. "I'm probably wrong," she said and went for the stairs.

"You're not telling then?" Freja said and rolled her eyes. "That's a surprise."

"It's not my place," Éloyse replied in a manner that suggested the matter was closed. "I mean, this is not the time." Subtle, ever so subtle, but definitely brewing, her ferocity trickled through the words. There was no reason to pursue the subject. Freja didn't want to make herself an enemy, or even fall into a trap door of distrust. Like it or not, this Master was probably her life line tonight.

"I wish there was an elevator," Freja muttered as they began their descent.

Outside, the city was quiet, as though nothing strange was occurring that night. The moon was strong and hung in the dark sky, keeping dawn at bay, and the air was crisp and fresh, a bit cooler than expected for a summer's night. It had rained recently, a fact told by small puddles here and there in the untended holes of the tarmac. The water was dark brown, spoiled by pollution from exhaust and radiation, Freja guessed. It was strange though, because despite Lulja and Tryll's irritated skin at the power plant, Freja had felt nothing of the kind on her own. Not even as much as a mild irritation had occurred in her. Then again she didn't know if itchy skin was a common symptom of radioactive affectation or if it had been a reaction from the proximity of the Strays. When the inevitable consequence of these thoughts finally struck, a thick fog entered. If it was Strays, she would be expected to be exempted from the physical paralysation that locked someone like Lulja or Tryll.

That locked a *human*.

She focused her mind on the street, where they traversed the city from Linden Plaza through to the east parts of Amérle, taking particular care to avoid the places they knew were under CCTV coverage. After all, they couldn't be sure who else was watching the footage. On a corner, Éloyse stopped. Freja leaned against the wall, the world returning to straight lines and monochrome with every desperate blink. When the letters had stopped swaying, she saw that they were on the corner of Great Street and King's Avenue: the west corner of the Great Square.

"It's not too late to turn back," said Éloyse. "You look a bit pale."

It certainly felt too late, Freja thought. Instead she collected her thoughts, held them together in her mind with willpower like super glue and tape. They only had to stay together for a short while. Then she would let them fall apart in whatever way they liked.

"If this was any other night," Freja said tentatively, not sure what she was asking, "if this was any other Curfew, what would happen?"

Éloyse looked as though she didn't understand the question. "What would happen?" Freja nodded. "We would collect energy from your organic wells," said Éloyse. "The tree sends energy here and we take it back to Ma'zekaï. You have other energy sources." She sniffed the air. "All these smelly ones."

Freja frowned, incredulous. "That's all?" she said. "That's why people go ... Why my mother was removed?"

"I wish I could give you another answer, Freja, but that is the way it works. I should go." She hugged Freja quickly—to both of their surprise, she deduced from the brevity of the hug—and went around the corner into the square.

When she was gone Freja felt far too alone for her own liking. Perhaps she should have let Lulja or Tryll come with her? Then again, this battle was not theirs. Topster had called her name. Now he was calling another one. Though she didn't dare look, Freja heard a male voice—Topster—calling for Éloyse. It was cool and callous, as sharp as the edge of a leaf through the silence of Curfew. Freja leaned back against the wall and closed her eyes. She would wait for a few minutes before going to her judging. A few deep breaths.

Let's spell it out, she thought. Once, just once.

She wasn't human. She mumbled the words to herself. "I'm not human." At least not fully. She was half Master. She had the Essence. She was half Master. "I am not human."

Strangely, it didn't result in the crumbling sense of tearing confusion and split self-perception as expected. It gave her strength. The Essence was strong within her, so Elflock had said. It was why she wasn't affected by the Strays and why she had been able to access the energy in the Willow leaf that time. It was strong and it made her strong. It was as close to super powers as she had ever been and all of a sudden she felt it pulsate inside her, sending out adrenaline with every beat. The Essence was everywhere: every bone, every vein and artery, every nerve ending secreted and absorbed the substance. It was part of her; nothing could give or take it away. Topster could do anything he wanted with her, but she had the Essence. When she opened her eyes it was to a new vision. The moonlight had become clearer, illuminating the night as bright as day. Curfew was a memory, suppressed to the back of her mind. She was of the Essence. The daughter of a Lord of the Élan. She decided it was time and turned to the square once more. Adrenaline made her jittery and she had to turn to controlled breathing again to calm down. One, two, three. Her heart slowed down, but the Essence continued to rage within. It felt good.

Just as she was about to step forward with all the force she had, a hand clasped around her mouth from behind and panic burned and scorched the edge of all power. It blossomed like a weed, threatening to overturn all the assurance she had tended so gingerly only moments ago.

Not now. Not when she was so close!

"It's me, Freja—I'll let go now."

The familiarity of the voice did little to soothe Freja's frantic internal activity, like a hurricane sweeping the woods, cutting down the trees of calmness by the dozen. The rough skin, beaten by hot trays and cold flour for decades ought to touch some soft spot inside her. It ought to trigger a subconscious sense, but all it did was add force to the storm, which now operated in all four directions, unbound like wildfire. An agent of the senses untamed by reason.

Yet, when the hand retreated, she swung around and wrapped her arms around her father's neck. Instead of seeking the absent scent of baked goods she steered her memory in that direction, back to forgotten days of ease and ingratitude. If only she could extinguish the present for a second, just a second to feel what she was fighting for—for the world she was defending … She held on as though in fear he would vanish into thin air if she let go for even the slightest moment and his arms grasped her just the same.

As though on cue, both of them let the other go, without

breaking body contact. He looked wearier. He also sported a new branch of wrinkles extended from the corners of his eyes when he smiled. And he smiled; he smiled at the sight of his daughter, at the touch of the flesh and blood he had thought lost for good. He had been unlucky once, and so had she; but this time fortune had put the odds in their favour.

"Tej?" she said.

"My Master name," he said. "That's what they used to call me."

"It's what they call you now," she said in a low voice, hardly daring to look at him. But she did. Master, no, Lord Tej. Her father. She saw him but recognised nothing. Not one bit of him seemed familiar. The creases around his mouth, now thin lines as he wasn't smiling, his handsome face—the blue eyes just like hers. The grey masterform gave him an alien look. Her eyes watered at the thought, but she pushed back both tears and ponderings. She had to be strong, unbiased. Lord or not, her father was still Otto Evenson in part, and he was not the running away type of man. That was probably the quality that made him a great and appreciated Élan Lord, thought Freja and that strange light appeared again; the one that lay like a filter confined to the vision of her father. It bathed him in a glorious light as if the sun had taken the night shift, solely to illuminate him. He appeared taller and younger—and there was no scent of a heated oven. The filter took his memories and his scent away. She rubbed her forehead, pushing back the tears. Curse those easily tickled tear ducts. Not now, not now, not now.

"I wouldn't let you go alone," he said with a smile. "It's after Curfew."

A wave of something sweet and soft covered the raw soreness like a band aid.

When she looked at him again, tears straddling in her eyes as though unsure of what way to choose, she saw him not only as Otto Evenson, devoted husband and father, baker of excellency, and lover of board games with red and blue pieces—she saw a Master, a Lord in fact, who had left it all behind for love and now saw a chance to be true to himself again. She had too many questions pressing, but now was not the time.

Her father, the Lord, stroked her cheek. "You are so like your mother, Freja, and yet so much your own Master."

Freja shook her head. "Our world is falling apart, for what? Because they want stolen energy?"

"'They' are not the Lords, if that is what you're saying," said her father, surrounded again by that peculiar light, filtering away Otto in each peeled layer of fantasy it placed upon him. "Yes, I heard what Elflock said, but I cannot believe the Lords would accept such a thing."

"You would know," she said and instantly regretted it. Like water on a curved surface, the light slipped off and left her father behind, the ghost of what he once had been. "Sorry," she muttered.

"Masters collect energy to stabilise the Energy Network," her father continued. "Nothing more. Those were the rules. Curfew was set in place after the nuclear accident as a safety measure—partly for radiation and partly as a legal correctional system. If the people of Vildaell found out about Masters it could risk the whole balance." He paused until he saw doubt flare in his daughter's face. "What the Flÿght is doing has nothing to do with the Lords, Freja."

"Are you sure about that?" she said and recalled what they had seen at the power plant. "I saw them, I heard them talk about splitting Strays and being blackmailed."

"I'm sure," her father replied and she bit the inside of her cheek, not saying anything further. If he wanted to be blind, she'd let him. For now.

A loud yell came from the square, like before. Topster was

once again calling for Freja. Her name sounded first, but then Topster said another one as well—Tej. He must have seen her flinch at the mention of his Master name, for her father took her in his arms again. "I'm sorry, Freja," he said. "I love you."

All at once the filter vanished and she fell into his arms, allowing the tears to escape for one moment only. The next, she wiped them away and broke free from his arms. "Shall we?"

"I guess we must."

So they walked together through the short underpass into the Great Square of Amérle. Moonlight was guiding their way in the last passage before the storm. A cloud passed by the shining orb and darkness swallowed them. In the blink of an eye, the path was lit again. They reached the square and the centre of a box, surrounded by the walls of suspended pedestrian paths. Above them, on one of the bridges, stood Topster with Klobb, Florin, Éloyse, and Klepta by his side, all peering down at Tej and Freja as they came into the arena. It was like stepping into a photograph. She had seen it on the screens in the tower, and the Transporters stood as before, but the CCTV footage had omitted the silence, the chill of the night, and the smell of a dying city.

Dust to dust, Freja thought again as she met the unsympathetic gaze of her previous host.

CHAPTER 41

Less than three hours until bell eleven

"WELCOME, FRIENDS—OLD and new," said Topster in his crystal clear and cold metallic voice. "What a pleasant gathering we have here. Miss Freja, returned from the Obbsborn filth, and Tej, returned from a long absence of insanity."

"I do not expect you to understand—"

"Understand what?" Topster interrupted. "You are weak, Tej. There is no future in Ma'zekaï."

"Heim will not surrender."

"They will have no choice. The Essence will rule." Topster snapped his fingers and Klobb stepped forward, carrying a square object. Topster remained by the railing, hands behind his back, perfect poise, staring down at the bottom of the Great Square. Fierce glares were shot between her father and Topster, but their conversation was drowned out in Freja's mind. All she could do was stare at the Master, the traitor not only of her and Lulja, but of Klobb too. Nothing she said could fully represent the black disdain she felt for this man, once the object of her admiration, but now only an icon of fierce hatred. The Master caught her eye and she saw that he recognised what was in her mind, his smirk so zealous it threatened to break his perfect porcelain face in two.

"Out with it," said her father. "Why have you called us here?"

A short moment separated them from ignorance and knowledge. A brief pause of life, where only the moon was alive in the midst of the dying world; nothing but time infolded into itself, passed by its opposite in the temporal vacuum we call 'a moment'.

Then Topster spoke at last and suddenly Time had abandoned them all.

"There was a time," he said, "when Masters and humans lived together—we will have that once more. There is hope for all of us, all generations, if Masters rule this world—and one of you will lead it."

Freja felt every second like a wave of motion pass through her, pass in her, with no exit wound.

Topster, again. "Two Champions—one will live, one will die. Whoever stands victorious will be the Master of the human world—the Lord of Heim."

Freja frowned, in spite of all the hundred other physical responses tugging at her psyche in that one moment. It was not a conscious choice: her eyebrows seemed the sole mobile unit on her body, yet able to receive and process information from her brain. Everything else had gone cold. The surroundings, ever so familiar, transformed into a landscape never before travelled, but with an uncanny resemblance to her home town. The pavement was new, the sign pointing to the local library and the highway was new—she was new. New was the proposition, nay order, just presented to her ears, they, too, unused and chafing as though she'd never noticed their presence before. Sound contorted into a hollow echo as if from a fish bowl.

It was ridiculous, of course. A battle against her father?

When she looked at him she felt a surge of energy flow

through her body. He was a Master. She was a Master. She had the Essence. And she would not be biased. She adopted a poise worthy of a Master and addressed Topster. "Why would I help you? You have done nothing but deceive me."

"Why would you trust me?" Tej filled in beside her, stepping up to her side and knitting his hands behind his back. A true Lord. "I left you once already."

"*Ka-ka!*" said the unforgettable cackle of Klepta. "You think this is about you?" She let out a laugh like a mad hen. "Selfish and greedy, just like they say. Humans!"

"We are not human," said Freja, feeling the truth of her words fill her with courage.

Her father joined in. "You need us, I see that clearly—but why do we need you?"

Topster lifted his chin and jutted his jaw, as though stretching it for a long speech. The Master was not one for those, however, and he left it short. "The future of the Master race. Your race, might I add."

"Of the Flÿght, rather," said Freja, not afraid anymore. She took one step closer to the bridge. "That's been your goal all along, hasn't it? The latches, the Strays—all so that the blue population can rise above all other colours." She stared into the cold eyes of the Master, fighting the urge to look away. They were not equals. She had human values in her as well as the Essence. In her world, lineage was not important. Whether the son of a tradesman or aristocrat, the human value was the same. Jahran was different, Buria as well, but the soil upon which they stood now vouched for all beating hearts of humanity. They were not equals. Topster, who could see no further than the blue fog of his masterform could never fully understand humans.

Topster's eyes were still on her, but shifted when Tej spoke. "We will speak to the Lords, ask that restrictions on the Flÿght are lifted."

"A traitor's promise," Topster hissed at him. "You have no rank, you have no say—you are nothing."

Tej took a step forward. "My masterform is grey, is it not?"

"Have the Lords condoned your treachery? I happen to know they have not."

"What insight have you with the Lords?" Tej snorted.

"Much more than you think, traitor."

"He is not a traitor," said Freja, cutting the verbal gunfire short.

Topster sneered. "You are quick to forgive, Miss Freja, for all the lies he has told you."

"That's—"

"Bias," interrupted Topster, spitting it like a foul-tasting word. "Weakening bias."

Freja countered, "It's not weakness to love."

"No one strong has ever had their heart biased except to himself."

"I know one," Freja said and glanced at her father, who opened his mouth as if to speak, but only left it half-open, unspoken words flowing from its interior like wisps of smoke never materialised.

"A true Lord of the Élan can control his inner life."

Called out of its hollow, Freja's own bias crawled out and nudged her to step forward. The ferocity in her voice was unplanned and uninhibited. "What about Sofia?" she yelled and saw Topster's lip curl. "That's right, I know all about it. Don't think you are any different." Topster's eyes went dark in an instant and he glared down at the girl in purple. Hatred flared from his entire being. It was the most uncontrolled Freja had seen him, but she was not afraid.

"You will help us, Miss Freja—" his calm was infinitely more frightening than fury— "because you are one of us. One future—one race."

"My father was a Lord of the Élan, yes," said Freja. "I know that."

"And your mother?"

"She disappeared," she said, clearing her throat one time too many than seemed natural. Incredulousness scrabbled over Freja's face, removing all stitches and seams to her half-Master courage. It melted away like oil in a hot pan, scorching her skin and leaving nothing but raw flesh behind. "She missed Curfew."

"She doesn't know?" Klepta cackled. "*Ka-ka*! How sweet."

It made Freja wonder if she knew that her Pojk was dead. No, she decided, Klepta didn't know. If she did, it would have been visible in her face, like it had been on Freja's father. On Mrs Aitken.

"Topster—" said Tej in a low drumming voice. Topster ignored him with glee in his voice.

"It was no Curfew trespass, Miss Freja. Has anyone told you the history of Masters in Heim?"

Freja shook her head, not trusting herself to speak. Let him speak, she thought to himself. Let him say too much. Her silence inspired him to go on, a jeering smirk flowering on his face. Let him speak, Freja repeated to herself like a mantra. Let him say too much.

"When Ma'zekaï began its decay many generations ago, the Lords sent delegates to the other *landskapës* to represent us. For then, we were one. These representatives were unseen to the authorities of Heim and the Red World. Here, the Masters were ordered to blend in with humans, to study them, to learn from their mistakes and successes." He shifted his gaze to Tej, but only for a second. "The thing is, a Master in this world becomes subject to its finiteness—as well as its bias. His protective Essence fails in touching the polluted energy flows. It makes him weak. Because of this, it was said that the Masters who came here for longer than one generation would stay until the end of their life: settle down and become part of the human community. They settled, married humans, had children."

"That does not make them traitors."

"I am not finished," said Topster. "You have the Essence, Miss Freja—correct?"

"Yes."

"It is," said Topster, "by blood acquired. With one parent of the Essence and one without, it may not be present in the offspring." His lip curled and he let his eyes sweep over Tej. "But with two parents of the Essence—"

Freja searched for hope, for explanations, in her father, but his sad eyes told her no other truth.

"It is true," he said and averted his gaze. "The Essence is a natural presence. You can't force it."

"So I got it from you then?" she said, still not willing to grasp the full extent of what was being said.

Then she remembered: the old Lord had left Ma'zekaï with *another Master!*

"What happened next," said Topster, disregarding the obvious signs that Freja had grasped the truth at last, "the Lords ought to have foreseen. These Masters, now in the human world, began to betray us, siding with the humans and forgetting their—our—legacy. Of course they were highly trained and knew every thread of the Energy Network. A trusted person was then sent by the Lords to terminate the President and ensure that Heim was ruled appropriately."

"Too bad the 'trusted person' failed," said Tej.

"I did not fail," snarled Topster.

"The Lords beg to differ."

"Everything that was promised was delivered. President Colerush was replaced by a Master and we could begin our proper rule and control the Network again." He told the rest of the story. The new President, Fiende, made the situation easier to handle. The Lords steered from Ma'zekaï and the Network was adjusted and established to favour Ma'zekaï. Curfew legislation ensured continued secrecy. However, despite all their efforts, the Master valleys went into decay and one by one they died. The Flÿght lost the majority of their population when Wind faltered, the wall was built, and many lost their lives pounding the bricks from the outside.

"Where exactly does my mother come into all this?" Freja asked.

"For generations we have collected energy here under what you know as Curfew," said Topster. "Without the energy from the Willow, there is no Heim. Humans need us. Because of those people—" he pointed to Tej— "our future is at risk."

"What 'people'?"

"Biased people," said Topster. "Your mother was a Master of the Trew and Lord Tej failed to control his bias to her. Your father brought Ïoletta with him and left his lordship behind. Left his life behind to filth and mortality."

"Ïoletta—her Master name?" Freja asked, and her father confirmed. "Not Marja?" He shook his head.

"So you see, Miss Freja," said Topster. "That you are one of us—a full Master of the Essence."

Freja inspected herself and saw a new self; a self-swathed in the same filtering light as her father. The masterform was her second skin, the gems her rightful ornaments. Nothing by halves; she was a full-fledged Master with the Essence flowing inside her, fully deserving of the amethysts. When she had traced the energy in the Willow leaf it had been a reaction by instinct. By blood. Unlike the other unhomely light, this one was fresh and bright—and welcoming. Like the first warm morning in spring or the fresh buds in the soil once the snow has thawed, she felt renewed. Recycled, like a plastic bottle given new life in a new shape. "You knew?" she asked Topster. "You knew I was a Master?"

"I needed someone with the Essence to collect the latches," he said.

"The shadow … The one I followed—that was you?" She anticipated the answer before it came.

"No," he said. "But it was on order from me." He let the information sink in before continuing, "You see now why you must help us, Miss Freja?" He gave Florin an order and she left. Klobb stood at the railing, clutching it like jail bars, peering through it down at Freja.

She thought of Elflock and Ravn, of Cecelya and Pojk motionless on the beach, of the thousands of Obbsborn imprisoned, of Jaspir and Mrs Nagel forgotten in the abandoned Valley of Wind; then she thought of her father, the Master Lord, and her mother, Ïoletta, of the Trew. She thought of herself, a Master offspring, disengaged to her heritage, strewn away like pollen into a world that wasn't her own. No, she did not see. She wanted no part of their evil plans.

"I don't care," she said.

"Too many words come out of your mouth," Topster replied, untouched by her coldness. "Keep your voice to yourself for a moment and I shall explain why you care."

"No, I will not. It isn't weak to be biased," she said, slowly and with careful articulation. She wanted it to hurt, to really seep into his very pores and penetrate his Essence, crack it, break it. End it. "I'm sorry Sofia died, loving her might have made you a better Master. A better person. So no, Topster, I will not keep my voice to myself and I do not care."

"I think you do," he said and snapped his fingers. In a moment Florin returned, pushing a girl in front of her. The yellow masterform said enough and Freja gasped.

"Lulja!"

Gagged and held back by the brittle but strong Florin, Lulja's eyes were wide and frightful, tears drawing stripes all the way down to her chin. She must have been captured on the way to the house. How far had they got? Where was Tryll? Freja could only hope he had managed to escape. With his maimed leg, it was unlikely. Lulja would be quicker than him. If only her father had been with them, they would have been safe, she thought and felt guilt surge through her body. Then again, she had not asked him to come. A justifying thought that was inefficient in relieving what she felt inside.

Lulja squirmed in Florin's grip and managed to spit out whatever it was that had kept her silent. "You tricked me," she screamed, struggling to tear free so that she could tear at Topster. "I didn't tell you the truth, Freja. My father was a Master, of the Trew. He was a deserter of Valley of Water and fled to Jahran when it fell. They told me that if I helped, I could come back and be a full Master."

"And you shall," said Topster. "Once we take over Heim, you may join our forces—if you win."

"What?" said Lulja and stopped fidgeting. Florin took the opportunity to grip her firmer. A small wince distorted Lulja's face as Florin's arms wriggled under her armpits and grabbed her shoulders. "Win? What do you mean, win?"

"Of the three *landskapës* we will, as dawn breaks, have two in our possession. Heim and Ma'zekaï will be ours."

Florin pulled at Lulja's hair, causing her to whimper in pain. Fresh tears dripped on the pavement, making dark blotches.

"This world is not yours," said Tej. "You can't just take it."

"We already did," said Florin.

A dangerous thought flashed in Freja's mind as she watched her friend being assaulted by the beautiful Master. Florin's delicate hands were strained by bulging veins, colourful through her pale skin. Her strength was not natural.

424

When the penny dropped it did so with a terrible weight. Perhaps Topster saw it—or heard it in some metaphysical dimension—because he gave the realisation words as it dawned upon Freja.

The battle ...

"I brought you to Ma'zekaï to make you a Champion," he said.

was not to be—

"And this is the moment we have been waiting for."

between her and her father—

"In the end, there can only be one Champion—one human Master over all of Heim."

it was between her and—

"The other Champion is—"

"Lulja," whispered Freja.

CHAPTER 42

Two hours until bell eleven.

ÉLOYSE LEFT TOPSTER'S side and collected the large object Klobb had brought forward. It was wrapped in brown cloth and appeared to be of hard material. Meanwhile, Florin held Lulja steady up on the bridge until Topster ordered her to go after Éloyse down to the lower part of the square, where Freja and Tej stood motionless. It looked unwieldy and not at all as effortless as Florin did, with one hand around Lulja's shoulders and the other knitted into her hair. Florin, unlike Éloyse, was a natural at keeping things—people—hostage.

With only a few steps between them, Éloyse came to a halt and let the object slide to the ground, where it landed with a low thud on the concrete. She looked at Tej without emotion, and he met her eyes. Then, without any warning, Tej turned on his heel—and ran. It was so sudden that no one reacted for several seconds; not until Topster yelled for someone to follow him. In an instant Éloyse handed the object to Freja, passing over the weight of it into her hands, and followed in the direction of Tej. At the same time, Lulja managed to push Florin off her, but was soon caught again at the wrist, whimpering at the pain of Florin's powerful fists.

"You're tearing her hair out!" said Freja. "Let her go!"

"Very likely," said Florin and laughed. "So you can run off again?"

"We didn't run."

"They never do."

When the steps had died out there was silence. The night sky had nothing to say to its street walkers. Clouds were passing the moon as though reminding them of the passing of time and the approaching bell. Her father had run. He had left her—again. Left her to fight her dear, dear friend *to the death*. It was impossible to conceive—almost as impossible as a night without Curfew—but Freja feared what might happen if she refused. The Obbsborn had shown her ample proof of how cruel Masters could be when they felt so inclined. Jaspir Nagel's fate was forever etched into her mind. And Cecelya—

Freja glanced at the tall buildings around them. Behind every secured window and every locked door, bar the offices, there were humans sleeping, humans unable to sleep but reading, humans doing whatever it was humans did during these dark hours. What was it she used to do after the Signaller had blinked red and the blinds had been pulled? With what tool had she killed time in her other life, before Ma'zekaï? She couldn't remember. All of the humans behind the windows, unaware of the commotion outside; blissfully enveloped by dreams or nightmares that would end in a few hours, as opposed to the very real one playing out here in the open.

"Let Éloyse bring him back. Klobb, set it up," said Topster from above, sending the little man to join them below. Without speaking, he took the object from Freja and she let him. A dark blob settled in Freja's chest and sank into her bones as Klobb unfolded the cloth. His small fingers were clumsy and it would have done him well to look at what he was doing instead of

Freja. Yet, he kept his gaze steady and unfolded the cloth and, once off, put it in a neat pile on the side. In a minute, his work was done. Freja had watched with mixed fascination and fear when he set up the playing board that had been hiding underneath the cloth. "Gimme that, will ye?" he said and pointed to a dark pouch that had fallen out. When she gave it to him, they exchanged another look and she saw at last what he was thinking: she would be safe. A glint, a glitter, the smallest twitch of the mouth, let her know that she could win this game. Klobb opened the pouch and began to deal out the red and blue pieces.

The playing board itself was square and set on four low legs that had been folded into the hollow of the playing field. Dots and stripes made up the centre and would steer the pawns, now set out by Klobb, across the game. She could have navigated it in her sleep. It was her mother who had taught her and each night after Curfew she had sat down with her to play. When she was removed, they hadn't finished their game so Freja's father had taken over the seat. Freja had never known he could play— and he did cheat—but he was almost as good as her mother. Come to think of it, she had never played or even seen the game outside of her house. "A local game," Lulja had said in the village. For the first time she realised that it was a family secret—a Master secret.

"Is ready, Master," said Klobb as he had placed the last blue pawn on the board.

"Excellent," said Topster. "Florin, place our Champions."

With some force, Florin managed to seat Lulja and Freja opposite each other: Freja in front of the red pawns, Lulja blue. In her friend's eyes Freja saw shining terror, glazed and ready to crumble at any minute. She tried to give Lulja a comforting look but saw none of it reflected in the depths of fear.

"You will play one round. The winner is our final Champion," said Topster from above and gazed east between the buildings. There was still no sign of breaking dawn. Time was choosing the enemy.

"And the loser?" Freja asked, but was ignored.

"Are we ready?" Topster said instead.

Think. She had told her father she wanted to stall Topster while Elflock and Ravn worked their ways in Ma'zekaï.

"Wait!" she said. "I want to know where my mother is, or I won't play."

"Topster, this is ludicrous," said Florin who had stayed beside the two girls, perhaps to ensure no one ran away again. "Can we not simply take the yellow one—she is not making such a fuss."

"She is frightened out of her mind," said Freja. "If she could make a fuss, she would." Lulja was frozen in her seat. "Lulja, you won't play either, will you?" No reply. Paralysis had claimed her body, almost as if Strays were nearby.

Florin pulled a leaf and held it against Lulja's heart, glee shining from the Master's pale eyes. "Are you ready *now*?"

Freja's breaths became shallow. She gave a short nod, realising she had no choice.

"Enough nonsense," said Topster. "Florin." She let go of Lulja and lay down a pile of silver-shaded leaves in the neutral circle in the middle of the board where, usually, you would put pawns that were claimed by your opponent.

"Each time you lose a pawn," said Topster, "you will pick a leaf. These have been grown and selected to work at short distance. That is, they will not be able to harm us."

"So it is not worth trying," said Florin and stepped back to what Freja assumed was a safe distance. "And do not run again."

"I said we didn't run from your party," said Freja. "Klepta showed us the way out." She turned up to Klepta who had been unnaturally quiet. Red heat flushed into her cheeks now and she pushed herself against the railing, waving her finger down at Freja. When she spoke, it was to Florin.

"I put them in a safe place," she said, then turned to Topster. "Master Topster, Master Florin—I showed you there, didn't I? *Ka!* The girl is a-lying. Don't accuse me for things I didn't do!"

"Regardless," said Topster with a look that thrust Klepta back into silence, "we will get started. Champions, if you look around you will see a guard at each exit. Do not attempt to run."

Freja saw that he was right. A dark figure blocked each of the four exits from the square. They were trapped. She wondered how the guards had got there so fast, and did it mean that Elflock and Ravn had failed? Then she remembered the infinite latches. Breathing became easier. It might not be over just yet. Nevertheless, there was no running away now. Topster repeated this thought in words. Opposite her Lulja looked as terrified as Freja felt. Her brown eyes were empty and glazed and she was trembling, staring at the leaves in the circle. Like daggers. Each player had ten pawns and three Lords (Freja now realised what the grey 'queens' really were) to lose. Thirteen stabs with the leaf daggers was the fate awaiting one of them unless they came up with a plan. If Topster was telling the truth, and she suspected he was, Freja was a Master by blood. Lulja was only half. Would that give Freja any advantage at all? Immediately she shook her head. The thought was not only horrendous but fearsome for herself. Lulja was her friend and there was no way she would help hurt her. She knew what the leaves could do.

"Play," said Topster from the balcony. "Blue begins. Play!"

When nobody moved, Florin grabbed Lulja's hair and tugged. Both Freja and Lulja screamed but Florin's fingers tightened their grip and she ordered Lulja to make her first move. With shaking hands and no other option but to obey, Lulja moved a pawn—straight into a 'hop, switch, roll' killing position.

Freja saw it before her opponent even let go of the playing piece and going by Florin's little snigger, she had seen it too. "Your move, girl," said Florin and released her grip on Lulja.

Freja considered the board. She didn't have to take Lulja's pawn, at least not yet. She calculated at least four different options, one of which would compromise her own position. When she reached to make a safe move, not quite ready to have her skin torn just yet, Topster cried out for her to stop.

"That is not the move," he said in his cold, calm voice. "Make another move, Miss Freja. This is a competition."

"Would you like to take over?"

"Make another move," Topster repeated slowly.

"I don't see another move," Freja lied.

"Florin, point it out for her." Neither of them looked at the board as Florin stretched out one thin finger and rested it above a red pawn to the right of where Freja's hand had been heading. "To here," she said and pointed instead to Lulja's pawn.

"Oh, thank you," Freja said, making Florin smirk.

"Just do it," said Lulja, croaking and fast. Her voice was breaking and sweat glistened on her forehead. "Do it quick."

With a nod Freja reached out and moved the pawn. Its metal surface felt cold against her skin. She placed it next to Lulja's pawn and paused a moment before removing it to the circle. As a replacement she took a leaf and breathed in. "I'm sorry," she mouthed as she squeezed it between her palm and thumb and held it up towards Lulja. The energy trembled inside and the next moment the leaf scorched into ash and Lulja gave up a chilling scream. A bright white stripe appeared on her neck, running from chin to collar bone. With a jolt, Freja realised how Florin must have got her scar. Tears fell from Lulja's eyes while, above, Topster clapped his hands.

"Excellent," he said. "Well done, Miss Freja. Now Lulja, it is your turn."

"Make a move, doll face," Florin said in a menacing voice. "Or I will take a souvenir myself."

"You look focused," Lulja continued as if she didn't register the threat. "You always look focused."

"Except when I crawl into a ball and cry," Freja replied with a grin.

"We all cry from time to time," said Lulja.

"You okay?"

"Yeah … Feel a bit strangled, that's all. My move, right?" Freja bit her lip and nodded. Lulja had five options, one of which would give Freja another 'lucky' draw. Lulja hesitated. "Kind of makes you wish the Strays had eaten us, right?"

Freja smiled. "They don't eat people, you know. They suffocate them."

"Same difference. I feel eaten though. Like it's eating at me from within." Her last words were drowned by a choking sound and Lulja collapsed on the ground, clasping her throat. Her eyes went blank. She was staring out into thin air, not seeing Freja at all. Gone.

Then Freja felt it. A slight tremble, nothing more than a regular cold would cause, lingering like a thin blanket over her ears and eyes. The world became subtler, less distinct. Up on the balcony Topster flinched as Klobb fell to the ground, his body convulsing. At the exits, the commotion made the guards retreat, exchanging worried glances. They felt it in their Essence, as did Freja.

Something was on the move.

It didn't take long for them to come.

CHAPTER 43

THEY ROLLED IN on the lower part of the square, a dark cloud of beings running, racing, speeding, across and over everything in its path. The Strays stirred the air, spinning every living thing off balance with their breath of demise. Freja threw herself to the ground, clutching Lulja's hand as she went down, pulling the paralysed girl with her. She watched as the Strays grew and expanded like bulging smoke from a silent explosion. Many faces appeared in the crowded darkness: old and young, happy and sad. A likeness to a familiar face appeared one second in the mass as it divided, only to be swallowed up again as the part re-emerged and swelled up towards the bridge and the Masters.

Topster was facing them. "You are early," he said.

"Master," the Strays said in unison. Even their voice sounded like a thing not living; hollow, as if an echo from another dimension. "The latches are prepared. We are prepared. Separated by the axis, as agreed."

Something glimmering entered Topster's eyes, which even Freja could see from below the bridge. She had dragged Lulja half way under the playing board and she was peering up from behind one of its legs.

"Show me," said Topster. "Show me the separation."

"Master—"

"How else will I know it has been done properly? Show me."

"Are you questioning the Lords?" The cloud of Strays hovered threateningly as it spoke, faces protruding here and there from the darkness. The familiar face remained within.

"Are you questioning me?" Topster asked and took a step towards the Strays. "Are you questioning your Master?"

"When all this is done, you will be our Master no longer," said the Strays—now channelled through one voice, one face.

"Naala," said Topster and smiled. "What a pleasure."

"It is not mutual."

"Show me."

Naala sighed, which stipulated itself as a heaving of the entire mass, and then retracted into the cloud. For a moment everything stood still. Then, with a creaking, breaking sound, the Strays separated. The air filled with the sound of broken-ness. Like the unfolding of a row of paper cut-outs, the Strays disconnected from each other like parts glued together: slowly and painfully. Everything about it seemed to scream unnatural, like pieces of a jigsaw puzzle being pulled apart in all the wrong places. Yet it unfolded, piece by piece, ripped at the seams.

Soon they stood separated, one by one. Alone together. The dark shadows, sole and independent, stood on top of each other, beside each other, below each other, as though gravity was powerless and yet some other magnetic force wouldn't let them be too far apart. The difference now was that there were spaces in between where the city was visible. The shadows had faces. Naala's was beautiful. "There," she said and a wave-like motion rippled through her and the others. "We are as separate as can be. But we will move together, as is our right."

"Fascinating," said Florin as she came up to Topster. "It is truly fascinating."

"Lonely Strays," puffed Klepta. "*Ka!* I've seen it all now."

"Quiet," said Topster and the others fell back at his voice. Such authority, such terror. He reached out a hand towards Naala and although she flinched (and the rest with her), she remained still as he caressed her face. The darkness was stunning and enchanting. "Remarkable."

"The latches are ready," she said. "Now stop the splitting and let us live."

"And the Trinity Latch?" Topster had slipped out of his trance. His hand went back behind his back, clasping his other one, but not likely to forget the touch of a Stray.

"There was a problem," Naala said. "The Lords …"

"You did not bring it?"

"The Lords do not have it in their possession," said Naala. "It is lost."

"Is that so?" said Topster, pondering. Then his eyes narrowed into thin slits and he spoke with steel-like chill. "Then I have no other choice but to let the Lords split you into little, little fragments and watch as you are digested by the Network and become an invisible part of the Trinity at last."

A ripple of shock swept over the Strays, oscillating like an electric wave across their opaque being. Though separated, they were still one in that remark. Naala's voice trembled. "Our agreement was—"

"That is all, Naala."

An expression of disgust and disbelief mingled into the swell of disbelief. Even if Naala's features were blurred into obscurity, Freja saw how her face sunk and collapsed into disdain. The Stray was then swallowed up into the masses once more and a low rumbling filled the square. The Strays were conversing in melodious murmurs.

Topster, unconcerned, went over to Klobb, still lying motionless from the effect. He then took a leaf from his pocket and put it on his heart. Soon Klobb woke up in a spasm, and flung his arms out towards some invisible body. Klepta helped him to his feet.

All the while Freja remained on the ground, not quite sure what to believe. That something was wrong and that Topster had involved her in some activity well beyond the substance that she was aware of, was evident. What it meant, however, was still uncertain. Her aching head refused to make sense of it, and she decided she would listen for once, and not speak. Beside her Lulja's eyes were blank and vacant. Freja gave her a smile, intended for reassurance, but it felt more like a grimace. She didn't even know if Lulja could see her in this state.

Naala spoke again. "We do not like being fooled, Master," she said. The other Strays had joined her side now in an elongated row of dark matter.

"I am yet the Master. I am yet the Lord."

"You are no Lord," said another Stray who protruded from the mass next to Naala.

A shadow of strain crossed Topster's face and he stretched his neck as if in search of support from his companions. When he received none, he looked stern and faced the ghostly woman. "It is hardly prudent, Ïoletta, to speak in presence of the Champions," he said, indicating towards Freja and Lulja. "I have already liberated you and now you shall help liberate us as promised."

The name rang like a false tune in Freja's ears. She knew what it signified but its meaning had not yet settled in her mind. Ïoletta of the Trew, her mother Marja Evenson—one and the same. She wondered if her mother had seen her yet. Did she know her daughter was lying under the board game they had shared for so many years? Did she know she was there at all? She wanted to yell, to cry out, anything that might divert the attention from Topster to Freja. But she remained silent. She couldn't choose the words. There were so many of them, lost in over two years of separation. A black hole of missing had swallowed them whole, digested them, and refused to recycle. So she watched, instead, how Ïoletta stretched out as far as the mass of Strays would let her go, then a little further on pure willpower, reaching out with her arms towards the Master, claws extended and ready, but was pulled back by the force still keeping the Strays close.

Topster smirked.

"Perhaps it would be prudent," said Ïoletta, her dark strands of hair shaking as she pulled as close to Topster as she could without being flung back by the invisible force, "to speak in plain words." She was spitting the words. "You have betrayed us, your own kind."

Naala joined her overextended position. "The Strays will not forget."

The response was a chuckle. Topster approached them while keeping careful check that he avoided their reach and sucking magnetism for all that lived. Oh, they tried all right. He leaned against the railing, over it, as though speaking to a child, and smirked.

"You are the past haunting the present and it was doomed to end when the future arrived. Once Masters have this world, there will be no need for Strays, dear. A new era is coming and yours is, as it always was, a thing already gone. Hide if you wish but know that you will be found eventually. Now leave. We have a game to play." He turned away from them and said something inaudible to Klepta, who cackled in reply.

The Strays gave up such a cry that Freja flinched and banged her head against the bottom of the board. Rubbing the sore spot, she peered out and watched how the Strays merged once more with a squelching echo, fusing into one again. She crawled close to Lulja and wrapped her arm around the cold body. Her own flesh was vibrating, shaking to the bones. Her brain was skipping and slamming into her skull. It would happen, she thought. Whatever happened next, it would happen to them together. The cry grew and multiplied as the Strays became one being again and the noise filled the space like a sharp liquid. The whole world trembled. When they moved, they moved together. An endless cloud of Strays surged in from under the bridges and joined the ones on the square. Though Topster tried to dispel them, he could only hold them off for a few moments until he, too, sank to his knees, arms over his head, trying to fight the clutching Strays. Freja felt her mind begin to drift again as the force of the Strays became larger and more intrusive. They could evidently affect Masters outside the wall, so why hadn't they rebelled before?

A cold hand dismissed the question as it wrapped around her wrist and she let it pull her away. As long as Lulja came with her, she'd go anywhere. A voice, one of the ones that had spoken earlier, whispered in her ear. The breath was chilled, but smooth. It said she could trust them. "That's what they always say," Freja mumbled under the spell of Master souls.

"I'm forever sorry, my love," she said and Freja mumbled the foreign name signifying that familiar piece of longing. "We took you away once, but never again. We are free now," she said. "We do as we please."

A white light descended upon Freja and she lost her grip on Lulja. However hard she tried to move, she couldn't. There she was, right in front of her. Her presence was strong and visceral, and yet Freja could not reach her. Not see her clearly. She had forgotten her face. Two years, and she had forgotten her mother's face. She was out of reach for the living. Topster had touched Naala, but Ïoletta of the Trew was out of Freja's range. Two lonely tears ran down the sides of Freja's face. "I can't reach you," she whispered.

Ïoletta spoke to her—and her alone. "You are of the strongest earth, Freja. Never forget that."

"Mum ... what happened to Mops?" Without replying, Ïoletta smiled in her own sweet way and stroked her daughter's cheek. No sensation admitted the touch on Freja's skin. "You can't reach me," Freja said. "And I can't reach you."

"No," said her mother in a soft voice.

"You're going to have to leave again, aren't you?"

"Let me worry about the Strays, my sweet. For now we must take you away from that treacherous man."

The world around them slowly darkened, like storm clouds rolling in on a clear blue sky. Beside her, Freja felt her friend's limp fingers touch her own. "Are you taking Lulja too?" "Yes, both of you."

"Thank you," Freja managed before she lost consciousness altogether.

CHAPTER 44

Less than two hours until bell eleven.

THE MASTERS ROSE in silence as the Strays left the square. When Topster came to his feet he brushed off the dust from his masterform and smoothed his hair, his curled lip evil and cruel.

The horizon had yet to reveal the rising sun, but a faint glow indicated the new day was not far off.

"We will find you," Topster murmured into the city. He glanced into the CCTV camera even though he knew that the tower was most likely empty by now. They wouldn't be so stupid as to return there.

He turned to Florin who was plucking dirt out of her blonde hair. "We do not need them or the latch or the Lords," he said and sliced the air with his flat palm. "Let it begin anyway."

Florin froze and let her hair fall down in a, for her, unusually tousled manner. Her cheeks were pale and she wetted her lips several times before speaking. "No," she said, shaking her head. "It is—No." She received a glaring look in return.

"Do not oppose me, Florin."

She opened her mouth and closed it anew. Swallowed the

truth of her emotion, selecting what truth to present. "Ever since the beginning we have known that a human Lord is the only path to success here. I refuse to compromise on that, Topster. Even coming from you." If there was ice in her, it melted from the heat of his scowl. Hot and desperate in a fierce way that suggested he would enforce any measures necessary, it bore into her like no other Master, except Skylar, had done before. She couldn't utter another syllable. A tongue tied by—what? Her eyes wandered instead to Klepta and Klobb, who remained silent. Where were the others, Florin thought? Éloyse? Ravn? Their allies?

"Florin," said Klepta at last. "Topster is right—this is it. It's now or never."

"And the window is shrinking," Topster said, pointing to the horizon between the council house and a tall office building. A thin line of light had appeared above ground; the sun had begun to rise. Florin saw this too and frowned with a sigh.

"It is too risky," she said. "They will not comply."

Topster came close to her, so close that she smelt his scent. "Florin," he said and lifted her chin so he could access her eyes. "We have thousands of Masters just waiting for our signal. As many latches, handmade by latch welders. They come here, with Transporters, and we carry out the plan like we have said—do you think the humans will have any choice but to comply?"

"They are many." Her words wandered lost in the darkness of his eyes.

"So are we. And we are stronger."

"They have weapons."

Topster smirked. "So have we. Florin, we are ready. Believe in us." He came closer and lowered his voice further; whispered to her ears only. "Tej has lived here for a long time. If necessary, we can use him."

"Then let us wait until Éloyse brings him back."

"It could be too late then," said Topster. "Florin, be reasonable. As soon as the Lords incorporate the Strays into the Network, it is too late." He paused and waited for further objection, but Florin said no more. After a contented pat on her shoulder, he turned to the others. "Masters—" Topster spoke to his comrades on the bridge— "we cannot wait any longer. The Strays have betrayed us and they will face punishment for it. In the new world, there will be no place for lingering death. But when that sun rises upon Heim we must have this city in our control and therefore we will proceed without them. Please take your positions."

Without any question or protestation, Florin and Klepta took a Transporter each and headed off in different directions, one west and one east. Below, the exit guards left to occupy the northern and southern parts.

"When the world wakes up tomorrow," Topster mused to himself as he stepped onto a Transporter, "it will be to a day like no other. A new day and a new age—the age of Masters."

From his side came a loud "NO!" as Klobb pushed his sausage fingers into the flesh of the Master, pushing Topster off his Transporter. He stumbled for a moment, then regained his balance and stared at Klobb with fire. "Master, you shan't proceed," said the little man. "This world en't yours, and it en't yours to take either." A waft of the scant hair fell into his face in his agitation and Klobb puffed it aside.

With careful and deliberate hands, Topster released the tousled bun and let the white-blonde strands fall down around his face before tying them back up again. Before this tall being Klobb stood firm, but a closer look might have revealed a tremble at his hand.

"Klobb, my dear friend—would you like to retract that?"

"No," he replied. "I re'tact nothing. You come and take me away from my Sora and my wee ones, and you says, 'Klobb,' you says, 'come with us and we'll make you a great man.' A great man! Now, I'm not a very great man in myself, Master, so I welcomed it. But you en't made me no great man, Master, have you? I'm as small as even more crippled than I used to be."

At first Topster could do nothing but stare up and down at the rambling man and his sudden rebellion. Nothing but air separated them. Air—and the evil protruding from Topster's narrow eyes. He looked at his former companion, now seeing clearer than before. The inner stuff of his servant was lying like an open book for him and he saw all the human filth that riddled the space like a cancerous tumour. Bias was part of it. And Klobb was full of bias; it penetrated his every cell, the fool. No emotion flashed in Topster's face to reveal what he had seen, but a cool indifference spotted his perfect complexion, and his eyes were shut to all intrusion. He was not weak like others. Narrow and square, his eyes observed the defiant Klobb. The true colours of the Master were out in the open—and they were dark; indeed darker than anyone could have imagined. The illusion was broken—for both of them. There was no going back now.

"What is going on?" Florin came rolling back at the commotion.

"You have let me down, Klobb," said Topster, ignoring her.

"I en't letting you steal. It en't right! If Miss Freja was *hooman* Champion, it would've been different. It's her world—it en't yours. Master." Despite everything, the soldier still made honour.

Topster put a slender finger to his mouth and hushed slowly, closing his eyes as though relishing the moment. "It is all done," he said in a low voice and went down on one knee, level with Klobb. "Forget not that I know your weakness." From a pocket on his masterform he produced a pressed blue flower. Klobb snatched after it but Topster held it out of his reach, teasing, for a moment before closing his fist and crushing the dry flower to pieces. It fell to the ground, broken, in front of a speechless Klobb.

"Give me your hand," Topster said to Florin, who had been observing the whole thing, and gripped her arm.

"I believe you have it already," she snapped back and received a meaningful scowl in return.

"You are young," he said as he inspected her palm, his fingers tracing the veins visible through her pale skin and masterform. "You have a strong Essence. A wise choice for the Élan."

Before another word was said, before Florin could thank him for the praise, before she realised that he had put a fresh leaf in her palm and placed it on Klobb's forehead, Topster had accessed the core of the leaf and sent a wave of energy through the little body, so strong that it was lifted off the ground and hurled through the air several metres back. He did not have time to utter a single cry for help, or disdain, or even as much as a final growl or muttering. It was so quick that nobody but Topster fully grasped what had happened until the poor creature flew back in a void of recognition and landed with a dense thud on the small patch of artificial grass. Until it was all over. He was dead before his feet left the ground.

*

From a higher point, not too far away from the Great Square, lay two dark figures engulfed by shadows cast by the amicable buildings around them. Unseen to Amérle, they had a clear view of the city. These four eyes perceived the same scene as Topster, but it instilled another emotion altogether.

Éloyse cried out as the deed was carried out and then watched in mute tears as the unintentional murderer waved her finger in front of Topster's face, most likely berating him for taking such liberties. The villain only scoffed and brushed off his assassin. Éloyse's gaze wandered to the little frayed creature on the ground, nothing more than a bulgy lump now. Her Master heart ached at the sight of it all, platonic bias burning through her membranes like toxic water, and she made as if to run towards him. Tej pulled her back with a gentle tug at the shoulder and brought her into his embrace. The scene was partly concealed behind a blurred curtain of wetness for both of them.

She had caught up with him around the first corner from the Great Square, which was lucky because after that the Queen's Parade merged into a crossing with three streets spreading out into three different directions. Of course luck had nothing to do with it; she had merely followed the plan devised back at the house: if anything happened they were to meet in a particular spot. For several eternities they had stood there, trembling and panting, waiting, expecting Klepta or Florin to turn the corner and discover them. Neither had come. Topster's trust in Éloyse was impeccable. On another day she might have found this a reason to smile, but not today.

"He was an ugly thing but he helped us," Éloyse said while drying the last tears. He went against his Master for us and he died for it."

When she turned to plead for Tej to feel with her, she saw that he already was: he just didn't have words for it. Perhaps humans felt more with the inside, Éloyse thought, and it had rubbed off on him after all these years. She took his hand and felt that it was trembling and wet.

"We need to go," she said without making any attempt to move. Their hiding place was on top of a small elevation, in the midst of a group of houses subject to dereliction. The streets here were different from only a few blocks away: dirtier, more bumps and bruises. The physicality of it all was astounding.

Tej leaned into her, so close she felt his trembling as though it was part of her own, and whispered in her ear. He had words at last and the ones he spoke calmed her heart without condescending or belittling it. He knew her; knew what she needed to hear, as painful as it was.

"I hate him," she said. "I really do. I wish—"

"No good wishing," said Tej and moved away from her immediate presence. "You are right, we need to leave. They will come for us soon."

"What about Klobb?"

"What about him?"

"We can't leave him there!"

Tej knitted his eyebrows, gestured towards the square. "What do you suggest we do? Waltz down there, shake Topster's hand and take him? He is right next to Topster and unless you're willing to fight him—" Éloyse raised her eyebrows. "You're not going down there. End of discussion."

"Maybe for you."

"Éloyse!"

"Do you even know what you did when you left? What you did to Ma'zekaï—to me?"

"Éloyse—"

"No," she interrupted. "You can't flee this time."

He took her elbow and came closer. "I'm not going anywhere."

"Unless you think of a way to reach her," said Éloyse with a slight smile.

"Unless I think of a way," he said and paused for the length of a sigh. "There isn't a way to stop them, is there?" His voice was hollow, like an echo without a source. "The word he used—'digested' …"

Éloyse couldn't help but admit that she had wondered the same thing herself. If the Strays were divided, their power would decrease, but what that meant in practice, she couldn't figure out. "Maybe there is, maybe there isn't," she said, unsure what sentiment to best convey. "What about Freja?"

"Ïoletta will take her and the other girl to safety."

"You have spoken to her?"

Tej shook his head. "I know her," he said with a wretched smile. "Taking Freja from Vildaell was a collective decision by the Strays, or perhaps she believed she acted in earnest. If it is the last thing she does in this world …" His voice trailed off as the weight of the possible consequences of split Strays landed. "I trust her."

Silence ensued. Perhaps there was a humming in the air, night bugs singing their melody, or something of the kind. Perhaps the night was silent. All this standing still set the mind works going. They needed action. Right then they got their chance.

"This is it," Éloyse whispered and pointed towards the square again where Topster was again alone, seemingly in a contemplative and most of all distracted moment of stargazing. "We need to go," she said and wriggled free from Tej's arms. Both of them cast a last longing gaze towards the Great Square, but not for the same reason. She knew he felt guilty about leaving his daughter there. At the same time she knew that it was necessary, and that he realised this as well.

She turned back to the square, where Topster was scanning, searching, scouring the city for his lost allies and enemies, now scattered across the *landskapës* in the fight against him. She pursed her lips. New determination moved in her core. "This is when we leave," she said. "We go back."

"Back? No, I need to find Freja first."

"She is a capable Master and, besides, you said yourself that Ïoletta will make sure she's safe," Éloyse said and guided him away from their hiding place. "There may be only one valley left in Ma'zekaï," she added as they descended from the hill of desolation, trying hard not to equate this fate with Ma'zekaï, "but it has the Willow."

"Where all these problems started."

Éloyse stopped in her footstep and put a hand to his chest, preventing him from moving forward.

"The Willow is where all the problems will be solved, too," she said frowning. "Where all life comes from; the origin of air, water, and everything you see. You and I included. The problem is the Flÿght. I think you are right: what the Lords are doing is just a reaction to their insanity."

"They're not all evil. You just happened to pick the worst of them."

"I'm starting to believe you can't choose your bias," said Éloyse. "I know I didn't."

Both of them knew what was nestled in her words and that the little crease above his nose reminded her of everything that had been. Everything that could have been, maybe.

"Come," said Éloyse.

She had been told of an infinite latch close to Linden Plaza—the opposite direction from the Great Square—and asked Tej to lead the way there. In silent agreement neither of them spoke much, afraid that wandering Masters would catch their voices. Every corner was a danger.

"I think Elflock struggles with bias too," said Tej when they stopped two-three blocks away from the TV tower, having made sure that there were no CCTV cameras around. They couldn't know if anybody was watching. The eleventh bell would soon ring after all. "For you."

"Élan?" Éloyse said. "I wouldn't mind."

She winked with one eye and he laughed like he'd done so many times before. For a moment time went back a generation, to a simpler era which wasn't at all as dark.

With a smile Tej took her hand led her past the last corners to the latch, hidden in an alley filled with overfull dumpsters with smelly sacks of foul stuff. Dodging the last revelatory slivers of moonlight, Tej and Éloyse disappeared from sight, away from the city, hand in hand.

*

At the Great Square, on the balcony overlooking the crater below, Topster stood upon his own Transporter, alone. Every now and then he would playfully spin it round, as if on a leisurely ride, sometimes casting an eye to the gilded horizon, but not as much as once looking at the remnants of his servant. The lifeless body of Klobb lay there, wet from dew, like a discarded trophy. The haggard face had sunk into the bones and illuminated a kind of sincere misery, spotted with sordid indignity. It was ingrained in the wrinkles and creases of the face, even in death. Nobody had taken care to close his eyes. They were now staring into eternal nothingness and the hollow echo of the anticipatory afterlife. There was no longer any longing to go to that place of his past: Klobb had finally come home.

As though receiving a secret signal, Topster suddenly came to a stop and killed the engine on the Transporter, drowning its hum with the coming steps of day. They were moving fast now. All his allies had betrayed him. As always, the Flÿght stood alone. He stood alone.

He lifted up a hand towards the sky and shot up a jet light of energy. Ten leaves worth colluded into one stream of power and bent the air molecules one by one to stretch up towards the constant light in the sky. In the distance began a low rumbling, as though the belly of the world was awakening and craving breakfast. A hunger so severe and ravenous filled the silence with pops and crackles cutting through the peaceful city from all directions, like fireworks without the colours.

At the same moment, Éloyse and Tej stepped through the infinite latch to Ma'zekaï. What they didn't know was that as Topster released the stream of light, a cycle was set in motion.

It was beginning.

CHAPTER 45

One hour until bell eleven

THE LOOK-OUT could see everything according to its sign, but when Freja peeled her eyes open there was nothing in front of them but a dull grey haziness. Only when pulled to her feet by Tryll did she realise that they were on that self-proclaimed all-seeing hill. After having made sure that she was without severe injury, Tryll went back to Lulja and crouched next to her. The effect of the Strays had gone deep into her and she was still, so still, lying pale as a sheet, with fear frozen in her blank stare. All they could do was wait until it wore off.

Freja took a look around the place. The Strays were gone. The Look-Out was off CCTV camera coverage and a good place to hide, if there ever was one tonight. She sent a thought of gratitude to their rescuers, to Ïoletta. Freja wondered where her mother would go now that she was set free, if she would ever see her again. It depended on what being 'set free' meant at all for the Strays.

A cold wind passed by, rustling the grass and bending the straws so that they flexed like lithe acrobats in the late night. Dawn was approaching. Its apostle was slowly rushing on the horizon, painting its surface golden and glimmering beyond the city. The new day was breaking and, in less than an hour by Freja's estimate, the sun would rise and bell eleven would ring. To what scene was still the moon's business. Freja hardly wanted to think about it. Fatigue was riddling her mind and body alike and all she wanted, really, was to go home, blind the windows and sleep. She laughed to herself. The city was still under Curfew and she was outside. What had she said to Robin on that last day? *Just imagine.* She had imagined and here was her fantasy wrapped around her, handed to her by forceful feeding. She took one breath—not more, nor less—to take it all in.

Beside her Lulja was coming to, and Freja chased away the thoughts of yesterday. Lulja was struggling to control all her limbs (once swinging her arm precariously close to Tryll's face) and extremities, and tried—and failed—several times to sit up.

"It's like a full on body-lock," she said, slurring somewhat. "Jeez. I'm fine, Tryll. Let me try myself." Tryll was trying to pull Lulja to a seated position, meanwhile she was slapping him off as much as was possible with her rubber arms. He looked up, met Freja's amused expression, and broke out in a soundless laugh. It was only lucky that Lulja was in no position to see this reaction, or she might have yelled at him. The next couple of tries failed in equal measures and Lulja tumbled back and forth like a beetle in trouble until, at last, grudgingly, she let Tryll help her up.

Freja kneeled next to them both with a smile. She asked how Lulja was and her eyes welled up with tears while claiming she was fine, ever so fine.

"I'm so sorry, Freja," she said. "I should have told you. I only told Tryll at the cottage when you were speaking to Elflock."

"Don't apologise," said Freja and stroked her hair. "In fairness I didn't tell you the whole truth either."

Instead of being consoled, Lulja covered her face with her

hands and moaned. "I knew, Freja, I knew you were a Master."

Freja froze. "What?"

"The pu-purple latch," Lulja stammered and broke down into convulsing sobs again. "Only a Master could have collected it, that's how important it is. It's some sort of Essence-related protection."

Freja lifted her head to Tryll. "You knew?"

He shrugged at first, then after a reproachful look, nodded. In vague signs he gestured to his heart then to his lower arm. Lulja took a break in her sobbing and twisted her neck to watch him. "He suspected it as soon as he saw you in the Turf," she said. "He recognised the Essence. I was thinking about it too when Ravn said you had the Essence so I asked Tryll about it and he told me it's not something you just get or are given. I don't have it."

"But your father was a Master?" said Freja.

"I guess I got my mother's genes. I shouldn't be so affected by the Strays either, but, well." She let out a sniffling laugh and wiped her face.

On request from Freja she told her story—the true version. Born in Jahran to what she had been told were criminal parents, Lulja was adopted by a teacher couple at the age of three. When her father lost his job and her mother turned to the bottle for consolation, Lulja left her safe haven at the age of seventeen. She travelled around Jahran, trailed the border of Vildaell to Buria, and when she came back to Jahran she decided to search for her biological family. By then her adoptive parents had drifted apart, had become alienated from each other—and from her. Documents from the adoption and a couple of old addresses took her through a series of dead ends. She was about to give up when a man turned up out of the blue. He was a private investigator, a converted Master, and wanted to help, free of charge. "His interest didn't lie in money," Lulja said. "I was suspicious at first because, I mean, who does anything for free? Especially in Jahran, that's nobody. But he actually found my real parents." Her father had been called back to Ma'zekaï when Lulja was three and that's why she was adopted. "This guy showed me these beautiful letters from my father to my mother. I think he really loved her." She sighed. "My mother was already dead; I went to her grave and everything. Any grandparents I had were gone too. I asked the investigator to take me to my father and that's when I met Ravn. He showed me the task of the Élan and said that if I helped, I'd become part of them." She paused. "And here we are."

"Ravn didn't trick you," Freja said. "What he said was probably true. The Élan wants to open the borders, remember? It was Topster who made it all wrong." She pondered for a while and gazed towards the TV tower where the bell would ring soon.

"Did you speak to your dad?" Lulja asked.

The question hit, but missed by a hair's breadth. Freja had forgotten all about that. Somehow, among the confusion over her mother and the Strays, she had pushed out of her mind that her father was not Otto Evenson, but Master Tej of the Élan. A Lord, even. "I hope he doesn't hate me," she said at last.

"Why would he hate you?" said Lulja.

Because for a moment she had hated him, Freja thought to herself, but settled for a small smile as reply. With a shrug she closed the question and let Lulja hug her. She had regained all function now and was using it to squeeze the pain out of Freja. The tightness of her chest shrunk a little when Lulja's heat mingled with her own and her arms wrapped around her back like the glue that holds a person together. She inhaled and felt the warm scent of her friend. At least some things were familiar.

"It suits you," said Freja and smiled. "Lulja Bellamy of the

Trew."

"Freja Evenson of the Élan," said Lulja and laughed. "Crazy."

"Crazy," agreed Freja.

Tryll had gone to the fence where Robin had once stood and was looking out over the city. He cleared his throat.

"Sorry," Lulja said and laughed as she dried the last tears. "And Tryll St. John of the most admirable Burian Peninsula." He made a theatrical bow and turned his back to them.

Freja smiled and looked around her. Everything was so different now. The telephone booth from which Robin had made secret plans with Enton had been sprayed with black graffiti. Now a foul word decorated the yellow surface. On that phone Robin had spoken the words out loud: Cecelya was gone. If all went well, Freja would have the honour this time. She rubbed a sore spot at her chest.

"Pretty different from Buria, huh?" she called to Tryll. She could only imagine what he was thinking of the tall city landscape and grey dullness of concrete. From pictures she knew that Buria was colourful and bright. Tryll turned around and gave her thumbs-up. She looked to Lulja, who translated this gesture as 'this is better'. "Liar," Freja whispered to Lulja, who laughed. "Never heard anyone who thought Vildaell was prettier than Buria."

She pulled her knees to her chest, wrapping her arms around them, pushing away, clawing to dispel the thoughts in her head. The chill of the nocturnal world was still in the air in the no-man's-land between night and dawn. The grass was moist with morning dew, reminding her that day was coming. On another occasion it could have been a beautiful morning. Her first sunrise in Vildaell was not what she had expected.

"Buria's beautiful, but gaudy and artificial in a way," said Lulja who was seated in a lotus position with her arms resting in her intertwined legs. "And Jahran's only dust and dirt, but Vildaell has something else." She paused. "Do you think they're going for Jahran and Buria as well?"

Freja thought of Klobb taken from his home, his family left behind. "I think they've got Muspeldal already, or parts of it," she said. "So it's not unlikely."

A whistle from Tryll got them to their feet. He waved them over and they rushed to the railing to join him. He pointed down to the bottom. "You've got to be kidding me," Freja mumbled and drew a deep breath.

"I thought you were fine with heights?" said Lulja with a cheeky eyebrow raised.

"Shut up," Freja muttered. The height slapped her deeply but she forced herself to stay where she was. No time for fainting, little one, she thought.

"What is that?" Lulja asked. "Are those—people?"

At the bottom of the drop they saw two human shapes slouched against each other. On this other perfect (and imagined) morning where Freja experienced her first sunrise under completely different circumstances, she might not have recognised the people, but there was no doubt of their identities now. Last time she had seen them had been far away and under no more amicable conditions. She felt her heart drop in equal measures relief and grief. She had helped someone; amongst all the losses was this one victory, though tainted as it was.

"Jaspir!" she shouted before thinking and instantly clasped a hand to her mouth. The night remained still, but below neither the man nor the woman stirred. Freja shouted again, shriller this time, crouching next to the railing. She didn't care whoever might hear her. "Jaspir!" If there was, if she could—she had to. Still no movement. Jumping to her feet, she rushed towards the wooden staircase that led down the hillside to the pedestrian path. How many times had she raced Robin down these steps? Once, that's how many. Only once in her life had he convinced her to run down the side of the Look-Out, and never again. She had lost then, as she felt she was losing now with every step, despite her being the only runner. The wind rushed in her ears as she took two steps at a time, so fast that she almost tripped several times. A fall wouldn't mean death, but a few broken bones at least. Calculations were distracting her from the logistical nightmare in which her limbs found themselves. She was out of breath before she was half way down.

She yelled his name. His mother's name. Nobody replied. Not one voice. Not even an echo came in return. She was losing in her victory.

At the bottom of the steps she understood why no reply had come. The two lifeless bodies were already cold and pale from death. Jaspir held his mother affectionately, one arm hooked in hers, the other resting as a bar of protection across her frail body. Her thin and useless legs were splayed in such a way that they could have belonged to either of them. Despite the macabre gruesomeness of it all, they looked peaceful and unharmed. The latch must have opened up nearby. But they didn't survive. Freja had saved them from the Valley of Wind but not from their own world. She had led them into a suffering death. Falling to her knees, she bent over Jaspir's body and let the tears fall. Except there were no tears. Because somewhere deep within she knew that she had at least given them a chance of surviving. She had given them a way home. Given the opportunity again, she would do no different. "I'm sorry," she whispered and closed the eyes of both Jaspir and Mrs Nagel. "You're home now."

Tryll and Lulja had followed and were standing behind her, quietly observing. When she stood up, they joined her side. "You knew them?" Lulja asked on behalf of them both. Freja could only nod and sniff as the tears came at last. Tryll spoke the only language he knew and embraced her. On the other side came Lulja and wrapped her arms around her too. They stood like this for a long while before breaking apart.

Tired, dirty, puffy eyes from crying—she was a mess and so were her friends, but as long as Topster was moving, so would they. Already, much time had been spilled. Each one of them was searching for ideas of what to do next. Freja assumed her father had escaped to join the Masters in Valley of Wood. Instead of being here with her, he was fighting with his own kind. Check that: their kind.

Suddenly the sky filled with a jet stream of light and for a moment Freja thought the world had imploded. Later she would wish it had. The light was gone as swiftly as it had appeared. "What the—"

Pop.

Freja swung around. There was nothing. But something stirred inside her. Like stretched threads vibrating.

Pop.

Lulja and she exchanged panicked glances. There was definitely something. Lifting herself up to a crouching position, resting herself on her finger tips, Freja peered out from the little opening where they were seated. Nothing was visible in the filtered light.

Pop.

When the source of the sound became apparent, Freja lost her breath for a second. Elflock's words echoed in her head: whenever a latch is used, it reverberates in the Essence. And latches were being used right now. Fully grasping the situation, she stood up, hunched, and exhaled in one word, "Hide."

With no other option available, they left Jaspir and his mother lying like carcasses on the prairie below the hill. Crouching in the bushes they saw Masters literally *pop* into sight one by one on the pedestrian path. All in black masterform, they were Masters she had never seen before. More and more gathered below the Look-Out. In a hopeful moment she thought they might be of the Trew; that Elflock and Ravn had done it, that they had convinced the Lords and this was aid coming from another world. She murmured this to Lulja, her pulse accelerating at the idea. Lulja replied what she knew already: they were of the Flÿght. She had seen some of them in the village, sneaking into the house in the middle of the night to speak to Klepta. They had been wearing blue then.

Freja's heart sank to new depths in her seemingly bottomless chest pit. These were Masters of the Flÿght. She didn't have to look to Lulja or Tryll to see what it meant. Topster had latches and the Flÿght were moving through them, straight into Amérle.

CHAPTER 46

Less than an hour until bell eleven

AFTER A FEW minutes the pops and crackles stopped. No more Masters appeared out of thin silvery air and those who had entered already soon ventured into the city on Transporters.

Freja led the way from the hill, down to the bridge, and then across to the other side. They were moving south, towards the nuclear power plant, and that was the second last place she wanted to be. Instead she took a left turn and sought the steps, the wet steps splashed by the water from the river. The air instantly became colder as she guided them down to the water-line. To their right lay the river black and gloomy like a serpent wriggling its way in and out of the city, and Freja shuddered, but for another reason.

The Flÿght were taking over her city and the Lords could not be trusted. In fact, she wasn't sure who to trust anymore.

"Where is my bag?" Tryll gave her the one he had slung around his shoulder. He had taken care of it when she went to the square, he signed. The other two must have been forgotten in the TV tower. In one way or the other, Topster had more latches than they had collected at the Bank and Wind put together. There must have been at least thirty Masters on that path and if there were thirty of them in that place—where else were they, and how many?

"So we lost," Lulja said and took Tryll's hand. "I can't believe it's over."

Freja gazed into the black river. It was indeed a tough piece of information to swallow. Everything they had done, all that effort—all for nothing. If only her father had been there to comfort her. She was more human than Master in that way. Unlike them, she needed affection, emotional interaction. She couldn't imagine a life without the rush of gladness she associated with Robin or the warmth from her parents' hearts. The cold heart of a Master was not for her. Perhaps when that sun rose it wouldn't matter. She would never see her father again, or Robin, or her mother. Those who had paid or would pay the price of love. The Flÿght would reign with cold and heartless terror, she knew it.

"Eeek!"

Lulja cried out and shuffled to her feet, her flinging arms swinging at Tryll who almost lost his balance. He stumbled backwards and swayed, his arms waving, before finding his footing again. About to shout at Lulja for making sudden movements, for screaming, for risking them being discovered, she opened her mouth, but closed it again. Not solely because she had done the exact same thing fifteen minutes earlier at the Look-Out, but mostly because she saw what had caused Lulja's reaction. At first it looked like a cat, but when it crept closer its rodent-like appearance became clearer. It was black and blended in with the curved shadows whose depths this creature now came. Teeth like a flesh-eater by nature glimmered when the fading moonlight hit them, sending a promise to the three standing in its visual field. From the way its eyes moved, it became clear it was searching for something. For someone. All three of them were backing with slow steps into the assumed protection of the bridge, knowing full well that it was completely irrational. To scare a rat, as large as it may be, all they had to do was make noise.

"Freja." Lulja hissed when Freja had leaned forward. "What are you doing?" When her name was uttered, the creature stopped for a second.

"It's not a rat," Freja said, echoing her own mind. She crept closer, slowly, remembering that they would scare easily. The creature, black and leathery, stayed still. When she was close enough she reached out a hand and offered the creature her palm. His glistening eyes blinked. Then he scuttled on to her hand and she took him up. Behind, she could feel Lulja's flabbergast expression before she saw it. "It's a batsër," said Freja as she came up to Lulja and Tryll who were both looking at her with traumatised astonishment. "It's Pollux."

They stared at the batsër, still not convinced he wasn't a rat in disguise—or worse. Waiting to release his message, Pollux wet his jaw, sticking out a little pink tongue and slobbering it across his invisible lips. At this sudden movement, Lulja skipped back a step, into Tryll's arms. Her cheeks flushed red, but whether because of her jitteriness of a harmless animal or where it had taken her, was impossible to tell.

The message was short. Three sentences only. Elflock.

"The Flÿght are moving in. We're turning to the Obbsborn. Remember the third," Freja repeated to her friends, who looked as concerned and confused as she did. "They're asking the Obbsborn for help," said Freja with a smile towards Tryll. "That's good." He nodded and smiled back and she hoped he did indeed think it was the right thing.

"'Remember the third'?" said Lulja, looking at Tryll, who seemed equally oblivious.

Like she usually did when thinking hard at something, Freja played with her necklace, the spirit of her mother surging in as a comforting force. Well, it used to, before she knew the truth. "Remember the third." Elflock was clearly trying to say something important, begging her to remember. The charm felt warm.

The third?

The third.

"The third!" she said aloud, causing Pollux to stir in fear. She stroked his chin and he calmed down. The charm. That it hadn't struck her before! "The third, of course the third. Here, Pollux." She brought Pollux to her shoulder like a parrot where his little claws dug into her masterform without causing pain. After making sure he was happy to perch there for a moment or two, she turned to Lulja and Tryll with a new glow in her eyes. They, on the other hand, looked as if she had gone crazy. Maybe she had. Right now, however, her (in)sanity was less important. She lowered her face to her chest and held out the charm. In Lulja's glimmering eyes Freja saw that she had no idea what it was. "It's an open latch," said Freja. "I'm guessing infinite too."

It took Lulja a minute to digest and accept. "That's a surprise."

"Didn't even know I had it until hours ago. My mother gave it to me. She must have felt I would find out one day."

"If we have an open latch," Lulja said, shifting between Tryll and Freja, "we can go anywhere?" Tryll nodded with excitement. "Not just Ma'zekaï?" Tryll shook his head. "And it'll take all three of us?" Again, Tryll responded in an affirming manner. "And it'll last forever?" At this, Tryll used a flat hand to show that it was only partially true.

"Infinite latches are only called 'infinite' because they haven't ended *yet*," said Freja, understanding the concept for the first time. "But just because it hasn't ended yet doesn't mean it'll last until tomorrow." She sucked her cheeks in and plucked at the charm. Remember the third. She had barely been listening. It would most likely be immensely difficult, not to mention dangerous, but she also knew they had to try. Elflock had sacrificed a lot to help them in the Latch Bank, and she could never leave the Masters—her own kind—for something so selfish as fear.

The rising hum in the air reminded her of their purpose and she knew what to do. There was nowhere safe around to open the latch—just concrete and bricks as far the eye could see.

"We have a latch," said Lulja. "Many latches." She nodded towards Freja's bag. "Where do we go? It could go anywhere, right?"

"The third *landskapë*," said Freja with determination. "That's what Elflock meant." She gave Pollux a stroke. "We need to be one step ahead now that Vildaell looks lost. The brothers of the Red World swore off all connection with the Trinity ages ago, but maybe this will get them going again." Though she didn't say so out loud, she added in her mind: it has to. "We want to go before bell eleven." She crawled out from under the bridge and into the light. It wouldn't be long now. Between the buildings glimmered the gilded horizon, now with a clear line of sunlight, though not yet any sign of the upper curve of the star itself.

"Not a second to lose," Lulja said. "About half an hour until the bell."

"Thirty minutes?!" said Freja. "There's something I need to do first before we can go. Follow me."

Once upon a time she would have given anything to play a dangerous game of hide-and-seek under Curfew hours. But circumstances changed. With a trembling heart and on shaky legs, she managed to lead them north again. They had to go past the Great Square (though at a distance of maybe twenty blocks) and all the time listen for the hum of Transporters and Flÿght Masters crawling through the city. By luck or by chance, they encountered no one bar the dark shadow of a Flÿght Master turning the corner at a distance, and bent the shadows to their advantage on the way from the bridge and the river to Freja's neighbourhood. She avoided looking at Mr Nagel's house as they turned the corner into Mauve Road. It was too painful to think about. Number 15 came up on their right and Freja steered them into the gravel front path.

"I'll stay here," Lulja said. "It's creepy."

It was hard to disagree with her. Freja watched her childhood home with a heavy heart. The house was dark, desolate, and dismal; a ruin of shadows in the midst of the garden to which she was so accustomed. There was some air of emptiness around it all and the cold of the night suddenly came to her like a retroactive pull; penetrating into her very bones, breaking a shiver through her core. This bleak shape was her house, her protector during Curfew, and yet not at all. "There's a space under the steps," she said without looking at Lulja. "Don't stand out in the open."

The steps creaked as she ascended to the front door. The ten bells of Curfew had sounded long ago, but she still pressed down the handle of the door. It swung open, soundless like a ghost without its rattling chains. She stood on the outer side of the threshold and looked into the darkness within. There was no light to reveal the interior, but she could see it clearly. There was the bureau to the left where photos of herself, her mother with Mops in her arms, and her father stood lined up on a crocheted cloth with floral details around its border; opposite that was the coat rack where her father's chef's hat had taken its place for as long as she could remember; there was the striped rug, leading guests from the hallway into the sitting room where two three-seater sofas, a large table with magazines usually cluttering the surface, and a cushioned chair welcomed you to sit down; the two doors to the kitchen, connecting it to each room in the downstairs area. Her own room above. All of this she saw from outside, and she was afraid to cross that threshold, without quite knowing why. Then again, the answer was right in front of her: the door was open during Curfew. It was the ultimate sign that this morning was a far cry from the usual Curfew daybreak.

Ignoring the chilling sensations it stipulated, she went inside the house, leaving Lulja and Tryll under the steps outside. She made every attempt not to look at the familiar things, the bureau, the chef's hat, the kitchen, and instead went straight for the drawer with writing paper and envelopes. Without choosing she pulled out a decorated kind normally used for special occasions, grabbed a pen, and started writing. Once finished, she went out and looked over to the Aitkens' house, concealed behind the neighbouring villas. It had become clear to her that she couldn't leave without telling him. Not again.

"I'll be right back," she said to Lulja and Tryll as she crouched down where they were hiding, closely huddled together.

The envelope with the letter was tucked inside her master-form and she felt it pulsate with every step as she snuck down the street towards the house where the Aitkens lived. Lulja had asked if she wanted company. There were several reasons why she had pushed away the voice screaming 'yes' and turned her offer down. One of them was in that envelope.

At the gate, she listened for sounds in the night, but all was calm, and she crept up to the door. She pushed the envelope through the letter box in the front door and it landed with a thud on the other side, but nothing in the house stirred. Just as well, she thought. "Please, get this," she whispered. "For Cecelya."

Was this response enough to Cecelya's last question in life? Freja wondered. The one Cecelya had posed right before they separated for the last time; the one Freja had not answered? The one she was afraid to answer. "Am I in—" she began, but shook her head and turned away from the door standing between her and Robin. Now was not the time.

Before heading back, Freja climbed one of the apple trees in the garden—just like she had done so many times in her youth. Her feet found each branch by instinct and she reached the top without trouble. This time she stood alone and gazed towards the city and though the vision was limited by buildings, it was enough. Connecting the view with what she knew was like watering a monstrous plant: the picture grew to a terrible ogre and soon she had lost all control of her senses. An inner force, the Essence perhaps, created a scene in her heart so vivid it might have been playing out below her very feet. She put the image aside for the time being and slid down the tree. Running as quietly as possible, she soon returned at number 15. Dawn was so close she could sense it.

Lulja and Tryll came out at her request and she led them to the side of the garage where her beloved Thunderball X770 stood under the plastic cover. "We agreed then?" Freja said and brought out the charm. "To the Red World?"

"Wait," said Lulja and frowned. "What about Jahran?"

"What about it?"

She exchanged a look with Tryll. "We talked about it. Jahran and Buria. We can't just let them be taken too."

Freja stared at the two. Clearly leaving them alone had been a bad idea. "What?" she said.

"We should warn them," Lulja repeated and sought support from Tryll, who gave it willingly. Freja groaned. Mostly because they were right.

The image returned. If only she could have relayed it to

them: Amérle was drowning in the Master presence. Unseen and unheard to the citizens, herds and herds of Flÿght Masters had stepped through from Ma'zekaï on Transporters, and were now spreading out in the city on Topster's orders. They were stationing guards outside each closed gate, each locked door, each shut window, in short each and every way out or in. A Master on every corner; Masters going down in the gutters, beneath each grate, and many more spreading through the underground sewer system like a disease; they climbed to the top of the houses, occupied basements; altogether claiming every open space from the ground to the sky, awaiting the imminent dawn of day when humans would wake up to the new world. Their freedom recoiled, drew further into the depth of submission, and meanwhile, the dreams of humanity remained unharmed in blissful ignorance of the nightmare occurring on the other side of their walls. Soon enough there would be no Amérle left that wasn't under surveillance from a Master. They had all worn black—one Master race.

They would invade Jahran next, she was sure. One country wouldn't be enough for all the Masters if Ma'zekaï fell. Even if he didn't possess the Trinity Latch and could move on to the Red World, Topster would not be satisfied with Vildaell. Jahran was the closest and perhaps easiest target.

The hum in the air was growing louder. They had to leave. Now, no—sooner: they had to leave ten minutes ago.

She didn't quite believe her own words when she said, "Take the northern route," and pulled off the plastic cover of the Thunderball. Its black surface caught the approaching daylight and glistened. Incredulous looks met her statement. "There's no time," she whispered. "Take the northern route to Buria. No," she added as Lulja began protesting, "Buria. The Queen has more power than all of Jahran put together. Go to Buria."

"Are you sure?" Lulja said, and Freja heard it wasn't a question for her, but for Tryll. He looked to Freja for support this time. He pointed to her with a question mark on his face.

"And you?" he seemed to ask.

She said she'd go to the Red World, as Elflock instructed. "I have Pollux in case something happens." The batsër was still clawing onto her shoulder, sound asleep.

"You have the Trinity Latch as well," said Lulja. "That's worth more than anything. Keep it safe, yes?"

Freja thought of the letter lying on Robin's doormat and didn't reply. With a small gesture Tryll reminded them of the pressing time. The sky had now exploded in a blanket of orange and red. The line of light on the horizon had become brighter and within minutes the golden orb itself would appear and rise to a new day. A wholly different day.

Freja smiled at her friends but felt the corners of her mouth disobey and turn downwards. "Good luck," she said and gave the key to Lulja. "You ever driven one of these before?"

Lulja took her hand and broke out laughing. "Never." Tryll and she put their helmets on and straddled the motorcycle. Both Lulja and Freja struggled to find those important last words. Nothing came. Instead, Tryll reached forward and ignited the engine. At the same time as it came to life, the world detonated into a raging hum. It shook its very foundation as Transporters rolled into the streets outside the property. Next thing Freja knew, Lulja was steering the motorcycle out and around the corner in the opposite direction to the approaching Masters.

Freja watched them for as long as she dared before hurrying into the back garden, alone. Clasping the charm, she brought it out with steady hands. It had been given to her for a reason, she knew it. Her mother was, after all, a Master. Freja was a Master.

Not quite willing to crush the charm itself, Freja observed the leaf shape. A thin line at the top told her there was an opening. She closed her eyes and felt the cool glass. With a small click, it came open. The latch came floating out in a ball of all kinds of silvery shades. The intense shimmering was so bright it was blinding. Freja took Pollux from her shoulder and held him tight. "Hold on, Pollux," she whispered as the humming thundered around her. A flash of black flared in the corner of her eye as she reached into the light. The next moment the world sprung into a million pixels and dissolved everything around her in a drizzle of colourful squares. The humming faded and was replaced by a subtle *click-click-click*.

She was gone.

Epilogue

A minute earlier

Across the city in the highest building of the town, a stout man appeared in the top office of Amérle's TV tower. He looked around his space. Someone had been there, recently. The desk was a mess and the neat row of pencils he had left that morning was not so neat now. While correcting the linear pattern, pencil by pencil, he checked the time. Not yet.

After order was restored he lit a cigarette and heaved himself into his chair. It had his imprint now. Well, that made it comfy. Smoke swirled up towards the ceiling and the white cylinder he had been told was a fire alarm. If it worked, it was switched off. Smoking hadn't been a problem in the past five years, and probably wouldn't be today either. The monitors showed Masters rolling across the city as the Flÿght took over.

Poor humans, he thought and then laughed until the smoke sent him into a coughing fit. He was a funny one, so he'd always thought. He drew in the smoke, felt it fill his lungs.

Poor humans, he thought again and grinned to himself. The myth of the Ringer was as deeply rooted in human culture as in the *landskapë* of Masters. And now they'd never know. He was the invisible man to all but two people. His bosses were not the open-door type of executives, but they gave him the freedom he wanted and let him deal with his job on his own. With his experience he hardly needed a babysitter. They were fair, too, and rewarded good effort.

Tonight's events would surely be of interest to them.

He laughed and coughed, smacking his bulging stomach, as one of the Masters hit the kerb and fell off his Transporter and tumbled to the ground, after which he received what looked like a scolding from a comrade. With a flick of the switch he opened the sound channel and heard another Master yell insults to the one on the ground. He laughed in such a violent manner that he dropped his cigarette. Cursing, he bent down to retrieve it before he set the whole place on fire.

He found the cigarette all right, and also a strap. As he pulled it out he saw it was a bag made from fine fabric: a craft trade-marked by Master hand. Interesting, he thought and unbuckled it, the cigarette butt hanging from his lips. Even more interest-ing, he thought as the content came into view. This was some-thing for his bosses. He swung to face the keyboard and tapped a short sequence of numbers, resulting in a dialling tone.

After three rings two faces appeared on the screen to his left. They were identical save for a scar running down the left brother's temple. Ugly things, they were too, but the man was no beauty himself so he reserved judgement. Except for that scar, the brothers' white locks, the pale green eyes—everything was identical. The Ringer greeted them, excited to tell them what he had found.

"Brothers, forgive the lateness. I was just up in the office to ring and—"

"It better be important, Volsces."

Oh, it was important all right. He held up the bag for the brothers to behold. One look at the glimmering silver crystals sufficed. The Duo closed the connection and Volsces got ready to leave. His time had come at last. Only one thing left to do in Heim before he would be out of here for good.

He checked the time on the monitors. 05:59:55.

The man pushed a button. Five seconds early would not make any difference. Not today. Before the final bell had echoed out over Amérle, he stepped back into the latch, not even noticing the tiny squares breaking apart one reality and building the next. It was all routine to him now.

Before the latch closed, he chucked his finished cigarette on the floor where it glowed in the dark. He didn't look back. For all he cared, the tower could burn to the ground.

And over the city of Amérle rang the final bell to mark the end of Curfew—

Bell eleven.

END OF BOOK ONE

Thank you

At last, I'd like to express thanks to a few of those who helped this book come to life.

First of all to Bharat, who read and re-read again, demanding that I answer all the tough questions. Without him, this story would have made a lot less sense.

To my sister Emma who read even though she doesn't care much for fantasy fiction, to Diane who was the first one to love this story, to Judith who pointed out to me that two times ten is not thirty, and to Hal whose hugs are simply the best hugs in the world.

And finally to you, reader, for exploring The Landskapë Saga with me. I hope you will continue to join me on the journey across the *landskapës*!

xoxo Nina

Connect with Nina!

Facebook: facebook.com/ninajlux

Twitter: @ninajlux

GoodReads: goodreads.com/ninajlux

Blog: ninajlux.wordpress.com

If you enjoyed the book, will you please help more readers discover *Bell Eleven* by leaving a review at Amazon and/or GoodReads? Thank you!

Made in the USA
Charleston, SC
17 April 2015